The memory of that afternoon is my sanctuary now. It is all I have left. I watch my children play in front of me as if the illusion were real, as if I could reach out and touch them, as if I could change everything; as if I am still their mother.

For the rest of my son's brief life, my daughter's lead was the only one he would follow. Hers was the understanding heart he sought; her soul a soothing refuge for his pain. If he wandered, he returned to her. When he was lost, she found him. Since time immemorial there was no precedent for the love they owned. Few could possibly mine the unspoken depths of their affection or the secrets they shared. They were born for one another.

Neither knew how to live without the other. Neither did.

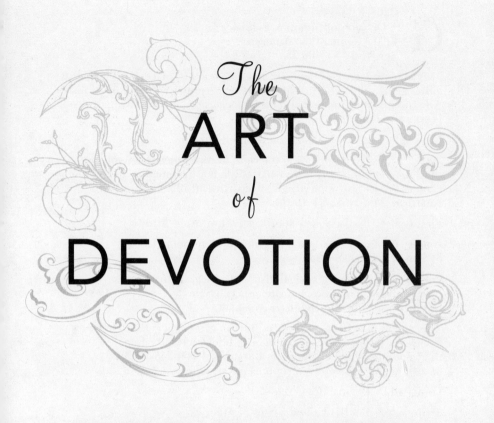

The
ART
of
DEVOTION

SAMANTHA BRUCE-BENJAMIN

G

GALLERY BOOKS

New York   London   Toronto   Sydney

G Gallery Books
A Division of Simon & Schuster, Inc.
1230 Avenue of the Americas
New York, NY 10020

First Gallery Books trade paperback edition June 2010

Gallery Books and colophon are registered trademarks of Simon & Schuster, Inc.

For information about special discounts for bulk purchases, please contact Simon & Schuster Special Sales at 1-866-506-1949 or business@simonandschuster.com.

The Simon & Schuster Speakers Bureau can bring authors to your live event. For more information or to book an event contact the Simon & Schuster Speakers Bureau at 1-866-248-3049 or visit our website at www.simonspeakers.com.

Designed by Davina Mock-Maniscalco

Manufactured in the United States of America

10 9 8 7 6 5 4 3 2 1

Library of Congress Cataloging-in-Publication Data

Bruce-Benjamin, Samantha.
   The art of devotion / Samantha Bruce-Benjamin. — 1st Gallery Books trade paperback ed.
      p.   cm.
   1. Summer — Fiction. 2. Aunts — Fiction. 3. Secrets — Fiction.
4. Mediterranean Region — Fiction. I. Title.
   PS3602.R8326A89   2010
   813'.6 — dc22   2009048055

ISBN 978-1-4391-5394-9
ISBN 978-1-4391-7075-5 (ebook)

For my husband and my mother

Acknowledgments

First and foremost, I must thank the wonderful Anthony Ziccardi, whose kindness, perspicacity, and passionate advocacy ensured that this novel not only would be published but that it would be edited by the brilliant and wise Kathy Sagan. I also owe Louise Burke a tremendous debt for further championing my cause. I would also like to express my gratitude to the delightful Jessica Webb, Sarah Reidy, and everyone at Simon & Schuster who contributed to the publication of this novel.

Normally, the publishing thanks would end here, but the creation of the Gallery Books imprint proved a marvelous blessing for this novel: primarily, it brought me into contact with the hugely talented Jennifer Bergstrom, whose extraordinary passion, generosity, insight, and belief in this story inspired me to greater heights than I ever imagined possible. This merger also enabled me to work once more with Kara Cesare, who I have long admired for her integrity and vivacity, and whose succinct editorial suggestions proved a godsend in honing this novel.

I also cannot praise highly enough the following people, who, over the period in which this novel was written, displayed astonishing bravery when broaching the tricky subject of criticism with this fledgling author. In addition they offered encouragement, editorial guidance, and, above all, faith in my abilities, which I will not soon forget: my divine sister, Juliet Bruce, was my first reader and proved unfailingly enthusiastic and discerning; Emma Davidson, Kirstie Macrae, Colin Turner-Kerr, Patricia Moffat, and Jennifer Healy were all hugely supportive; the gifted Anna Valdinger came along at just the right moment and propelled me forward with her astonishing passion, dedication, and insight; John Ziccardi proved that business savvy and kindness are not mutually exclusive; Jirair Tcholakian and Piet went above and beyond the call of duty for me; Sasha Bell-Flynn proved unfailingly inquisitive, asking all the right questions at all the right times.

As ever, I am humbled in the face of the love I have been shown by my family and relatives, without whom I would certainly have not been able to write this novel. I would like to thank my wonderful father, Stuart Bruce, the really, really good-looking and exceptionally talented Calum Benjamin; William, Susan, Gary, and Romy Bottrill and their families; Sandra, Steven, and Stuart Bottrill and their families; Alexandra Bruce-Dickie, Alistair Dickie, my grandfather, William Robertson Bruce, my late and beloved Grandad and Nana, William and Barbara Bottrill, and, of course, my grandmother Ruth Bruce, who was my first, and without doubt, best storyteller.

Finally, if there is an art to devotion, then it has surely been displayed by my husband, Dr. Arthur Benjamin, and my mother, Linda Bruce. When all is said and done, I owe them everything.

So we beat on, boats against the current, borne back ceaselessly into the past.

—F. Scott Fitzgerald, *The Great Gatsby*

Characters

Adora

Oliver: Adora's husband
Sebastian: Adora's brother
Sophie: Adora's mother

Miranda

James: Miranda's husband
Genevieve: Miranda's daughter

Jack: Oliver's business associate

There is no truth. There is only perception.

—Gustave Flaubert

PROLOGUE

Sophie

An island in the Mediterranean Sea, 1940

For each of us, there is a moment: what we see at the last, before God closes our eyes forever; an entire existence distilled to one perfect memory. We anticipate its promise all our lives.

Some are entirely unprepared for the joy that dances through their souls and wince with regret at everything they missed during those final seconds. Others peacefully acknowledge something they long suspected but never truly realized, content to venture into the night enlightened. And then there are those, like me, who know exactly what they will see, who welcome the end for the privilege it will contain. Yes, for each of us, there is a moment. This is mine:

They are there in front of me on the beach. A tiny boy and a tiny girl bronzed from the sun, their hair white-blond. At the edge of the shore they stand, holding hands. They are singing a rhyme I have taught them in French: *Odeur du temps brin de bruyère/Et souviens-toi que je t'attends.* Fragrance of time sprig of heather/Remember I wait for you forever. They sing the song every time a wave approaches, attempting to jump over it before it breaks against the sand. My daughter invented the game, and my son, as ever, is content to play with

her. Not simply content, ecstatic. They are childhood personified, childhood as it should be. They are the innocents of the
world. They are laughing. They turn to each other and squeal
with excitement every time they jump. Their curls fly up in the
air as they ascend and fall over their eyes when they land.
Odeur du temps brin de bruyère/Et souviens-toi que je t'attends.
Fragrance of time sprig of heather/Remember I wait for you
forever.

I call to them from the balcony of the Hôtel des Anges
that it is time to go home for their nap. She looks at me over
her shoulder, a familiar look of mischief in her eyes, and
tightens her grip on my son's hand. He would have come to
me. She will not let him. And what is the harm? Why not let
them play until they are so exhausted they can barely stay
awake? They are only children. This is, after all, their time. Up
and down they go, completely oblivious to me or any of the
other assembled guests on the veranda, entranced by their
game.

Sebastian is six, older by two years, but still he waits for
Adora to jump before he follows. I can see his little legs shaking while he waits for her cue, afraid that he might ruin the
game by leaping too soon, remaining throughout a beat behind
her. His face floods with relief as he lands, but he does not look
to me for praise or encouragement to try again, only to her. The
sun moves down in the west of the sky as the game continues.
It will stop only when she decrees it so.

I sit there, my hand resting on my parasol, basking in the
glow conferred by my children, so exquisite they eclipse all
others. I feel the residual heat of the day slip away like a silk
cover being pulled carefully and slowly from my body, the
breeze kissing my cheeks as dusk approaches. I care little for

the murmurs emanating from the more staid American tourists who have stopped on our island as part of their Grand Tour. *It's not quite proper, don't you think? Really, their nanny should bring them in.* Most of the visitors seated around me are as transfixed by my children as I am. Yet as much as I want to linger on, I reluctantly check my complacency when I realize that it is growing late and their father and I are dining with friends this evening. I call to them again to come in, knowing I should insist, but something stops me. Something in my daughter's eyes, as she turns toward me, framed by the dusk beyond, stops me.

It is thirty-five years since I watched them play on our island in the Mediterranean Sea. Yet it doesn't seem possible that I am no longer that enviable woman sitting on the balcony of the most exclusive hotel in Europe in 1905, unquestioning of who I was, my morality, my judgment. Life then had done nothing so cruel that I could not recover. I considered everything I had ever been given to be a right and not a privilege. Not for me to toss in my bed at night asking myself, *What have I done?* That would come later.

The memory of that afternoon is my sanctuary now. It is all I have left. I watch my children play in front of me as if the illusion were real, as if I could reach out and touch them, as if I could change everything; as if I am still their mother.

For the rest of my son's brief life, my daughter's lead was the only one he would follow. Hers was the understanding heart he sought, her soul a soothing refuge for his pain. If he wandered, he returned to her. When he was lost, she found him. Since time immemorial there was no precedent for the love they owned. Few could possibly mine the unspoken depths of their affection or the secrets they shared. They were born for one another.

Neither knew how to live without the other. Neither did.

Genevieve

New York, 1940

Everyone agrees that nothing less than the Metropolitan Club will do. The marble palace situated on the lush boulevard that is Fifth Avenue and the home away from home for the Morgans and the Vanderbilts is considered enough of a statement, in what my mother judges to be a suitably understated British fashion, for my marriage tomorrow evening to that most daunting of species, an American millionaire.

I did protest at first, somewhat violently, that the gesture was too grand, the cost too high, but my mother would hear none of it: "Genevieve, this is what we would have given without a second thought had—" and here, glancing at me nervously, she stopped in midsentence, checking what she had intended to say "—had nothing ever changed," my mother concluded, swallowing the words as if they were medicine and turning back to the seating arrangement.

I let the matter go without further comment. I simply couldn't bear another scene. My nerves haven't quite been right of late, and I know better than to work myself up over things I can't change. Instead, I sought solace in my father in the hope that he might understand how important it is that my marriage to the man everyone loves so much should be free from any worry on my part. "Nothing you can say will deter me from giving you the fairy-tale wedding we have always imagined for our only child," he said and smiled, tapping me gently on my nose, as if humorously reprimanding a naughty puppy. "Besides, this wedding is also a gift for your future husband, and we can't possibly let him down now, can we?" By way of a reply, I beamed my brightest smile, just as he expected me to.

In the face of my parents' generosity, I gave up, accepting how important it is for them to show everyone with this lavish wedding that I am making the right choice in marrying this man, a man I once longed for and loved more than I could possibly have imagined. Looking back to when we first met, I could never have predicted we would end up here, about to commit to spending the rest of our lives together—especially considering all of the obstacles thrown in our path. Yet as my father so often tells me, my fiancé is far wiser than I in so many ways and I should listen to him. It is safe to do so with him by my side. In an odd way, despite my concerns, I must confess to feeling somewhat relieved that the day we have waited so long for can still bear all of the glorious hallmarks of what we once knew so well. On the surface, at least, nothing has changed.

It has been somewhat eye-opening moving permanently to New York, such a different place from the countryside of Sussex, England, where I grew up until two years ago, and a world apart from the island in the Mediterranean Sea where I spent the summers of my youth. Inevitably, more than a few eyebrows were raised when my fiancé returned here, after so many years abroad, with me, whom he presented as his future wife. His acquaintances were completely taken aback by the announcement, especially as they knew nothing about me, save for a mention in a telephone call while he was away. I don't believe they ever truly realized just how private a man he is. It was obvious by their collective reaction that they thought they knew everything there was to know about him. Their noses were rather put out of joint by the realization that I, a mere twenty years old, appeared to be the keeper of such knowledge in place of them.

As we have both painfully learned, however, the opinions of other people mean little, which is probably why my fiancé is my constant companion. He has borne the brunt of so much jealousy as a result of his phenomenal success, even more acute considering he started out with nothing more than a dream and the overwhelming conviction that he would achieve it, in spite of how difficult it would ultimately prove to be.

As for me, I choose not to dwell now on the difficulties of the past. My eyes have been opened to much over the course of my relatively short life, and I know whom I like and whom I do not choose to cultivate as a friend. In truth, I find many of the people who surround us now rather unkind but, as I tell myself when I'm tempted to react, it is only to be expected in a place as competitive as New York that one-upmanship might figure prominently in the lives of those who have less than we do, so I turn a blind eye. It might sound strange, but I have been somewhat amused by the various rumors I've overheard regarding our marriage. One of the less pleasant consequences of being a strange girl in a strange town is that my life is open to so much conjecture. I have given nothing away, which I attribute as much to British reserve as to a desire to keep my cards close to my chest, so to speak.

My fiancé dotes on me, rarely leaving my side for a minute, and many have commented on how attentive he is. I wouldn't disappoint him for the world. In fact, the very idea fills me with a creeping dread I find hard to shake off and, at such times, although I know I shouldn't, I frequently struggle with my own feelings of inadequacy. Despite how often he reassures everyone that I'm doing everything right, still I fret sometimes that he's just saying such things to be kind. I expect it's only natural, however, to question myself, given how perfect everyone considers him to be and how lucky I am by association. I tell myself off frequently that I have everything to be happy about. So many girls would give their eyeteeth to be me.

I can't lie, however, and say that everything is perfect, but if there has been any unhappiness at all for me during the run-up to my wedding, it comes from the knowledge of who will not be there to share in it. Growing up, I had always kindled a romantic notion that grandfathers and grandmothers would still be alive when I finally married but, unfortunately, that is not the case. Nor will Sophie be coming and, far more than that of anyone else, her absence has dealt the keenest blow. I miss Sophie terribly. I dearly wish she could be here, considering how much she tried to help me in the past.

Sadly, Sophie is only the first of the cherished faces that I will not see as I walk down the aisle, which causes me untold sadness. It is a sorrow that builds to an agony when I dwell on it—especially when my thoughts turn to you, my Beloved, and why you are missing.

I haven't confided my regret to anyone; to speak of my private thoughts would serve only to make my family worry, and that would cause such terrible trouble. Moreover, my fiancé would be so unhappy if he thought that I was dwelling on those events of the past he has tried so hard to help me forget, always encouraging me to focus only on the future.

Strangely, however, I don't consider the interior life you and I share, my Beloved, to be a betrayal of him or of my mother and father. It is, after all, all that remains for us. I have had to be careful not to give anything away, and I think I've been success- ful, although there have been occasions when I've given myself up to memories of you and had to jolt myself back to the pres- ent for fear of arousing concern. Curiously, it has only been in the last few weeks that the reality of your absence has truly hit me. Prior to that point, so much of my time had been taken up with planning the wedding that I had willingly closed the door to you, content to let the past stay where it was. And then, when things started to calm down, after flowers and dresses and seat- ing arrangements had been confirmed, I found myself slipping, recalling things that seemed years old, only to realize with a dis- concerting shock that they had happened a mere few hours ear- lier. I wondered for a while if I was going mad and, for some reason, found the notion oddly consoling, almost a relief.

But no, my absentmindedness, this inability to remember what I am doing from one moment to the next, is solely because of you and what might have been. I suspect that the trigger was Sophie, thinking of her and what her opinions might have been, remembering how close she was to my mother, almost like a mother to her in so many ways. I thought I was safe in doing so, but I recognize now how wrong I was. For remembering Sophie has inevitably led my thoughts to you, and so you have been my companion along the path toward this pivotal moment in my life, cloistered behind my eyes in the depths of memory.

At first I thought I might be able to cope with your reemer- gence in my thoughts. I allowed myself a reprieve of sorts to cast my mind back to all that we shared together. When I real- ized, however, how much you had come to dominate my thinking, I tried to keep you at bay, but it has proven too difficult a task. Now, everything I see seems to invite a memory that pulls me back to those better times, despite how my fiancé insists that everything seems so only in retrospect. But I find it impossible not to think of what once was. You are everywhere and nowhere, the intangible force that beckons and denies me in equal measure. It is almost as if you are here with me, guiding me, showing me what I have blinded myself to.

Today, the eve of my wedding, is to be no different. For as I emerge from behind the heavy velvet curtain draped over the entrance to the ballroom that faces Central Park, a shadow on the staircase in the Great Marble Hall of the Metropolitan Club catches my eye immediately, inciting a memory that was the beginning and end of everything; a memory so powerful that I immediately retreat behind the velvet so that the perpetrators of the shadow do not see me. I can barely catch my breath as I feel your familiar presence return beside me, your arm around my waist, your head resting against my shoulder almost as if you are here again with me. And although I desperately fight the pain of remembering you, it is no use. I am consumed by you again as you lead me back through the pathways of memory, a road so painful it seems shrouded in nettles. And yet, every sting, even now, still feels like a kiss.

Your name, Adora, meant beloved. Nothing could be more true. In spite of everything, you are and will always be, my Beloved Aunt.

But there is no one in whom I can confide this, No one who will listen to anything more to do with you. I tell this story only for myself.

Miranda

New York, 1940

To say I've had my hands full with my daughter is the least of it. But then Genevieve is so highly strung—although she didn't get that from me, I'm pleased to say. I've always been a steady sort, thank heavens. No, it's prewedding jitters, that's all, and she seems calm enough now and all set for the big day tomorrow. I rather think her fiancé and I deserve a resounding pat on the back for steering her through all of this without a scrape, no mean feat considering how difficult she has been.

To be fair, it's not really surprising that it's proven such an ordeal trying to get Genevieve to think of the future and turn away from the past, especially when everyone, it seems, never stops asking about it. Well, you can't blame them for wanting to know about our time on that Mediterranean island; it was, after all, such a seemingly enviable existence, and my husband, James, and I—and, of course, Genevieve—were very much part of it, treasured guests every summer for nearly twenty years, the lynchpins of Adora and Oliver's inner circle.

What were the parties like? they always want to know. *Was Adora really as breathtakingly beautiful as everyone makes out?*

And what of the tragedies—did you ever have any inkling about the truth behind everything? Miranda, Miranda, they beseech constantly, barely able to conceal their curiosity, *tell us everything.* . . .

Ironic really, that I, of all people, should serve as the mistress of ceremonies when it comes to Adora, especially considering everything she put me through. But people do ask, and it's so important to me that they not be misled.

I tell them that it was a world of privilege such as you could never imagine and that Adora and Oliver were indeed considered to be the most glamorous people of their day. I tell them it's true that the moneyed and the sophisticated flocked from all over the world to be charmed by them, that their world glittered with a sheen of entitlement everyone clamored to be enveloped by. And all Adora and Oliver ever asked was that their guests worship at the shrine of their exquisite existence; such was the price of admission: a price to which I was never quite equal.

And then I add that it was never my choice to be there; that if I had had my way, I would never have set foot again on that godforsaken island, which despite its intoxicating allure was a place of unparalleled cruelty. Yet I had no say in the matter. My husband was Oliver's lawyer and his best—and most trusted— friend of years' standing, and Adora and I, as different from one another as we could hope to be, were thrown together and just expected to get along; a role I was forced to play until . . . well, until it was no longer necessary.

So every year we would visit from our home in England and attend to Adora and Oliver as if they were really the king and queen of that island in the Mediterranean Sea. Of course, people ask me why, how on earth I put up with it, and, whereas

I struggle on occasion with certain other questions they ask of me, I find the answer to this one by far the easiest: "Devotion," I tell them. And for some reason, that singular response never fails to satisfy them and we happily let the topic drop and move on to talk of other things.

PART I

Adora

1919–1938

Adora

The olive grove, an island in the Mediterranean Sea, 1938

I have lived my life surrounded by love. I have traveled over oceans. I have watched the clean, white light of the sun filter through the shutters every morning when I awake. I have heard the angels singing in the bougainvillea bushes on my daily walks. I have had a lifetime of the most enormous love imaginable.

My darling Oliver proposed to me after only two days. I was nineteen, he twenty-six. I met him purely by chance. He was on holiday from England, and I had returned briefly to visit the island, my childhood home, from Paris, where I was living temporarily. Two years earlier, I had been crowned *La Reine d'été*, the Summer Queen, of my island, and I had been carried through the streets to be met by my family at the door of the Hôtel des Anges, where a banquet was held in my honor.

Without my knowledge, that day a journalist had sent my pictures to Paris, and my career took off shortly afterward. I was photographed by *Vogue* and acclaimed as the foremost beauty of my generation. My face opened every door to success, but I closed them all when first I saw him. I did not need photographs and fame to sustain me, only the touch of his lips, the sound of my name whispered into my hair when he held me. It is true that one other man had touched my soul before I met Oliver, but it was Oliver's touch that returned me to life.

I was consumed by his gentle grace, his attentiveness, and by the aura of sadness he tried so carefully to conceal but which only I could possibly understand. We willingly left our careers behind in Paris and England and moved back to my island to live together. I married him because I was madly in love, passionately jealous of all other women who came near him, dedicated wholly to the ideal of our life together.

They called us the king and queen. People flocked to us then, inviting us everywhere, wishing to be invited back to our home in return. Of course in those early days we could not entertain quite so grandly, but our veranda had such a magnificent view and, as long as I could see the sea, as long as the bougainvillea flowered in the pots outside and he came home to me, I was content.

On the weekends, we went to the beach, smothered ourselves in olive oil, poured lemon juice on our hair, and basked in the glorious sun of our youth. As with so many things, we did not know then that what pleased us would ultimately harm us. We shone in the sunshine like gilded idols, staying up all night, dancing until dawn, drinking champagne. We were feted by everyone who met us.

With his charm, my husband quickly proved successful in business. But Oliver had more gifts than the ability simply to flatter; he possessed that enviable talent of making everyone he spoke to feel special. In addition, he was beautiful. Men wanted to shine by association and women simply wanted him, but he was mine and nobody questioned his devotion. I was as much of a prize to him as he to me. All the pleasures of life were ours for the taking, and we took them all, surrounded by our smiling friends, cheered on by passersby who simply liked to look at us.

But no children. Except the one I stole.

Genevieve

Throughout your life, Adora, you had suffered enormous loss. Of these things you never spoke; you wrote about them instead in your diaries at the end of the day, interning yourself in the past, lost to all trespassers. How many times did I slip by your library door to see you seated at your desk, framed by the enormous window that offered the blue, blue sea in the distance as a view, scribbling away, completely oblivious to sound and to whoever might creep past to catch a glimpse of a woman immersed in grief.

Most of your admiring friends never knew this about you. It was a testament to my privileged place in your life that I did, for I was invited to share in the ritual every summer. No, your friends saw only the incomparable beauty of a woman who had lost practically everything, yet beamed graciously through it all. In all honesty, I don't think they cared to look much deeper than the image you projected or the magnificent generosity you displayed. They were too busy reveling at the lavish parties you held or taking siestas in the exclusive hotels you pulled strings for them to stay in, during their sojourns on your island in the Mediterranean Sea.

Your house was located on a cliff overlooking that same sea: a white villa, enormous in size, home to the priceless artifacts acquired during your travels throughout the world. It was the house you had grown up in, a wedding gift from your mother. But it was the view from my window that beguiled, that haunts me still: the view that encompassed the expanse of the island beyond and the pool below, inlaid with turquoise marble in the shape of dolphins, the distant whitewashed houses dotted down the hills, your olive grove and, finally, the bougainvillea flowers.

All summer long, you would wear bougainvillea in your hair. From the first summer I can remember until the last, you would place a cluster behind your ear, always of the deepest pink, and wear it to dinner. You elicited awe whenever you appeared; your blond curls, which would turn whiter as the season progressed, cut into a bob, your drop-waisted dresses, always white silk, and the ubiquitous diamonds you adored marked you as entirely of your era: a time whose demise would be deeply mourned if you were any indication of its magnificence. It was easy to imagine you dancing the Charleston or wafting, cocktail in hand, over perfectly manicured lawns of a summer evening. Nor could there be any doubt that you were the guest of honor: the exquisite creature the party would not be complete without.

It's hardly surprising that I approach life in the way in which I do considering that the foundation of my education was provided by the romanticism of your life. You were so beautiful beyond compare, so cultured and refined, that I sought to emulate you in everything, which must have provided quite a spectacle when I was a child. I would mimic your speech and feign your accent, thinking myself too, too sophisticated until my mother's reproving glance would remind me of what I was not, nor ever could be: you.

It was inevitable that I would idolize you. Everything you did provided a vision of elegance that proved completely unforgettable. Nothing was ever mundane in your world. People were never pretty or good-looking; they were *beautiful.* No one simply loved; they *touched one another's souls.* Nor did anyone ever die; *their light receded.* I can still recall the lilting rise and fall of your accent as you voiced your opinions, the soft French tones that so bewitched whoever was lucky enough to listen to you. Nor can I forget the evening's vision of your walk with your dogs through the olive grove to the edge of the cliff that overlooked the sea, bordered by the marble balustrades. It was, I was to learn much later, the cornerstone of your day and I was forbidden by my mother as a child—absolutely forbidden—to ask to go with you.

My mother explained that your life had been so sad, you had lost so many loved ones, that those walks with your dogs were when you thought about them. So I would watch you from the house as my parents and Oliver chatted, drifting toward the olive grove where your greyhound, Linford, would always sit at the entrance waiting for you. He was your favorite; you called him your guardian. "He stops me from going too far," you'd always say, whenever asked. I had no idea what you meant, but the way you whispered it, as if you were saying a silent prayer of thanks, made me think that it was important.

You spoke like that, dramatically, intoxicating to most people who listened—but not all, I learned. I vividly recall one visitor rolling her eyes at her friend, a rather plain woman who stubbed out her cigarette with a smirk when you told them the same thing. I hated them for doing that, for mocking you, and I remember scowling at them and glancing nervously to see if you had seen their reaction, but your implacable demeanor gave nothing away. Nobody would ever have known what you were thinking. You seemed to be always looking past everyone to somewhere else, high above the general proceedings, to an enchanted private world. Wherever it was, if you lived there, I wanted to go there too.

My mother wasn't much help on the issue either. I remember saying that I loved the way you spoke, Adora, "so lee-ri-cal," I swooned, in imitation of the bright-blue-eyed, charmingly world-weary French man who had sailed his yacht to the island just to pay his respects to you. "*Chérie,* how could I not? Are you very annoyed?" he had asked as you strolled up to meet him and, by way of an answer, you held out your golden arm and led him away, serenely listening to him adore you.

"It's not so lee-ri-cal when you're starving to death and waiting for her to come in, Genevieve," my mother had snapped, admonishing me with a hard stare. I ignored her. Even in the beginning, I couldn't see past you. It was easy to turn back to you.

The light was always fading whenever you visited the grove, a hazy gray-white that seemed to envelop you as you strolled toward the sea in your white silk dress, Linford at your side, your fingertips resting on his back as he walked perfectly in time with you, your diamond bracelets glinting in the approaching dusk, followed by your collection of dogs rescued from the streets all around you. And you would stop at the edge of the cliff, in front of the marble balustrades, your back to the house; you and Linford perfectly still, both so delicate and refined, like statues watching over the sea beyond. I used to wonder what you were looking at, but I knew it was captivating, whatever it was. And I remember clearly wishing as a child, in all my innocence, for a tragic life just like yours. If I could grow up to be that beautiful, if I could wear bougainvillea in my hair and diamonds on my wrists, crying silent tears in the olive grove for all that was lost, what a life that would be.

Bougainvillea. It might as well be your name because it is what I think of whenever people speak of you. You loved those flowers so, allowing the branches to grow unchecked until they enveloped the house with their fuchsia petals. I wonder now if it was their delicacy that appealed to your mysterious heart; they withered so quickly once cut, after all. But while they lived, they provided an image of beauty that seared the souls of those who gazed upon them. Like you.

Perhaps they provided a bright spot on which to focus your heartbroken eyes. But they also found an outlet in me. I recall perfectly how your head would turn toward me, the fuchsia stem of bougainvillea behind your ear a searing slash of color against your white-blond curls before the brilliance of your aquamarine eyes would find mine as I waited at the window for you to return from your evening walks. From my earliest memory, they seemed to feast. I was never scared. I let you wrestle me from my mother's arms. She was the one who clung, I the one who ran willingly far, far away to the splendor of your flower-strewn world.

Sophie

It is the dogs I remember now. Inexplicable how they always chose our carriage to run alongside. From all over the island they came, the unloved, homeless orphans nobody wanted, most of them left behind by capricious tourists, some bred by the islanders hoping to make money, but most discarded for some reason or another. Long before we lived there, when we only holidayed on the island each summer, every time we ventured out they followed us, racing the carriage, barking excitedly to attract our attention. Sometimes they followed us all the way to our destination and, as soon as we disembarked, they would crowd around Sebastian, quieting only when he petted them, basking in his care and attention until we went home again. I called him my little Pied Piper, my golden-haired son, whose soul whistled a tune that soothed the lonely dogs where we lived. Such a charming notion; I never expected him to take me seriously. Every year when we returned from Paris, where we lived, to our summer house, it was the same. The dogs were always waiting for him.

I can't remember precisely when it started, but the dogs grew more confident with each summer as they chased our carriage, and several times, on seeing Sebastian inside, they tried to jump in and were caught under the wheels, the poor creatures trampled to death by the horses. Sebastian was inconsolable. The situation grew so grave that I actually considered not leaving the house, fearful that more animals would die and that my son and daughter would never recover. *Why? Why, Mama?* my precious son would ask me, tears flowing without end down his perfect little face. Nothing I could say consoled him and, as time went on, he showed no signs of recovering; not even Adora could elicit even a whisper of a smile. He blamed himself. He thought their deaths were his fault. Nobody could convince him otherwise.

It was Adora who cured him, who offered up the little white lie to mend his broken spirit. I had left her for the afternoon with some friends at the Hôtel des Anges while I took Sebastian to the doctor, frantic at how much he had withdrawn from the world that summer. He was only ten. So much sadness, I thought, couldn't possibly be normal in such a young child. I shall never forget watching her race up the steep stone steps to our villa, a vision of hope and prettiness, a secret in her pocket. "Sebastian," she called, searching around for her brother as she reached our marble veranda, where I was sitting, brooding. "Mama," she exclaimed seeing me sitting there, "I know why."

"What do you know, Adora?" I asked with little interest, too distracted by the events of the afternoon.

"I know why they die—the dogs," she explained excitedly. "A lady from the island told me today. She knows about us; everybody knows about us and about the dogs dying. The islanders think that the dogs choose to die."

"*Ma chérie*, whatever do you mean?" I scoffed, irritated by her persistence. I wanted to be alone to try to reconcile what the doctor had suggested to me. "How can anybody possibly know what a dog wants?" I watched her face, seconds earlier alive with promise, crumple into disappointment, tears not far from the surface, but I was too upset to bother with her. I had more pressing issues than Adora's fancies to deal with.

I had no idea that Sebastian, who had retreated to his room as soon as we arrived home, had come out onto the veranda at the sound of Adora's voice. "Do they really?" I heard him quietly ask as he came up beside his sister. She blinked back her tears hurriedly before she turned to him, something in her even then understanding that he could not cope with sorrow. "Yes," she announced, nodding her head vigorously. "It's true. The lady at the hotel told me today. She said that everybody, even dogs, has a choice about when they die and that they always die with the person they love the most. The dogs chose you because they love you the most, like I do."

I watched her watch him expectantly, to see if her little ruse had worked. I didn't believe there had been a woman at the hotel. Adora was always so fond of stories. I was sure she'd made it up herself. Yet Sebastian, for the first time in weeks, smiled at her. It was a smile suffused with relief, as if she had saved him from a precipice he had been tempted to jump off.

"But why do they die, Adora? Some of them are only puppies," he asked, warming to her theme.

"Because nobody loves them when we're not here," she replied simply. "They're frightened you'll leave and never come back. That's why, Sebastian. It's because they love you the most."

I watched the scene in front of me with a mixture of awe and skepticism, expecting Sebastian to break down in tears again, as he so often had whenever I tried to console him. To my surprise, however, he took her hand and followed her off down to the olive grove, peppering her with questions as they left.

"Did the lady know any of their names?" he asked his sister who, happy as ever to oblige, launched into a lengthy fairy tale in answer to his question. "Do you remember the little dachshund with the red hair? Well, his name was Geordie and he was born in a cherry blossom tree in Japan and all of the flowers came apart from the branches and made a nest and they sailed him here because they heard about you, Sebastian, and how you would love him. . . ."

I almost fell under the spell of Adora's story myself. What a talent she had, even at that tender age—a talent to beguile—for her brother, Sebastian, listened as if spellbound as they moved further and further away from me. I can still picture them in my mind's eye, slowly walking down the steps to the olive grove, with me following them at a remove, delighting in their private scene. I vividly remember Sebastian's little hands, still plump with childhood, smoothing the ground as if he were making a silk bed for a king and announcing, "Geordie shall sleep here," looking for approval up to Adora, who was hovering ever near as if ready to rescue him from dangers unseen.

"And Lala; where will you put her, Sebastian?" Adora cajoled, understanding this was the type of activity that he needed, that would bring joy to his fragile heart. In my memory, I watch Sebastian struggle to decide and blow the memory a kiss, leaving them behind in that perfect idyll where they were once so happy.

I thought that would be the end of it, but it wasn't. In fact, Adora's story was only the beginning of how my children became the rescuers of every homeless dog on the Mediterranean

island where we came to live permanently for the sake of Sebastian. As soon as we left the island at the end of that summer
to return to Paris, he relapsed into the terrible melancholy that
had plagued him until Adora's story released him. He could not
cope with leaving the dogs of the island. He would have terrible nightmares and screaming fits in his sleep about his beloved pets he had left behind, whose lives, he believed,
depended on his happiness. I took him to every doctor we
knew, but none could assuage my concerns.

Finally, I asked my son what he wanted, what I could do to
make him feel better. "To live forever on the island with you
and Adora and my dogs and her stories," he replied. Nothing I
could say would dissuade him. It was all he wanted and, despite
how I cajoled and bribed, he remained disconsolate for
months, until his father and I finally gave in and I moved there
at the end of 1909, my husband staying behind in Paris until he
could take leave of his job and visit us.

Before he was killed, my husband, Alexandre, was a politician serving the French government. We had met at a ball in
Paris, where I had recently moved from Nantes, where I was
born. At the time, I desired the life of a philosopher, to commit
myself only to books and education, things I thought I could
find only in the city. As is so often the case with love, however,
when we met everything changed. To be with him, I abandoned
everything. Together, we traveled the world, dined at the great
palaces and embassies of foreign lands. My hunger for knowledge was sated by the brilliant men and women we met. It was,
quite simply, the most extraordinary existence. My children,
however, forced me to reconsider my priorities. Sebastian, especially.

Once we came to live on the island, the change in Sebastian was remarkable; it was as if he had found a purpose that fulfilled him completely. His health, his spirits, his education all improved, and although I missed my husband with a passion, I couldn't regret my decision on witnessing the transformation in my cherished son. I congratulated myself that my children would not become spoiled nomads so representative of the children of politicians, but nymphs of the sun and sand, who would grow to become part of the simple culture of the area.

Now, when I recall their childhood, I think not of the impediments to the normal life I once craved for them but rather of the spectacle they provided each week of bringing every dog on the island back to our house. Rescuing the dogs was Adora's idea. If they could save them, then they could love them and, if those poor creatures were loved, they wouldn't need to die so young. Like clockwork, Adora and Sebastian would appear at 4:00 P.M., in time for their afternoon nap, with a half-starved animal ranging from a Doberman to a Pekingese. The poor thing would have been named before its arrival, conferring an intimacy that made it impossible for me, despite how I protested, to turn the bedraggled creature away in the face of the tears welling precariously in the enchanting eyes of my children.

"But Adora says that she was born in Scotland, where it's so very cold, Mama, and they left her outside and a polar bear found her and carried her on his back all the way here," Sebastian would plead, full of one of Adora's latest inventions. "Nobody wants her, Mama. Please let me save her."

And so we did. How could I refuse such compassion or imagination? Especially when it was all that he had? Not for my son to play with toys or the other children, only the simple, soundless spirits he rescued and his besotted sister, who seemed to cradle him like a snowflake, terrified he might disap-

pear. Our house, an enormous whitewashed villa on top of a
cliff overlooking the sea, became a sanctuary for the lost and
lonely animals of our island, cared for by my two golden-haired
children. Every morning, I would go to their rooms to wake
them, only to find they weren't there. After the first time it happened, when I almost died from the shock, I never worried
again because I knew where they were: in the olive grove, asleep
with their dogs on the ground. Sebastian's favorite dog, Titania,
a doe-eyed greyhound, refused to sleep there alone and came to
his window every night crying for him. So Adora found the solution and took Sebastian there to sleep, too, so that Titania
would not be alone. Perhaps something in my daughter understood even then that living without Sebastian would be unbearable. Eventually, when it became obvious that they would find
any way to leave their beds at night and hurry to the olive grove,
I bought a hammock, and every morning I found them there,
softly swaying, their golden arms wrapped around one another
in the incomparable dawn of a Mediterranean day.

Yes, it is the dogs I remember now; every name and story connected to all of my children's pets. I can remember, with vivid
clarity, how many years my golden son, Sebastian, had spent
on this earth when they brought home each new addition; how
many summers were left.

Years later, the summer just before my daughter died, I asked
Adora whether there really was a woman at the Hôtel des Anges

who told her of the myth that saved Sebastian. "No, Mama," she replied resignedly. "I made it up. I wanted to believe it too."

"Why?" I asked.

"Because the alternative was unthinkable," she replied, her eyes filled with a sorrow impossible to quell.

Yes, it is the dogs I remember now. I remember them too because they encapsulate the only time in my life when I can recall being grateful that I had a daughter, instead of wishing her gone.

Adora

Whenever people ask where you are, Sebastian, I always tell them the same thing: My brother lives in the sea, like a dolphin, I say. And it is true, my love; it is where I know you live and it is why I have stayed here on our island, so that I am always with you.

Your life was comprised of simple pleasures, enviable for me, who coveted everything, to witness. I followed you everywhere. You never tired of me, although you were a quiet soul. I remember asking you once if my endless chatter bothered you. *No*, you replied, *I love to listen to your stories.*

Now all I have left of you are stories, which I do not share, for to share them would give others the opportunity to comment, and they simply would not understand if I were to relate the love we had for one another. Their minds lack the purity of your own. You could not conceive of such insensitivity, such lack of depth, my poor, beautiful brother.

Every afternoon of my life, I have gone to my library to write down the story of my day. I have done this for you, Sebastian, because the ritual makes me feel as if you are still alive with me; everywhere I have ever traveled, you have journeyed too. I do it to keep the memory of our love alive, however elusive the recollections become, for I am growing older, Sebastian, evolving further and further away from the eighteen-year-old girl you last saw before you left me nearly twenty years ago. I am glad you did not live to see my hair dull or regret stain my eyes. Yet I know that everything I have is because of you and, in spite of the anguish I have suffered each day when I awake, I am so thankful for all of the things you have given me. Nothing I coped with in my life could possibly compare to what you endured, and so, as thanks for the blessings you made sure I own, I have lived my life for you because you couldn't, because I took it from you.

I failed you. The punishment I pay now, I accept completely. If it would bring you back, I would pay it every day of my life. All I can say, Sebastian, is that, if you had been with me, everything would be so different. I would never have erected this prison from which I cannot escape; the prison borne of the relentless sorrow I feel for your loss.

Sophie

When first we settled on the island, every day we were stopped by the villagers. My God, how many times did they ask of me if my divine children were twins? It was exhausting. Sebastian was older than Adora, only barely, by two years, I would tell them, but they refused to believe. They would stand and marvel at them, at their hair of the whitest blond, and their eyes of aquamarine, which distinguished them from anyone such people had ever before seen. All of the people would flock around them, wishing to touch their fair skin as if they were sacred statues sculpted of gold in a temple.

It was so very shocking, the attention they attracted from the local people. At first, I failed to understand how uniform their lives on the island had been before our arrival, accustomed as they were to centuries of unstinting sameness. In the village where we lived, Sebastian and Adora were revered as holy by dint of their exceptional difference from the norm. I could never have imagined that I, too, would be crowned like a queen, an object of veneration by virtue of bringing the closest things to angels the islanders were ever likely to see in this arid landscape. My desire to keep my son and daughter humble was ritually tested in the face of the locals' admiration. Each day, they would return home from school laden with gifts presented to them by everyone from their teachers to the local shopkeepers. I was so exhausted after months of futile attempts to quell the tide of goodwill toward them that I finally gave in and allowed my children to develop a sense of entitlement normally reserved for royalty.

It is I who must be reproached for the nature of their existence. For as with most children singled out, through no fault of their own, for reverential worship, they became inseparable. I was frequently absent, hidden behind the doors of our home poring over books, so involved with the improvement of my mind that I let them run free, telling myself it would only prove beneficial to them. Thus, each provided the understanding heart for the other, the sounding board for their unique woes, the protective hand to grip in the face of spectators who studied their every move. Nothing I provided could compare. The sea was their true refuge. There they could hide underwater, pretending to be dolphins, communicating through signs. Every day after school, they would scour the beaches for hidden coves where they could sit undetected, Adora's lovely head nestled into Sebastian's shoulder, where she would watch for signs of mermaids and he for that elusive whale, Moby Dick.

Sometimes I would feel guilty enough to interrupt my studies and venture to their sanctuary on the beach. I would discover them drawing floor plans of their future houses with twigs in the sand—Adora's ornamental and imposing, Sebastian's austere. From there they would initiate their afternoon ritual of receiving one another for tea, something they had learned from me, for whom the education provided by frequent visits to the British Embassy had proven indispensable. Always these visits would fol-

low the same pattern, Adora tut-tutting about the mess Sebastian
had made in his kitchen, her brother content to sit quietly in the
sun on her marble veranda, a collection of his dogs at his feet.

The two became known as *les petits voleurs* — the little
thieves — to the islanders, a nickname affectionately bestowed on
them because sometimes they rescued dogs that were not homeless and, of course, irate residents would show up at our door
demanding to take their family pet home. I can still picture my
little boy, clad only in his swimming costume, interrogating those
who did come about their love for their dog, only releasing the
poor animal back to them when he was completely satisfied
nothing would harm a hair on its head. Nor did his compassionate vigilance end there. For weeks afterward Sebastian would spy
on the land surrounding their homes, Adora at his back, to ensure that the dog was well treated. If ever he saw it chained outside the house or a makeshift dog kennel in the back garden, he
would march up and reclaim the animal, forcing me to deal with
the subsequent ravings of incensed owners until they would
eventually give up and stop seeking to take back their mistreated
pet, who had found a sanctuary with my son.

I did not question my children's intense need for one another. I did not ask why they never brought other friends home
from school, why Adora gripped Sebastian's hand with a feroc-
ity that bordered on manic possessiveness. I simply reveled in
their appearance every afternoon outside my study window,
their bouncing golden curls flying in the air as they ran up the
stone steps to our villa, framed by the incomparable blue of the
sky, their white and navy blue school uniforms pristine in the
sun, the babble of their voices as they laughed mischievously,
each the owner of the other's secrets. Secrets they would never
share with me.

Adora

James was my husband's best friend. I never questioned his affection for Oliver. They had been friends since they were five years old, boarders at the same private school in England. James handled all of Oliver's legal transactions; Oliver trusted him implicitly. I refuse to believe there was ever as much love between two friends as they shared.

James was the first friend of Oliver's I ever met. They were both holidaying on the island together. Of course, Oliver never returned to England. James did, to set up his law practice, with his wife, Miranda. It is no secret that Miranda and I never cared for each other, although we always appeared to for the sake of our husbands. She resented me, and I never could fathom her. Whereas James was there always when we needed him, ready to go out at a moment's notice, Oliver often complained about how distant Miranda seemed, endlessly citing her daughter as an excuse to leave early and get back to the hotel. It was very much apparent she disapproved of her husband's friendship with us; Oliver and I would often see her pull a face when James offered to drive us somewhere or help in some way. As I told my darling husband at the time, how-

ever, I could not imagine why she acted as she did. I never professed to understand her.

Regardless, they always visited the island every year for
their summer holiday and, in spite of whatever troubled Miranda, we truly did have the most wonderful times: days spent
on the beach, the two men playing tennis, the *thwack, thwack* of
the ball keeping rhythm with their laughter. Then lunch on the
beach, home for a siesta, a quick change before dinner, a meal
outside in the Mediterranean night air. How life should be
lived. How we did live it for all those years.

It was difficult, of course, with our not being able to have
children and watching our various friends announce the seemingly frequent arrival of their babies. More than difficult; I was
devastated. But I have been privileged in my life to love and be
loved, and I have been so blessed, so very blessed in so many
different ways. And, of course, there was always Oliver.

The way he used to look at me . . . people would comment
on it. They had never seen anyone so profoundly in love as Oliver, they told me. They told me I was the luckiest woman in the
world. Always, he watched me. I can still recall the passionate
thrill his attention inspired in me when we first met: the curiosity in his eyes, his handsome face contemplative, unsmiling.
Before I knew him well enough to understand his moods and
emotions, I would always worry I had annoyed him and would
beg him to tell me what he was thinking as he watched me. Yet
I never had anything to fear, for my darling Oliver would always
reply, "I was simply thinking how lovely you are." And he would
kiss me so gently and smile so reassuringly that I could almost
dispel my doubts. Yet despite his constant support, I was always
in fear of not living up to the enormous love he showed me.

Watching Genevieve—or Gigi as I always called her—grow

up, however, changed everything for me. What I had learned to accept—my barrenness—ripped me apart again. She was the loveliest child I had ever seen, and James's and Miranda's joy in her savaged my heart in ways I could not possibly have imagined. I had never felt such love and such regret at the same time. Naturally Oliver, knowing me so well, understood what I went through during that time, and he bought me the most magnificent diamond necklace for my twenty-third birthday when, after three years of trying, I was told categorically by the doctor that I would never have children. I wore it for my party, when practically all of our friends had made the trip to the island to celebrate it with us. Oliver's gift was the topic of conversation for the evening. In fact, I think the women still talk about it: how considerate he was to buy me such spectacular diamonds because I could not give him children. To think they envied me for a necklace. Despite how much I wanted to put on a brave face, I retreated to our bedroom and wept. Oliver was so upset when I told him why; he accused me of trying to ruin the party he had planned so carefully for me, of making him feel inadequate. It was one of the few times we ever fought, but it was all such a simple misunderstanding. Oliver forgave me completely when I explained properly why I was so distraught. He had reacted only because he thought I was criticizing him, which I would never do. After all, I chastised myself, what else could he have given me under the circumstances?

Genevieve

Oliver was widely considered to be almost impossibly handsome. Debonair is probably the best way to describe him, but he was never slick. He was the kind of man destined to improve with years, the deeper auburn of his hair weathering to the color of sand, each wrinkle adding character and lending distinction to what was, in certain lights, although I have never mentioned this, as nobody ever dared criticize Oliver, a rather weak face.

From a very young age, I can always remember wanting to impress him, my "uncle." Of course, he was nothing of the sort, but Adora would insist that I call them "aunt" and "uncle." "I always think of you as mine, somehow," she would say, and I was more than happy to pretend that was the case. I did dances and turned cartwheels and showed Oliver how far I could swim underwater while holding my breath, anything to attract his attention. Not that my uncle ever said much in response to my efforts except "Well done" or "Really, did you?" when I would boast about my achievements. But I had seen how a smile from him lit up Adora's face, and I longed for the same. I would follow him and my father everywhere they went when I was little, swimming with them and collecting the balls when they played tennis but, much to my delight, Oliver never treated me like a nuisance. Just when I thought he had forgotten about me, he would smile in my direction or tickle me and I would feel exactly as I imagined Adora did all over again.

Even when I was small, I knew that my father wasn't like Oliver. Everything about my uncle, the way he stood—his legs apart, leaning back, his arms folded—seemed relaxed, unhurried, whereas my father was constantly buzzing, making jokes, telling stories, anything to please his friend. My uncle walked with an indolent grace, fluidly, effortlessly—everyone else seemed clumsy in comparison—and he always dressed impeccably in cool white linen suits and open-necked pastel shirts that made him stand out amongst the tourists and locals sweltering in the heat. He knew everyone and always greeted them warmly; he was the island's only celebrity alongside my aunt. He had trained as an architect and had founded a business on the island with a group of financiers, gradually buying over the existing houses and renovating them to even more luxurious standards than before to sell to the aristocracy who flocked to our paradise annually. Yet it always seemed as if others were in need of him, were chasing him down to say hello when, in reality, as an entrepreneur, it was Oliver who needed them. Such was his effortless charm that nobody ever seemed to mind.

It was his generosity, too, that encouraged further the adoration of his friends. Oliver never allowed anyone to pay for a meal, even if the assembled party amounted to twenty or more. The men of his group used to dash from the table when the orders were taken to settle the bill only to find that Oliver had arranged for everything to be charged to his account. And his kindness, his affability, the way in which he made everyone feel welcome, as if the elaborate parties he and Adora held were simply for people Oliver genuinely liked instead of the "right" people who could help him in his career, confirmed his status in the minds of his friends and acquaintances as the best of men.

My father adored Oliver. Even as a very small child, I can recall feeling a glowing pride whenever I would hear Oliver refer to my father as his best friend, as if I, by association, was singled out for that honor too. They did have other friends, those from school with whom they had triumphed on the cricket pitch. None of them, however, despite how hard they tried to impress, enjoyed that special place reserved in Oliver's life for my father. And they knew it. Of course, this certainly never stopped them from trying to come between them. They would offer endless invitations to Oliver that excluded my father. At the time, I could only imagine that Oliver initially accepted assuming his best friend had been invited too, because he was always astonished when he found out my father wasn't going but, by then, he could hardly refuse to go. My uncle was the perfect gentleman, you see.

Sophie

My husband, Alexandre, was my life, and when he died suddenly, I disintegrated into nothingness. To protect myself and indulge my grief, I abandoned my children, locked myself away from their touch, from the vision of what my husband and I had created. I knew that being near them would only impel me to recover, and all I wanted was to die.

Committed to him from the first; always we had been together, our minds, our passions inexorably intertwined. For him, I provided certainty, assurance that my soul would never waver in its desire for him and only him. In return, he adored me with the insatiable lust of a teenager, always by my side, forever mine.

I was not with him. It was the year after I moved with the children to the island in the Mediterranean Sea. Never before then had we spent a moment apart. He asked me to go to Norway with him, to leave the children with their nanny. Yet I had left our new home at the drop of a hat whenever he called that first year; I missed him terribly, and he was so busy with his work that I only saw him if he visited or if I accompanied him for a diplomatic meeting. It was guilt that led me to stay and not go with him, as he asked. I couldn't leave my children again for the fifth time in as many months. I rationalized that I had visited Norway before with him. I loathed the country, the people, the insufferable white nights. What was the point, I said, of being miserable while he worked? It was only a trip to last three weeks. He would come and visit us on his return. Just this once, I would stay, we agreed. I did.

I did. Not for me to die with my husband in a capsized ship in the black North Sea. Not for me to clutch his hand as we plunged to the seabed, never to resurface. No opportunity to tell him again how I loved him beyond words.

For months afterward, I resented my children: their need for me, their incapacity to care for themselves, their grief over their father's death; the fact that because of them I had been forced to leave Alexandre and move to that loveless island. Adora was nine years old, Sebastian eleven. I grew resentful of their incessant questions, their tears, their inability to understand the unfathomable. I could not cope. I needed my husband beside me. I needed his voice, his touch, his mind. Never to be mine again. I loathed God, Fate, Circumstance. I wanted to bleed myself of the agony of losing him, scratch my skin until it festered with decay. I relinquished life completely.

I was insane then. My brilliant mind failed me when I most desired insight, compassion, affection for my children. It was at that time Adora moved away from me forever, joined only to Sebastian. She did not seek me out or come to say good night. I terrified them both, but Sebastian never neglected me as I did him. For months, Adora hid from me. Sebastian, despite his fear, still came.

It was too late when I recovered sufficiently to be like a mother to Adora again. Too late to kiss and cajole her into loving me once more. Always she was wary of my presence. The guilt I endured was unappeasable when I realized the extent of the damage my absence had caused to them both. I longed for Sebastian to come to me as he always had, tapping gently on my study door, wriggling around it, and coming to rest his head on my lap, his hot, little boy breath delicious against my hand as I would smooth his hair. I should have appreciated what I had, how divine my children were, instead of blaming them for something they couldn't possibly understand: my grief.

I pushed them away after my husband's death because they reminded me of him. I couldn't bear to look at them and re-member him in them. I recall feeling proud when I realized why I had behaved as I did, almost ready to excuse myself for something entirely unforgivable. But it was too late; the bitter-est rub of my husband's death was yet to come. In my absence, Adora had lured Sebastian away from me like a sorceress. She had convinced him that she loved him more, offered him the love I had withheld. He did not want to believe, but he followed her anyway. Always he followed. Or so I was content to believe. Content because, by blaming her, I could forgive myself.

Adora

When Oliver and I would meet Miranda and James at the port to say good-bye at the end of their holidays, Gigi would sob and sob. Oh, whenever I think back to the tears streaming down her little face, I can't stand it. I could never bear to see her leave, but I did not let anyone know. All I lived for was the next time she would arrive on our island and run into my arms, when I would tell her that she grew prettier every time I saw her, when she would babble away about her trip and her school and her horse and all of the things that fill the minds of little girls.

As they walked away toward the cruise liner over the years, I would want to run after her and hold her one last time, my darling girl. She was all I wanted, all I could never have. And then the thought came to me, when she was eight years old, after years of being forced to watch her leave me, a thought that was perfect, impossible to deny. As I watched Miranda trying to calm her and Gigi crying and crying, begging to stay, the temptation welled up inside of me to say it, simply state what I wanted more than anything. So I did. I said: "Why doesn't she stay with us until the end of the summer and Oliver will bring her back to England when he has to come and see you, James, for business?" It was perfectly reasonable. We were, after all, her parents' closest friends, our love for her was not in dispute, and she was so, so terribly upset.

"No," Miranda said immediately, looking to James to help her. "She's too little. I've never left her with anyone," she protested.

"But please, Mummy. I'm eight. I'm old enough. Please let me stay," Genevieve begged, entranced by the idea. "I want to stay."

"James," Miranda pressed desperately, *"please . . ."* But James was not looking at her.

I held my breath as I watched the scene unfold in front of me. Miranda continued to protest, but I saw the light dawn on her husband, the light that said, *Why not? Why not?* Miranda saw it too. Understood as Genevieve's pleading grew louder, as her tears dried up and the prospect of staying seized her daughter's imagination, knew as soon as her gaze met mine that she was defeated.

It was wrong of me to take her only child, but at the time I pushed the thought far away, rationalized it to myself that we would take the best care of her, give Miranda a rest, time for her and James to enjoy each other. It was, after all, only six weeks until the end of the summer but, more than that, I could see that Oliver was in love with the idea, in love with me for thinking of it, and that he would never question why I had asked it.

So I took her. Took her in my arms, her head against my chest, and carried her away from her mother, who was helpless to protest in the face of our kindness. I did not look back. I knew if I did that I would melt in the face of Miranda's distress, and it had taken so much to finally feel peace again that I would not have given it up for anything.

That was the start of our summers together. Gigi and I had such a fabulous time that it was decided she should stay on longer every year after her parents left. At first, Miranda tried to holiday elsewhere to avoid leaving Gigi behind, but James insisted on coming to see his best friend. I'm so grateful to him for doing so, because I lived for Genevieve. I lived for the summers when she would rush toward me off the boat, her pretty little face alive with excitement and her heart inexhaustible in the love she offered. She was the blessing that made me forget everything I had lost. Those summers were the happiest times of my life.

Miranda

How could I have denied Adora? Especially when she presented the idea as the most reasonable thing in the world, in that matter-of-fact, entitled way she and Oliver always spoke: *Why ever not? Who could refuse us?* Genevieve was always practically hysterical about leaving; Adora standing there, beaming that they would be so happy to keep her, to give me a break for the rest of the summer, time to focus on the house, time to spend with James. How could I be seen to refuse a woman who would never have children a mere six weeks with the child who had stolen her heart?

I won't lie; I was distraught that she took Genevieve from me. I delighted in my daughter. I never needed a break from her. I loved to watch her play in the garden, to listen to her endless chatter, and she was so funny: naughty, yes, but funny along with it. Genevieve was always special. Different from the other children at school: gorgeous and terribly clever. A born actress, she was the star of all the classes she took. We always thought that she would end up on the stage. Everybody said so. Well, those who loved her did. Besides, I suppose in some ways she did.

She had a terrible time at school. The other girls were so nasty to her, taunting her about her airs and graces, all picked up from Adora, I have to say. The others were just jealous, but that's hardly an excuse. They would gang up on her and turn her friends against her, follow her down the road from school calling her spiteful names. I complained to the headmistress and even tried to reason with the parents. We did everything to try to stop it. Nothing worked, and it never stopped. Yet in spite of what she was forced to put up with, my daughter went to school every day and held her head high. I don't know how she did it, but she had a resolve at the youngest age to succeed, even in the face of outright wickedness. Although she cried in private and was often forced to sit alone, she never let those girls see how much they hurt her. She was almost impassive, her face registering no emotion when they teased her. I used to worry all the time about it, terrified they'd destroyed something vital in her, but Genevieve came alive as soon as she was home or with Adora, and I suppose that they would consider the life she leads now a success, even in spite of all of them.

I have only ever lived for her happiness, which is why I let her stay, although many of our friends simply can't understand what I was thinking at the time. Naturally, I don't confide that I had no real choice, that my hands were tied. Besides, when I said no at the port that day, nobody heard me—which is really just another way of saying that nobody cared.

Genevieve

You even wore your diamonds in the swimming pool, Adora. The way the sun glinted off them, you seemed suffused with light diving down to touch the blue mosaic dolphins on the bottom of the pool. Perhaps it was your golden skin or your refined bearing that saved you from looking ridiculous, ostentatious even. Not for you, my Beloved Aunt, to look as though you were trying too hard, like so many other women I have seen over the years who seek to make up for their lack of natural beauty with a profusion of stones dripping from their ears and wrists. But then, you never were like other women.

It seems odd to me now that I can only remember a handful of conversations we ever had. It wasn't as if you were quiet. When something piqued your interest or moral outrage, your voice certainly rang the loudest. Not that you were always right, but I don't think that thought would ever have occurred to you. You clung so fast to your beliefs that even if a mass of contradictory evidence had been presented, you would have dismissed it all with a wave of your hand performed with such grandiose finality as to stop the speaker from continuing. Less insightful people would say that your sense of your own intelligence was exalted; I would simply say that the essence of your life, the knowledge that sustained you, could never be questioned. What you believed to be true was true forever. Who you loved, you loved forever.

I think I exhausted you that first summer. As much as you seemed to want me there, I disturbed the tranquillity of your days. You were a thinker, "deep," as my mother used to say pointedly, although I don't think she meant it kindly. I would find you every day in your library, staring out the window at the sea beyond, lost in thought, the operas you loved playing on the gramophone. And if I ever asked what you were thinking about, the answer was always the same: "I am thinking about when I was a little girl, like you. . . ." And you would turn back to whatever you were doing, lost to further questions, compelling me, the intruder, to slip gently away.

But when you came out of your trances, you would be possessed by a manic need to busy yourself, which was bliss for me. For your idea of busy involved swimming or dressing up, strolling into town in the late afternoon to buy me things from the merchants in the square. For a time, the focus of your energy became all about pleasing me. Nothing was more sublime than holding your hand and being led through the narrow, whitewashed streets of the town, all eyes on you, all shop owners thrilled to help you. And like Oliver, you were charming to people. Not that you really needed to indulge in conversation with them. All you ever had to do was show up and smile.

Your smile was a rare and cherished thing, impossible to describe accurately. It was haunting. When you did not want to speak, you simply smiled and, for some reason that I have never understood completely, it seemed to answer any questions I might have, fulfilled unspoken desires, made little girls feel special in a way that later lovers do.

You used that trick on me many times that first summer, whenever my demands escalated to the point where you, like most mothers of talkative children, felt the need to go and lie down in a darkened room. It was a smile that conveyed how important I was to you yet forbade me coming nearer. It was a smile, I recognize now, that was designed to distance love until such time as you could cope with it.

Adora

The first summer Gigi belonged entirely to me, every morning she would run into the kitchen, where I would meet with our staff to plan the day, and I would squeeze lemon juice on her hair to make it go blond in the sun. I had told her that Oliver and I used to do that whenever we went to the beach and, from that moment on, she insisted I perform the ritual each day. Afterward, I would send her out to the pool to play with the dogs or splash around with the toys and balls I had bought for her. Yet five minutes later she would be back with me in the kitchen, demanding to know "Is it blond yet? Has my hair turned blond like yours?" I could not disappoint her. Her hair was so dark that only bleaching would ever make it light, so I would tell a tiny lie each day, marveling at how blond her hair had become. It hurt no one. It was the worth all of the riches in the world to see the smile spread across her face.

I adored solitude, but I adored Gigi more and could not deny her. I was enchanted by her attempts to copy my patterns of speech and movements. Her mimicry made her seem more completely mine. I fed her stories in the afternoons before she took her naps; those I shortened from my favorite novels, such as *Death in Venice* and *The Age of Innocence.* All of the stories I loved which she came to appreciate as well, asking that I tell them over and over again. Like my mother, I instilled a sense of culture into our days. I took her to the local art galleries, taught her how to speak a little French, dressed her in white silk dresses like mine. She drank in everything that I taught her, never complaining, always wanting to know more.

She was such an extraordinary girl, so distinct from other children of her age. I would let her sit at the table when we had guests over for dinner so that she could listen to our conversations and learn something. Of course, she was only a child. I smile when I recall the evenings no one else could speak because she chattered gaily on about her day and showed off, doing impressions of the merchants in town or one of the maids who came to clean the house. She became the star of our show, and I willingly gave up the stage to her, almost relieved not to be the center of attention for a while. I loved to listen to her. I would have let her stay up with us until the early hours of the morning, anything to keep her with me. It was always Oliver who reminded me of her bedtime and who was forced, poor thing, to take her to bed in the face of her protests and tears. I was always so sad to watch her reluctantly climb the stairs to her room, her tiny hand lost in his. I never could bear to watch her leave.

Sophie

Never did my children need me. I was envied for my lifestyle by other mothers; the independence of Adora and Sebastian liberated me to pursue my own interests. If they wanted something, a drink or a snack, they asked their nanny. If they required assistance with their studies, they asked their teacher. I spent entire mornings reading with nothing to disturb me. After their father died, they were strangers to me.

Yet once I emerged from my period of mourning, deep within me something had changed; I wanted them to need me more. I needed their love to fill me as their father's once had. More than anything, I longed for Sebastian, so similar to his father in countless ways. For him to come to me would restore my happiness in life. He was absent, however, save for the evenings, when we dined together. Adora occupied his time from sunrise to sunset, providing everything I had withheld over that terrible year.

As recompense, I tried to make them love me as they should. For the flimsiest of excuses, a scream or a cry, a book dropping to the floor, I would rush to see what they were doing, only to find them completely content in each other's company, the mishap part of their private game, something I would never be told about, despite how persistently I asked. I wanted my devotion to them to be apparent, for them to understand what two such tiny spirits never could: my grief, my solitude, my absence. But they were lost to me forever. Sebastian would never return to me — only to Adora.

I make them sound like strange children, something damnable. To any such grotesque stereotype, they were the opposite: completely delightful, loving, self-possessed, independent, everything a mother could wish for. I loved to spy on them, hovering around the corners in our home to eavesdrop on their conversations. If ever they stumbled upon me in my hiding place, they would simply hug me and run off to play somewhere out of reach, a place beyond my gaze.

I accepted failure. When I felt kind, I acknowledged Adora's influence over Sebastian as the necessary consequence of the terror my grief had inspired. When I felt vindictive or bitter, I resented every solitary thing she did. Yet I tried never to dwell on my distaste. She was born of me. The responsibility for her conduct belonged to me. Everything was my fault, I told myself. But still . . .

I tried to accept their unique bond. In public at least, I made a display of being fiercely proud of their love for one another, imagining myself a lioness. As fickle and unsubstantial as love can prove, together they owned far more, I boasted. Yet there was a truth to what I said: Between them, there did exist something inexplicable in words — a spiritual element that binds two people together forever. They were two halves of the same soul. The emptiness I felt after Sebastian's death was nothing compared to what my daughter suffered. It seems inconceivable that Adora should ever have continued to breathe without him. Never was her role to follow like some medieval pilgrim searching for religious sustenance. Despite the Herculean strength she projected onto Sebastian, he did not lead. Always, he waited for her. It is a dark thing for a mother to admit, but I couldn't bear to think of him being alone. I never escaped the feeling that Adora failed him by living only to serve his memory. Indeed, by continuing to live.

But I must stop, because it is unbearable to think of what life might have been if she had never been born, if I had never experienced the rapture of watching her tiny fingers wrap around mine, or watched her unrivaled beauty develop with each year, or reveled in the overwhelming love she offered as penance in her life. Now that she is also gone, I can accept that my daughter is everything. Just like her name, she is beloved. Always, she was somehow larger than life, impossible to ignore, and Sebastian never could. Everything that happened was borne of love, but for years I found that the deliverance only complete forgiveness could bring constantly eluded me.

While Adora lived, I could never allow myself to love her completely; first out of resentment, later out of fear. After the tragedy, I was afraid to because she was broken. Hers was the kind of devastation that could harm people because she loved so ferociously and couldn't let go. For everything she brought to the world, something was destroyed in order to do so.

And yet, I accept now that to be loved by her was an exceptional and special thing, complex and difficult to cope with, but entirely unique, completely unforgettable. Without her, people withered.

Genevieve

That glorious first summer I spent alone with you slipped away, and winter's barren arms enveloped me. You kept your promise and returned me to my mother, but I was an entirely different child from the one she had left behind. Gone were the voluminous party dresses she had made for me, to be replaced by the white smocks of sun-kissed children and bare feet. I had picked up more of an accent, in imitation of yours, dear Adora, which I put to good use by talking endlessly, coupled with sweeping hand gestures to emphasize my firmly held beliefs. I requested my meals in French and asked my father, in all seriousness, for diamonds for Christmas. In short, what was presented to my mother after six weeks of absence was a mini-version of you, my Beloved Aunt.

My newfound personality made my mother nervous. During my first days back, she fluttered around me, making herself available for games and trips to see my pony that she would never have had the time for before that summer. But soon, the warm familiarity of our house lured me back from the charms of my holiday. I was once again clothed suitably for the weather, no longer in need of afternoon naps and, straitened by my mother's exasperation after several weeks of demanding behavior that was certainly not to be indulged, moderately well behaved. With the nights growing darker, I turned my attention to wishing for snow for Christmas.

Yet I still remember the unhappiness of coming home to England after that first extended summer. Everything seemed lacking in comparison to the bright loveliness of your world, Adora. I loved my mother and father more than anything, and I certainly never lacked attention, but I was lonely. School continued as it always had; me left out by the girls in my class, the object of hurtful jokes and imitations. I walked home every day in tears. Nothing I could do would make them like me. All I longed for was you, Adora, my best friend, my other mother.

Your letters were everything I looked forward to, how I made it through the weeks. You would tell me how you were counting down the days before you came to England for another visit; what a glorious time it was on the island, although you missed me terribly; how the dogs kept going to my room to see if I was there; that there was a dress in town that I simply must have; and how the bougainvillea were flowering again. Such was the familiar flow of your thoughts. You told me of the books you had read; the swims you took in the afternoon; the shells you had found on the beach; the paintings you had seen that you knew I would love and, finally, always, how you longed to see me. As if by magic, all of my troubles would disappear when I read your words. Simply the sight of a letter from you made me feel special.

Perhaps retrospect has meddled with my memories of those years, for I can't recall arriving home from school to find a letter waiting for me without seeing my mother wince.

It never occurred to me then that love could cause such distress. I just thought I was lucky to be so loved by someone as captivating as you. I appreciate now how much it must have hurt my mother to listen to me sing your praises at every opportunity, yet she accepted it all with quiet serenity. She still does.

Miranda

James always thought me paranoid, I think, whenever I would comment on the change in Genevieve when she came back after her summers with Adora. It wasn't the accent or the dresses or the demanding behavior that troubled me, it was what I can only describe as a distance between us that grew greater with each year they spent together alone. I felt as if I was losing my only child to a life I could never provide, to a woman I could never compare to.

I told myself not to be so foolish, obviously, and tried not to dwell on my insecurities. A relatively easy task, considering I had such a unique daughter to raise, a demanding social life trying to compete with the other wives as the hostess du jour, a husband to look after, and a house to keep up. More than that, too, was the fact that Genevieve was so miserable at school. So I am to blame for allowing her relationship with Adora to become so deep, so meaningful to her. It was the only thing that made her happy, what she looked forward to the most. It was all she ever talked about, and I could hardly let her in on my own private feelings about Oliver and Adora, and the sacrifices I had been forced to make for that pair. God, whenever one of

Adora's letters arrived, I would want to rip it to pieces, but then Genevieve's excitement would check me and I'd feel so guilty. Then I'd think about Adora and force myself to stop. The full tragedy of her life would hit me and I'd reproach myself for grudging her the little pleasure Genevieve offered. Besides, what else did the woman have? Oliver? Well, that's a laugh, but I don't suppose there's much point in talking about any of that now.

No, I'd just sit there and listen as Genevieve would read the letter aloud, Adora's distinctive gentle French accent audible behind the words, cooing away to my little girl: "Gigi, it is only sixteen days until we're together again. I can barely stand it. . . ." And I'd watch my daughter read as if hypnotized by the magpie that had stolen all of the precious, gilded objects from my life. I never asked for them back. I let Adora keep them. I had no choice. For Genevieve's happiness my silence was bought anew.

Sophie

I learned everything at a remove, from Paris, where I moved after Adora married Oliver and I gave them the house, through letters from Adora. I visited every summer at its end just before Genevieve would leave to go home, but it was safer for me always to keep my distance. When those summers started, I should have intervened. I should have interrupted whenever I overheard Adora say "If you were mine, what I wouldn't give you, Gigi. If you were only mine . . ." I should have shaken Gigi by the shoulders whenever that child replied, with infinitely more conviction with each passing year, "But I am yours, Adora. I am yours." I should never have allowed the fantasy to continue; I owed that much, at least. At the time, I told myself it was guilt that stopped me—remorse over the past and the things I had not provided for my children, but I was, as ever, lying to myself. It was fear that stopped me, cowardice. I could not confront Adora; I simply couldn't do it.

Of course, I adored Genevieve, but I simply couldn't bring myself to disillusion her even though I have always prized honesty above all things. Yes, Gigi was charming and pretty enough as children go; a little poppet, cute, but not a beauty and never would be. I could see that from a very young age. Yet Adora seemed intent on conferring her own attributes onto the child; citing her in the same exquisite vein as herself, as intelligent, as emotional. None of it was the case. Genevieve was ordinary and, as she grew up, as I watched her grow, it became more and more obvious that Adora was simply blind to the truth about the girl she loved, just as she was blind to the flaws in all of those she loved.

I told myself there was no point in interfering. Adora had never listened to me, and it wasn't the first time she had idolized someone to distraction, which, in truth, is what concerned me so very much. Whenever I would visit, it was all I could bear to watch Adora and Genevieve together. I was so full of pity for Miranda. How the poor woman coped was something I could not fathom. To me, it appeared as if Adora had completely succeeded in replacing Genevieve's mother. I never once heard the child ask for her. As she grew up, it was always I who inquired after her parents. Genevieve never volunteered any information. Still, it was so very important to me to be close to her during those summers, considering everything. I did it for Miranda. So I never scolded Genevieve for her ambivalence about her family. In fact, nobody ever reprimanded her—a pity now when you consider it.

Perhaps because of Adora imbuing her with foolish notions, Genevieve grew up with a greater sense of self-worth than was justified. Every summer there were more stories about the terrible trouble she had at school, but she never seemed to lack confidence. Genevieve always seemed so strong, so capable, so impervious to harm, which is probably why I kept my silence; I thought she could cope. Yet as Adora always insisted, such confidence derived from having constantly to de-

fend herself against the unpleasantness of others. I understood
the logic of Adora's argument but, despite how much I loved
Gigi, I never felt it rang true or understood everyone's tacit acceptance that Genevieve was the innocent victim of schoolgirl
malice. Not once did one of us ever ask why. Why Genevieve:
What was it about her that made people turn away?

It seems to me that for everything in life there is a reason—
every regret and disappointment, something we do contributes
to it. Perhaps I lack the compassion to understand what Gigi
was forced to tolerate. It's certainly possible. After all, I have no
illusions left about myself or of what I am capable.

Adora

I have felt my heart break. I knew it was possible long before I experienced it, but I do not think I ever believed such a thing could be felt. Now, of course, I accept it totally. It is that moment when you see a thing so beloved in the process of leaving you, its light receding before your eyes. It is a dull sensation, your heart breaking, like the sound of a pebble dropping on the sand. Not a shattering, not a tearing apart, there is nothing shrill or grandiose about the sensation. It is merely an internal realization that something treasured you never knew you had is leaving forever.

I find it reassuring now to comprehend that I have loved so well. I find comfort in knowing that, for that moment when I saw such great love recede before my eyes, I felt something so profound. It is my only solace. For afterward I felt nothingness, as if I was hollow and the breeze could blow straight through the empty chambers of my once full heart.

I scoff at these screen actors and teenage girls who wail about their hearts breaking, as if they could ever know what it really means. For such a thing to happen, you have to have loved blindly and completely, utterly without selfishness. Your whole life has to have been bound up in that one person without whom you cannot live. I have had that honor, to love to distraction, to worship the object of that love without thought for myself. And I have suffered the effects of such love: I have been crippled by its death. Not the death that creeps up over years and takes you when you are old, but the death that is self-inflicted. The beating heart that is stopped by its owner because the love you offer is not enough, despite how hard you tried, despite everything you gave up to do so.

I live my life knowing that the pedestals on which I placed my idols were not high enough; my love a fraction too little to engulf them, to anchor them to me; myself, my smiles, my words not enough to save them. Twice in my life this knowledge has appeared at my door: first with you, Sebastian, and finally with my husband.

It was because of me; I had grown arrogant, trusted that the worst was behind me. After you, Sebastian, I thought I might be spared. Gigi had just arrived for the summer, had been with us barely a week. It was the very start of the season, and she had come in mid-May, instead of July, because she had finished school, having turned eighteen earlier this year. How I had so looked forward to it. It had been such a heavenly day, perfectly warm, and Gigi and I had spent the afternoon trying on my jewelry, swimming adorned with treasures until the early evening, when my darling Oliver came home. I thought myself so blessed for living as long as I had, for the efforts I had made to atone for all my sins. I was overwhelmed with gratitude at the beauty of my existence. I should never have taken it for granted.

I recall meandering over here to my olive grove, playing the day's memories again in my mind, for once not calling to you, Sebastian, simply being happy to live. What I wouldn't give to return to those moments now, before I knew, before I was confronted with the truth about my life and those I loved.

All serenity, all calm was shattered when my gaze met the vision of my husband slumped against a tree, a makeshift noose around his neck; I felt as if every organ was being cut out of my body with scissors, the horror was so acute. He seemed to be sleeping; I didn't know what had happened or how, but I was possessed totally by the need to bring him back to me. I held him in my arms, willing him to be alive, begging him to stay until his eyes opened and I knew he was mine again. I could not lose him just as the summer was starting; I would never be able to live through the season again. Not after you, Sebastian. After all, I have stayed alive only because you couldn't, so that I can tell you everything when we meet again as I wish every day that we might.

Hadn't I done everything right, I questioned as I held him. For Oliver, I would have done anything; he had rescued me from my insurmountable grief, shown me what life could be; turned me away from the past and its demons. And yet, he was leaving me; death was preferable to being with me.

I had to pretend that Oliver had fallen when Genevieve came running up from the beach below, appearing suddenly at the top of the hidden stone path, shielded by bougainvillea, which led down from the olive grove. I had no idea she knew about it; you and I used the path as children, but I'd let the flowers grow after you died because I couldn't stand to see anyone emerge at the top who was not you. I set the mystery aside, however, as I protested Oliver's fall to her, and in the pretending we both convinced ourselves that it was what had really happened. My husband had tumbled, but he had got back up. He was with us still.

What an incredible gift I was given that evening: the opportunity to restore life, to love again with renewed passion;
more than I had a right to expect. We talked for hours after Oliver came home from the hospital, my perfect husband reassuring me that only my love had kept him alive, although it was
also my love, or lack of it, he confessed, that had driven him to
it; he had found me so distracted and thought me uninterested
in him. He needed me to sustain him, and the fact that I had
saved him only confirmed what he had always known since first
we met: Without me, he could not live. I was devastated that
he had not told me of his despair. I made him promise that he
would never hide anything from me again and, of course, he
agreed. Our marriage will only become stronger, he said. Confronted with what we might have lost, we would treasure our
love all the more, he promised. *Of course, my darling Oliver,* I
replied. *Of course.*

We held hands again, we smiled, we danced to music on
the veranda late into evening, I even changed my routine to
join him and Genevieve at the beach to walk the dogs the next
Sunday. Our lives resumed their blissful rhythm; we swam, we
laughed, we adored one another as we always had. The memory
of that terrible evening was laid to rest and none of us ever
spoke of it again. I told myself to be proud that the love such as
Oliver and I were blessed to share could provide salvation. I
told myself that over and over again until I believed it.

And yet, I couldn't forget what I'd seen, the scene I had
witnessed in my olive grove; the truth that had suddenly become apparent and was impossible to ignore. It is a dull sensation, your heart breaking, like the sound of a pebble dropping
on the sand . . .

Genevieve

If I had known what was to come, would I have lingered in the olive grove and memorized every leaf? Would I have stood in the doorway to the veranda, the white chiffon curtains ballooning in the breeze, just to feel their touch against my freshly tanned skin? Would I have linked my arm through yours, Adora, on our strolls in the old quarter of town and nuzzled my face into your neck to commit to memory once and for all the essence of your perfume? Ultimately, would I have made a different choice, one that might have saved you?

That summer of 1938, when I was just eighteen, I had not yet had to say good-bye to the people I loved. I could let blissful memories carelessly drift behind me, thinking that there would always be better ones to come. I had not yet found the eyes of the man whose devotion would compel me to remember every movement, word, and deed we shared. I did not possess the calm that is the offshoot of acceptance. I had never woken to a new day without anticipating, in all the glorious arrogance of my youth, a world of endless pleasures.

We were, all of us, that summer playing out our roles against the familiar backdrop of everything we cherished, collaborators in what we thought the truth of our lives to be. Nothing had disturbed the tranquillity of our assumptions. We basked under the luckiest of suns, swam in benevolent waters, slept soundlessly on white pillows seemingly untainted by guilty consciences. Everything that brings ease and contentment to a life belonged to all of us. We had never been forced to look back with the wincing regret of those forsaken by luck.

It was the last summer I was ever to spend with you, my Beloved Aunt; the last of the bougainvillea and the blue, blue sea and the vision of you framed by the picture window in your library lost in all your yesterdays. I can remember every curl on your head, the way the light played with the white-gold strands trimmed into a neat bob. I can remember the look in your aquamarine eyes as you turned toward me the last day I ever spent with you, a fuchsia stem of bougainvillea behind your ear. I can remember the infinite forgiveness I found in those limitless depths the day I left your island in the Mediterranean Sea and you, never to return.

I imagine all of us there—my father and mother, Oliver, you and, of course, that summer's visitor. We are framed as in a picture in my memory, figures brighter than the sun, arms linked, smiles radiant, the infinite view behind us fixed eternally, falsely promising never to change. This memory is the most precious thing I own. It is all that is left, an indelible image of the endless pleasure of true friendship, the depth of the greatest love, of delight in what we had been given. We watched that last summer die, blissfully oblivious to the fact that the light that had loved us was leaving forever.

Adora

I have tried to lose track of the years since your death, my dear Sebastian, although I make a pilgrimage to church to light a candle for you on every anniversary. I have tried to stop counting because the years of absence between us bring only fresh grief; the accumulating days and months attack me with a renewed sense of loss every time I seek to tally how long it has been since last I saw your golden curls. Sometimes I marvel at how entirely a life can be ruined, the ceaseless agonies of having constantly to remind myself that you are never coming home.

How can it be, Sebastian, that so many days and hours now separate us in this life? I admit I lack the depth to understand the mysteries of the universe, but still it seems inconceivable that you are not here and I am so much older—no longer the girl of eighteen you last saw with the world at her feet. So much of my life now requires effort, where once I could wake, without a care in the world, and run out to find you wherever you were. The familiar pattern of my days now saps my strength where once I delighted in welcoming people to our home for dinner, never having to spend more than minutes on my ap-

pearance, and indulging my passion for conversation and entertaining. I know they look at me and find me lacking. Would
you, if you were here?

For all the happiness I have been given, I have sought you
around every corner, looked for a trace of your incomparable
presence in everyday activities, some coincidence in the mundane rituals of life that can assure me you are still near, not lost,
not somewhere I can never find. In the grand scheme of this incomprehensible life, I am now closer to the end than the beginning. Maybe your greatest lesson to me was to dispel any fear of
dying. I look forward to the end if only to see you once again.
People will grieve for me, I know, but there is no one I cannot
bear to leave behind. I have loved this life, yes, but only because
I believe that with each minute which passes I move closer to
you. This conviction is my assurance that I was always yours,
what I felt as a girl confirmed in age as real and enduring.

I wonder, sometimes, what might have happened if one day
I had gone to town for a few hours instead of submerging myself in memories of you? Would some chance encounter have
rid me of the burden of your loss? Could I have experienced an
epiphany one afternoon while walking through the narrow
streets that would have helped me to overcome my sorrow?

Yet for all of the joy you brought me in this life, you also
left me with the most hideous knowledge: of how you died and
why. If I was not so convinced of your love for me, if the evidence of it were not manifested in everything I touch, I would
think that I had been cursed for loving you.

PART II

Genevieve

Summer 1938

Adora

I can still hear the sound of his footfall on the steep stone steps as he climbed up into our world for the first time, the white butterflies fluttering in and out of the bougainvillea as he made his way toward me. I had heard the same sound once before and had waited to hear it again ever since. He wore a pale blue shirt and the face of hope as he climbed the stairs behind my husband, weaving tantalizingly in and out of view. I stood there waiting for him on the veranda, trying to pretend that it was just another day and he any other visitor, but even I, who was so accustomed to performing, doubted the credibility of my performance. What vision met his eyes as he arrived on the island? I wondered. It soothed my nerves to imagine what impression the stark white of the beaches against the blue of the sea had made on him as his boat pulled into the harbor. Had the breeze kissed his golden curls that morning? Had the idealistic dreams packed in his suitcase been fulfilled as he surveyed his new surroundings? And when he first reached the top of the steps and, slightly breathless, turned his delicate, inquiring face to mine, did he know in his heart that he had come home?

I had expected nothing of our visitor, an American engi-

neering graduate named Jack recruited by Oliver to help manage the construction of a luxury estate on the island. I vaguely
recalled Oliver telling me it was a favor of sorts for friends of
his family in America, where my husband had been born before moving to England. The boy came from an enormously
wealthy Philadelphia Main Line family and had run into some
sort of trouble. His parents had hoped that a trip abroad and
gainful employment might set him back on track. I barely
blinked. We entertained strangers endlessly. Seldom did any of
them make an impact. I put his arrival from my mind, anticipating only a series of meals at which we would entertain him
and introduce him to people before letting our visitor go off to
live his own life.

I said uncharacteristically little as Oliver made the requisite
introductions and led Jack to the table under the white awning
where we would lunch, transfixed by the scene unfolding before me. I smoothed my skirt, regretting how careless I had
been with my appearance, having thrown on an old white shift
dress and my usual necklaces, finger-waving my unruly curls
into submission. The days were at an end when such inatten-
tion wouldn't have made any difference to my appearance, but
I was too preoccupied to care that morning. Besides, it had
been one or two years since I had last elicited envy in our
friends and acquaintances. More often than not, I saw a mote of
pity flicker over their faces when they turned to greet me, that
my once trumpeted beauty had dimmed so considerably. In
others I witnessed triumph that I was no different from them,
despite my gilded existence; I was still subject to time and its
inherent brutality.

I had woken sobbing that morning, crying so hard I almost
choked, my only relief that Oliver's side of the bed was empty

and I wouldn't be required to explain myself. I sat in the dim light of my bedroom, shutters drawn to the brilliant day beyond, and mourned everything my life had become; the burden of your loss, Sebastian, was simply unbearable. I felt such enormous guilt that I had spent almost twenty years without you, sometimes even being happy. I couldn't fathom how I had been able to do it; nothing seemed to make sense for me anymore. How I had passed the hours without you by my side, how I had even thought to live.

I couldn't confide in Oliver because he had prompted what I can only describe as a deep passivity in me, a giving up of life, relinquishing my hold on it. The catalyst for such sadness had been the shock of my husband trying to take his own life and everything I witnessed that terrible day barely a month earlier. In the weeks that followed, the full weight of responsibility I felt for his decision had overwhelmed me, and the terrible memories of my past had come back to haunt me with renewed force. I longed to return to the life I shared with you, Sebastian, before you left us—to change what I did, to save you from my devotion. My every day was torturous, spent crucifying myself for all of the things I could never change. I began to believe that it was time for me to follow you at last, my precious brother.

I was not young anymore when Jack entered my life. I was thirty-seven years old when I first met this twenty-one-year-old boy, and yet it was as if someone had plucked me from the present and gently set me back in the past, where I belonged. Everything felt momentarily unsullied again, as if I had never once experienced disappointment or betrayal or had to wake to a new day knowing you were not in it. I had never thought to experience a sense of hope again, but I did, and my eyes glistened with tears as I watched Jack in conversation with Oliver, almost unable to contain everything I felt. For the first time in years, the future seemed suddenly possible again and the living of it a joy rather than a chore to be completed. I knew how this boy would love; I could predict every romantic step; I understood the happiness that being with him would bring. Yet more than that, I understood that you, Sebastian, had given him to me so that I might have a second chance to rectify all of my mistakes, to console me in my endless grief. It was the only possible explanation for Jack's arrival in my life.

I yearned for my youth again that day with a fervency that astonished me. I wanted to be kissed again for the first time, to experience again the incomparable feeling of being loved by the person you want the most, of committing to memory every move that person makes, every sentence they utter to be replayed in your mind when you are not with them. I studied him from the opposite end of the table, reveling in the remarkable similarities. It could have been twenty years earlier on the same veranda, the same boy alive with anticipation of the life he was about to embark upon. I thought to live again as I accepted Jack's presence. I no longer felt exhausted or enfeebled by despair. I wanted to shine again, to make an effort and learn every infinitesimal aspect of this young man's personality so that I could steer him to the brightest possible places. My mind was overwhelmed by ideas and dreams and excitement as I gave myself up to the bliss of your gift.

What a merciless trick life played on me that day, allowing me to believe there was still time for me. It was as if you had died all over again, Sebastian, the pain I felt as I realized how mistaken I had been about Jack's place in my life. As I watched the scene unfold, I could only yearn for what was long lost, and

I found little consolation knowing that the child I loved the most would know it now in place of me. For with a flash of envy that burned through me, I saw that Jack had fallen in love with Genevieve the moment she appeared through the French doors.

She was wearing one of my dresses. Yet she hadn't asked to borrow it. Genevieve had simply helped herself to my things as if it were her right.

Genevieve

I don't think you had ever looked more beautiful than that day, Adora. I couldn't imagine that anyone could fail to fall in love with you, regardless of age. Next to you, I felt plain and always had, despite how often you praised me. Sometimes I became conscious of imitating you, of feeling like a fraud, but I never stopped. You delighted in the fact that we were so similar. People frequently commented that I was mature for my age. Only in intellect, however: I knew nothing about emotions save for the enormous love I felt for you, my teacher.

I never expected to eclipse you then: I always regarded myself as second. I didn't yet understand that there are all types of beauty in the world. For me there was only one: you. It is incredible the effect that collective opinion can have. You were, from the first, set up as the ideal image against which everyone else was compared and found lacking. This fact of life struck me as entirely normal, and no one ever disputed it.

As I watched Jack stand up from his chair to meet me, I saw someone else, the face of a man who was not him: I remember the moment vividly as he walked toward me, an image of perfection that stirred something in me; a perception which ultimately vanished as he came nearer and I realized that what I had seen was almost a mirage, almost a different person entirely. It is astonishing for me to admit that I was initially unimpressed. I regard him now only as the most special person I have ever known. But I was eighteen and shallow, and my ideals were culled from the manicured images of actors powdered and primped to portray such perfection. Jack lacked polish to my mind. It was easy to be dismissive. From the first moment we met he disappointed me. He was not what I was used to.

"I didn't know you had a daughter," Jack remarked in surprise. I sucked in my breath, recognizing the tension his clumsy remark would generate, but Oliver cut me off before I could say anything.

"No, no, Jack. She's not ours, I'm afraid. Although I'd like nothing more than to adopt her," he replied, winking at me, "but I'm rather afraid her father, my best friend, would want her back."

Adora said nothing, which I found odd. Usually, she was delighted when people mistook us for mother and daughter.

"Oh, I see," Jack said, glancing again at me shyly, although he still clearly had no idea what I was doing there. I was aware of Oliver watching me expectantly, but I had no interest in continuing the conversation. Yet I knew Oliver would tell me off for being rude if I ignored our guest, so I felt compelled to make an effort.

"I come here every summer," I said casually, taking my seat. "It's my second home," I continued, turning to smile affectionately at Adora. She was looking not at me but at Jack. I felt rather put out. Normally she made such a fuss of me around guests.

"Well, as you know the island so well, perhaps you can

show me the sights sometime," Jack ventured lightly, but he was a poor actor. The apprehension in his voice gave him away, underscoring his fear that I'd say no and he'd look a fool. Something in me felt momentarily sorry for him, and I was about to agree when I noticed Oliver watching me, a stern expression on his face, and I thought maybe he wouldn't want me to be involved with an employee.

"I'm afraid I wouldn't be much of a tour guide," I apologized a little sheepishly, aware that Oliver and Adora would know I was lying. "I can't even drive," I added hastily. I wasn't so cold that I wanted Jack to look stupid in front of Oliver, whom he clearly wanted to impress.

"I can," Jack blurted out impetuously, and I felt my heart sink. He obviously didn't understand yet that we took our lead from Oliver and that he would need to do the same if he was to succeed.

"That's nice," I said quietly, privately cringing with embarrassment at his faux pas and desperately wanting him to turn his attention away from me, if only for his own sake.

"I love to drive," Adora interrupted at just the right moment, saving Jack from the humiliation of searching for something to say in response to my subtle rejection. "I race through the mountains, you know; those steep curving roads just thrill me."

"Addie," Oliver admonished jovially, "you know that you're an awfully naughty girl for doing that. How many times have I asked you not to?"

"I forget," she replied flirtatiously, beaming at Jack, and I can still recall the whisper of disappointment that flickered across her face when she realized he wasn't listening to her, he was lost in me.

• • •

I was completely unnerved by Jack's constant attention toward me throughout lunch. It was almost as if he had never seen a girl before, the way in which he looked at me as if I was some rare creature from another world. I grew increasingly irritated by his lack of ease, doing a poor job of hiding my frustration, which only made him more nervous, stammering over the questions he asked of me. Next to Oliver's impeccable manners and effortless charm, he was an infant, with everything to learn and nothing, I thought, to teach me. I was hardly kind that day, dashing the optimism that shone from him with careless responses to the questions he struggled to find the courage to ask me. I kept up my end to a degree but only to avoid being impolite in front of you, Adora, and Oliver, fearful of appearing lesser or, even worse, of being mistaken for my mother. Yet I barely glanced at Jack. I couldn't. The last thing I wanted was to encourage him. I was retreating from him from the first. Yet still he persisted in making me dislike him more and at the same time eliciting an emotion, similar to shame, that I could be so callous to someone who was trying so hard to please me.

For all of my bravado, the fact that Jack was interested in me was alarming, but I concealed it better than he did. I recognize now that what I felt was the early stages of love, as experienced by the novice heart. My instinct was to run away, to get him out of the house, to return to the comfort of life before he entered it. I didn't have the experience to feel flattered that he seemed to like me so much. I needed him to be more: more confident, more mature, more unlike me.

You seemed different that afternoon, Adora, infinitely happier, almost buoyant. Both Oliver and I had been concerned about you; you had seemed so withdrawn of late. I felt relieved that everything was back to normal. Oliver played his habitual role of intrigued host, effortlessly drawing out information from his guest, although he was less warm than usual, even uncharacteristically allowing the conversation to dry up on occasion. I thought that it was perhaps because he was dealing with a business associate rather than a friend. It must have been so difficult for Jack, desperate to impress Oliver, realizing how young he himself was in comparison, terrified of putting a foot wrong in front of Oliver, you, and me: a trinity connected by a history he had played no part in.

Luckily you spared Jack any of the awkward silences that Oliver strangely did not seem overeager to fill with conversation. Typically, you were content to play a secondary role to Oliver; he was always the ringleader of entertainment, you his admiring audience. Yet it was almost as if you couldn't stand to let Oliver speak, betraying a tiny glimmer of frustration whenever a business-oriented comment was made that would turn the conversation away from Jack and stories about himself.

You were undaunted by his lack of confidence—which I recall made me feel somewhat small in comparison—warming to his youth, I presume, as he fumbled his way through the labyrinth of years when you had not known him. And there was a moment I shall never forget when I recall Jack turning to you with a combination of relief and gratitude as you filled an impending silence with your own thoughts on America. As he talked with you, encouraged by a familiar theme, I saw your eyes melt as if you had fallen in love with him yourself. The two of you seemed distant, enclosed in a world neither Oliver nor I could enter. Some shared kinship developed between you in the face of the underlying tension contributed by us both. You provided the warm embrace of kindness to him, instinctively aware of how much he needed it. It was almost as if you were two old friends catching up after years apart.

"Tell me everything, Jack," you urged charmingly. "I always insist on knowing strangers inside out. Tell me news about America," you beseeched, like a child asking for a bedtime story. "Tell me about *you* in America."

Jack flushed bright crimson. He didn't understand that your flirtatiousness was part of who you were, something you turned on for all visitors. Perhaps he was daunted by the attentions of someone so beguiling; he'd probably never seen anything like you. Yet I understood that you were deeply interested in him; you were no longer acting. You meant every word.

"Well," he began awkwardly, "I finished my engineering degree at Yale and then I was introduced to Oliver through my family. They live in Philadelphia," he added hurriedly before realizing that he'd already us told that earlier. "I'm sorry," he apologized shyly, looking at me. "I don't seem to be much of a storyteller. I'm not making this very interesting for you."

"Don't be so silly," you soothed. "You're better than you think. Please go on," you urged sincerely. Jack looked at you then, and there must have been something in your expression that was invisible to me, because he nodded imperceptibly, almost as if you had asked him something else entirely, and he continued with the story of his past with more confidence, following your lead. Such was your effect, I thought and smiled to myself. I clearly hadn't yet mastered the art of making people feel special, although I was trying.

We learned about Jack's family in Pennsylvania, which led you to remark how much you loved to see pictures of the cornfields. He had hated growing up there though, for reasons he didn't go into, nor did you press for them. Jack had been planning his exit since the age of eleven, although he was at pains to point out how devoted he was to his mother.

"I think your mother is so lucky to have you," you said simply, your chin perched on your cupped hand. Strangely, without knowing anything about you, Jack seemed to understand the poignancy of that statement. The way he looked at you was so full of compassion and of a sorrow I did not yet understand, as if he could read exactly what you were thinking, understand completely where you had been. How could he possibly have known you couldn't have children? That I was the closest you would ever come to being a mother? You let the conversation die there. Perhaps you didn't think that anything else needed to be said.

"How's your game, Jack?" Oliver asked. He had unexpectedly left the table during Jack's speech about America and returned with two tennis rackets.

"Not as good as yours, sir?" he deferred jokingly, which I thought rather brave. It had never occurred to me that he could be funny.

"I knew I liked you." Oliver smiled. "Come. I'll introduce you to the tennis courts. Ladies, we shall take our leave," he said as he bowed his head. "I'm sure we've bored you enough for one day. Genevieve, come and watch later. You might learn something," he added paternally, forcing a grimace from me. Oliver was always knocking my game, which was atrocious despite the fortune my father had lavished on lessons. He put his arm around Jack's shoulder and moved him off, rather forcefully, before I could object.

You did not linger at the table with me as you usually did. You left moments after them without saying a word. I thought I must have done something to offend you, as it was inconceiv-

able you would ever treat me in such a way. You had never reprimanded me, only advised or instructed me in your soft, lilting
fashion. I rather thought to blame Jack. I couldn't help that he
liked me; I'd made sure to do nothing to encourage him. I was
certain I hadn't been rude, but you clearly thought differently. I
reconsidered the afternoon in my mind, analyzing my responses to see if I *had* been too abrupt, experiencing the familiar fear of disappointing you. There was no other explanation
for why you would be annoyed with me. Worse than that,
though, it wasn't as if we wouldn't see Jack again either. Considering how you had behaved over lunch, I knew that your
great liking for him would guarantee his presence in our home
again soon. Irrationally, I felt replaced. You had always reserved
all of your affection for me. I'd never had to share you, not even
with Oliver. I felt tears prick at my eyes; familiar feelings of
being ostracized made me vulnerable. I privately acknowledged
the prospect of Jack's company with dread.

I had to know what was bothering you and left the veranda
to seek you out. Maybe I could bring you back around, I convinced myself. Maybe your mood had nothing to do with me.
My only thought was to return myself to your good graces.

I found you in your library, framed by the huge picture
window that offered the Mediterranean Sea as its only view.
You never allowed your employees in there, so unusual for a
woman of your enormous wealth. You insisted on doing all of
the cleaning and organizing yourself. Nobody knew why, nor
did you ever offer any explanation. I approached your side gin-
gerly. I could hear my heart pounding in my ears. So high was
my regard for you that I would never have known what to do if
you were really displeased with me, except offer up everything I
owned to try to win you back.

You did not speak, but something in your silence, in your calm smile as we stood together, precluded my saying anything, made me think that to mention anything about the lunch or Jack would be to taint something you regarded as sacred. I decided to leave, to go and ponder my feelings of self-pity and unworthiness somewhere else, but then you said something that stopped me: "Gigi, I love you more than anything."

I had always accepted your love as a fait accompli, but I realized then that you had never said the words out loud before. Equal to the relief that filled me, I also felt a shadow fall over my assumptions; perhaps there were other things I took for granted without knowing the truth. I didn't have time to say anything, to respond in kind; you turned back to your window without further comment. I dallied in the doorway for a second, knowing that something momentous had just passed between us; something had irrevocably changed, though I didn't know what. I studied your silhouette; you seemed so tiny compared to the immense sea beyond. It was the first time I had ever looked at you as you were and not as I projected you in my imagination.

Despite the upheaval caused by Jack's arrival, I felt such calm as I walked across the endless lawn to the tennis court, secure of my place in your affections. I stopped at the gate to the court and was struck anew by the beauty that surrounded me: the distant whitewashed villas and the bright flowers and the deep, deep blue of the sky and sea. I no longer felt nervous, only peace that nothing had changed. But I turned back to the house rather than join Jack and Oliver: my first act of defiance.

• • •

"Of course, you'll join us again tomorrow, Jack?"

Every day, you ended our lunches with that same rhetorical question. If Jack had ever desired a life beyond our table, it was unlikely he could find it with you as the guardian of his time. And of all people, who could ever deny you, my Beloved Aunt? Especially when you cast those glistening eyes, wide and long-lashed, in the direction of any man alive.

I would feel my spine tighten every day, like clockwork, as you made your pronouncement, my fists clenched underneath the table, longing for Jack to find some reason, a feasible excuse why he couldn't return. He never did, nor did Oliver ever provide him with one, which disturbed me far more than Jack's constant presence; he seemed as keen as you to throw the two of us together—not that he ever left us alone when Jack did visit. Nor, for that matter, did you.

So every day at lunchtime Jack would come home from the office with Oliver and swim with me under the heat of the midafternoon sun. My performance would start at two and end at four, when they left to go back to work. I so resented the disturbance. Before Jack arrived, I used to read under the consoling shade of the awning before wandering into the living room to talk with you. With my routine shattered, we talked less and less. I would often find Jack ensconced in a chair next to you, instead of me. You always seemed to find some excuse to ask him to bring you something or help in some way, leaving me sitting with Oliver, who was always grateful to pick up the paper as a reprieve from entertaining. Jack's presence began to make me feel like an intruder and, to my private distress, you never asked me to join the two of you or help like you once did.

Familiar feelings from school of being left out contrived to make me highly emotional. The mere sight of you together prompted instant, bitter tears, and I would retreat to cry in my room. I could never stay there too long, however, as my disappearance would be noted, especially by Oliver, who was somewhat useless in the dual arts of perception and tact. Several times, he inquired loudly why my eyes were so red, drawing suspicious looks from Jack and you, and forcing me to lie about too much chemical in the pool or too little sleep.

I felt as if I was in the process of being slowly, painfully stripped of everything I held dear. The peace of our little world disintegrated into the cacophony of noise provided by the sound of your laughter: the exclusive party to which I had not received an invitation to attend. I accept now that I was somewhat overreacting. I could have, indeed, should have, joined you both, but my emotions were too raw. I needed time to deal with the changes that were occurring, time to be by myself.

I make it sound as though Jack was barely interested in me, when exactly the opposite was the case. He wanted me there with him; he used any excuse to include me in your discussions. He was ever solicitous of my feelings, constantly attentive to my moods, and although I was aware of being awful, hurtful even, I despised how everything had changed with his arrival. What frustrated me most, though, was that I could see that you were so right about him; he really was lovely, there was nothing I could detract from him despite how much I wanted to hate him for turning everything upside down. Having made a stance of sulking, however, I was too proud to concede anything good about him in the beginning. I saw that my cool distance disturbed him and made him try harder. I enjoyed it. I enjoyed inflicting the pain I was feeling onto him. It horrified me that I was capable of emotional cruelty, yet I couldn't help myself.

I was conscious then of never making you aware of my

whims, Adora. You did not see my quiet belligerence when Jack and I were left briefly alone together. What he saw in me, considering the way I treated him, to continue coming back for more continuously puzzled me. I would certainly never have stood for my behavior. I had not reckoned, however, on what he knew or what he had seen.

Adora

There is a strange and melancholy comfort that comes with age, with watching young people embark on love. Every thrill experienced comes flooding back to fool the spectator into thinking that it is not too late to own it again. But it is gone; the overwhelming excitement of the first experience is never replicated. As we grow older, so we become the watchers of time, relegated to the audience, equipped only with a fruitless sense of longing for what can never be repeated.

From the day I met him, I accepted Jack was a gift from you, my dear Sebastian; an act of consolation as well as atonement. At first, I could not comprehend why you would give me the boy only for him to be bewitched by another. After the endless years of yearning, it almost destroyed me to know that, again, I would have to share someone so perfect. I acted as I did in the past, almost as if I was still that young girl: a girl of Genevieve's age, covetous, manipulative. I refused to let Jack out of my sight, inviting him to our home every day, monopolizing the conversation, spiriting him away to my side, drowning in his presence. Yet for every effort I made, I could see he bore me true affection but not the love he held for her. I couldn't believe that I would never come first for him. Why, I asked, almost driving myself insane, would you ever do this to me, Sebastian? Have I not paid enough?

Days went by during which I tried to forget all of the terrible memories that resurfaced whenever I thought of you and that summer of our youth, the summer you left us. And then it came to me, the reason for Jack. How could I ever have imagined that you would let me down? I knew, too, that you would never be unkind to me, and once I began to reconcile the curious circumstances of his arrival and his choice of Genevieve, I understood the blessing that you, wiser than I in so many ways, had offered me. Forgive me, my love, for not having realized your intention. Of course, Jack must love her and Genevieve must love him back. It was the answer to everything.

Once I accepted my role, I grew restless waiting for their love to begin. The heat clung steadfastly to me, my books remained unopened, my pen lay idle. I spent my days watching, waiting for her eyes to open to the possibility of joy. Genevieve trained them elsewhere, anywhere but where she could find him. She began to hide in the shadows of my rooms, exasperated when disturbed by his arrival but, in truth, afraid because of what she understood it meant.

I had to force her to wear her pretty dresses or to put on some lipstick. In the end, I laid her clothes out for her, left jewelry on her dressing table to bribe her into making an effort. I could see during the dinners we invited Jack to that Gigi's breathing was shallow, that she concealed her trembling hands whenever possible in the folds of her dress. He was oblivious, however, to her charade. Genevieve projected an air of supreme confidence to disguise her nervousness, only adding to the infatuation her sophistication had elicited. Her intelligence emerging with every statement, he grew quieter, lapsing into the role of inferior suitor desperate for a trace of a smile from her lips. Of course, he had never met anyone like her before. I had raised her that way. In the face of his discontent, how I wept for him. How I longed for Genevieve to be older, wiser, more attuned to the rarity of the possibilities he possessed.

My patience gave way to frustration. Why did she not run to him? What made her retreat from the future? Had the tables been turned, I would have smothered him with my desire. Genevieve seemed intent on ignoring his perfection, on sidestepping his attentions, on fleeing far, far away from life. But I had not been hurt as she had. I could not understand that my darling girl's greatest fear was of being found unworthy of love. She had been shunned and ridiculed and ostracized and, although she was praised to the rafters by those who loved her, something of the others' spite had stuck to her. She could not rise above the negative voices that had informed her of her lack of worth. Genevieve had learned to dismiss happiness before it turned its back on her.

"I wouldn't know," she replied coolly, catching Oliver's eye as she looked down at her plate, her cheeks flushing with embarrassment.

I almost slammed my napkin down on the table in frustration. It was another dinner we were suffering through with Jack, Genevieve's face a picture of unhappiness. I wanted to give her a slap, the silly girl. Could she not answer the poor boy's question civilly? Could she not see what she was giving up with her surly behavior?

"It was just . . . I thought Adora had told me that you like to write stories too," Jack ventured apologetically, looking to me for help.

"Genevieve is a natural-born storyteller, Jack," I soothed. "She learned it from me," I added, staring directly at her, meaningfully. "Genevieve, are you feeling unwell?"

"I am a bit hot, I think," she replied, nodding, and it was then I realized that Gigi was staring down at her plate to conceal her tears, although what had prompted them, I had no idea.

Despite everything and how angry I was with her, I melted at the sight of her in distress. I saw her in my mind, that little, bright-eyed child who used to run toward me every summer she arrived on our island, and I just tumbled back into love with her. She needed me, I realized then. How could she possibly live or know what to do, if I didn't help her?

"I think you should go and lie down, darling," I suggested softly, trying to convey that I had forgiven her, to put her at her ease. "Come, I'll take you and tuck you in," I offered, holding out my hand and leading her up the stairs to bed just like Oliver used to when she was a little girl. I turned back at the top of the stairs to my husband and Jack, who were sitting in silence, watching us leave.

I wouldn't have said anything were it not for Jack's expression, one of wistful regret. As he watched her walk away, he gave up believing she was lost to him. It was understandable; Genevieve had offered no encouragement over the previous weeks. It was then I knew I had to intervene. I ached at the possibility of losing him. It was an act of desperation on my part, like someone rushing to catch a falling object before it shattered.

I tucked Gigi in, pulling the white cotton sheets tight around her, so tight she could barely move, talking all the while as matter-of-factly as I could, considering how much depended on her compliance.

"Genevieve, it's only natural that you are afraid, my love. You're an innocent. No boys' rough lips have bruised your own," I said, tracing the outline of her mouth with my finger. "You are everything I ever hoped you would become, like a swan, so poised and graceful, so similar to me in countless ways that it feels as if I did give birth to you. It's so funny how people mistake us for mother and daughter; it thrills me, as you know." I smiled. "I have so much to teach you about life, what you should seek to enrich your own and where you should never search if you don't want to be terribly hurt." I let the words linger in the gardenia-perfumed air of the evening, waiting to see if she would offer anything to me in response. When she said nothing, I continued, confident that she understood my meaning. "I don't think we've ever been closer than we are now, wouldn't you agree, my darling," I breathed softly, almost as if I was lulling her to sleep. "We understand one another perfectly, do we not? I know how unkind people have been to you, but not me, not ever—betrayal is something I, too, understand far too well. The blow of the ax still smarts, regardless of who wields it, long after the wound has healed. It's something I would *never* wish on you," I said reassuringly, standing up to leave. "Do you know why I so adored you as a child, Gigi?" I asked. She shook her head. "Because of your innocence; you were incapable of malice. I reveled in your purity. I still do. Everything I can give you, I will. My steps will match yours wherever you go to make sure that nothing ever clouds your happiness; your life will be a rainbow revealing itself after the storm if you only do as I ask.

"Love him," I instructed, opening the door to leave. "You've seen the worst in people, appreciate the best now that I've found it for you," I concluded, closing the door behind me.

And Gigi did, my darling girl. Her dedication to love was enchanting to observe. I like to think that she learned it from me.

Genevieve

I was terrified into loving him, pushed by a force so strong it overwhelmed me. The rush of new emotions he stirred in me was frightening, yes, and confusing, but that wasn't what moved me to hold on tight to him. I sensed your disappointment in me, Adora, felt the regard you held me in dissipate every time I pushed him away, watched your love diminish every time you looked at me. This is why I went to Jack in the beginning: I could not bear to disappoint you.

Our first afternoon alone together was masterfully contrived. Having invited Jack over for yet another lunch, through which I knew I would be mortified, you telephoned to say that you'd met some friends and that he and I should spend the day with each other as you wouldn't be back until very late. I was powerless to object, you having presented the prospect as if it was entirely natural, indeed, expected of me. I saw his car pull into the drive, watched him hop out full of expectation and excitement, and felt my stomach turn at the prospect of what I must do—what you had instructed me to do.

As I watched him cross the drive toward the steps, I felt a pang of compassion for him. He liked me, that was all. He didn't deserve to be duped into thinking I was attracted to him when I wasn't. Couldn't he find another girl who had genuine feelings for him? I dallied on the veranda instead of walking down the steps to meet him. I couldn't stand to watch the delight he would take in knowing that he had me all to himself. In fact, the thought made me feel ill.

I was pretending to read a book at the table when, after he had called through the house several times to no response, he came out to the poolside. I felt the hair on the back of my neck bristle as I became aware of him standing behind me by the door, not moving, not saying anything. I was about to turn around, ready to cast a cursory glance before telling him of the change in plans, but he beat me to it. Leaning over me, he placed a stem of bougainvillea beside my book.

"A peace offering," he said. "I know Adora always wears some in her hair. I think it would suit you too. You're always saying how much you love these flowers. Besides," he said, hovering beside me, trying to catch my eye, "Oliver doesn't pay me enough yet to buy you a proper present." His kind face optimistically searched mine to see if I would respond favorably to his joke.

I didn't know what to say. My mind flew in every direction trying to figure out what he meant. And then Jack sat down in the seat reserved for Oliver at the head of the table, with me at his left, and began to talk.

"Look, I know I annoy you. Oliver and Adora seem deathly keen to throw us together, but let's just say you don't need to pretend anymore to like me. I can see I'm not your type, although," he said, pretending to stretch back indolently, in a gesture of complete entitlement, "I must say, you *are* the first." Something in his statement reminded me of Oliver, and the way Jack subsequently looked at me, eyebrow raised, a rueful smirk on his face, made me warm to him as I never had before.

"I think you're exceptional," he continued, more seriously. "I've never met a girl like you; you're so cultured and know everything about books and art, and I can see you've learned a lot from Adora. Girls where I come from aren't like you. At least not the ones I've met. They're more interested in country clubs and making perfect matches of surnames than anything more intelligent. I just find you interesting, but that," he continued, "is all. I release you from the duty of having to be polite. I am going to vanish now, like someone very noble, but I'll probably trip on the way out and ruin the effect." He smiled jovially, standing up to leave. "Friends?" he asked, holding out his hand to shake mine.

Something in me died at the sound of his words and at the same time something new was born. I left childhood behind me that afternoon. So many people don't, perhaps because no one forces them to. I was touched by what he'd confided in me, more so because I hadn't expected the Jack who emerged; I had braced myself for the tongue-tied, wet, wholly unsophisticated lapdog I had created in my imagination, because that way it was easier to dismiss him. Yet the surprise of learning there was more to him—depths I hadn't credited—and that what my behavior had actually roused in him was sadness—sadness that he felt responsible for my unhappiness—humbled me. That he had come to me in order to reassure me, to accept without being told that I didn't consider him good enough, filled me with something akin to affection. I don't believe that anyone before him had ever been so kind to me, at least, not without wanting something in return. The gesture was entirely unselfish. He was not sly. It was not a tactical romantic maneuver to lull me into a false sense of security as he attempted to seduce me. It was an act of compassion, made out of insight into the ever-shifting emotions of a spoiled girl who could not appreciate what she had. And it surprised me into behaving in a way I never had before.

I took his outstretched hand and, as I touched his skin for the first time, a delicious shock went through me, like diving into the ice-cold sea on a scalding hot day. "You are more than that, Jack," I replied, clutching his hand tighter. "I just don't think I'm good enough for you."

I meant it. I almost wept because I meant it so much. I had been fighting him from the moment he arrived, lying to myself about how lovely he was, how nice, how interesting even. I had to; if I thought for a second that there was anyone else in the world beyond the idealized image I worshiped, I would be lost. I could have let him go then, defied everyone, spared him. But he kissed me, and I liked it so much that I willingly turned a corner into the dark, not caring for a moment that I didn't know my way out. And then he told me everything and I listened for hours as the sun died in the sky behind us.

Later, we went night-swimming, the only illumination the candles on the table.

"Does your hair turn white-blond in the sun in the summer?" I asked, swimming on my back toward the deep end of the pool.

"Yes," he replied, swimming beside me. "I hate it. It's too curly. I go through a jar of Brylcreem a day."

"Don't be silly," I teased, splashing him. "I love your hair. It's just like Adora's."

It was the wrong thing to say, bringing you into the conversation. It was like waking up from a blissful dream, only to realize none of it had happened. I suddenly felt self-conscious, as if I was being watched. Was I playing this scene correctly? Was I doing it as well as I was expected to? What was I thinking in the first place, allowing any of it to happen? As soon as I invited you in, the evening was ruined.

"Gosh, it's cold," I said, feigning a shudder. "I think I'll get out now."

"You're cold?" he asked, slightly confused. "It's so hot still. Here," he said, racing to the steps and climbing them, "let me help you out."

I felt the same shiver of something as I did earlier when I gripped his hand for support, only this time it felt like foreboding.

"I'm so sleepy," I apologized, "would you mind if I go in?"

"Have I exhausted you that much with my declarations of undying love?" he teased, putting his arm around my shoulder.

I forced a smile. "Yes. It's all been far too much for one day. Would you mind?"

I could see he was disappointed. It was still early, only 9:30, but I suspect now that he didn't want to press me for fear of scaring me away again. We walked together to his car, where he kissed me again, but this time I didn't feel anything—my mind was too full of other things. As I turned to climb the steps back up to the house, I had the feeling that Jack was watching me leave, waiting for me to turn around, that he would be disappointed again if I didn't—yet I couldn't. I told myself it was for his sake.

The next morning, the bright sunlight flooded me with fear at the steps I had taken too far the night before, experiencing the familiar sense of suffocation I felt at being loved by Jack. But it was too late; everything had been set in motion, including the yearnings of my heart that had allowed the possibility of him in.

After that first day and evening together, which I was careful to relay in sufficiently enthusiastic detail, your behavior toward me returned to the way it had always been. In fact, Adora, if it were possible, you appeared to love me more. You seemed so relieved. I had made everything better for you. I was once more in your good graces, your darling girl. I had done as I was told.

Jack invited me to the annual summer ball, which thrilled you, Adora, as you had been crowned *La Reine d'été* at one years before. I could barely contain my nerves; whenever I was apart from Jack, it was the same: I constantly feared having made a mistake, of having got in too deep. Yet every time we met, all of my doubts disappeared — as long as I was away from you. When it was just us two, Jack and I, we were perfect. I can barely remember what we talked about during those evenings, only his face and his listening intently as I did most of the talking, my nervousness causing me, I'm sure, to twitter on endlessly about rubbish.

Yet what I do remember is his calm. His affection for me was obvious, the way in which he would light up when I spoke, his laughter, unforced I think, whenever I made a feeble attempt at humor. But there was something else in him, a deep understanding of my inexperience, that made him stay to try again to win me over, and I found myself thinking of such instances long after he'd left me. It was almost as if he knew my secret; there was a sadness behind his knowing smiles that lingers even now.

The evening of the ball, I remember dressing and then wanting to rip off my elegant clothes, smear my makeup, wash off my perfume. The image of me gussied up like a woman, not a girl, filled me with self-loathing. I didn't want to be looked at, I merely wanted to hide. You and Oliver were waiting with Jack at the foot of the stairs, and I deeply didn't want you there; I had no idea how to behave when you were around and I was with Jack. It was as if I couldn't read what you really wanted me to feel. I have never been as nervous since.

I don't know how I made it down the staircase; I had a momentary impulse to throw myself off the landing. I felt the pressure of everyone's expectations so keenly. And there he was, waiting for me, beside you both, dressed in white tie, a smile full of delight on his unquestioning face. Yet what I remember most is the image of you, my Beloved Aunt, smiling at us both as we prepared to leave. Yours was not a smile full of pride. It was one of naked desire, as if you wanted to devour us both. Such was the strength of your love.

Adora

I believe I was with him, part of the air Jack breathed, at the summer ball where I was once crowned queen. Gigi could not have made a more stunning impression that night; her youth, her nervousness, so deliciously perfect, so in tune with the beginnings of first love. I was mesmerized by the scene that unfolded in front of me, recording every microscopic detail so that I might remember it always, long after he had disappeared from my view.

I traveled in my mind to my own first nights of such love, the glorious beginnings untainted by sorrow, recalling the affection in the eyes of another as I descended a similar staircase of my youth. You, my darling brother, were waiting for me there, always, your hand reaching out to take mine and lead me away to the world of the grown-ups, away from the confines of childhood homes and the innocence of inexperience. I remember the delight of chivalric gestures: a stem of bougainvillea placed behind my ear as I reached the bottom step of the staircase, a car door opened for me, the winding road down to the old part of town and the table set up for the two of us, always the best seat in the house. The night air enveloping us in the heavy, perfumed scent of the island as we talked ever on, of our hopes and dreams and my overwhelming desire always to travel with you wherever you might choose to go. And, of course, your delicate, inquiring face, suffused with the kindness and compassion of acceptance, watching me, listening to my girlish foibles, understanding my foolishness. How I long for those days again.

I waited for what seemed an eternity for the two of them to come back that night. Cloistered in the shadows of my bedroom, I anticipated the vicarious thrill of love from a safe distance. And when I watched Jack kiss Gigi here in my olive grove that evening and pluck a stem of bougainvillea from the tree and place it in her hair, I could have fainted from the surge of emotion and nostalgia his simple, touching gesture stirred in me. I loved with Jack, felt the tremble of anticipation in my bones as if I were her; my darling girl was to experience the same love I had been blessed with in my life. I was delighted, ecstatic that she should know such romance with someone so divine. I felt alive again, delirious with excitement. But after the rush of exhilaration, the wonder I felt for Genevieve's discovery of such love, a pall descended over my thoughts. The realization dawned, like a spider crawling up my spine, that it was I who needed him most and how ferociously I longed to be her.

Genevieve

I had been cosseted by you during the preceding summers, never allowed to venture out into the alluring world of nighttime. I suspect now that you had been saving me for an experience like that first evening. The ball was held at the Hôtel des Anges, the grandest hotel on the island. It had played host to most of the notable people of the last century, all of whom were immortalized on gold plaques displayed in the lobby. Everything was white, even the light reflected from the lanterns strewn throughout the trees and the huge canopy that had been erected on the balcony that overlooked the sea. As we pulled up, glamorous people spilled out of the entrance, a mass of diamonds and silks, swaying to the tunes from the band beyond. I was surprised that the staff seemed to know Jack—and not only that, but to welcome him. What had I imagined he did during the evenings when he was not with us? It was my first glimpse into a life beyond ours, as if such a thing existed.

Our house had evidently stifled him because once he was removed from the straitjacket of having to behave in a certain way, I saw who he really was that night: someone everyone wanted to know. It wasn't simply because he was so good-looking but because, like Oliver, he charmed all comers. Yet the two men differed completely in their approach; there was nothing contrived about Jack's kindness, whereas Oliver's attention, in comparison, seemed practiced, his reactions rehearsed over a lifetime dedicated to meeting and greeting strangers. I recall being horrified when I first realized the difference between them. I had never considered Oliver as anything less than perfect. I mentally slapped myself for having dared to fault him, chastising myself for some internal demon that prompted me to think critically of Oliver, so rarefied in the minds of everyone who knew him. Yet the perception would not dim, and I remember thinking Jack far more of a person than Oliver as I watched him enjoy himself that night. And the fact that he wanted me, against a backdrop of a life I had never known before, made me feel special, as if loving him might be a privilege and not a duty.

Our island was known for attracting the so-called *beautiful people,* and I felt naturally insecure, surrounded as I was by starlets and socialites, even some minor European royals. But Jack never so much as glanced at them, even when, as was my wont, I pointed out the most attractive girls, privately hoping that he would dismiss them but needing to hear him say they weren't his type. I labored the point so much that I could almost hear your voice in my head, Adora, telling me to stop it. I couldn't help myself. He was becoming someone new, almost someone I hadn't met before, and surrounded by a world of temptations he already knew all about, a world I had played no part in.

"I know the type of girl," he said, somewhat ruefully, "but I've left all that behind now." I was curious as to what exactly he'd left behind. Jack never really spoke of Philadelphia or his family. I had learned very little about them, save that he had an older brother, who had died some years earlier. I felt him watching me, somewhat quizzically, as if attempting to make sense of the image I projected, perhaps to fathom if it was safe to say what he did say next. He turned back to look at the dance floor and the sea beyond it, not at me, but his hand reached for mine across the table. "Genevieve, I love you," he said, and there was a certain reserve in the tone of his voice, a restraint, as if he was bracing himself perhaps for rejection. Often when Jack confided his feelings in me, I would feel an oppressive shadow fall over me, a terrible fear that I would fail him. I felt my breath catch in my throat, a snag in the happiness that surged up to overwhelm me. But that night I pushed it all the way back down because something struck me as I studied his profile; a horrible premonition that he would not stay, that I would not get to keep him. And I asked myself, How many times will I ever be told such a perfect thing by someone so lovely who asks so little of me? Jack was entirely unlike anyone I had ever known and, while that terrified me, finally the thought of losing him unnerved me more.

"And I you," I whispered, clenching his hand as if it were something secret that we would both be punished for if anyone ever found out.

Jack danced with me then, despite my protestations because I didn't want to make a fool of myself in front of everyone, but he insisted, pulling me to my feet and onto the dance floor. There was a man singing a folk song whom I had seen come into the ball earlier, almost an original island settler, much older than anyone else present that night, his skin leathery from the effects of the sun over the decades he had spent there. Yet he had that certain something that made people look at him and want to know more.

I wondered whether he knew you, Adora; if he had watched you glide past struck dumb with longing, the expressions I had seen on the faces of so many others over the preceding years. And I thought how thrilled you would be for me when I told you about this evening, not embellishing stories simply to please anymore but telling the truth about dancing with Jack to the strains of a French song I couldn't understand and how good, truly good, it all was.

In the face of all my girlish silliness Jack simply loved me, thought me different from everyone else, and told me so, despite the risk to his heart and its desires. I can still feel the strong grip of his hand as he led me onto that dance floor, the feeling of being protected so acute that I lost any sense of self-consciousness.

It was a night that should never have ended, but I was just a girl and governed by curfews and protective guardians, so we left just before midnight. I remember meeting him outside, having gone to the ladies' room to straighten myself out as I'd drunk far more champagne than I ever had before, except for once. Jack was standing with his back to me, and just as I was approaching he turned around to me wearing an expression that is indelibly imprinted on my memory. It was a half smile, sad, winsome; as if he was watching me leave him, not meet him; as if he'd dropped the strings of a kite and was forced to watch it drift farther and farther away, knowing it was lost forever and someone else would find it where it fell and claim it as their own. I asked him what he was thinking, but he simply smiled and shrugged and opened the car door for me. "I was just thinking how stunning you look," he said. I didn't believe him, but I let it go. There would be time to find out everything. I believed that then. We drove home in silence.

That was the night Jack placed a stem of bougainvillea in my hair, just like you wore it, and kissed me one last time in the olive grove before I climbed the steps to bed. I recall almost arrogantly enjoying the sensation of being loved on my way to my room, powerful with the control Jack had given me over his emotions. I felt the tickle of the flowers on my face as I carried the tail of my gown in my hand, full of a confidence I had never before experienced. It was then, as I was crossing over beside the pool, that I looked up and saw Oliver sitting and smoking a cigar on the balcony outside his bedroom. He stood and leaned over the railing, smiling in his habitual fashion—that sentimental smile, his eyes crinkling, a mischievous smirk dancing somewhere in their blue depths.

"All hail the new queen of the summer ball," he said, bowing his head down. But he was not teasing me. I could tell when he raised his head and smiled so fondly at me that he meant every word. And I remembered all over again why I loved Oliver so and experienced something approaching shame that I had ever thought ill of him.

Miranda

James and I had been duly informed of Genevieve's beau before our arrival that summer in mid-July. I was excited to meet him, naturally, and curious to see whom my daughter had chosen for her first love. Oliver had come to pick us up from our hotel that first morning of our holiday and, characteristically, had little to say beyond how much they seemed to be enjoying themselves together. It never ceased to amaze me how Oliver had become so successful. He was hardly a great wit. Most of the time, he bored me rigid, but then I was never a fan of his particular brand of charm and, in all fairness, he had never considered me worthy enough to bestow it upon.

I had actually spoken to Jack. He had answered that morning at Adora's home when I'd telephoned from the hotel to speak to Genevieve. He sounded young, and his conversation was somewhat stilted, which surprised me. It sounds ludicrous to base assumptions about someone on a telephone call, but he didn't come across as the sophisticated businessman I had imagined, with the American gift of the gab. When I learned of his age, I was even more surprised that Genevieve had fallen so completely for him, considering that she'd always gravitated toward charmingly world-weary, older men like Clark Gable and Errol Flynn, but only in her imagination, it has to be said. I very much doubted my daughter had ever been kissed. I decided it was best to reserve any further judgment until we met in person, but I was terribly intrigued and, generally, predisposed to like him considering how well he appeared to be treating Genevieve.

It was the first time in years that I arrived at that magnificent villa without a sense of dread. I almost felt carefree. I enjoyed the steepness of the drive and the vivid contrast of sky and bright flowers as we climbed in the car toward the house. My first sighting of Jack was in the olive grove as we pulled into the graveled driveway. His back was to me. He was playing with the dogs. I scanned the immediate surroundings for Genevieve, but she was not with him. Adora was instead, sitting on the stone bench, more stunning than I had ever seen her. I'm sure I saw something approximating triumph flash in her eyes as she caught sight of the car, waving to us, almost rushing to greet us as we got out, something she would not have done if Jack hadn't been there. Ordinarily, we were ushered into the house and forced to make small talk with Oliver while she prepared herself for an evening with us, not the easiest of tasks, considering. Every time, she would make her entrance from the top of the stairs, and we, the chorus, would be expected to provide her admiring audience—a role I could never quite bring myself to play with any passion. I left that to James; he was always so eager to oblige.

As soon as Jack turned to meet me, any residual surprise at my daughter's choice disappeared. Almost involuntarily, I closed my eyes tightly shut. It was too much for me. I felt as if I'd woken up from a comfortless dream to be confronted with

an even more painful reality. The young man standing in front
of me was perfect, almost incomparably so, and his shy warmth
as he walked toward us, the nervousness which he tried to conceal as he greeted my husband, only served to shed light on
what I had not understood up until that point. He was simply
magnificent; light seemed to radiate from him, kindness, integrity, depth.

Life sometimes offers up individuals like Jack, vulnerable,
not quite secure in their place on this earth, although only a
very few perceive that in them—their attractiveness is too dis-
tracting. But I saw it in him as I stood there in her driveway on
that perfect summer's afternoon. I almost mourned for Jack
and his choices and what they meant for us all with a depth of
feeling I hadn't experienced in years. I say "almost" because I
quickly blinked away the tears I felt welling up, checking myself for being so silly as to give Adora any inkling of what I was
thinking.

I chuckled ruefully at how I had thought myself happy for a
moment. How could I have been so naïve as to expect such a
thing on that island? Even so, I felt half of my heart soar for my
daughter that she had found such pure joy as keenly as I felt
the other half disintegrate beyond repair. Everything suddenly
crystallized: fragments of conversations Genevieve and I had
had before I arrived came flooding back; perception, instinct,
cynicism rushed over me. I understood the charade; I was familiar with the players. I had seen it all before. I played the
fool, accepting my punishment.

I don't know what impelled me—perversity, perhaps, but I
offered up a kiss to his cheek instead of proferring my hand to
shake. The sensation of his soft cheek against my own was so
familiar it startled me. And there was Adora, resplendent in her

finery, her gaze fastened on us, savoring her victory. I have always thought how lovely it must have been to be her that afternoon. I had certainly never envied Adora more than I did then. Nor do I believe that she had ever enjoyed the pleasure of my company so much. She was positively enamored of me, intent that everyone should know the esteem in which she held me. What a clever woman she was, knowing how pleased Genevieve would be to see us getting along, fully aware that, if I had subsequently said anything negative, I would have been pinned as the jealous shrew.

Even so, others have turned away from me in bemused disgust when they learned I kept my silence, allowed the masquerade to continue, knowing the pain it could cause. The reason is simple: I let Adora win. If I had not, I fully believe that I would have lost my daughter forever.

Besides, Genevieve was so evidently in love with Jack that I knew this lesson could only be learned, not taught. I let everything play itself out, secure in my knowledge of its inevitable outcome.

Or so I thought. I had not bargained on my own flesh and blood.

Adora

They were inseparable. Oliver complained that Jack was paying less attention to his work as a result, which almost prompted our first fight in years. We were dressing for dinner in town, where we were to meet with Jack. Oliver was fastening the clasp of my necklace when he mentioned it to me.

"Don't be ridiculous, my dear," I teased, desperate to change his mind. "They're young and in love. Don't you remember how late you were for work when you first married me?" Oliver could be intransigent once he got an idea into his head, and it was so important to me that Jack stay in our lives that I could not listen to anything, not even from the man I submitted to in everything, that might detract from him.

"She's not as crazy about him as you want her to be, you know," Oliver admonished. "You really should stay out of things that don't concern you, Addie."

"Oliver," I soothed, "anyone would think that you're jealous."

I waited for him to rebuff my joke, but before he could say anything Genevieve came in, asking to borrow my bracelet.

"I'm going downstairs to get a drink," Oliver said, "and Genevieve," he added, matter-of-factly, "make sure that boyfriend of yours knows that we're meeting tomorrow morning at eight sharp. If he's late, I'll hold you personally responsible."

Genevieve must have nodded, because she didn't say anything and I didn't look up as I was rummaging through my jewelry box. It was only when I did that I realized my necklace had been fastened far too tight. I could barely breathe.

That evening, I couldn't sleep; too distracted by Oliver's growing dislike for Jack and what I feared it meant. Who could not praise him? To me, perfection shone from his every pore. Genevieve did not see that entirely yet. She was young; it was understandable. Sometimes, she would pull a face if Jack called to say he was going to work through lunch and could not meet her, or if he arrived five minutes late. But I understood. He was dedicated, and as he spent every waking moment of his spare time with her, there was no reason for her to be anything less than understanding. I made sure whenever he did come to dinner, which sadly was less and less frequent an occurrence than before, to praise his work ethic, even checking Genevieve, on occasion, with a stern look if she started to whine about the hours he was away from her.

Jack and I seemed to agree on everything. From art and music to literature — my passion — he had a surprising instinct, considering his youth, for the layers of meaning inherent within certain works. I think Genevieve, although incredibly intelligent for a girl her age, must have felt left out, because the conversation often exceeded her knowledge of certain things. I surprised and shamed myself sometimes by completely dismissing her opinions, something I had never done before, having praised her in everything. I found Jack so stimulating that her ignorance, on occasion, infuriated me. Afterward, I always felt terribly guilty for being so harsh, but I found myself unable to stop. Her presence at the table served as a distraction for Jack, an interruption in the flow of his thoughts. Even so, he would always listen to her, even if she disagreed, and would accept her opinion as valid, despite how much I wished Jack and I could talk freely, without anyone else present. Yet I didn't dare. I willed myself to accept my place on the margins, grateful only that I could watch.

The weeks went on, and with each one came a fresh complaint about Jack from Oliver. I kept it all from Gigi. There was no need for her to know that Oliver was not happy with Jack's work. I had always conceded everything to my husband, but I thought him terribly wrong in his analysis, especially considering how impressed his associates seemed to be with the young protégé. I initially thought that making excuses for Jack might allay Oliver's concerns, but as time progressed a stubbornness I had never before witnessed rooted itself deep in his mind. All of my pleading could not convince him that he made the right choice in employing Jack.

I thought it so unfair that Oliver gave no indication to Jack that he was unhappy. My husband rarely had a bad word to say about anyone, but on the subject of Jack he could cite endless errors of judgment, which seemed to me entirely inconsequential, to support his growing lack of confidence in Jack's abilities.

I knew Oliver so well that I was terrified I might not be given the opportunity to learn more of Jack. As much as I tried to stay away from him, knowing the damage I could cause if I didn't, I was forced to accept that we could not keep Jack if I did not step in to help. If I guided him, I convinced myself, he would be fine. Genevieve was too young to know how to reason with Oliver; I could make sure that Jack did everything right, but I needed to be closer. All day, every day, I ran through every possibility in my mind—what I could do to help without getting too close—but every time I tried to find a solution, I realized that I would have to involve myself with him personally, and I would recoil from the idea, like a creature kicked away from a feast.

In the end, Jack found me. I was thinking about you one evening, dear Sebastian, here in my olive grove, cradling Delilah, a little black-and-brown dachshund I had found at our gate, in my lap.

"My mother always told me that you give your heart to a dog to break," Jack said.

His voice did not startle me; I was so accustomed to replaying every little thing he said that I didn't actually realize he was standing behind me and not a ghost whispering in my ear. I was not even drawn out of my trance when he placed his hand on my shoulder, reflexively reaching for it as if he were you when we were young. I turned around expecting to see your face in my memory, anticipating the wincing remorse of knowing that you were not there, that I had imagined your presence, when I realized that it really was Jack behind me. And the first thought that came into my head was that he had found me, taken the responsibility out of my hands and come to me. I smiled up at him, grateful that he had shown me the way home without my having to beg.

No one ever disturbed me here; they understood it was my sanctuary, the only place left after you died where I ever felt truly at peace. I have always felt closest to you here. It's where the dogs sleep every night, something they have done ever since you left us. Long after the dogs that were still living when you died had followed you to paradise, the new animals I res-cued would instinctively lope here to the olive grove every night to rest, spread out on the dry earth and wrapped around the trees. I used to worry that they would wander too close to the edge of the cliff, and so I had marble balustrades installed, but I had nothing to fear. Our dogs kept their distance; the only time they went close to the edge was when I would sit here each evening, all of them lined up beside me as I whispered stories of you to them, so that your legacy would endure long after people ceased to talk of you.

"That's a touching sentiment," I replied. "Is that what you believe too?"

"No," Jack responded thoughtfully. "I think it's the other way around. I think they give us their hearts to break."

"Why?"

"Because they die first. They have to say good-bye first. I think that must break their hearts, to leave behind those they love the most."

I struggled to keep my emotions in check. I had never thought to be surprised by grief, but what Jack said made per-fect sense, although I had not conceived of it before. I only ever thought of the sorrow of those who must mourn those they loved, thinking them somewhere better than the place they left behind. Is this what you wanted me to learn, Sebastian, my love? That your heart was broken the day you slipped into the Mediterranean Sea and never came out. Heartbroken because of what I did to you.

"Adora, are you all right?" Jack asked, his concern touching me so that I shook my head in reassurance. "I didn't mean to upset you. Genevieve told me that nobody is allowed to bother you in here, but it was the only place I could speak with you alone. I wanted to ask if you would help me organize a surprise for Genevieve. I really want it to be special, and I know that you'll know best what to do."

I was lost with you somewhere, Sebastian, as Jack chatted on. I agreed absently to his suggestions, slowly and by degree waking up happy to the present and how things had turned out. Jack had found me. Jack needed me.

"Of course, you'll come to lunch tomorrow," I remarked, just as I always did. But as our eyes met when I stood up to leave, we both knew that it would be an entirely different lunch from any other we had shared. Nobody else would be there. Jack had found me and I had let him. We were not the heartbroken dead. We were the lucky ones who had been allowed to stay.

Miranda

I feigned migraines to avoid going out with them. I had managed to get through one afternoon without betraying the truth.
I intended to keep it that way. I am quite sure my absence was
barely commented on. Adora and Oliver would naturally com-
miserate with James and send their love, no doubt secretly
pleased that they wouldn't have to make an effort to take an
interest in someone they didn't care for.

I ruined James's holiday, I know. When it came to Oliver and
Adora, nothing could be allowed to upset them. If I had been
dying of some insidious disease, I would still have been expected
to crawl out of bed to entertain them. And I had. For nearly
twenty years, I had kowtowed to them, desperately trying to keep
the mood light, the conversations flowing. No easy task when we
had nothing in common. But no more. Not for me. After what
Adora had done, I granted myself an excuse note, and I intended
to honor it until James's patience was entirely exhausted.

Genevieve was furious with me, with justification. She, after
all, was placed in the uncomfortable position of having to live
with the two of them. Each day she came to visit me at the
hotel, sometimes with Jack, who would loiter in the adjoining
living room of the suite until I made myself decent. I must have

embarrassed her beyond belief. I didn't care. In my mind, as irrational as it was, I considered my own daughter Adora's accomplice in the ongoing plot to destroy my life. Over that period, I relinquished my role as her mother. It was the only way to save what was left of me.

I would luxuriate under the cool cotton sheets, the fan on full blast, the shutters half open to let the clear light filter through, glorying in my disobedience. Avoidance was my revenge, causing embarrassment for my husband, disappointing my daughter. All of these things brought pleasure to me in those dark hours. I would delight in my husband's plea to *please* come downstairs and Genevieve's hopeful expression when she entered my room each day to see if I was feeling better, only for it to vanish when I told her no. I suppose you could call it a meager victory for a narrow mind tainted by bitterness. I no longer cared what anyone thought. My days of seeking approval were at an end.

For all my indifference, however, I could not escape the ghost Jack inspired. I would watch him speak and experience that familiar sensation I once knew. I could almost feel the touch of my old chiffon scarf fluttering in the breeze against my skin on a beach with sand so white it blinded on a day long before. I grew ever more silent during these times until Genevieve, out of sheer frustration, finally lost her temper and told me she wouldn't come to visit me again. I remember when she told me of her decision that I felt a scream rise within me. No! Come back, if only for one more day. But I said nothing. I merely held her gaze until she pivoted on her heel in disgust, slamming the door behind her, destroying what was left of peace.

I turned my face to the wall and sobbed as I had all those years ago. The familiar pain once more at my door, pushing its way in, refusing to take no for an answer.

Adora

I was not upset when he arrived slightly early. I knew Jack would, if only to make a good impression, because he cared so much about the people Gigi loved. He brought me white orchids, commenting that it was the first time he had bought flowers for anyone other than Gigi. They were all the more magnificent to me for it. I kept one and pressed it later so that I might remember our lunch always.

I sent Gigi off in the morning in my car to the market on the other side of the island. She loved it there. All of the artisans hawked their wares every Tuesday and, invariably, she returned home at sunset laden down with unique gems of clothing unavailable in England. Oliver was away for the day to Nice for business. We were entirely alone.

"So, I've taken care of everything," I assured Jack, serving the lunch. "Les Amants is the most exclusive restaurant on the island and, as I know the owners personally, they are going to lavish you both with attention all evening. And," I continued more seriously, "everything is already paid for—" I shook my head disapprovingly and held up my hand to prevent him from interrupting. "Everything is already paid for and so you need not worry. Now, tell me," I continued brightly, sitting down opposite him, "do you think she'll be thrilled?"

Jack was entirely touched by the gesture, as I had known he would be, and full of thanks. It was so heavenly to sit with him, imagining Gigi's delight, our imaginations running away with us as visions of the evening played in our minds.

"I can't thank you enough," he said with a smile, clearly surprised that anyone would go to such lengths for him. "I worried that I'd upset you the other day with what I said. You seemed so distant. I wasn't sure if it was right to ask you to help."

I put down my glass, intrigued by his insight. "Why would you think I wouldn't? I would do anything to help you."

"No, no," Jack protested, clearly afraid he'd offended me again. "What I meant was that you always seem so preoccupied; I worried that I was disturbing you—that helping me, I mean," he corrected himself, "would disturb your routine. It seems you like to be alone a lot."

"I don't like to be alone," I answered honestly, directly. "It's just that I so often am."

"I know how that feels," he confided. "When my brother died, I was seventeen—I felt like there was an invisible wall put up around the whole family and each of us individually. We were just alone after he left. Nobody could talk anymore or do anything together. I didn't understand it at the time. Now, I think my parents just couldn't cope and couldn't bear to get close to anyone else."

Yes, I thought, exhaling all of the pent-up stress and frustration of years under my breath, *this is why you came. Because you understand what it is to be alone. And nobody since Sebastian ever has. . . .*

I wanted to take Jack in my arms and hold him there, to whisper everything I understood and share it with him, but I stayed where I was. I had known you had given Jack to me for a reason as soon as I met him, but I could never have imagined why. Finally, I began to grasp why we were so similar. We had both experienced the same isolation, the same regrets, the same excruciating loss. Of course, I was right to think I could help him; only I would be able to relate to what he had endured. But I had to do all of this for Genevieve, so that she could benefit from my wisdom in guiding Jack to a happy life. I would not have wished him to live with the endless regret that consumed my days.

Yet even as I aspired to noble acts, just talking to him and watching the shifting expressions of his delicate, inquiring face inspired such love in me that I wished I were young again, like Gigi. I wished that the discovery of love and all of its blissful pleasures were still mine to be had. I wished that my face, once alive with youth, still retained something of such splendor instead of slowly eroding into middle age, only a whisper of what it once was. I wished that I was sharing lunch with you, Sebastian, as we did every day years before, and that nothing had ever changed and you were still with me. And it was then, inexplicably, that I began to cry and the afternoon's task of helping Jack was forgotten as I found myself pouring forth my memories of the evening when you first took me to the restaurant I had chosen for Jack and Genevieve.

I checked myself at first, trying to control the heaving sobs, the suppressed grief of years rising inside of me, but Jack did not appear frightened of such agony. To any other boy of his age, indeed to men or women much older than he was then, the desire to flee from the horrors of such a tragedy would have been inevitable. The fact that he stayed, placed a consoling hand on my own, listened to me in his innocence as I talked ever on made it one of the most humbling moments I have ever shared with anyone. Not even Oliver had witnessed the true depths of what losing you, Sebastian, had done to me. I had held back over the years from revealing to him the inner torture I struggled with, instinctively aware that he would not be able to cope with it. It had almost been a blessing to be forced to put away my memories, not to have to be reminded at each story's end that you, my beautiful brother, were gone forever. I was always afraid, too, that Oliver would run from me if he knew the extent of my sorrow—but that Jack stayed for the entire afternoon, in spite of the trouble his absence might cause, made me love him more than I ever imagined I could.

"My brother lives in the sea, like a dolphin," I began, scanning Jack's face to gauge his reaction. He didn't flinch or turn away, embarrassed by my behavior, and so I continued. I told him of our childhood on the island, the unique relationship we shared. I relived every moment, it seemed, that we had ever spent together. Jack said nothing, simply listened, only his expression revealing the extent of his empathy.

"You can't know what this means to me," I told him, exhausted from crying. "I've never been able to talk about Sebastian with anyone. I tell the story of his life to myself, every day. No one else will listen. I'm so grateful that you stayed with me this afternoon, but you're going to get into terrible trouble from Oliver if he finds out. It's so late." I realized with alarm that I had kept Jack for hours, castigating myself for causing him problems when all I wanted was to help.

"Adora, I couldn't have left you," Jack said. I waited for him to add something like "not considering the state you were in" or "because you needed a friend," but he didn't say anything more. He just said, "I couldn't have left you," and that was all.

I stood up and took his hand to lead him out. He accepted my damp palm in his without comment; he didn't flinch or flush with embarrassment at my forwardness.

"Leave Oliver to me," I said. "I'll tell him that it's all my fault you were late back to work if anyone says anything to him when he returns from Nice."

"I could stay longer, if you want," Jack replied. He sounded concerned, and I wondered for a moment just how unhinged I must have appeared to him. "To help you," he added softly.

"Come back again," I replied almost before he finished his sentence, unable to conceal the desperation in my voice.

I knew that I shouldn't demand any more of him. I was aware of what might happen if I did, but I couldn't help myself. I needed him. I didn't look for a reaction as I felt my stomach knot in expectation of his response. He'll say no, I told myself, and then it will be out of my hands. I won't need to wonder anymore. I'll accept that what I've been given is enough. Be grateful for the afternoon; don't be greedy. Remember, I told myself, you are doing this for Genevieve, for her happiness. He is not yours. He won't stay. But Jack's voice rescued me from my doubts:

"I'll come back."

I never asked myself why he agreed to come back, whether he felt obligated or if he really did want to spend time in my company. I just accepted that he would as if it was meant to be, as if you, Sebastian, were guiding him.

"Thank you," I murmured, standing in the half-light of the hallway, the shutters slightly ajar to keep out the midafternoon heat. I stood on my tiptoes, leaned in toward him, and kissed him good-bye at the door. His cheek felt like down against my skin, deliciously cool, unblemished by time. I pulled back and almost reached up to smooth his golden curls as I used to with you, but what Jack said stopped me:

"My mother stopped kissing me good-bye after my brother died. Even when I left to come here."

He was resigned. I could hear the disappointment in his voice, but I could think of nothing to say in response. The light blinded me, flooding the room, as I opened the front door to show him out. I watched Jack leave through an unreliable prism, the sunshine in my eyes distorting his image as he receded from my view. I waited for him to turn and wave as you always did, even when you were just leaving to go to the kitchen or out to the pool. There was always that moment when you turned to me and waved one last time before you disappeared. I waited. But he never looked back.

Later, I convinced myself that I'd made a mistake. Of course, he had turned to me one last time. I had been mistaken. After all, I was blind.

Genevieve

It was the most simple of gestures, Jack lying down on the sand to place his head in my lap. It was then that I defiantly just let it happen, the love; I couldn't fight it any longer, despite the cost to myself; I loved him and that was all. Nothing else made any sense; when I was apart from him I was lost in a fog of confusion, when I found him again I understood everything. Perhaps he reminded me of a child, of me with you, Adora, seeking a safe place to rest, a place of trust. Or perhaps—and this thought ruins me now—I wanted to save him.

I remember feeling such perfect tranquillity that afternoon as Jack lay there in silence, the sun on his face and white sand in his hair. My fear slipped quietly away as I learned, for the first time, what it is to love completely, knowing that I could do no wrong, that I would be forgiven if I did.

"I can understand it now," he said sleepily, "what it is that you love about here. It's like being lulled to sleep, knowing that it's safe."

I was startled out of my trance by his words. He had never seemed unhappy to me. "You didn't like it here? When was that?"

"Oh, don't worry," he assured me, rousing himself to sit up. "It was before we started going out together. I felt out of place, that's all; I wasn't sure of certain people. Yet recently, I've started to feel as if I belong. I find it comforting. There are so many things I've come to love about this island."

I was unsettled, not reassured by what he had revealed. "Who were you unsure of?" I pressed. "Did someone do something to you?"

"Never mind," he said, sounding a bit annoyed, standing and shaking the sand off his clothes. "It's nothing. Everything is perfect now." He held out his hand to pull me up.

I walked with Jack to his office, the siesta hours between two and four at a dispiriting end, his hand in mine, no words passing between us. Usually, he spent his lunchtime telling me how much he adored me. I felt uneasy that he hadn't said anything like that; he seemed distant, and I felt as if I was racing to catch him up. He kissed me good-bye in front of the glass doors of the building where he worked and I watched him fade through them, like a ghost. I had nothing to live on, no lovely compliments to replay in my head until I saw him again that convinced me Jack still felt the same and, yet, I loved him; I had just realized how much. The thought that I might be already losing him unnerved me totally and utterly.

I ran after him, the sound of my heels reverberating off the marble floor, into his arms, where he held me for what seemed like hours. People stared at us, the two lovers who could not bear to part saying one last, lingering good-bye. A woman smiled knowingly at me, but she couldn't have known. She saw a young girl refusing to let go of her lover, reminded perhaps of a similar scene from her own youth. She couldn't have known that it was an act of desperation on my part. But I got what I

needed; I could replay Jack's astonished reaction, the graceful
turn of his head, in my mind all night, breathing in the memory
of his smile as if it was the only thing in the world that existed
or mattered.

After I left, I walked to my parents' hotel to tell my mother
everything in the hope that it might make her feel better and
because I felt guilty about how I had lost my temper the last
time I had visited her. I told her how I had dismissed Jack at
first, why I had fallen so completely in love at last. She listened,
her face expressionless. I tried harder to make her understand,
babbling brightly, pouring my excitement into the room in the
hope that it would raise her spirits. Still, she said nothing.

"What *is* it?" I finally insisted, dangerously close to losing
my temper. I just could not understand her. She was ruining
everyone's happiness. "Don't you like him? I thought you
would have been thrilled for me. Why can't you pull yourself
together? Every time you come here, Adora and Oliver make
such an effort and you're always so difficult with them. I just
don't understand you."

I knew I had gone too far and braced myself for her to slap
me; I had never spoken to her like that before. Yet she just stayed
sitting on the bed, her shoulders slumped as if I had beaten her
senseless, her eyes curiously glassy, fixated on nothing.

"Please," I pleaded. "I so want you to love Jack and be
happy for us and be happy yourself. Adora is thrilled. I just
don't understand why you're not."

My mother turned her face up to me then, and there was
no mistaking the terrible bitterness in her expression. "Adora?"
she scoffed, her voice dripping with sarcasm. "Yes, Adora, of
course, is thrilled. Go to her. She'll tell you what you want to
hear, but leave me alone, Genevieve. You're good at that, after

all. Let's not pretend that you ever needed me. Your entire childhood revolved around your summers, and you never made any attempt to hide that fact or think about my feelings when you left me every summer without a backward glance."

I tried to protest, but she stood up and pushed me toward the door. I thought she had gone mad. My mother hurt me terribly as she hustled me out and, despite my tears and begging, slammed the door behind me. I stood there for a time, banging on the door, demanding she let me back in. But in truth something in my mother appalled me, and the longer I waited, the more afraid I became that she would open the door and I would be confronted by her unaccountable anger again. So I did the only thing I could do, what I was always so good at: I ran to you, my Beloved Aunt, and told you everything.

Adora

She was in a terrible state, considering what Miranda had said, and I did my best to console her, attempting to make sense of her mother's behavior. It was incomprehensible to me that Miranda would not appreciate the poignancy of Jack and Gigi's relationship or even feel grateful that such an extraordinary thing could ever have happened. I couldn't waste time, however, trying to fathom Miranda's motives, especially not considering Gigi's revelations about her feelings for Jack. I listened, my chin perched on my hand, my eyes alive. That Gigi had finally understood what she had been given in Jack moved me unutterably. There could be no doubt now that he would stay in our lives. Not even Oliver could be so ruthless as to break Gigi's heart.

I felt as if I had returned to what I considered to be the beginning of my life, my late teenage years, when everything happened for me. I couldn't separate myself from her. It was as if we were the same person. Everything that was happening was so familiar it was as if my life was starting all over again.

I scrutinized the changes to my face in the bathroom mir-

ror each morning, trying to find ways to fix them. Although the
loss of my youth and its related beauty still caused the pressure
of depression to grip my shoulders, I found that I could conceal the worst of it with rouge and eye shadow, things I had
never had to use before. My confidence slowly returning with
each admiring glance I received from people I met, I began to
feel more attractive than I ever had. I walked with renewed
confidence, went shopping almost daily for new clothes and
makeup, and sunbathed for the first time in ten years. I felt impervious to decay, to harm.

I did not blame Gigi for clinging to me in her mother's
emotional absence. Where else could the poor thing have
gone? Unlike Miranda's, my love for her was never withheld,
even when I so disapproved of her conduct. I do regret the
pain Miranda experienced during that time, but there is nothing I can do about it now. It was never my intention to hurt her,
ever. Yet I doubt my apology would mean a thing.

No, the way the events of our lives had occurred made Gigi
seem like she was mine, and I accepted this vaguely abnormal
state of affairs unquestioningly. I hardly ever probed anything
in my life. You see, when the mirror looked at me, I knew exactly what it saw. I knew who I was and where I had been and
what I had done for love. Without Gigi, Jack would never have
stayed in our lives. Besides, what she did not know was that so
much of her happiness was orchestrated by me. Jack had come
to rely on me more and more over the course of our meetings; I
advised him on everything, even how to love her—especially
how to love her.

How many times in our lives can we say that a perfect soul
saw the future in us and waited for us and no one else? And
how many times can we ever say that we willingly ran to them

without fear, only expectation? Some people are never given the privilege. Some consider it a hindrance. I, on the other hand, have always understood the blessing. And this is what I taught him, among so many other things, during the incomparable snatches of time afforded to us by the benevolent Gods.

Miranda

The day I turned my daughter away, I finally hardened myself to having failed totally and utterly. I could not stand to listen to what I already knew: that, in Jack, she had found her perfect partner. For I was certain he was; there wasn't a doubt in my mind. Just as I was convinced that my lack of approval had destroyed something of the delight she was feeling. But I thought it best that she understand disappointment before it inevitably found her.

I believe she thought I had barely any knowledge of him. After all, I certainly didn't make conversation or even leave my room sometimes. But I knew him. I could even see the things Genevieve could not: his seriousness, concealed then behind a veil of happiness; a depth of suffering she could not begin to comprehend. Jack was damaged, balanced on a knife edge. One wrong word, one sullen argument, one crippling disappointment would destroy him.

It is both a curse and a blessing to have such an instinct for people. I always knew which friends would turn on Genevieve equally as well as I understood who privately loathed my popular husband. I was always guilty of saying what I thought. I could never stand the injustice of watching the people I loved the most put their faith in those so unworthy. I did try with James in the beginning to enlighten him to the fair-weather of spirit who surrounded him, who, to be quite frank, used him. He could never see it, and terrible arguments would result where I came off as the bad girl, marring his joy with my skepticism. So I learned to hold my tongue, never more so than that summer. To say anything was pointless; there was too much love involved. I was unsure whether my family would ever open their minds to the truth and, if I'm to be honest, I felt completely unloved, as if all my years of raising Genevieve had amounted to nothing. Adora's arms were the ones she had wanted from the first. So I let her love her, kidding myself that I was being a good mother by allowing it, but really resigned to a battle I knew I would never win. Nothing in my life had ever made me change my opinion of Adora: Everything she had ever wanted had come to her, even things she didn't deserve.

My thoughts returned frequently to Jack. I harbored a wish that, perhaps, I was wrong, that everything might not turn out badly, but my instinct told me otherwise.

Sophie

I had not yet arrived for my annual holiday when I learned that Oliver had purchased, finally, his most coveted desire, the apotheosis of all he had worked so hard for—the yacht. Funny how no one ever questioned how much he deserved his success. The evidence of his dedication was obvious to everyone in the extraordinarily long hours he worked and the frequent trips he had to make. He was envied, yes, but not despised. There was a general absence of jealousy, the offshoot of spite, for what he had achieved. Perhaps, as the more cynical among us might privately have thought, because his friends were invited to share in his wealth.

He had always been a god to his associates and friends. He had no detractors. Amazing considering how easy it would have been to hate him. Whatever the reason, whether his generosity or his affability, no one close to him ever would. He was one of those people things came easily to, and he was worshiped for it.

He called the yacht *The Titania,* which made Adora cry, naturally; Titania was the name of Sebastian's favorite dog, a loping greyhound who had been terribly beaten and brain-damaged by its owner. The two were inseparable although, in the beginning, Titania barely seemed to function. What Sebastian learned she could still do was fetch pebbles if he threw them for her, and that is what my darling son did, for hours each day, anything to please his crippled pet. Titania was the dog who died two days after Sebastian, who refused to leave the beach where he drowned. Adora was forced to sleep with her there, the two of them heartbroken on the sand, destroyed without him. Titania died at Adora's feet while they slept, the closest the poor creature could get to Sebastian. Adora, despite the fact that she refused to eat, survived, but only barely.

The yacht was Oliver's gift to my daughter for their seventeenth anniversary, although he gave it to her several weeks early, unable to resist sailing it during the height of the summer. It was unveiled in the harbor in town, surrounded by well-wishers and the attendant fanfare Oliver so loved. After Adora's initial emotional response, however, nothing more was ever mentioned about his inspiration in naming the boat. It was to become, instead, a home away from home for them as they sailed to the tiny islands that surrounded their own, private gems of white sand and clear seas. Adora wrote frequently telling me how Oliver would steer her to the hidden coves of her childhood, where she used to go with Sebastian. She rediscovered the beauty of her home, the caves nestled into the cliffs on which the island was built, the magnificent mountains crystalline in the sunshine rising high in the center of the tiny paradise she adored, and everywhere, always, her brother's memory.

She never learned to sail, leaving the task to Oliver who, in keeping with his talent for all things, took to the job as if he had been born to it. She would buy enormous amounts of food and wine before they set sail and cook it over a barbecue on whatever beach they alighted upon. My daughter was always at her happiest cooking, perhaps because it delighted her passion for solitary pursuits. Genevieve and Oliver would swim and play beach ball and tan their skin as dark as it would go, leaving Adora in peace for hours until they were called to lunch.

Their lives were comprised of the kind of simplicity that can only be acquired by tremendous wealth. Money dictated their pleasure, for who could not rejoice in the relative ease of wanting for nothing? But Adora began to grow skeptical, something she could never have been accused of before that summer.

"Mama," she wrote, "I cannot help but feel that we are so arrogant to overlook the price of such comfort. I fear that Gigi is growing spoiled; she seems to believe that everything is hers for the taking. Yet I suppose she has learned this from us and we are all guilty of loving the glittering sheen of our existence, sometimes to distraction. Except for Jack. He always appears sincerely grateful. In this regard, Mama, and in so many others, he differs completely from us. Sometimes, I am frightened for him."

I had not met Jack when she wrote me that letter. Nor did I consider the effect sailing over that sea and visiting the places of her past would have on Adora. I should have known.

Adora

He bought me *The Titania* to mark the anniversary of your death, which was also our wedding anniversary. Oliver was always of the opinion that, if something awful happened, we must commemorate the day at some point in the future with something wonderful, so that happiness would override sorrow in our memories. So I replaced the agony of your death, my brother, with the joy I shared with Oliver by marrying him two years to the day that you died, but it didn't really work, although I would never have confided this to my husband. I couldn't disillusion him. I wept, of course, not for the gesture but for the fact that nearly twenty years had passed without you by my side. On seeing my response to his overwhelmingly touching gift, my darling Oliver immediately offered to return it. I would not allow it. This present to me reconfirmed our grand love. Only a husband who deeply understood his wife would ever conceive of giving such a thing, with all of its happy and unhappy associations.

Certain friends thought the gesture tasteless, although they never directly said so. They did not need to. I could tell by the looks on their faces. They were wrong, of course. Oliver had given me the yacht and in so doing had allowed me to be close to you once again. You were part of the sea that surrounded us. The sea we had adored as children, which I continue to love now.

My heavenly life balanced on a precipice for me, ready to be lost at any given moment. I cannot help, considering what I have lost, conceiving of existence in this way. Although I am still capable of finding enjoyment in everyday things, it is tinged with a wariness that only comes from having lost too soon the people to whom I gave my heart and mind.

This is my life. I have been blessed and condemned in equal measure, but I have never lost hope. Somehow, sailing over that sea, my hand skimming the water that claimed you, Sebastian, inspired not grief but a longing for the future and what it might bring. I felt deeply loved and closer to you than I had ever been. It was almost as if my head was once again resting on your shoulder as I told you stories. In my mind, I closed the door on the past and immersed myself, for the first time since your death, in the glorious anticipation I used to experience whenever you walked into the room. We were together again. Everything had come full circle.

Jack and Genevieve would sometimes swim with the dogs out to the tiny islets just as you and I had done when we were their age. He was a strong swimmer like you, dolphinlike in his grace, leading the way for Gigi to follow. Whenever she tired, she would cling to him as if for her own life, and I would watch them, the two lovers of the sea, from my chaise on the deck of the yacht, and marvel at the incomparable consolation I felt at knowing such love was still possible in waters that could claim them but chose to support them instead.

Sometimes I swam out to meet them on their return or merely waited for them, towels ready to envelop their glistening, golden bodies, on the deck. And I would listen to their stories, their dreams, over dinner and thank God I had stayed long enough in this life to know such ecstasy again.

Sophie

She would sob in my arms whenever Sebastian went out, as if she would never stop. She was fourteen, he sixteen. Always she considered it her failing that she had not kept him safe. She cultivated a sense of abandonment, her once taut grip on his love waning. She refused to imagine a world where they were not together as they had been in childhood, resisting it, despising time for the changes it had brought to their once perfect life.

I knew that I had to let Sebastian wander despite my fears for his safety. He would disappear for days. He had no friends other than Adora, but it seemed so important that he try to find a life beyond her. Our island was not expansive, but one could get lost on it, and the first time he didn't come home, I feared the worst. Yet when he appeared again, Sebastian seemed so proud that he had managed to live away, if only for a few days, that I considered myself right in letting him be free, in letting him be free of her.

But while I nurtured one child, I began to destroy the other. Adora could not cope without Sebastian. I was at a loss to know what to do with her. Yet Sebastian was always patient with her as she pleaded with him not to leave or to take her with him.

"You are with me, Adora," he would say. "I hear your stories everywhere I go." He would wipe the tears from her face and carefully unprise her hands gripping his arms. I felt so deeply for him—Adora made it so difficult—but I pitied her too; she genuinely struggled to live without him. After Sebastian would leave, no bribe could console her. Not even our treasured dogs loping up to her for attention could distract Adora from Sebastian's unbearable absence. She would go to the olive grove and sleep there with the dogs, spending her days by the edge of the cliff watching for him to return.

Everything she needed was found in him. "My brother was born half asleep," she would explain if ever anything was mentioned, "but I was born wide awake. And that is why he loves me, because I tell him stories to keep him from falling asleep completely." People smiled consolingly whenever she said that; sometimes the truly compassionate even turned away to hide their tears from the blind little girl who loved to distraction, who loved a simple boy too beautiful for the world in which we lived.

Adora

Every time we met, I exulted in the vision of him waiting by the sea's edge on the sand, his back to me. In the beginning, it was so painful to watch Jack turn around and not be you, Sebastian, but later, as we grew closer, it was almost impossible to tell the two of you apart. Whenever we met it was as though what had been lost was returned to me for the few, brief hours we were together. After all of the years of solitude, I had found someone who granted me the freedom to speak of the past. I took him there with me over the lengthy luncheons we shared, sadly only once or twice a week, but all the more special to me for their rarity. He seemed a willing co-traveler, as if he knew the places and stories well, as if he had been there before himself.

I divested myself of years and plunged back into the ocean of happiness that was my youth, unafraid, for the first time, of drowning because Jack was by my side. As with Gigi, he became the one constant of my existence and, like her, I felt the sheer bliss of knowing he would come to me whenever I asked. Such was his incomparable kindness; he could not bear to disappoint those who needed him most. He would watch me as I spoke as you used to whenever I told you stories, intent and curious, filled with compassion and love.

Yes, he had grown to love me. This I knew long before he did. It began as he turned to meet me on the beach. Every meeting, his excitement, his smile grew until he was delighted to find me slipping down the dunes, my white dresses caressing my skin as I walked toward him.

I took him to the last beach of your life, where you said good-bye to us. It had to be that beach. I had followed Oliver's advice, superseding the terrible sorrow of the memory where you died with the joy of helping someone almost indistinguishable from you.

He was afraid, I know, as time moved on that Gigi might find out about our meetings. Jack could not stand to keep anything from her, but as I told him then, only a petty, immature mind could possibly misinterpret the innocence of our time together. I impressed upon him what a relief it was to find someone so empathetic after years of concealing my private thoughts from those closest to me. I could not imagine, if Gigi were to find out about the hours we had shared, that she would think any less of him for trying to help someone she loved like a mother.

It was simple to soothe him, like cradling a babe to sleep. He was content, I thought, to slumber in my world, listening ever on to my stories of long ago and of you. Jack's sadness as he listened convinced me of how right I had been to keep him always near us on our island. His quiet grace, the simple nods of his head as he agreed with one of my many interpretations of loss, was intrinsic to his spirit. Some of us are born knowing our fates, possessing a deep-seated understanding of life and what it will bring to us. As he sat with me, I believe he saw his future open up in front of him, confirming what he already knew about his own life and where it would lead.

Genevieve

The more Jack grew to love our island, the quicker he began to succeed, swiftly becoming the star of my uncle's show; an innovator whose ingenious ideas were met with astonishment, as a result of his youth, and glee for the money they would ultimately generate. He met the elaborate compliments that were showered upon him by Oliver's associates with utter humility and a touch of what seemed, to the naked eye, embarrassment; attributes that caused Jack to be compared frequently to Oliver. People would often say how well Oliver had taught him and that a fine future awaited him by virtue of their similarities. Except Oliver. His distance decreed that Jack still had much to prove.

I agreed with them at the time, allowing Jack to shine, careless of my arrogance. I was living your life, Adora, and I loved the power I felt when I was with him, just as you must have yourself with Oliver. I was a princess-in-waiting, ready to be crowned, ready to step into your shoes when the time came.

I bought entirely into the myth in the process of being contrived around us. Oliver's business associates even suggested that Jack had the makings of a junior partner, a statement that made you beam with delight. I saw a future of ease and contentment opening up before me: a life just like yours. One that I would never have to struggle to make sense of, that I had already seen lived; where I would never be taxed again by troubles or doubt or guilt, where I would be able to drift along free from worry. With each success he enjoyed, I became someone who was welcomed, not spurned.

I was still so naïve and oblivious to how much I had to learn, what was lurking on the horizon to challenge us all. Looking back, I should have paid more attention to how uneasy Jack was made by the escalating hoopla that accompanied his triumphs. I should have asked him what he wanted instead of carelessly dismissing anything that might upset your plans for him, Adora. I was obviously learning far more from you than I even realized.

I know he did everything for me because I revered you. Jack had seen my family splinter that summer: a mother who was disinterested, a father consistently embarrassed by his wife's absence, a daughter rebuffed by the very person she needed most. Acutely perceptive, he understood that I needed to feel calm, and he gave it to me by his silence, by refusing to upset the applecart. I did not love Jack for such qualities then, it was only later that I realized the enormous sacrifice he made for me. What I loved was an intangible element, almost impossible to explain, precariously sentimental. When I rested my head on his chest, I could sense a quiet strength, a deep peace that stilled my fears. But it was much more than that, and here is where I risk sounding ridiculous: His heart seemed to beat for me. As long as I lay there, I required nothing else. I felt a sense of completion, the irrefutable knowledge that I had found my home.

We would lie together, the only sound the *swish, swish* of

the hammock, swinging slowly, barely talking, drifting together. It was enough. It was everything.

My mother kept her silence right through to the end of her time on the island. On the last evening of my parents' holiday, she made a show of attempting to come down for dinner, which was aborted due to the sudden return of her thirteen-day-long migraine, the only cure being to lie down again in her darkened hotel room. You offered to go and sit with her, Adora, even to call the doctor in to see if anything could be done. My mother flatly refused, or so I presumed, because the call my father placed to their room ended abruptly after barely a minute. In the face of such outright bad manners, you and Oliver smiled on, your carefully constructed masks designed to conceal what you really thought of her behavior.

I was relieved she wasn't coming. I neither wanted nor needed to confront her disapproval, to have my happiness diminished chip by chip for the hours we would have to spend together. Oliver drove us all deep into the island to an old converted mill only the locals knew of where we dined outside in the garden. My father was his usual merry self, more so considering the welter of business Oliver's investments had generated for him. Over the years his law practice had grown as a result of their friendship. He handled practically all of Oliver's legal affairs which, considering Oliver's success, ensured a steady stream of referrals and new accounts. They were involved in a huge property investment at the time, some project Oliver was spearheading and Jack was working on, which was substantial enough to almost guarantee my father's early retirement. Life, for him, was good, not, in truth, that it had ever been anything less. Yet helping people, especially Oliver, was what fueled him. Frankly, I think it was why he got up in the morning.

Jack was unusually animated that evening. Often he seemed shy in the face of our familiarity, but I believe that my acceptance of him made him feel safe to enjoy involving himself more deeply in our lives. Even though only six weeks had passed, I had loved him enough to reassure his doubts about whether or not I would stay or go. Although I was only eighteen, my family seemed to accept that marriage to Jack was inevitable. Nobody had pulled me aside to ask me if I was sure about committing myself at so young an age; not a word of discouragement had been uttered. Apart from my mother's ridiculous behavior, nothing had troubled us. After the initial upheaval his arrival had caused, everything seemed to be falling perfectly into place.

I watched him talk and grow ever so slightly drunk on the champagne that was a constant at Oliver's table. I realized how familiar he seemed, not because of our growing intimacy but because he did indeed remind me of someone I knew and loved. Jack might have emulated Oliver in business, but it was my father, James, he was most like in terms of personality: he had his sincerity and desire to please. In fact, the more I observed, the more I came to think that he was exactly like my father, even down to his fondness for you and Oliver.

I watched you, Adora, and Oliver seated side by side at the head of the table, a picture of success, enviable in your perfection. Yet you both seemed suddenly old next to Jack's youth and energy. We were starting, I realized, where you were ending. It was our time to shine now, to bask in the attention people gave us, the interest they had in Jack—and me, by association. I could play your role, the adoring partner to a brilliant man. Maybe I could even play it better, I thought. I worshiped you, of course, but you could be difficult, hard work, as my mother often said. It was well known, although never spoken of, that Oliver had had his hands full with your mercurial moods over the years, and there had been rumors that the fact you didn't have children wasn't because you couldn't, as you alleged. I realized that I was growing up, able to discern more than the surface glamour of your lives. I would never deny Jack children or recluse myself to wallow in the past. It vaguely horrified me to question your personality; I certainly never had before. But you had turned on me slightly that summer; I was not as gullible as I once was when it came to your charms or your virtues.

I drank Jack in; he was so handsome, golden, the picture of summer in his white linen shirt. He was better looking than Oliver, I realized. He had an honest face, whereas Oliver's concealed something that I was no longer sure was nice. It was then that I finally allowed myself to cast aside any doubts my mother may have inspired in me and submerge into happiness, to experience the incomparable glow that came of knowing Jack belonged to me. With a complete lack of self-consciousness, I leaned over and kissed his cheek, causing him to go bright red with contented astonishment. It was my way of saying, yes, once and for all, in full view of everyone whose acceptance I coveted. Oliver smiled at me, as if he had once known the feeling himself, silently approving where it would lead. I smiled back at him, and I remember thinking how lucky we all were to love one another so much. I reached for Jack's hand, turning to him, but he wasn't paying any attention. He was fixated on you, my Beloved Aunt, staring out into the distance as if your heart was broken.

Miranda

James found me waiting in the hotel lobby on the day of our departure, suitcases at my side and the car to the port booked. He was astonished I had been able to get everything ready considering that he had thought me totally insane over the course of the previous two weeks. He was also suspicious. I was aware that my pulling myself together to leave, appearing to be as sane as ever, would invite him to speculate on whether all I had really wanted to do was ruin his holiday. I already knew, however, that I would never be forgiven, whatever the reason, for committing the cardinal sin of snubbing his best friend.

My husband was not a bad man, far from it. He was everything any woman might wish for in a spouse, but he had one fatal weakness that had caused an irrevocable rift between us over the years: his love for Oliver. It's not fair to say that I never liked Oliver; it was he who disliked me. I wasn't placid or plain enough for his taste. He required James to marry someone quite dull, so that he could shine all the more in comparison. Oliver needed his best friend's wife to be as sycophantic as everyone else who surrounded him, certainly not a woman who wouldn't go out of her way to satisfy one of his wishes. Nobody will ever convince me, as James has tried so hard to, that friendship is founded on living one's life solely for the friend.

Frankly, the fact that neither of us particularly cared for the other should have been allowed to pass unnoticed. I could have carried on, smiling politely, ambivalent about his company, had he not tried to ruin my life. Perhaps that statement is too dramatic. Better to say that I wouldn't have cared a jot about spending time with Oliver had he not destroyed my marriage.

We had been married only three years when we decided to try for another child. Genevieve was just a toddler. Adora and Oliver had just been told that the chances of Adora ever conceiving were highly unlikely. Despite everything, I did feel for Oliver. After all, what was he really guilty of at the time save for a certain dismissiveness toward me? We were holidaying on the island when they received the news and, obviously, James was called upon to help Oliver through such a difficult period. As usual, I found myself left alone—Adora always insisted James bring Gigi when he visited the house—for most of the holiday as my husband dedicated himself to his duties.

I recall, however—and it's funny how certain throwaway things impress us, call upon our instinct to pay attention— Oliver unexpectedly dropping in on James one evening at our hotel and asking him to come for a walk. I watched them from the balcony as they talked together by the pool, two tiny figures in the distance dressed for the late afternoon in their pale summer suits, Oliver's casual grace evident in the way he ambled alongside my bumbling husband, his arm around his shoulder. I recall Oliver catching sight of me as he turned to leave my husband, nodding his head in a mock bow, and smiling, dare I say, fondly at me. In spite of myself, I was thrilled. Perhaps he did like me after all. I began to realize why people raved about him so much; when he singled you out for attention, there wasn't any feeling quite like it.

Yet there was something in James's bearing that day which made me question exactly what had been said. Something told me that there was a lot more to what had transpired during their meeting than James was letting on, but he didn't elaborate when he came back to the room. I pressed him at the time, but he wouldn't tell me and I was forced to let the issue go.

Years later, however, I believe Genevieve must have been about eight—in fact, yes, she was, for it was the first summer she had spent alone with Adora and Oliver—after a drunken evening out with friends, James came home and let slip what had really happened that afternoon by the pool. He told me what Oliver had asked of him that day. His best friend had requested that James and I not have any more children. He felt that their friendship might be destroyed as a result of he and Adora not being able to share in the inevitable joy children would bring. And when I inquired if my husband had categorically refused such an abhorrent request, he was drunk enough to tell me that he'd said nothing. He had not turned his back in disgust that any friend could abuse their relationship in such a way as to deny happiness to a married couple, nor had he done what most men might have in the situation and simply punched his friend in the face. No, such was my husband's regard for Oliver that he had kept his silence and, by so doing, completely and utterly humiliated me.

I have had to remind myself frequently of the strength of their friendship to excuse my husband's cowardice. I have had to tell myself that James was probably so astonished by Oliver's request that he didn't know what to say. I have been forced to tell myself this, but I never really believed it because my husband never slept in the same bed with me again after the conversation he shared with Oliver while we were on holiday. I perceived his withdrawal at the time as an aspect of marriage many women must tolerate and thought it a temporary situation. But it was not.

As the years progressed, however, I began to consider myself responsible for James's lack of affection. I thought that I was lacking, not good enough, unable to please him adequately. Yet that evening, after my husband's confession, I came to accept that we all have one great love in our lives. For me, it was Genevieve. For my husband, Oliver. I should have been able to conduct my life without ever having to confront such knowledge. At the time, I condemned Oliver unreservedly for my being forced to accept that James's motive in marrying me was not what I had previously imagined. While my husband appeared, most of the time, to put me first—front and center, so to speak—it was only so that the true nature of the love he felt for Oliver never became apparent. I was a human shield, designed to deflect attention from the truth. I figured in my husband's life as little more than a plausible lie.

How ironic it is to consider that the one child we were permitted to have became the object of Oliver's wife's undying obsession. I never asked James quite how Oliver coped with Genevieve's presence, considering his distaste for the idea of us having more children. I often ask myself, considering everything, what Genevieve would say if she knew that Oliver might once have been more than willing to eradicate any trace of her; that, in essence, he wanted her never to have been born. It's funny how things change.

Genevieve

It was the first time I didn't cry when my parents left the island at the beginning of August. I refused even to go to the port to see them off. I remember feeling a great weight lift from my shoulders when I looked at the clock and realized their cruise liner had departed, as if the summer and all of its related pleasures could finally begin. Their visit had proved something of an ordeal, and I was glad not to have to deal with the perpetual guilt of knowing my mother was present on the island yet entirely absent, provoked.

Over the weeks that followed, after a couple of futile attempts to engage my mother by writing letters to which I received no reply, I decided not to bother again. Any concern I might have felt for her disappeared entirely and I was almost elated not to have to subject my high spirits to her pessimism. You said nothing about the situation, Adora, despite my efforts to glean an opinion. This hardly surprised me. I had never actually heard you criticize anyone. Your distaste at the mention of someone you did not like spoke volumes and warned the speaker not to proceed any further. Yet although you kept your opinions of my mother to yourself, you never allowed me to disparage her, saying only that migraine headaches were terrible things and I should consider myself fortunate not to have inherited them.

Nor was my father any help on the issue; the letter I received from him revealed nothing. As my mother refused to speak to him, he was as much in the dark as everyone else. Finally, I stopped asking, indeed thinking, about her. I thought that, sooner or later, she would tell me what had been wrong, if anything. I let the matter slip, which was easy considering who I had to occupy my time.

I really did not care about my mother that summer. I considered her a hindrance. In the face of the enormous effort you and Oliver always made for her, I thought her behavior atrocious and assigned my loyalties accordingly. I was pleased to be rid of her. Even though I was beginning to learn that you weren't perfect, either, I began to look to you, my Beloved Aunt, to guide me more and more. Despite your lapses into mild indifference that summer, you had allowed me all of the simple pleasures of youth without asking for a single thing in return, quite unlike my mother. Far more than her, you nearly always delighted in my every move, indulged my whims, showered me with praise without ever calling me to task, and exonerated me from any kind of responsibility.

Because of Jack, I was growing, evolving into a young lady who was watched and, sometimes, admired. I began to study you closely, analyzing how you behaved in certain situations, copying your smile in the mirror whenever you greeted somebody. It so charmed people when you did it; that "ah, here you are, and I am delighted" expression. It was so powerful a tool in your arsenal that, when you didn't greet someone that way, the full force of the snub was clearly felt. But when you did, the prize was their reaction: the way men's faces lit up, delirious to be individuals you cared to know. Of course, the women weren't quite so enamored; their tight smiles forced until they turned to Oliver and let their guard down completely and utterly.

I didn't realize then how much you were changing. You had never worn makeup before for the simple reason that you never needed any. Yet that summer, your bathroom became a cosmetics counter of rouge, powder, lipsticks, and face creams. You began to spend hours every morning in there, performing an elaborate beauty routine of masks, moisturizers, and facial exercises before you would emerge looking exactly as you did before you went in. I even started to use some of the same products until my face broke out in a severe rash and you had to rush out to buy something, anything to reverse the effects of whatever I had smeared all over my face in imitation of you. It hadn't even begun to dawn on me yet that the very idea was risible.

It was only later that I learned nobody could possibly compare to you, my Beloved Aunt. Nobody ever has.

Adora

At night, when I cannot sleep, I recite the list of our dogs' names to myself as far back as I can remember. First is Lily, the huge German shepherd, who was so emaciated we had to carry her up the steps to our house. Then Lucy, the border collie, who we joked was the worst guard dog in the world as she would roll on her back to have her stomach rubbed whenever a stranger walked through the gate. Bella, the brown and white beagle, refused to sleep anywhere except beside me and astonished all of the locals by following us into the sea and swimming with us for hours on end. Bailey, the Jack Russell, we rescued from the drunken butcher who used to beat him. When he made a fuss about how we had stolen his dog, Mama marched down to his shop and warned him never to come near us again. He never did. Skipper, another collie, loved to run around all day, every day, never growing tired until nine at night exactly, when he would fall down next to his favorite tree in the olive grove and sleep until sunrise, only to start his routine all over again. Bertie, the cocker spaniel, loved to be fussed over for as long as our patience allowed . . . and Mabel, the Pekingese, and Char-lie, the black Scottie dog, and Lulu and Fluffy and Tiny and

Rudolph . . . The names flood back to me until my eyes flutter closed and I dream about them—and you—all over again.

You thought you might become a vet, Sebastian, but you showed no aptitude for the sciences. "I'm not clever, like you, Adora," you would say despite how I tried to convince you otherwise. "I just like to be close to them." I suspect now that there was something of them in you, Sebastian, something elemental to the soul. The way you would lead those poor animals here into the olive grove and touch the ground to show them where they would sleep forever safe near you, and the way they followed you I think speaks of something far more than simply love. I think they knew that they had come home.

I still carry on your work, Sebastian, and now we are surrounded by Sasha, the gentle King Charles spaniel, and Bruckie and Rory, the Scottish border terriers who never stop barking until you pick them up and carry them everywhere, and Clark Gable, the black Labrador, whom Genevieve christened, and Linford, the greyhound, my closest friend, one of Titania's children's children, who meets me here at the entrance to the olive grove each evening and walks with me to the edge of this cliff, where we sit and watch the sea, lost with each other in perfect peace. And finally, our new addition, whom I found waiting by my car at the beach where you died, a small mongrel of tan and gold whom I named Jack so that he might always be with me.

Genevieve

It was nearly two months after we first met, the briefest space of time in the larger scheme of things but a lifetime to me then, when Jack began to change. He did not stop loving me. If anything he needed me more, holding me tight for hours, as if he was unable to let go. It was his mind where the trouble, the fear, was beginning to root. I am convinced that he sensed the end of happiness, could glimpse it on the horizon of our days. He was waiting for it.

It was our last lunch together because Jack had so many things to take care of the next day before traveling to the mainland, to Monte Carlo. He was leaving the following evening because Oliver wanted him to meet with investors regarding a potential project there. Although he really didn't want to leave the island, he had no choice. To think that two weeks apart seemed so long at the time. Neither of us could bear to part with the other—for Jack it was even harder than for me, and I had to reassure him, frequently, that I would still be waiting when he came back.

"Are you sure?" he pressed. "You know, I really wouldn't be able to stand it if you weren't."

I laughed involuntarily, wanting to change the subject back to something more cheerful. "Jack, stop it," I said, shaking my head. "You know how I feel. I'll be here, don't worry."

It was blissfully hot that day, a cool breeze coming in off the water as we lay in the secluded cove we had found one lunchtime on a beach to the north of the island. We loved it there, surrounded by the jagged rocks of the cliffs, the clear expanse of sea our only view. We were never disturbed there and, unusually, it was one of the few places where nobody in the nearby cafés or bars seemed to know you and Oliver. Neither of us mentioned our discovery to anyone, to protect our romantic idyll from being ruined by similar-minded privacy seekers.

"You know there's really nothing you could do that I wouldn't forgive you for," he persisted. "We all have secrets. We've all done things—"

"What have I done, Jack?" I laughed nervously, surprised by his seriousness and the line the conversation was taking.

He didn't immediately reply, and I grew more anxious. I was used to being held to exacting standards by my mother, even by you, Adora, always having to appear a certain way, but never with Jack. I pondered what it was he thought he knew, something he had seen in me that I had believed carefully concealed.

"Nothing," he said absently. "I was talking more generally. I suppose I'm going to miss you a heck of a lot," he said apologetically. "I'm getting nervous just thinking about leaving you."

"Is that all?" I cried in relief. "I'll be here," I promised. "Don't doubt that."

I nuzzled my head into his neck, teasing him about his insecurities as if they had no merit at all. But it was an effort, I remember, trying to convince him that nothing could possibly change the way I felt, not even his absence. Gradually, Jack submitted to my attempts to make him laugh, perhaps to please me, perhaps wanting me to remember him happy after he left. Uncharacteristically, I'd had some wine at lunch in my ongoing attempt to emulate you, Adora, and I fell asleep beside him on the beach. He was watching me when I woke up, resting on one elbow, as if he were studying me.

"What is it," I murmured, "what are you doing?"

"Remembering you," he replied, and I don't know why but my eyes filled with tears as I pulled him to me. All I could hear was the sea as I clung to him, and I did not let go until I was sure he wouldn't be able to see that I'd been crying for him.

I turned back at the top of the stone steps on my way into the house. I knew Jack would still be standing there, leaning against the car, watching me, remembering me. He wore a pale khaki suit, and, although he was so golden, he seemed pale, deliciously so; cool. He raised his arm in a gesture of farewell, and I knew even as he did it that I would never forget it; the way the late afternoon sunlight caught him, filtering through the haze, was perfect—just as he was. I felt something flutter in me, a lightness, as if somebody had breathed against my soul, had touched it. I felt the tears sting my eyes again before I turned away and, as I did so, I realized that I had left Jack somewhere between hello and good-bye: The way he had stood was like a gesture of welcome as well as farewell and, for some reason, I found it consoling.

• • •

The house was cool and dark, disconcertingly so after the brightness of the afternoon, as I walked inside. I felt as if I was sleepwalking as I passed through it. I found you in your bedroom; you were reading on your bed.

"I'm going to marry him, you know," I asserted, almost as if I was challenging you, Adora, as if I didn't quite believe it myself anymore.

You lowered your book, and I felt the warmth of your eyes as they feasted over me, as I let you. I waited for you to reply, to breathe, "My darling girl, of course you are." But you didn't. You simply stood up and smiled, kissed me on the cheek, and sent me out to the pool. I tried to push my disappointment to the back of my mind as I walked outside, scuffing my shoes disconsolately, troubled by the afternoon and your response. I thought about everything Jack had told me, his concern, and, after hours of soul-searching, finally managed to convince myself that all would be well, everything would work out as it was supposed to.

It was easy enough. I didn't know any better.

Adora

I have always hated to leave. Whenever I have to, I wake with an inconsolable dread that what has been anticipated is over, another part of life spent. There is no future in leaving for me, no hope. Even when I've had to go somewhere I was disinterested in or a visitor came whom we cared little for, I always dreaded the final good-bye, the last check of the hotel room to make sure nothing had been left behind. It is no surprise then, considering, how I come undone at the thought of someone I love leaving or of leaving them. The last days of Genevieve's visits were always unbearable. *All gone,* I used to think, the excitement, the prospects of adventures, happiness, done. I used to so resent when Oliver would mention dinners or meetings we would have to attend after she left, matter-of-factly projecting into the future oblivious to the fact that I wanted none if she was not with me. I would think to myself, *But she'll be gone then; all of this will be a memory; how can you ask me to imagine that?* And the days after the treasured visitor leaves, the unexpected tears when one drives into town for the first time or prepares the lunch that they will not eat, the thinking that it was only yesterday or a week ago or five hours ago that we did that together, that they were here with me, and now everything is mundane, rhythmic in its simplicity; the best is over.

I used to think the Gods so merciful for offering no warning that I would not keep you, Sebastian. I used to believe I could never have borne watching the minutes die knowing each one was a step closer to letting you go forever. Now, I think them pitiless to have left you alone to count the last moments of your life. I need to believe there was an angel with you when you left, someone to walk with you and hold your hand, to offer consolation before the night fell. I need to know that you were in the presence of love, that you were held in that presence, and that leaving was a relief, like slipping into the sleep I had tried so long to keep you from.

Jack was waiting for me here in the grove with Linford. I wasn't expecting him, yet something had impelled me to leave my desk in my library and go outside, knowing I would find him. All I could think of was the first day we met, his blue shirt and face of hope as he ascended into my world.

Did you know in your heart that you had come home, my love? I whispered to myself like a prayer, repeating the question my soul had first asked of him.

Everything around me, the trees and the stones on the ground in this shaded grove, felt somehow more real than it ever had, as if I was waking up for the first time in years. I was no longer gliding past in a dreamworld with Linford and the rest of my dogs, I was walking toward my destiny. The irrelevant facts of our existence meant nothing; not that he would leave me in three hours for Monte Carlo or that I would take him to the port with Genevieve to pick up my mother at the same time. Nothing.

I could tell that he had spent most of the day in the sun on the beach; he had that dryness about him, a sandiness, even in his hair. We used to do that, Sebastian, don't you remember? It was always such a wonderful feeling coming home and looking in the mirror to see how tanned we were, how white our hair had turned. Jack was just like us; it was all I could do not to smother him as I remarked the gold in his curls and his face wet with tears.

"Walk with me," I said, taking his arm in mine. He could barely move, stumbling beside me, and I realized he seemed drunk, quite desperately so. I didn't mind. As with you, Sebastian, I felt it was my duty to hold him up.

I never cease to admire the beauty of my olive grove, the way the trees touch at the tops, causing a deliciously cool darkness to fall over spots on the ground and the way in which the sea appears like a promise at the end; like looking through a telescope and finding paradise. And everywhere my dogs, wrapped languorously around the trees, some looking up to greet me, all of them safe.

We walked to the clearing and leaned against the marble balustrades, protected from the cliff's edge. It was late afternoon, my favorite time, and the day had been so perfect. Yes, it had been perfect, and no, I hadn't mourned Jack's leaving, I realized. I was astonished yet content to accept that something in me had moved on; I no longer regretted endings, good-byes. With Jack, there would be none. This I had known from the first. Just as I had accepted that he would come to me. He had.

Words had no import. The two of us were leaving something behind, and yet we were together and so I paid it no mind. Nothing he said surprised me. Something in me had always known.

"I killed my brother," he wept. "That's why they sent me here."

Filled with instantaneous compassion, I drank in his angry confusion, his terrible sorrow, and opened my arms to welcome him.

"Did you know in your heart that you had come home?" I murmured into his hair, clasping him to me.

"You don't understand," he sobbed. "I killed my brother. Someone will tell her. She'll never forgive me. You don't understand."

But I do, Jack, I do, I thought, the tears slipping soundlessly down my face. *I do understand. I killed my brother too.*

His arms reached up to wrap around my neck like a baby reaching for the reassurance of his familiar parent. The weight of him pulled me down to the ground and I let him, happy to fall.

"Yes," I breathed, accepting of everything and where it would lead.

With that, the metamorphosis was complete.

Genevieve

You were excited because Sophie was coming to visit from France. I couldn't help but compare your happiness with my ambivalence toward my own mother. I was so in love with you at that time; I had convinced myself I wouldn't care if I never saw her again. I was not as unfeeling as I supposed, however, and experienced constant twinges of guilt whenever I saw you doing things in preparation for your mother's arrival. But even so, I did not write again to mine. I may still have loved her, but I was not prepared to forgive just yet.

My mother and Sophie absolutely adored each other. In recent years, my parents had changed the time of their visits to the island from midsummer to its end in order to coincide with when she would be there. It hadn't worked out that year because of some commitment my mother had made to one of her charities, which I remember had upset her. Yet I always felt for you whenever Sophie and my mother were together; you seemed so completely left out. Sophie always seemed to prefer my mother's company to yours, and they would talk for hours, oblivious to whoever else was there, and to the enormous effort you made whenever your mother came to visit. Anyone could have been forgiven for thinking that Sophie was my mother's mother, not yours. Sophie spent so little time with you, after all. In fact, whenever my mother was there, Sophie didn't even seem to notice you. It was inconceivable to me that anyone might not want to be near you. Yet as wonderful as Sophie was, she was not the type of woman whose choices could be questioned. Nor were you, for that matter, so I never said anything.

I was also thrilled that Sophie was coming and pleased, too, for a different reason about my mother's absence as she couldn't stop herself from openly crying whenever Sophie started telling her stories about Sebastian, regardless of whether other people were there, which was always so acutely embarrassing.

I loved Sophie so and always tried very hard to please her, looking for things I could do to make myself useful. She was my storyteller, a gifted teller of tales, and I had spent most of the afternoons of my early summers snuggled beside her as she entertained me with story after story she made up according to my specifications. My favorite was "The Happy Prince," the credit for which belongs to Oscar Wilde, although I later learned Sophie had elaborated on it somewhat. Yet the original concept of the statue covered in gold with sapphires for eyes and the swallow who stripped the prince, at his request, of his finery to save the lives of the starving until the swallow stayed too late into the winter and died remained the same, save for Sophie's additions, which involved saving the malnourished dogs of the town.

She was antithetical to you in looks, being dark and pale, save for the omnipresent slash of red lipstick she always wore. Whereas you seemed to live an interior life, Sophie's expressions gave away her every thought, however inappropriate they might be. She had no patience for people she could not stand and blanked them accordingly, much to Oliver's irritation, as her distaste was most often reserved for his friends, *obsequious fawners* as she always described them, loud enough for them to hear. My family, however, was exempt from Sophie's wrath, and I can still remember vividly how she would cry out in delight whenever they walked through the door, which was most unlike her. She was never as affectionate with you.

When Jack and I learned that he was to be away for the whole of her visit, I had tried everything, through you, to get Oliver to let him come home early. I know you tried but, apparently, the trip was just too important. Jack had to go, you told me. "Besides," you said to cheer me up, "there will be so many other times when my mother and Jack will meet." I was disappointed, naturally, as I wanted to hear all of Sophie's thoughts, and rather astonished; you always used to be able to persuade Oliver to do whatever you wanted. Something had obviously changed.

The evening that Jack was to leave, I had made my way to the car only to be surprised to find him with you at the entrance to the olive grove. The original plan had been for you, Adora, to drive me to his apartment and then on to the port, where he would catch his ship to the mainland. I was relieved when Jack greeted me affectionately that he seemed a little more like himself again, but I could have sworn he had been drinking; he appeared slightly confused, a little bleary. I had been worried somewhat about what he had said at the beach the day before, about forgiving me anything. I had racked my brain to try to understand what he must have been thinking about, but I hadn't been able to come to any conclusion that satisfied me. As I looked closer, I actually wondered if he had been crying, but you, Adora, smiled so brightly at me that I didn't think any more of it.

"Can you imagine that I found him sleeping in the olive grove, darling?" You beamed, mock-admonishing him. "We had better not tell Oliver, had we?"

He smiled at you, relieved. I thought I saw something then, a look that flickered between you, something intimate, hidden. I couldn't be sure, but what I did see quite plainly was that he held an enormous fondness for you, far more than I had imagined. Momentarily, I felt annoyed; Jack had claimed he couldn't meet me that day because he had too much work to take care of before he left. He looked like he'd been at the beach—how long had he actually been at the house?

"I thought you couldn't meet me, Jack," I queried, unable to stop myself. "I thought you had too much to do."

Adora answered for him: "Jack can only have been here an hour or so, Gigi, darling. I was down here earlier before I went inside for a siesta."

"Yes," he agreed, a little absently. "I finished up earlier than I thought and wanted to come and see you; but the house was so quiet when I arrived that it looked like you were all taking a nap, and so I waited here in the olive grove and fell asleep myself."

I wasn't sure I believed him, and I had a sudden insight that he was in love with you, Adora, but I almost laughed out loud when I thought of it; of course you were so desirable, but you were so much older. It was ridiculous. And then, almost immediately, I stopped in my tracks. I would never have come to such a conclusion during the previous summers; the idea that you were in any way imperfect or human, even, would never have occurred. I was too busy thinking about that to entertain any more suspicions and, as Jack seemed fine, I forgot about what I thought I saw.

We took him to the port together as Sophie's boat was arriving at almost the same time as his departed. Although I would have preferred to say good-bye to him alone, there was no time. We were actually late. Jack had no idea where he was going to be staying in Monte Carlo; apparently, an associate of Oliver's would meet him there and take him to his hotel. Oliver was always so disorganized that things were invariably last minute. He himself had left for Italy on business, so there would have been no way of finding out before Jack left. I only realized my mistake later, but you reassured me that Jack would phone when he arrived and I could get the number then.

Was it Providence or Misfortune that permitted Sophie's boat to arrive early and Jack's to be delayed for the brief instance required for them to meet one another? All I know is that Sophie saw me kiss Jack good-bye as she walked along the quay to meet us and, as he looked up to smile at her, her face drained of all color before she turned away and took you in her arms. Jack had to rush because he had stayed too long with me. As I watched him disappear into the distance, I turned to find Sophie still clutching you to her, her knuckles white where they gripped your golden arms.

Almost as soon as we arrived home from the port, Sophie complained of feeling unwell and went to her room. Throughout the next day, she could barely rouse herself to move until you, beside yourself with worry, called the doctor, who insisted she be taken to hospital immediately. That night she suffered a massive coronary and, over the following days, all hope of a recovery began to fade. When we would visit, she resembled a wraith in her bed.

Every morning, on your instruction, I would bring bunches of bougainvillea to her room, placing them on the dressing table across from her bed, obscuring her image in the mirror. And every day you would ask me if she had woken yet, to which I was forced to reply, no. At night, you would leave Sophie's room with bundles of fuchsia petals in your hands, swept from the table where they fell, reminding me again to replace them the next morning.

Even the dogs were silent. It was as if our house, our island, was holding its breath. I had never known anyone truly sick before or been around the loved ones who retreat into a private world to cope. I found myself spending hours outside when we were not at the hospital, not moving, for fear of making a sound, of disturbing you.

You became a stranger to me during those days: a woman without purpose, unable to articulate even the briefest of sentences. I could not understand then what horror must have gripped you, the way memories of death must have tormented you with the knowledge of how it would be should your mother not recover. All I know is that I retreated from you. The romantic notions I had entertained as a child of your so-called tragic life were crushed under the foot of the reality I saw in you every day. In your grief, you were terrifying.

Worse still, he had not kept his promise. I had not heard a word from him.

Adora

In the face of another loss, I sought life. Jack phoned, as I had promised her he would, as soon as he arrived at the hotel. Gigi was out by the pool, staring into space, no doubt recalling the face of her true love in her memories. She had not heard the phone ringing as I had one of my operas turned up to full volume in the living room. As soon as I heard his calm, boyish voice, I knew I would never tell her. The image of him, of his delicate grace and beauty, his fragile innocence, overwhelmed me to the point where I sank into the chair by the phone, overcome with feelings of déjà vu so intense my whole body trembled. No more of this, I thought. I could not let her have him anymore. I could no longer subject myself to the agonies of watching someone so reminiscent of you, Sebastian, love someone other than me, who accepted him, flawed and broken, without question. She was too young, too careless: she was not exiled from peace as we were. Watching Gigi through the French doors to the veranda, tears in my eyes, I told him that she was out. I promised him I would pass on the message and his phone number at the hotel. I never did.

When he called again over the next few days, I would tell

him she was in town or in the shower, walking the dogs on the beach, anything, in fact, to prevent him from speaking to her. Initially, he would simply ask that she return his call, to which I would assure him she would. Then, when he phoned again, I would let it slip that I had, indeed, passed on the message, pausing just long enough I hoped to introduce doubt. And so our conversations began. "Does she know?" he begged me. "Did someone tell her? Is that why I've heard nothing?"

He had grown concerned, of course, at first by her silence, then upset, then almost frantic as the days went by without a word from her. I soothed him as one would a babe, reiterating Gigi's love for him, his foolishness at doubting her, and so on. I had no fear of her finding out what I was doing. I intended to deny everything, knowing she would never doubt a word from my lips. It was quite easy to keep her at bay. As far as she was aware, Jack had not telephoned and Oliver—the only other person who would know where to find him—was away, too, so there was no one who could tell her where Jack was staying.

I would watch her jump when the phone rang, only to be disappointed when I indicated it was a private call for me. I told him to phone at the same time every day, and I would send her out on miscellaneous errands so that she was never in when he telephoned. I made sure we were always together in the house. If I went to visit my mother, I took her with me. There was no possibility of them ever speaking with one another. Mine was to be the only voice he was to hear.

He grew to accept this; what we had shared that afternoon in my olive grove was the turning point we had secretly hoped for but never dared to expect: How silly we had been not to accept its inevitability. After all, I had called to him and he had come whenever I asked: the lunches, the pilgrimages to the beach, the stolen moments here in the grove. He was only a boy, and yet he had consoled me, waited for me, returned to me, confirming what we both had long suspected; the promise of one another had always existed within us, finally realized that day he placed his elegant, soundless foot on the step to my home and ascended into the purgatory I lived in. We were a pair, he and I, aligned by circumstance to comfort one another, to alleviate the burden of the losses we had caused. In the face of the overwhelming darkness I was gripped by, his voice, the promise of him, was the only thing that prevented me leaving this life. The same was true of him.

"You kissed me good-bye at the port, when I left," he said one day. I could hear from his slurred speech that he had been drinking again.

"No. I kissed you hello because I know you will come back to me. I could never kiss you good-bye, because I could never bear to watch you leave."

"I will always come back to you. I never left you in the first place. So you forgive me?"

I understood what he was asking of me, how his addled mind was muddling me with his memories.

"Yes," I said, "I forgive you everything."

"Thank you, Mother," he replied.

There was no need to correct him, for he had not erred. We all of us search for a touchstone to the past in the souls of those we meet in the course of every day; a flicker of an eyelid, a turn of the wrist that ignites within us the memory of what we miss so acutely; our perfect companions who have left or abandoned us. I was content to fulfill the role for him, and he offered no objection when I replied, "My angel, thank you for coming for me."

Genevieve

You always shocked me with your beauty, Adora. Somehow the mental image of how you looked was perpetually dim next to the reality of seeing you standing in front of me, your every feature glaring in its perfection. As the days passed without a single word from the man I loved, I began to realize how dismally I fared in comparison. If I had resembled you, the object of my love would never have been able to let a moment go by without speaking to me; he would have kept his promises.

In the house I cherished, perpetually near to you, whom I idolized, I had never felt so isolated. Somehow your despair had erected a barrier between us. I could no longer run to you to confide my fears. You were so ill with worry that it would have been selfish of me, wicked even, to burden you with my romantic troubles. Down the corridors of a hospital to the northeast of the island lay a woman whose life was inexplicably ending, who spent her days drifting in and out of consciousness, unable to recognize us should she ever briefly wake when we visited. A woman oblivious to the blooms we brought for her every day and placed on her dressing table, unaware of their slow death until their petals finally curled into ugliness by nightfall. It was inconceivable that I should bother you with anything in the face of what you were going through.

I thought about everything that had happened between Jack and me, presuming I had misread his feelings for me, allowing myself to believe that my initial ambivalence had hardened him in my absence. Perhaps some stranger in a bar had told him that I wasn't worth it after Jack had relayed the details of our initial courtship. Perhaps what I had thought of as sadness in him before he left the island was really disinterest. Maybe he had really wanted to leave me and simply couldn't tell me.

Yet if that were true, I couldn't understand why he had told me so often that he loved me. Nothing made any sense. Maybe I had just been a challenge to him. Despite what I knew to be right, as the days wore on without a word, I managed to convince myself that he was leaving me and allowed his insidious silence to plague me. I grew angry in my despair. I had dismissed him in the beginning for fear of ever being let down again. His promises, I told myself, had been vicious lies. Yet still I returned to the hope of him coming back to me, despite my misgivings and doubt. For if he did not love me, I honestly believed I would lose everything.

And so you and I were each immersed in our own private horror of losing people we loved without explanation. You were so distant with me, so cool, almost as if you were looking straight through me whenever you briefly had to speak. I had never felt so insignificant. I grew increasingly insecure; nobody noticed me in town the way they used to; without Jack, I was irrelevant, expendable. For some reason, I resented the fact that the same would never have been true of you; successful, brilliant partner at your side or not, you would always have been the guest of honor wherever you went. Dark memories resurfaced of Jack with you in the living room, in the olive grove, on the beach. Some instinct had told me not to trust him. Although it was vaguely ridiculous, I even considered that perhaps it was you he had wanted all along. Maybe he had only been with me to be near you. I was totally irrational, terrified at the idea of losing him and what it would mean for me. My thoughts began to resemble a tawdry melodrama where I subverted what I knew to be true to paranoia and resentment.

Destroyed by his silence, I accepted finally that he did really love you. I hated what I saw in the mirror, could scream with frustration sometimes at how completely I failed to resemble you, the only beauty I had seen heralded by everyone. Perhaps he had found someone else on the mainland. Maybe it would never be the same between us again. My perfect love affair seemed to be inexplicably ending, and I didn't even know if I would be given any kind of explanation. At night I would lie awake, consumed by the fear that he might never come to me again, that he no longer wanted me.

My only solace came from hoping that ultimately you would console me when you had recovered, tell me everything that I needed to hear. You would, in your inimitable fashion, dismiss him out of hand and draw me back into the comfort of your world, where it was always just the two of us. Thinking of life before the summer began was the only way I could make it through the day. Yet so much had changed between us, I could no longer be sure that you would rush to my rescue, and it was that awful thought that tormented me. *What have I done?* I would ask myself all through the night, unable to grasp an answer from the riot of explanations that could be found. And far more frightening was the ultimate question I tried always to avoid: *How will it be when Oliver comes home?*

Adora

Only the sound of my mother's breathing and the ring of the telephone roused me from my panic. I found it so easy to lie, almost as if I were playing a role, an actress in a film where everything would be resolved satisfactorily before the end.

Gigi stopped asking if Jack had telephoned; too proud, too stubborn, too afraid. After the first days had passed without a word from him, I witnessed her hurt give way to anger. I knew she would not forgive him because I knew her best.

My mother continued to ignore me, wasting away in front of me, refusing to wake and acknowledge my presence. I deterred Oliver from returning. For the first time in my life I did not need him. All I wanted during that dreadful time was to be alone, the guardian of a secret which was my only solace.

Jack continued to phone, the sound of his voice the sole bright aspect of my days. He was beside himself, of course, that Gigi had discarded him, as I had allowed him to believe, but he needed me so to dispel doubt, to confide in, to trust. I would not have given him up for all of the world. I had waited my entire life to share again such flawless compatibility with someone else, as I had when I was a girl.

I became what I despised in people: duplicitous, selfish, oblivious to the unhappiness of others. I told myself that I did it for them both; after what he had confided in me, Jack could not be with her; a girl like Gigi would never understand. And Gigi would only have been made miserable had they stayed together. Yet how she must have longed for me simply to hold her, to reassure her that perfectly reasonable excuses can be found to account for the bad behavior of men who break their promises. She needed me to confirm that she was perfect, lovable, that he was a fool. I offered no such comfort.

Then, suddenly, there was nothing; no phone call, no word. What had been given back to me was lost again. I called his hotel ceaselessly, but no one picked up. Finally, after three days had passed in which I had almost driven myself mad with worry, Oliver telephoned to say that Jack had left the mainland a few days early, his work unfinished, without a word. I sank to the floor, cradling the phone against my chest, and wept as I had done all those years before, stifling my sobs with my fist lest Oliver hear me. But he did, thinking I was upset about my mother. He insisted on coming home. I didn't deny him. I fell into my bed, insane, cursing Fate for offering me a tiny amount of hope, only to return me to my darkness again. I no longer knew where to find Jack. And if he was not near me, how could I possibly survive?

Genevieve

I began to spend most of the day out of the house. I visited places Jack and I had gone to together, the beach or the cafés in the old town, staying there until nightfall, astonished by my ability to allow time to speed by immersed in thoughts of what I couldn't understand. You never questioned my actions. For the first time since I had known you, you didn't appear to need me.

It seems barbaric to recall the anguish caused by a lover's supposed ambivalence as exquisite, but I did then. Each day, I derived a masochistic pleasure from playing through my thoughts of abandonment because I suspected there was still the potential for reconciliation, although I was completely oblivious then to the facts that would eventually allow it to happen. Suddenly the island became a place of barbed memories, tainted by his presence, beginning to resemble not a safe house but a torture chamber of regret and confusion. I didn't even know if I would ever have the chance to rail against his selfishness and the contemptuous way he had treated me.

On the day I did finally see Jack again, I thought that I had exhausted myself with tears, that my heart had closed itself to him and his mistreatment of me. When on that Wednesday afternoon, quite unexpectedly, he appeared at my table in the café we used to meet at looking as if he had run the hundreds of miles from the mainland, I had given up on everything. I had failed miserably in love, in keeping his interest, because I was not you: I was not exceptional.

He stood there with tears coursing down his cheeks, and I steeled myself against forgiving him as he sat down beside me. I knew that I should tell him to leave me alone, thinking that, in a similar situation, it was what you, Adora, would have done. But still, I had to know, despite the trouble he had caused, had to know why he had left me and ruined everything in the process. Jack poured out all of the details of the preceding two weeks, asking me to believe that he had phoned every day, only to be told by you, Adora, that I was not there, out, or else aware of his calls and completely disinterested. He asked me had I met someone else, did I no longer love him?

Despite my hostility, as he tried to explain everything, I kindled a strong wish that he might be able to make me believe. If Jack had stopped there, I might have been able to excuse your behavior as that of a grief-stricken, even desperate, woman. As he talked on, however, offering up details in his urgency to have me believe him, it turned out he already knew everything about your mother, the intimate details which could only have been revealed during conversations I had not been included in. Jack knew everything about your brother, too, things I had never been told, that he could only have learned from you if he had asked. You were a closed book when it came to your past. I had never dared to intrude upon your sadness by asking anything about Sebastian. Everything I had ever learned was told to me by Sophie. Yet Jack knew as much about you as he did about me. In the face of his protests, the dark fear I had harbored about his feelings for you convinced me during those moments that he had only been using me to get to you. When he started to tell me about how he would meet you for lunch, the die was cast.

"How could she do this to me?" I asked, astonished. "She was desperate for us to be together."

"No, no, you don't understand," he protested. "She loves you more than anything. Adora is too kind to ever hurt anyone."

"Why do you keep on saying her name like that, like she's some sort of idol, when she has totally betrayed me?" I continued, my voice rising, not remotely concerned who was sitting next to me. "I mean, she *expected* me to go out with you. I did as I was told, and all along you two were meeting behind my back, laughing at me?" I gasped, furious tears rolling down my cheeks.

I watched his disturbed reaction and enjoyed it. I was so shocked and hurt that I wasn't bothered that he'd found out how I had been almost blackmailed into going out with him in the beginning. "You know, Oliver was right about you," I said, not caring anymore about how cruel I sounded. "You really are a total failure. The only reason he kept you on was because of me."

"Why are you saying this?" he asked, clearly reeling from my viciousness. "You know that I love you so much. Adora—"

"Adora nothing," I shouted, causing heads to turn in the café. I checked myself in embarrassment and wiped the tears away from my face angrily.

"Listen to me," he pleaded. "Oliver isn't who you think he is. You have no idea what he's capable of. He's had so many affairs. I found out so much when I was away. He doesn't love her at all, and he's doing something that if he ever gets caught—"

"Enough," I snapped, shaking my head furiously, determined to prevent him from going any further. "That is enough.
I won't listen to another word. I want you away from us. I never
want to see you again." I wasn't afraid of Oliver's reaction anymore. I knew once I told him that he would accept my decision,
why I had to do what I did.

Jack continued to protest, begging me to believe that I was
so wrong, that for him there could only ever be me. He refused
to let me speak, offering up details and insights into Oliver that
were so unbelievable I sat there dumbfounded, convinced Jack
was a pathological liar. He was desperate to make me see the
truth, trespassing on everything I loved.

"Everything you love is a total lie; none of it is real—" Jack
protested, reaching for my arm to stop me as I tried to stand up
from the table to get away from him. I knew that what he had
impetuously blurted out was a last-ditch attempt to keep me,
and I almost buckled. He hadn't grabbed me with force as others might have to make me submit to him. I knew that if I sat
back down beside him, Jack would never hurt me, never in his
life. "None of it is real," he repeated more softly this time, "all of
it is a lie. . . ." At the sound of his words and the gentle touch of
his fingers on my bare arm, something quiet inside me believed
him. But I had known you all my life and Jack just one summer,
and I couldn't stand for what he said to be true, I simply
couldn't . . . and so, in the face of what I could not bear to hear,
I let him go.

"I never felt a thing for you. It was an elaborate hoax." I did
not shout. I spoke slowly and deliberately, knowing exactly
what I was doing, that it was time for everything to end. "I was
told to love you, and I did it to please someone I love more

than anything, despite the fact that I'm not sure they feel the same. Never come near us again. I hate you more than I've ever hated anyone."

I was humiliated and brokenhearted. I told myself that everything Jack had said was outlandish, appalling. I desperately didn't want to believe a word of it. In truth, we barely knew him. Surely it would be easy to forget everything he had said.

The taxi left me in the driveway, and I stood looking at the house before going in. Not mine, I realized. I am just a visitor here. Was any of it real? I asked myself, Jack's revelations pushing their way back to the forefront of my mind. Were we all hiding here from real life? I felt utterly defeated as I stood there trying to make sense of all the summers past and who I was and who I had become. My shoulders shook as sobs convulsed my body, chastising myself for everything I had coveted, every stupid thing I had been so content to believe in. Was I loved? I asked myself. Did Jack ever love me? Did you?

I found you on the veranda, tears streaming down my face; I didn't know what would happen. I didn't know if I could trust you, Adora. Who were you really? And what had you wanted with me? I stood there, preparing to resist you, steeling myself against falling again under your spell. I thought of what Jack had said about Oliver and, although I could never bring myself to believe it, I wondered if you knew or suspected. And if that were the case, then what unhappiness lurked within you? I was torn between hating you, loving you and, ultimately, pitying you. I was about to leave; the summer was over for me. Yet as soon as you turned that perfect head, the white-blond curls moving slowly to reveal the fuchsia bougainvillea and then your aquamarine eyes, I knew I wasn't going anywhere.

"Come," you said, opening your arms, the faintest of smiles on your lips.

Do you already know? I thought as I stumbled toward you. Are you mocking me? Or are you smiling because you know you have won?

I folded into your arms like a fighter felled in the first round, stunned senseless by losing. You held me there for hours, never letting go, the clear blue sky and sound of the sea beyond the only evidence of what I had once loved in my innocence, before the fall.

Adora

How could she not have tried to help him when he was so clearly in distress? I mourned with her when she told me, but not for her loss, for his. As soon as I could, I went to find him. He needed me more than ever. Clearly, Jack had tried to live without my guidance and couldn't. I drove around the island for hours, barely able to see through my tears, searching for him in every spot I could think of until, weary from driving, I found him at the gates to our house, slumped against the wall.

I didn't take him inside, even though I still thought that Genevieve might relent and forgive him for the sins of which he was wholly innocent. He had not rung the doorbell, I assumed because he was unwilling to risk being told to leave, preferring to wait outside in the hope that she would appear. I thought he might be wary of me, considering what he had learned, what I was guilty of doing to him, oblivious then to the whys and the wherefores, of how everything I had done was to help him, to save him. I thought he had come because he perceived me as the only person who could possibly rectify everything with Genevieve. I thought he had no choice but to join me in the car and come away to wherever I might choose to take him.

We went to a quiet restaurant in the hills where he refused

to eat. We drank together instead, in total silence, and I grew uncomfortable, laboring under the weight of how miserable I had made him by my actions.

"I loved her like a daughter," I offered, "but I can't explain why she left you. When she learned from you what I did, Gigi should have forgiven you. I would have. I can't explain it, I'm sorry."

He studied me somberly as I spoke, but I thought I perceived some pity in him. He grew more serious as I offered up a host of paltry excuses, transparent in their deceit, convincing myself that he was naïve enough to believe them, to need to if only to conceive of a way to get her back.

"You have nothing to apologize for," he said finally. "I loved her, it's true, but we don't need to pretend anymore, do we?"

I didn't dare believe that he had spoken such words or had reached the understanding of our relationship that I had from the first.

"Adora, you know I came for you," he said.

"I hoped," I said, losing myself in him.

"And you know that we must be honest with one another now. We must tell the truth."

"I know what you're going to ask me," I said, shaking my head to ward off the question. "Please don't make me."

"Adora," he urged firmly but kindly, no longer sounding like a boy. "Sebastian: How did it happen?"

I turned my face up to his, like a child in awe of its father, obligated to truth because of the extent of unconditional love offered. "Like this," I replied.

He accepted the simplicity of what I had confessed, asking for nothing more.

"Adora, would you like to go home now?"

"Please." I nodded, tears of joy filling my eyes.

Genevieve

In the aftermath of losing Jack, I tried to console myself with notions of all-encompassing loyalty and an innate refusal to ever participate in malicious slurs against those I loved. I conducted myself just as you did whenever anyone tried to instigate conversations destined to malign someone close to you: I waved a dismissive hand to Jack's words to keep them at bay, to indicate my utter refusal to participate. I tried to be blind but, as with all rumor, conjecture, or even lies, what has been heard cannot be forgotten, and suspicion sidles its way into our consciousness, polluting our blithe assumptions.

I was torn between believing that you could be capable of deliberate cruelty or that Jack was a liar who thought me an immature fool. Neither rang true to me, but sometimes I would recall the image of the two of you sitting together, a smile that had passed between you at dinner or lunch, and feel a sharp stab of something I could never confront. Yet whenever you smiled at me or hugged me in the morning, kissed me good night, my thoughts seemed ludicrous and I was left with the discomfiting notion that I had trusted a boyfriend who was not worth it. But still, I was astonished to find that I missed him; memories of the time we had spent together returned to haunt me with the happiness we had shared. I thought it might be easy to forget him but, despite how I tried to hate him, I found myself thinking about him again, worrying about what might happen. Everything seemed very real, irrevocable and, often, I found myself gasping for breath when I thought about what I'd done; suddenly it seemed wholly vicious where once it had appeared the only option.

I kept all of this from you. I didn't want to upset you any further. Your behavior became less unnerving, perhaps because I had a minor understanding of what it meant. I began to seek your company again, simply to be near you, and your willing acceptance of my presence filled me with remorse for having avoided you when you needed me. Gone were the memories of your dismissiveness during the first few weeks of Sophie's illness, replaced with guilt for not having tried to comfort you. It was, I told myself, something lacking in me, something I should watch for in the future that had caused your detachment. I had behaved abominably by questioning you, for daring to consider myself as more than you, to imagine that I could ever fulfill such a role. My unhappiness, I told myself, was nothing in comparison to what you had known.

The doctor continued to monitor Sophie daily, reporting no improvement in her health. Although she had been stable for the past two weeks and the doctors had been able to rouse her, she had never regained consciousness for more than brief periods and, even then, she did not appear to be able to communicate. Every day you would break down at the news, continuing to ask whether anything more could be done to help her get better. There was nothing to do, he told us daily, except wait and hope that she might rally. In the meantime, he suggested that we both should spend as much time as possible with Sophie, talking to her, although, based on his prognosis, neither of us was sure whether it would do any good.

"I'll stay with her, Adora," I offered one day after the doctor left. "Why don't you go home and rest?"

You were clearly touched by my gesture and kissed me on the forehead. "But Genevieve, keep the conversation light. Promise me you'll do that. I don't want her upset when she's so ill. Trust me on this, please."

"I promise, Adora," I lied, knowing as soon as she left I wouldn't be able to help myself. I'd tell Sophie everything just to ease my conscience.

Sophie

Since the Gods took my son, I have lived in a lesser world, devoid of brightness. Always, I am obliged to turn away from him, his image in my memories. To gaze upon him is like staring into the sun. I move further and further away from him, permitting of time the freedom to dull the intensity of the yesterdays when still he lived and breathed. Both my children possessed a vibrancy conferred by their unparalleled perfection, unbearable now to contemplate. All my life, I studied literature and philosophy, feeding off its nourishment, yet all of my education has proven worthless, for never can the words be found to describe the loss of a child. A life so damaged can never return to a semblance of what it once was: such a preposterous myth to suggest otherwise. All of the years since Sebastian died I have felt hollow, slower, as if only half of me still existed. While she was alive, what was left belonged to my daughter, through whom I lived at a remove, for nearly forty years.

A mother is ordained from the moment of conception onward to love and to forgive the foibles of their children, or so I have been told. I dedicated my life to this task until Sebastian died and I forsook all such foolish notions. Save for the sum-

mers, I hid from my daughter, making out of duty only one telephone call a week, fulfilling my role as her mother only barely,
as a consequence of both my ambivalence and the distasteful
combination of resentment at God and frustration at all my
frailties. Only my son had ever needed me. It was the secret I
held in my heart, a boundless love for one child over the other.
From the moment his perfect soul was handed to me by the
nurse, I understood that he was the reason I was born. For my
daughter too. He was the life force toward which we both gravitated and held fast: to fulfill our need for love and to be loved
selflessly in return.

I smirk now at the irony of the situation I found myself in
that summer of 1938: After nearly thirty years of being brokenhearted, it was only then that my heart weakened. During that
terrible time I spent in the hospital, only the darkness offered
any consolation; my eyes manacled shut by choice to the pain
of observation; I refused to wake and confront reality, and so I
lay in silence until it became impossible for me not to act.

How many years had I spent before then longing to die, to
escape the sheer futility of life without my husband and Sebastian? Youth was at an end for me. All that remained for me was
my recollections of the past, offset by the bitter sting of realizing everything wonderful was behind me.

This mysterious universe, its vast expanse, endlessly plays
host to such youths, young men who are almost Hellenic in
their beauty. Ostracized from the commonplace, all of them
singled out for worship or hate, their existence a blessing and
a curse. Always I have watched them, all my life it seems. To
nurture an unrealizable desire to see my son again, some concerned friends say I have hunted for boys like him in crowds,
in restaurants, at parties. Each one was lacking, which doesn't

surprise me considering that they were not and never would be him. No comforting warmth engulfed me when I found myself in proximity to some pretender to my son's crown, until I saw that young man at the port, flanked by Adora and Genevieve. Time slipped for me. It could have been twenty years before, when a similar scene played itself out in front of me on the same island. Then I was overcome with joy. This time, only horror.

Genevieve

Oliver dismissed Jack as soon as he returned to the island at the beginning of September. He offered no explanation, just grimly informed us over dinner and told us to leave it at that. Adora raised not one word in protest, which shocked me far more than Oliver's decision. I couldn't believe she would allow Jack to just be discarded like rubbish, because that's what it felt like; after all, she had been the most enamored of him of all of us, perhaps even me, which made me smart with shame whenever the thought crossed my mind. Suddenly any notion of reconciliation I had privately kindled vanished, leaving behind a haunting fear: I didn't know where he was anymore; I'd never be able to explain properly what had been going through my head that day he found me in the café, and I felt so badly that I needed to. The comfort of being angry with a lover comes from being able to go to wherever they are at any given time. With Oliver's decision came the realization that I had been playing a role since I left Jack, pretending not to care when, in fact, I had merely been biding time until I could see him again. That I might not left me inconsolable. I simply couldn't bear to have him leave our island without knowing that I had felt something for him.

Oliver became intensely protective of me. He felt responsible for the pain I had experienced over Jack. He really hadn't imagined that it would grow so serious, he told me, but he simply could not tolerate anyone who might mistreat me, and there were other things, which I did not need to know, that had contributed to his decision. Whenever anyone asked about Jack and what had happened to him, Oliver kept his silence, which they interpreted as the tight-lipped quiet of an irate guardian who felt guilty for not having protected me from disappointment. My copious tears plainly moved him when I begged him to tell me where Jack was so that I could at least apologize or say good-bye, but his decision was made and there was nothing more I could do about it, which proved rather unsettling. Adora would have been able to change Oliver's mind. I clearly lacked her powers to persuade.

I was supposed to leave that week, but Oliver insisted I stay until the end of September. "I blame myself for all of this, Gigi; stay on, let me make it up to you. We can't have you going home with tearstained cheeks now, can we? Besides, your father would never forgive me," he teased, forcing a smile from me even in spite of how miserable I felt. Oliver had that effect; I was quite convinced I'd eat spiders if he told me they tasted good. Yet although no one was ever in doubt about how I longed to stay forever on that island, this time my extended holiday was like being given a present of poison. What I needed was to leave our island and all the memories it contained, to forget Jack, to escape the self-loathing I felt, to excuse myself from the liability of knowing that I had cared more about myself than about him. I had never seen such ruthlessness in Oliver before. He had always gone out of his way to help people. Although I knew that Jack could not have stayed indefinitely after losing his job, I still couldn't quite understand why everything needed to be so abrupt, so ruthless, frankly.

I had no reason to mistrust Oliver. In fact, of everyone, he was the one whose company I craved more and more. And he mine. He hovered over me until the end of that summer, always near, as if he were afraid to let me out of his sight. Memories of Jack began to slip as I grew ever closer to Oliver, and the soothing kindness in him that made up for everything. It was so true to his generous nature that he felt accountable for my breakup to the point where he needed to jolly me along on a daily basis. Sometimes, I would turn around on the veranda to find him watching me from the balcony, like a guardian on high.

These gestures and others were what led me to understand your devotion to him. He had offered you the same love over the years. I envied you the knowledge that the man you loved would never fail you. By association, I enjoyed the same privileges, but it was not the same. Not even remotely similar.

Sophie

Impossible, to find again love remotely comparable to what Adora had shared with Sebastian. I had overlooked, however, how easy it was for my daughter to ignore the flaws in those she loved. In the annals of those profound eyes, a veil was drawn that precluded the truth from filtering in, sullying her romantic ideals. So she could love beyond the realms of reason, absolved from ever acknowledging what was real and disappointing in her life.

Instantaneously I knew when I met Oliver that she would marry him. Instantaneously I knew that he would fail her. Their courtship was reminiscent of the great tales of courtly love, flawless in its execution. There was no incident, no blemish in his perfectly constructed personality, to lead her to question her choice. Nor had she ever been involved with anyone remotely like him. Her life was the island. Before Oliver, there had only been Sebastian.

Numerous times over the course of my life, I've met his type. Such men proliferate in exalted circles, usually on the arms of rather plain, well-to-do daughters of diplomats or financiers. One might be forgiven for being easily duped by their ready charm, the attention they lavish on their girlfriends, who will inevitably become their wives. I never was. The deceit involved in pleasing everyone these men went to such seemingly great pains to do was entirely evident to me. Popularity is seldom conferred on those who have not orchestrated the plan themselves. To please everyone involves a perpetual subversion of one's true self. It is not enough simply to be as good-looking as Oliver. Such men must also be able to lie—to themselves and to everyone who surrounds them.

How fortunate for Oliver that my daughter was considered such a prize and that, in him, she found a counterpart ever attentive to her needs. To a point, one must add. He was not a man to whom she could reveal her deepest thoughts, her loves and regrets, the sadness that, before him, undid her. When first she revealed the loss of her father and brother, he made the requisite sympathetic sounds. After that, if ever she broached the subject again, he asked her to focus only on their life together. They should not live in the past, he told her, only the glittering future that awaited them. Even at his most selfish, Oliver was instinctively aware of the perfect thing to say. Breathless and excited, she came home to me after living in Paris with him for a time. She felt purged of her grief. He understood exactly what she needed. Nobody could be better suited to her than him.

Adora put all of her photographs of her brother and father away. Her old bedroom had evolved into a shrine as I had placed everything that ever reminded me of them in there, unable to contemplate them in photographs, knowing they were never coming home. Like an obedient child, she obeyed Oliver, never allowing him to see the images of men to whom he could never compare. At the first sign of potential disapproval from her fiancé, she erased the great loves of her life from view, but she didn't convince me at the time: The truth was that she could not stand to lose someone else, so she tricked herself into believing that Oliver's lack of empathy was, in fact, a virtue and deferred to him over everything from that moment on. To dissuade her from her course was not my place. Even had I tried, she would not have listened.

Adora was completely content to worship the ground Oliver walked on. She considered it almost sacrilegious if anyone, be they friends or family, defiled her perfect image of him with criticism. For her, the sun rose and set on his surface glory. Opportunities arose everywhere for them. The superficial of spirit clamored to befriend them, and Adora threw herself into creating the life he wanted with total abandon. They traveled everywhere, succeeded in amassing a fortune that provided a life of ease, seemingly enviable to those honored enough to be invited to share in it.

I was not remotely astonished when friends informed me of Oliver's various dalliances. After all, Narcissus himself seemed only mildly self-involved in comparison to my son-in-law's vanity. I kept the knowledge to myself. My daughter would have been destroyed if she thought that others shared in his affections. He was perfectly discreet. The women lived elsewhere, on the mainland, in Italy; those places he visited for business. He was fortunate, I suppose, for none of them ever followed through with their threats to tell my daughter everything. I expect he could have persuaded her they were lying had they attempted to do so. That she was never forced to confront the extent of the truth throughout their marriage was for the best. As with the legend, she personified Echo, parroting back to Narcissus the high opinions he held of himself. She carried on with her life, leading everyone to believe completely that Oliver was her savior, her great love. For me to have suggested anything unpalatable about him would simply have been spiteful, serving no purpose other than to ease my conscience or vent my frustration at her foolishness.

To Miranda, I confided my thoughts. So very kind, she was the daughter I never had. We were entirely in agreement with one another. She had seen through Oliver as I had almost immediately. Miranda was also condemned to observe her delightful husband be treated like a lackey by my son-in-law. Not that James ever considered that to be the case. Men like Oliver, however, have a knack for preying on the seemingly weak; those ill-equipped to intuit anything other than goodness in others; those who trust accordingly. Oliver made very good use of his insight, surrounding himself with the adoring chorus of my daughter and his best friend, enabling him to carry on with his life without fear of remonstrance.

It was Oliver who was weak. I saw that from the first. He was pathologically incapable of coping with anything that did not go his way, leaving others to clean up the mess he had made. Throughout his life, they were more than willing to do so. Every time, he emerged anew, spotless from censure of any kind, basking in the adoration of those who loved him, of those who helped him up on his pedestal. How preposterous I considered the concern my daughter and James showed whenever he was in a gloom-ridden mood because something had gone wrong, considering it depression, jumping through hoops to make him smile. How I pitied their lack of insight. Oliver was never depressed. Oliver was simply afraid.

Genevieve

It was then that you began to fade, Adora, the perpetual light
that seemed to surround you diminishing day by day. Your gestures were somnolent, moving an effort, save for when Oliver
came home and you would rally like the great actress you were
to present a façade of perfection that not even someone who
knew you as well as he did could pinpoint as fake.

I had no idea what the catalyst for your total disintegration
was. I often feared it was me, how I had disappointed you so,
but then I would shake my head to ward off the thought, convinced you couldn't possibly know the cruelty of which I was
capable. Something in me recognized that you were leaving;
you were certainly letting me go. No more were the days we
spent snuggled into one another, wrapped in the scent of mi-
mosa; no more walks through town, your arm tight around my
waist, your head nestled on my shoulder; no more delight
when people mistook us for mother and daughter. No more of
you, my Beloved Aunt. You were no longer the same. Sometimes, I would catch you looking at me as if you were contemplating a ghost, a whisper of a smile on your lips; not mean or
intimidating; heartbroken, I think now. I look back and long to

throw my arms around you, to eradicate that entire summer and everything that had happened and to return to the way it always was—just you and me.

At the time, it so upset me to watch these scenes, to know without understanding that everything was shifting, moving toward an irrevocable conclusion that would transform you from all to nothing. The effect on me was astonishing: I had let you down terribly, I realized, and the disgrace was overwhelming. It was something in me that had triggered your demise, I convinced myself; I hadn't fulfilled your dearest wish of loving Jack properly; I had run from you when Sophie was sick because I was terrified by the specter you cut. You would never have done that to me. You had always been there for me. I remember some days before I left, brushing my teeth in front of the bathroom mirror and catching myself, a look in my eyes, and really seeing myself as I was; I remember the chill that went through me, the complete acceptance of what I had done and what it meant, and I recall gulping hard and tasting the bitterness of knowing there was nothing I could do to change any of it.

You and I lost the capacity for speech during that time, each of us drowning in incomprehension. I would watch you in the olive grove with your dogs—Linford, contemplative and upright by your side, as you watched the days die—and wished you would turn around as you used to and come back to me, but you never did. And so we moved away from each other, the two of us mired in regret for entirely different reasons.

Sophie showed no signs of improvement. You mirrored her in your slow relinquishment of life. I felt like constantly weeping, for Jack and for you, to whom I could not speak for fear of hearing answers I could never withstand. I had only ever

known happiness on your island. Without you, however, I realized none could be found.

I was left alone to struggle with my thoughts of Jack. I had
to see him and be forgiven; I couldn't let him leave without ex-
plaining everything to him. I would look for him every day
when I went to visit Sophie, scanning crowds in the streets,
taking detours on the off chance that I might find him in a café
or shop. One day, I even went to the apartment where he had
been staying, hoping to find him there. I can still recall how
crestfallen I felt when they told me he had already left. I don't
know why I thought he was still on the island. Without a job,
there was barely any point in him staying. Yet some instinct
told me that he hadn't gone back to America yet. There was still
time, I believed, to find him again. I knew I had to, if only so
that you would think well of me again.

You insisted Oliver and I go sailing over my last weekend to
the surrounding islands, even though you were not to join us.
You pulled yourself together brilliantly in front of him; Oliver
wouldn't have believed me had I told him how altered you were
when he wasn't in the house. You assumed your habitual per-
sona for an evening, the mock skepticism you always displayed
when he told a bad joke, the charmingly raised eyebrow that
said, "Oh my love, you cannot possibly expect me to believe
that," as if you were reprimanding a charming little boy whom
you adored. Oliver agreed with you that the change in scenery
would do me the world of good. You felt guilty, you told me,
about the gloominess in the house, using it as a feasible excuse
to get rid of me for the weekend. I didn't object. Nor did I feel

slighted by your need to be alone. I, after all, understood you better than anyone. I almost felt as if I had your consent.

As I watched you wave us off in the drive, I experienced a nostalgic comfort in going away by myself with Oliver because I felt as I did when I was a child. I wanted to feel that way again, to be careless. As the house receded behind us, the burden of my guilt eased and I began to remember all over again what it meant to be frivolous and carefree. I handed up my enjoyment to him with both hands, relinquishing all control over my moods, wanting him to plan my days, to provide my enjoyment.

Nobody could have been better suited to the task, programmed as he was to captivate. He took me to the beaches of my childhood, each one containing an anecdote of better times spent there. He enjoyed the attention of the passersby who watched us as we strolled past, wondering who we were. He glowed as we walked into restaurants and all heads turned toward us, beaming with pride at his catch.

He made me eat things I was unsure I'd like, insisting upon it until I gave in only to please him. He forced me to swim with him further out than I felt comfortable with, pushing me on when all I wanted was to return to shore. He insisted I spend the hours between 12:00 P.M. and 3:00 P.M. in the shade, so that I would not burn and, in the evenings, he poured me a glass of wine so that I might sleep more easily. He pandered to my every whim, and in return I submitted to his every request. For all of his easygoing insouciance, Oliver was not a man you could refuse or, indeed, would ever want to deny. To do so implied a fall from grace, a turning away that would never be revoked. The very idea was horrifying to me.

We talked sometimes of you. He told me of how dearly you

had wanted me to go with him, your concern for my health after everything that had happened. He heralded you as a paragon of selflessness, concerned only with my well-being. You became even more impossible to live up to but, basking in Oliver's warm affection, I knew he held us in the same regard, that I, too, was reserved for a special place in his affections. It was a testimony to his great charisma that such a thing would even have mattered. Yet it did, especially for my father, you, and me. Fulfillment hinged on pleasing him, I came to discover. It was not an unpleasant notion. Rather, for some inexplicable reason I was too young to analyze effectively, it was everything.

Oliver had always been a peripheral figure in our lives, away on business or working late. He was someone for whom we were always waiting, the pleasant surprise who arrived mid-meal around whom the conversation turned constantly. I had loved him unconditionally without ever feeling close to him as a child, perhaps because I was inseparable from you. I had always sensed an invisible barrier between us, a guardedness in his affection for me that had finally slipped over the most recent summers. I felt as if I had been ushered into the inner circle of his private world and wanted by him. He let me be oblivious to worry or commitments. He wouldn't allow me to dwell on Jack. He listened calmly when I started to tell him everything that had happened, things he didn't already know. Afterward, however, he told me that in his experience it was best to put away sad stories: I should focus on the future, on the great weekend we were having. I was so grateful to him. I felt as if he understood me completely. His very presence seemed to instill a deep-rooted security in all who knew him that everything would be taken care of, nobody need worry for a moment.

I understood him to be an exceptional man then; hugely

generous, attentive, far kinder than anyone had a right to expect. In fact, the only time he may ever have been accused of being unkind was with regard to Jack. I had wanted him to try to help, but he made it obvious at the time that the situation was not to be discussed. After the wonderful weekend we had shared, however, I was loath to do anything to ruin it. I couldn't have wished for more. Such was his magic that, whenever I considered the situation, I grew increasingly convinced that Oliver had conducted himself impeccably, as always. I believed him when he told me that he had done everything he could to help. If I found Jack, I knew that I would have to help him accept responsibility for his actions. But I didn't tell Oliver that; I knew he wouldn't approve.

Adora

Do you remember, Sebastian, how you were born half asleep and I was born wide awake? Do you remember the stories I told you to keep you awake, so that you would never leave me? Jack began to slumber like you; every time we met, he was a little sleepier, and I would cradle him in my arms and tell him of our dogs; of Lilibet, who voyaged over the Tyrrhenian Sea in a raft with a dove to find you; of Bertie, who followed the migration of the swallows to our island to find you; of Isaac, who was always left out by his brothers and sisters but who heard of a place where you lived and ran all the way from Antarctica to find you. Jack listened, his eyes wide and trusting as I loved him awake, making him promise never to leave without me.

I met Jack always on your beach. The days were perfect, the sun blinding against the pure white of the sand. I would always take a second to stand on the crest of the hill looking down, searching for him, shielding my eyes from the glare conferred by nature. I would walk warily down the dune toward where he was, sitting in the sand, watching the sea. He always looked so pitiful, so defeated that I could almost sense his sorrow across the empty desert between us. My rapture at meeting him was always subsumed by a frightening wariness as I approached; the realization would strike me that, after the excitement of waiting for this day, it would end. I never knew if there would be more to come. Invariably, I'd consider turning back before he saw me, of letting him go and returning to the farce my pathetic life had become. I'd stand there, immobile, intensely aware of the seconds passing when I could still change everything. And then he would turn toward me, as you used to, desperate need in his eyes: the need I had understood in him from the first, the characteristic which had made me stay near, for I knew that it was only I who could save him and he me.

I had no thought for how much longer the days would last. Yet I knew soon everything would change. For the first time since I had met him, I felt the burden of responsibility for his well-being grip my shoulders like a vise, but I did not dare to confront him, to ask of him, when? Sometimes I feared he wouldn't take me with him, and so I'd make him understand all over again how much he meant to me, how his arrival in my life had brought such contentment for the first time in years. I offered only love, not truth, as an ointment for his woes.

Yet things began to change for the worse; not even my stories soothed him. I began to give him money, which he did not even try to refuse, snatching it from me greedily, almost arrogantly, as if it were his due. Sometimes he was kind, at others resentful. He could sit for hours saying nothing despite my frequent attempts to engage him. As the weeks progressed, he grew worse, his appearance slipping daily, the bright blue of his eyes dull with weariness. Only the sound of Gigi's name brought any sign of life, which cut me to the bone. I, after all, had stayed with him, nourished him when no one else, not even his darling girl, would.

I spent sleepless nights thinking of all the lovely things I could tell him about himself, to make him realize his potential. Yet when I saw him again, he would listen to me vacantly; nothing registered. I lived in constant terror that he would vanish and I would never find him.

I was consoled only by how much he seemed to need me. When he lost his apartment, I paid the rent on another one for him. But for all my good intentions, my love for him merely sped the progress of his decline and with it what was left of me. I forgave myself everything I was compelled to do to be alone with him. If I had been Gigi, I would have believed every word from his mouth. Nobody would have stood in my way to him; I would never have allowed it. He so completely resembled you, Sebastian; you were one and the same person. I wanted to right what I had done so terribly wrong all those years before, and so I clung to him.

I shut out all notions of myself as an adulterous wife, seeking the companionship of a boy almost young enough to be my son to recapture some essence of my youth. I knew that my actions would provoke such claims, if anyone were to find out. I was deceiving Oliver and Gigi, yes, but not for illicit thrills. Jack was not my lover; there was nothing sexual about my passion for him nor, as the depraved have whispered behind my back, for you, my incomparable brother.

We are taught early in life that love should be between a man and woman who have never met. Our entire existence pivots around our journey to each other. I know this to be true, for I have experienced it myself. But great love, the kind that overcomes all obstacles, can be for those we can never have, with those for whom we possess no sexual desire, only the purity of existing alongside a person who understands everything, for whom nothing needs to be explained. Such was my love for you, Sebastian. You were the ideal against whom everyone was measured. I had been so privileged to share my entire life with someone who was such a perfect match. Losing you was like losing my identity.

Oliver was my reward after your death. I knew that and understood it. I thought then that nobody could possibly steer me through the years better than he. I imagined us as kindred spirits, the perfect balance of need and generosity. We fed off each other. We completed each other.

Before Jack, I had never lied to Oliver, never spent a moment away when he was at home. Although our love appeared on display for all to witness, the reality of it was entirely private. Nobody could possibly have understood the depth of our awareness of one another, our mutual darkness, through which we helped each other. Nobody, except, of course, for James and Mama, knew Oliver suffered from depression, markedly worse over the years. For so many years, I considered it my duty to protect him from ridiculous questions from well-meaning snoops, hence our silence.

After you, after my inability to help you, I perceived Oliver as atonement. Not that his depression was ever evident until at least ten years after we married. Yet somehow, I sensed something in him beyond his beauty and kindness that only I could possibly alleviate. It sounds bizarre, I know, to confess that I actually felt gratitude to be of use to someone I loved so much. Our love has oscillated between great joy and tremendous pain. Oliver needed me to live completely for him, so I told myself it was a blessing that we could not have children. I used to believe that, of all the things I have done in my life, caring for my husband was my greatest achievement. Without me, I used to doubt that he would ever have survived.

Yet this summer I realized that he would have, and that is

when this all began, I believe. Something in me just gave up; I had no purpose anymore. I felt it fall, an element deep within me, and I woke up thinking: I can't fight this anymore; I need to go to sleep now. I cast my mind back over our years together and questioned them: there was no cause for his sadness, no terrible tragedy in Oliver's youth to prompt such blackness. You, Sebastian, simply seemed to own sorrow; the unhappiness of the world, life's injustices struck you harder than everyone else. You felt, in some way, responsible. I believe this is why you rescued all of the homeless dogs on our island. I used to think that Oliver shared the same attributes, that this was why he went out of his way to ensure his friends enjoyed their holidays on this island of ours. Both you and he, by your actions, seemed to be paying off a debt to something or someone indefinable, known only to yourselves. But I was wrong about Oliver, and this is why I falter now every day when I awake; why I taste disappointment every time I say his name; why I find it so easy to let everything go, to drift away on dreams of you, Sebastian, until the pain subsides and I am lost again in the consoling ether that memories of you inspire.

Genevieve

Those last few days of happiness were a trick, a lull that falsely promised a return to the familiar; a reimmersion in the past. I look back on them now with envy. Nothing truly terrible had happened, I recognize now. I had changed as a result of my first, aborted experience at love, but not so much that I was unable to start to enjoy again the pleasing rituals of our days. My weekend away with Oliver had restored my spirits. I no longer felt quite so miserable when I thought of Jack. Sophie began to show signs of improvement, Oliver was at home all the time, and you, Adora, resumed your evening ritual of walking the dogs through the olive grove, a bougainvillea flower behind your ear, your diamond necklaces glinting in the light from the setting sun.

We were all fooled by you because we wanted to be. The change in you was barely perceptible save to those who knew you best, and we chose to ignore it because doing so was easier. The idea that you might not fulfill your pivotal role in our lives was outrageous. You were larger than life in many ways, so much so that our lives *were* you. I have lost count of the times during those preceding weeks that I saw you crying when you thought you were alone, cannot even remember how often I turned away because I could not stand to confront what I knew to be true: You, my Beloved Aunt, so alive and vital to our existence, were becoming someone else, a person whose sole daily objective appeared to be merely surviving, not embracing the days as you once did.

It is unbearable to think of your loneliness, Adora, over the last few weeks of that summer. Oliver and I were culpable in willing you to be as you once were, in overlooking what was so obvious. You, despite the enormous love you were surrounded by, had assumed a role for us all over the years that dictated you could never change; you could never be real. You were a prisoner of the rapture you inspired in those who cared for you. In accepting the part you were asked to play, you denied yourself the possibility of happiness, of exoneration from the sins you felt you had committed, the terrible burden of your past.

The only times you appeared to completely assume the aspects of your glittering personality were when you went out to run errands in the afternoon. A hope seemed to shimmer from you that was nonexistent by the time you returned. As the days progressed toward autumn, such hope was replaced by a despair you confronted alone, never allowing any of us near. None of us knew how to help you.

Sophie

How can one adequately describe someone whose memory looms so much larger than their actual physical being ever did? The towering image of everything that was once special and now lost, a halcyon time; Sebastian has become that for those of us he left behind. He embodies the best of what we considered ourselves to be then. And yet, we were as insignificant then as we are now. That is the tragic truth of it all. We are not remarkable. We have existed, that is all. At best, we are mere people. Sebastian, himself, was just a boy.

Always, I was completely aware of what my children were capable of being, good, bad, or indifferent. Nothing about them escaped my attention, although I never revealed my insights. For Sebastian's sake alone, my silence was kept; I knew he would never have withstood my anger nor could he have borne to watch his sister chastised. Far too innocent to grow old in such a vicious world, that is who my son was. The dismal family secret, the failure: had he lived, that is what he would have become, the relative inquired after in hushed tones. Fortunate because he was heavenly to look at; there was no one immediately prepared to dismiss him in any way. From the rest of us shal-

low, flawed entities, he differed completely. He had been born
with a soul suffused with melancholy, which nothing, save his
sister, could possible alleviate. His mind was prone to despair.

My daughter was so young when signs of Sebastian's difference from us first manifested, but even then she possessed that
curiously dismissive quality, refusing to acknowledge Sebastian's weakness: his inability to ever grow up as she would. Not
for my son to have friends. He simply did not fit in. Despite
how hard he tried in his teenage years to leave her behind, to
permit her to find a life without him, he always returned.

Not the type of boy who could approach girls with the
other hormonally charged fools as they passed the bars in
town; despite his looks, Sebastian was cripplingly shy. A dismal
team player at cricket on the beach or tennis, terrified of losing,
he understood himself to be weaker than his peers. Inevitably
they tired of him; they gained nothing by the association. His
only comfort in life was his sister. For her, she believed the opposite to be true. In Sebastian she discerned complete perfection and looked to him to guide her. Desperately he struggled
in private to quell his intense need for her, but she never
thought of him in this way. To her mind, it was she who needed
him more than anything. Exponentially, the love she felt in-
creased every time he returned to her. My poor daughter
thought he had a choice when, in truth, for him, no such alternative existed.

We are guilty, all of us who lose, of elevating our lost loves
to godlike status in our memories, imbuing them with qualities
and characteristics they never possessed. To dishonor my son
in this fashion, I have refused to do. Just as he was, I loved him;
unbalanced, delicate, utterly ill-equipped to manage anything
beyond his immediate field of ken. All he had was his sister, his

dogs, and the succor he found in Adora's stories. He was remarkably kind, totally without malice, enchanting to look upon but, had he lived, would he have become an astonishing success? The answer is no. For Sebastian, the best I ever hoped was that he would find a woman who could love him as he was, who would understand his need for simplicity, peer beneath the surface of his beauty to the quiet, damaged soul within. That was my wish for my son.

Whenever I have spoken the truth about Sebastian, my confidants have fled in disgust, as if I have somehow defiled his memory by not exalting him to the heavens. I believe that, by loving him with total honesty, I have served him better than anyone. How can they understand what it is to wake up with the image of your son's face in your mind, knowing he is not, nor will ever be, there in the next room, waiting for you to wake him? Not for them to feel the pain of the images of him that pass through one's mind throughout the course of every day. Not for them to recall their incomparable son holding his sister's hand everywhere he went, or the look in his eyes when he gazed upon someone he loved; the desperate wish that they might never find him lacking. His entire, brief life, my son sought to please everyone. There is a whole world that will never know he existed. Yet he was mine for a time. I did not need him to become a searing intellect or a captain of industry. A life well lived, that was all I required for my son. Nothing else was possible for him.

Genevieve

My final morning on the island was perfect, which developed into a blissful late afternoon when I left the house to go and visit your mother. I had borrowed one of your white dresses, curled my hair and tied it back to make it look bobbed, and walked barefoot down the dirt road, my shoes in my hand, to the taxi stand. I remember vividly how I had loved, *loved* everything about the day: the quiet, the serenity I felt, the calm contentment I projected as I swished past the shops on the way to the hospital, the cool silk of your dress a scintillating kiss against my legs. People stopped to look at me; I imagined myself a dark imitation of you.

I felt a momentary impulse to run away when I arrived at Sophie's room; the image of someone ending her days collided viciously with my happy state of mind. She resembled a specter in her bed. I had brought flowers and was arranging them in a vase by her bed when Sophie's hand flew out and knocked them off the table. She did not mean to hit me with them, but the vase bounced off my hip, covering me in water and petals, bright pink against the white of my dress; my unspoiled day, my perfect masquerade ruined. I wonder now if that was her intention.

I was so frightened by Sophie's violent gesture, and the astonishing fact that she was awake and lucid for the first time in weeks, I almost couldn't catch my breath. She demanded that I sit in the chair next to her bed and listen to everything she had to say. She spoke harshly, as if she was about to tell me off for something I had done. I felt butterflies in my stomach; I had always hated getting into trouble. Yet looking back, I almost wish that I had been the one she was so furious at, so that I might have been spared.

She waited before she started to speak for me to sit down, and then she told me everything. Everything about you, my Beloved Aunt: who you had been as a child, your obsessive love for Sebastian, his illness, your inability to let him go, and the reason why her heart gave out that day at the port as she saw history repeat itself, only this time, I had been selected as the sacrifice. And then she embarked on the story from the past that was to crush every solitary thing I had ever thought of as truth. It was a tale of Sebastian and the woman he loved beyond anything, the woman whom you could not stand to share your brother with, whom you schemed to get rid of from the first moment they met.

Part III

Sophie

Summer 1919

Sophie

When Sebastian brought her home to meet us, I was elated. She was English, deliciously pale in the tradition of such girls, with flaxen hair and eyes so blue they startled. She had come to our island with a family of English aristocrats, although she was no relation to them. She was someone, it seemed, they had taken under their wing; it was never quite clear what her role was, something to do with the children. The parents seemed pleasant enough, albeit constantly drunk. Buffoonery, I think, is the term for such entitled debauchery. From what I could glean, she had lost both of her parents at the age of eleven and their family estate had been mired in debt. As a consequence, she was passed around well-meaning relatives, and by the time we met, when she was twenty years old, Sebastian's new friend was facing a future of servitude, not servants. She was quiet, observant, although not in an obsequiously timid way, and rather forlorn—understandable, considering. I wondered what she'd seen in her life, what obstacles she had been forced to overcome; there was cynicism—refreshing, not bitter—about her, a perspicacity that I thought would only serve Sebastian well; she could guide him, I thought, with a steady, sensible hand.

It was a *coup de foudre* for Sebastian, an instantaneous love that delighted me when I learned of it. I think it was perhaps because she was one of the few people he had ever met whom he could genuinely help. To my mind, love should occur instantly or not at all. It is not an emotion that should be worked at, least of all for someone as glorious as he was. Adora and he were strolling, as they habitually did, through town in the late afternoon after they had taken their siesta. They were a familiar sight there; often islanders would point them out to visitors: the two little dog thieves grown up into remarkable youth; that summer Sebastian was twenty and Adora, eighteen. So little happened on our island; in a sense, my children provided a form of entertainment, like viewing works of art in a museum. The day had been predictable enough; Sebastian and Adora had returned in time for lunch from one of their morning excursions down to their favorite cove; we had guests from the mainland, and Adora had led the conversation gaily; my children were divine, dressed in the cool white linens and silks they favored over the summer months. I don't know what had stirred such happiness in them, but Adora was in such a buoyant mood, and I remember watching Sebastian—quiet as was his wont—drink her in, enjoying every ounce of her and thinking myself lucky that my children had turned out so well, considering the grave impediments to happiness that had threatened to destroy us over the years.

Maybe my son had a premonition; perhaps he sensed that he was on the cusp of change, that no more would be the days when he remained a beat behind his sister, but as an equal at her side. Maybe he anticipated the treasure waiting for him in town, something he had never dared dream of or consider: another person who could love him in the way a woman should love a man.

"She was crying, Mama. Nobody was with her. I looked around, but it didn't seem as if anybody wanted her, so I thought I'd sit beside her and make sure she was not too lonely." That's what Sebastian told me the afternoon he returned home from town full of news. He had spotted her immediately sitting in an outdoor café and, for the first time in his life, had been unable to simply continue walking, content in his sister's company. Adora had felt him let go of her hand as he turned on his heel toward this stranger, this seemingly lost soul, moving as fast as he could from the tie that had bound him all those previous years.

I was frightened for him, naturally, nervous that this stranger might not appreciate his strengths and, of course, weaknesses. Sebastian was such a quiet, reserved boy, happy to allow Adora to speak for him, most content when he was soundlessly caring for his pets; I fretted that the attraction he felt for this girl would not be matched, that, perhaps, she might need more in a partner. I waited as the weeks passed, growing increasingly hopeful when he would return happier than ever that this girl might prove the exception to the rule we had resigned ourselves to with regard to Sebastian; it seemed she accepted his simplicity, nor did she appear to demand anything from him, sensing instinctively that he could never provide it. I was grateful that she allowed the attraction she felt for him to mature gradually, believing she clearly understood Sebastian must always be eased gently into any situation.

Sebastian took her to the beaches he had shared with his sister, the places they frequented, this time without Adora. They went swimming far out into the sea, the dogs joining them, which amused her, even though she was at first afraid of his insane collection of German shepherds, greyhounds, and mongrels. They loved her like he did, however, coming to her when she called them, curling up beside her on the beach or at her feet in a restaurant in town. Each night, he would come home a new man, full of her virtues, eager to tell them to all of us. For the first time since she was born, he was entirely oblivious to his sister. He did not notice that she listened with an ashen face, impossible to read.

From the instant we met, I adored her. For my son, I could not have chosen a more suitable girl. Simply, she was his destiny. I was overjoyed whenever I saw her smile shyly at him, the love in her eyes, the *please notice me,* entirely transparent despite how she tried to conceal the true depth of her feelings for my son. There was a familiarity in the way she treated him, as if she anticipated what he would say or do before he did. Most of us are not lucky enough to know when such love appears at our door. But I knew when I met their father what I had found. I was the exception. Nearly all of my friends, oblivious to what they had, had given up their true loves, thinking something better might exist somewhere else; those lesser, more entertaining souls who bring only unhappiness to hearts full of untainted expectation.

Like me, Sebastian's love was unusual because she recognized what she had found. Not for her to presume that there would be others who would love her even more. I thought her pragmatic. I wanted her for him as much as he did. Until the love that had been overlooked due to her arrival made its presence felt once again, she belonged only to us.

Yet for Sebastian, his own happiness was irrelevant; he thought only of his sister. "Adora won't need to tell me stories anymore, Mama," he said proudly. "She won't need to worry about me." My poor Sebastian. He finally felt his sister would be able to live a life beyond him. To go out without him permanently shackled to her side. All the years of his life he had considered himself a burden to her, despite the fact that she would never have entertained such an absurd idea. He thought he was helping her by letting her go. In truth, he was killing her.

And I failed to see it. When my two children needed me most, my eyes were trained on a future that did not, nor could ever, exist. I was blind to the truth. My daughter inherited that trait from me.

Adora

Since we were children, it had always been left to me to make sure that Mama did not see. Displaying an insight nobody would ever have expected of you, Sebastian, you made me promise, and I did as you asked. There were things you understood; I always thought it cruel and frustrating that you were so underestimated. I would argue with people, get involved in heated exchanges to try to make them realize how special you were. You would stop me, grab my arm, and lead me away. "It's all right," you would say. "You know me better than anyone. It doesn't matter what they think." Your words would mollify me, my anger at the ignorant dissipating next to your affection. And then, always, you would ask of me a promise that I knew was borne of a twinge of remorse: "Just promise never to let Mama see that I love you the most." And you would turn your delicate, inquiring face to mine, searching my face for a sign that I would never fail you and, finding it, as you always did, you would lead me away by the hand to the paradise we shared.

Yet it had to be: I knew it then and I know it now. The girl in town was inevitable. We were walking together, and I felt you turn and, although I didn't look to see what had attracted your attention, I let go of your hand. I didn't let it linger in mine and relish the last seconds of your touch; I let it drop knowing it was the most precious thing I had ever owned, bracing myself, in some curious way, as if it were something fragile, about to break. It was time. Yet would I have clasped your hand longer had I realized I would never hold it again? Would you have let me let you go if you'd known that it would be impossible to come back?

She was different from us, tiny, exhausted. Nothing about her was vibrant; nothing shone. Her eyes did not glimmer with joy when she turned her face up to you, as mine did every time I found you in the morning after the darkness of sleep had forced me to journey somewhere alone. Her expression held a simple request: *Please.* It was a plea of someone defeated. Who would have gone to her if you hadn't? She was surrounded by people, and they must have seen her crying, but yet they did nothing.

I watched you talk to her, pull up a chair, forget me, and it seemed to me familiar, as if I had seen all of this happen before. It was immediate; the girl, mousy and ordinary, suddenly became more attractive; her face grew interesting; hidden attributes were revealed under your doting attention. I had always known this would happen. It had to be. It was always going to be. I stood there, in the middle of the square, involuntary tears flowing down my face without end.

I was surrounded by people, all of whom watched me cry, but, yet, they did nothing. The girl who had stolen your heart and I weren't so different after all. And in that, like a starving spectator to a banquet, I found a bittersweet solace.

Sophie

Like my son, I thought it best that Adora relinquish her self-appointed role as her brother's guardian. I knew it would be painful for her, but it simply had to be. Their childhood was over, and I had indulged her every covetous whim of being with him, far too much so—it was time for Sebastian to be indulged. As she was older than when he first began to leave her behind on his forays, I never actually considered that she would object to her brother's good fortune, that it would appear to destroy her piece by piece. Adora had committed her every waking moment to pleasing him; I foolishly thought she might be relieved that someone else could assume her role. I also truly believed that my daughter would never stand in the way of Sebastian's joy, that she would only want the best for him. And yet where did I come up with these ideas? When had Adora ever confided in me? It was Sebastian's ear she constantly sought. As the events of the summer unfolded, I found that I had misinterpreted her love for him: I thought it altruistic when, in reality, it was founded on possession.

To ignore the signs was ridiculously easy. After her initial distance, she went to such enormous lengths to make Sebas-

tian's girlfriend feel welcome, lending her clothes, taking her
into her bedroom to talk for hours on end. Like the proverbial
ostrich, I contentedly stuck my head into the sand and convinced myself all would be well. I am impelled now to admit
that I didn't care about my daughter. I had resented her ever
since she took Sebastian from me when she was a child. It was
only when this delightful stranger arrived that he began to
grow close to me again. I reveled in the bond that grew each
day between us, delighted to be needed. Relieved that Adora's
influence was fading.

To love someone so much that everything else pales into in-
significance is not a cardinal sin. I have felt compelled to remind myself of this fact repeatedly over the years whenever I
have wanted to condemn Adora for everything that happened.
Nor is it wrong to presume, when one is told every day how astonishing is their beauty, that the object of their affection might
dismiss them in favor of another. She was young, barely eighteen; her life had been only him; she had never known suffering; she had never heard *no*.

Et souviens-toi que je t'attends. Why did I not listen? *Remember I wait for you forever.* It was their rhyme when they were
children. As they grew older, whenever they went out in the
evening, he would wait like a suitor at the foot of the staircase
for her to descend, goddesslike, to his side. I thought it charming that he was so chivalrous, emulating his father, teaching her
how to be treated by men. Always, they recited the line when
she reached his side, laughing, as if it were a joke: *Et souviens-toi
que je t'attends.* But it was no joke; my daughter had clearly believed it. The night she dressed Sebastian's girlfriend up and
walked with her down the stairs to where he was waiting impa-
tiently, she could barely hide her distress when he handed a

stem of bougainvillea not to Adora but to his girlfriend, when he said, *Et souviens-toi que je t'attends*. It was impossibly romantic, as he intended it to be. Of charm and sophistication in the realms of love, what knowledge did he have other than the playacting in which he and my daughter had indulged?

He would have been devastated to think he had hurt his sister, but he had no experience beyond her. Nothing in their lives had happened that they had not shared, indeed invented together. He had no concept of the despair that would lead to cruelty his simple gesture had set in motion. She watched them leave, rooted to the spot, her face a masterpiece of sorrow and what I construed as hatred. I thought she was sulking. I considered her entirely spoiled and left her to it. I was completely unwilling to fulfill my role as a mother to her, to hold her, to draw out the darkness that had settled on her mind, to offer a calm voice of reason. I thought only of myself and my euphoria that Sebastian would finally be happy. I had no doubt that would be the case.

For years, my only consolation was that, despite everything, my son did know love before he died, just as I perceived Jack shared with Genevieve before he slipped away into the morass of sorrow provided by my daughter.

Two young men so similar in looks who loved two women — a mother and a daughter. I still consider life intolerable in its cruelty.

Miranda did not need to watch her daughter suffer as she had. She had been punished enough.

Adora

You never could stand to hear the sound of tears. It was why I learned to weep soundlessly. And it was why, when we were children, we used to hide underwater in our swimming pool from Mama, whose unresolved sadness after our father died so disturbed you.

I told you that you were a dolphin, and when we were old enough, we went to the sea every day to disappear, so that you wouldn't hear the unkind things people said. Mama was so often away, or hiding from us; there was nowhere else we could find peace; the water was the only place that seemed to soothe you.

"My brother lives in the sea, like a dolphin," I wrote in a class essay when I was a little girl. I had to read it aloud and, as with all my stories, I read it to you, Sebastian. I don't remember the laughter now, the taunts from the other children; I just remember your face full of wonder that I had written a story about you. You thought you were famous, and you were, I told you. "Everyone else is just ordinary and that is why they'll never understand how beautiful you are."

I knew you were beautiful; it was all anybody said. "So

beautiful, such a tragedy. . . ." Often they cried, and as soon as I saw the tears, I'd grab your hand and we'd run to the beach and dive into that clear blue sea and swim for hours, until you were so tired that you fell into the hammock in our olive grove on our return, saved from the sound of tears—and the truth—for another day.

Nobody praised you; nobody said you were clever or exclaimed, impressed, at something you'd written or a gold star you'd received from the teacher, because that was never to be. I had to do all of it for you; I was the one who excelled, but only so that I would know how to lead you—because you didn't know how and because you wanted me to. "Promise me you'll always show me how to do things," you'd ask, "because I'll make a mistake and look silly." "You know things that I don't," I'd assure you before we drifted off to sleep. "You know how to make people happy without trying. I don't have that talent." And you said, "You make me happy, and I only like you so I think you have a talent too."

Yes, Sebastian, my special talent was always to make you happy, to show you how to do things, to save you from the sound of tears. I was devastated when Miranda arrived, but I knew that I had to show you how to love someone other than me. It wasn't really my place, and I was punished for it, but I did it for you. I gave up everything that I loved—our little rituals together—and told you to share them with her now. When you handed her the stem of bougainvillea that night, after I'd dressed her in one of my outfits to go out with you, I almost couldn't breathe; you had to leave me, but still I wanted so to keep you. You did as I said and greeted Miranda at the bottom of the stairs as you used to greet me, handing her the flowers that were always mine. I saw how proud Mama was and how touched Miranda appeared by your gesture, and I comforted myself that I'd done the right thing by both of you. Yet I was desperate for the two of you to leave so that I could rush to my room and give in to my unhappiness. I grimaced in pain, and I saw Mama throw me a quizzical, irritated look. I bit my lip hard to try to steel myself against losing you, but then I heard you say something I had not suggested:

"Et souviens-toi que je t'attends."

It was too much; it was our rhyme, our childhood song. It meant everything to me, I would never have asked you to share it with her. That I wanted to keep. I almost gave in then and there, right in front of you. Yet when I looked up at you, I found, to my surprise, that, although you were facing Miranda when you said it, you had uttered the line for me, just like always. And it was all I could do not to grab your hand the way I used to and run with you into the clear blue sea to save you from the sound of my tears.

Miranda

It was the only time in my life that I ever truly enjoyed myself. Afterward, I became a pessimist, pouring cold water on any excitement I felt, reminding myself that it wouldn't last; something would ruin it. When I first saw Sebastian, he was walking with a woman so spectacular, I thought him out of his mind to even cast a glance in my direction. And then, when he left her to come and talk to me, I almost couldn't believe it. Next to her, I was nothing. I don't say that so people will jump to disagree; I know I was pretty, but her kind of beauty was unparalleled. I knew I would never compare. Yet somehow I did.

When I found out that she was his sister, I was flabbergasted. They had seemed like two lovers walking along together. She was so obviously madly in love with him; everything, the way they held hands, their intimate way of talking, almost as if they were murmuring promises of passion, struck me as nothing like the way a brother and sister behaved. They were so perfect; they were almost unreal. It was unnerving, to be honest. More, when he had left her to come to me, the expression she wore was one of complete shock, almost horror, like that of a jilted lover, her eyes trained on him in disbelief. Maybe I should have paid more attention to my initial instinct about the two of them. I've learned to do that since. As a consequence, I'm very seldom disappointed by people anymore. I expect nothing. I'm happy to keep myself to myself.

At first, I didn't really think it would begin, let alone last, between Sebastian and me. I thought he might get bored. There were so many dazzling people on the island that I felt like a nonentity in comparison. But he wasn't interested in them, never even looked at anyone else. Gradually, I let my guard slip after my initial suspicion. He never did a single thing to make me doubt him. I even began to believe that we would always be together. Actually, I believed it totally. I didn't have a care in the world. I was madly in love with how my life was turning out; a girl in my position would never have dreamt of such an existence. I thought we were meant for each other, that somebody had finally thought me good enough. Nobody ever had before.

I've always been a reserved type of person. I don't trust people willingly. Never did. I think I inherited this from my father. He saw through everyone, was the first to point out hypocrisy in others, to question supposed kindnesses. I began to look for the same traits in people, watching for chinks in personalities that revealed the truth of their thoughts. Dirty looks cast at my mother in church because her dress was prettier than everyone else's, friends at school whispering in corners about other girls, the wife whose smile dried up the moment her husband left her side—all of these things I caught, sometimes without even looking for them. I suppose some people would call it insight, perceptiveness. I've often considered what might have been if I'd simply turned the other way, welcomed life instead of steeling myself against it. And yet I did know once what it was to yearn for the days of happiness, each one better than the last. I learned my lesson when they all ended. I learned never to let my guard down again.

Something told me not to trust Adora, but she was a brilliant actress, I'll give her that. I pushed aside my instinct. Adora was so interested in me that I allowed myself to be duped. I was so thankful to her for being kind to me, involving me in the life she led with her brother, leaving nothing out, I thought. For the first time in my life, I shared everything with another person, confided to her all of my thoughts and feelings for Sebastian. I even told her about my lack of trust in people and how happy I was to finally find a family who were so uninhibited. And, my word, they were: I'd never seen anything quite like it. When we would go swimming, she'd stand and dry his hair when he came out of the sea. Every time she spoke or suggested plans for the evening, Sebastian would watch her as if following music, almost as if she was a conductor, showing him how to play. I know that sounds ridiculous, but it's true. Nobody else really commented on it, though, least of all Sophie. I told myself that maybe this was the way things were done on the continent but, still, I could never quite shake the worry that Adora might turn against me and ruin everything.

They were so different from the people I had grown up around. Even though I loved my parents when they were alive, they were cool in their affections, strict with me. We didn't discuss things openly like they did in Sebastian's house, where the whole family seemed to know everything about each other. Things were discussed behind closed doors in mine. My parents were old-fashioned; children were to be seen and not heard. After they died, I was simply the charity case who lived with various relatives—each set more distant than the last—

during the holidays when I would come home from boarding school. Not that I inherited much from my parents; in fact, what they left barely paid for my education and that was all: I had no dowry when I finished school. The best I could hope for was a teaching position with a good family or else to become a companion to a wealthy dowager.

For most of that summer I thought I had found the family of my dreams. I loved Sophie from the first time I met her. I'd never felt so welcome before. Initially, I was insecure; I thought she might not consider me good enough for Sebastian, but the opposite was true. She was more intent than I, I think, on us being together. She treated me like a daughter from the beginning. And Adora acted like a sister, offered me such warmth that I cast all suspicions aside and, for the first time in my life, put my complete faith and trust into another person.

It was mid-July; we'd had six perfect weeks together. Sophie had insisted I leave my employ shortly after I met Sebastian, which I was more than willing to do. I believed in our future completely. I trusted Adora implicitly. I forgot how she cried when he first left her; I overlooked how he searched first for her approval before he did anything, how she hovered around us whenever we went out, even if she wasn't invited, just to make sure, she'd say, that everything was fine. I wanted everything so badly that I forgot every lesson I'd ever been taught.

Sophie

I was outraged by Adora's behavior. She would not leave them alone. Every time I inquired of Miranda how their evening had been spent, invariably I would hear that Adora had arrived mid-meal or earlier to steer the focus of Sebastian's affection from Miranda to Adora again. It was entirely apparent to me what my daughter was up to, the same thing she had done to me when she was a child: tempting him away with her stories, determined always to get her own way, whether it was best for him or not. The more I heard, the angrier I became, until I knew something had to be done.

I suspected that to introduce suspicion into a relationship where there was none was Adora's sole intent; in this way she could ensure that Sebastian would never leave her. She was devoid of compassion for Miranda. By befriending her and becoming her confidante, Adora could study Miranda's every weakness and play on it. Such, I deduced, was my daughter's game. Yet nothing she did could be questioned. She could not be accused of anything other than enjoying the company of her brother and his girlfriend.

When they were all together, Adora would reminisce over

the countless stories from their past, of the places they had visited, of parties at which Miranda had not been present. At first,
Miranda was excited to learn everything about Sebastian, so
obliged to his sister for sharing their private years with her. She
often confided to me how much she looked forward to meeting
with Adora during the day and to her companionship in the
evenings she spent with Sebastian. Yet it was only a matter of
time before Miranda began to feel left out and became aware
that the conversations my daughter instigated evolved only to
completely exclude her. If ever Sebastian and Miranda vaguely
disagreed on a subject, my daughter sided with him. If Miranda
went to say something, Adora interrupted her to tell another
anecdote about Sebastian. Miranda was far more experienced
than my children; she had spent time with diverse people, both
kind and unfeeling. Adora's constant presence succeeded in
sowing the seeds of doubt in Miranda's mind. She grew to understand that, for Sebastian, she would never come first; Adora
would always be there, would always be deferred to in place of
Miranda. The best my son's girlfriend could ever hope for was
second place in his affections.

Adora became a rival with whom Miranda could not compete, which resulted in a jealous streak that was justifiable yet
completely unattractive. Worse, gone was the calm that had so
sustained Sebastian; Miranda forgot herself, and her burgeoning distaste for Adora triggered the onslaught of his despair.
That he knew his sister better than anyone was the simple
truth. While he was not sophisticated enough to understand
the extent of Adora's childishly Machiavellian antics, what he
did know was that he was destroying her. She had never before
been spiteful. Sebastian was guileless; if Miranda said Adora
was nasty to her, then he believed her, which only contributed

to the terrible confusion that resulted. All he had ever received from Adora was selfless love. He had only ever known contentment in her company. He blamed himself. If not for him, not only his sister but Miranda would be happy. His inability to bring joy to the two women he loved the most started to devour him. The vision of the future he thought he had found began to fade in front of him.

He was, after all, a fragile boy, unbalanced in manifold ways. That he could have found someone so caring and sensible had grounded him. Not understanding what she needed caused the disconcerting gloom of failure to descend over his mind, which had found brightness for so cruelly brief a time.

In any other instance, I might have forgiven Adora's actions as those of an immature girl who had been far too spoiled. Our reality, however, had consisted of constantly balancing the moods of my precious son, who illuminated our lives. To deny him the love he so deserved was tantamount to killing him.

I was not surprised when Miranda came to me; I had been on the brink so many times of extending an invitation to her, stopping myself at the last minute only because of a fear of betraying my children. It was so very important that we know one another well: to share our thoughts on how to help Sebastian, to discuss how to minimize Adora's influence.

"You must come to me, Miranda, if you have concerns or if you need advice," I urged her that day. "I will do anything to help."

"I just don't know how to overcome her influence," Miranda confessed, clearly bewildered by the strength of their bond. "She is the Queen, after all, isn't she?" she exclaimed with a mixture of awe and good-natured humor. "That is, I'm just a guest, aren't I? How could I possibly compare?"

"Oh, my poor child," I commiserated, "you are so much more than that. You have made Sebastian's life so full, so rich. I never expected anyone to love him as you have."

She looked at me contemplatively. I could see that she was nervous about saying something. "I just wonder—" she began. "I mean to say, I just think, perhaps—Oh, I don't know what I mean," she said in exasperation, starting to cry. "It's just everything's always been taken away from me. I couldn't bear it if I were to lose Sebastian. I don't know what I'd do."

I crossed over to sit beside her on the chaise and consoled her as best I could. She was so deeply distressed, and I shook my head in irritation that Adora again had caused such trouble.

Yet I knew that separating Adora from Sebastian would hurt him terribly; I wasn't sure if he could survive it. At the same time, however, what chance would he have without Miranda?

"It's just that they're so close," Miranda remarked. "I mean, I know it's not my place, Sophie, but people comment on it. I mean, they're awful people, hideous, but I want to spare Sebastian from ever hearing something he might not understand. It would be so terrible to do that to him. I just wonder if they could spend a little time apart . . . ?" She let the sentence trail off, entirely unaware of what she had said, I'm sure.

I'd heard the same; it was inevitable given how they were inseparable from one another. It was different when they were children, but when they were grown, they seemed more unusual, and puerile minds made ridiculous assumptions. Yet it was also utterly risible. Inconceivable. Besides, the very idea that Sebastian could even—Well, it was just not possible.

"Do you hear these things a lot?" I asked quietly.

Miranda wiped her tears and took a breath. "More than I should."

I covered my face with my hands, knowing I had to act but oblivious as to the best way to do it. "It would devastate him to be separated from her, you must understand that."

"I do, I do," she protested. "I just wish we could have some time so that I can help him as she does."

"Yes," I agreed. It didn't seem so unreasonable, although I was completely ignorant as to how either Adora or Sebastian would deal with being kept apart from one another. Yet I knew I had to do it—for Sebastian.

"I'll try," I said. "It's so important that Sebastian have a life free from worry."

"Sophie, that's all I want for him too," Miranda agreed earnestly, taking my hand.

I found her sincerity touching. People were so vile, sniggering at things they didn't understand. I felt so protective of both my children, but I knew that Sebastian needed my help more than Adora. "Leave it to me," I replied, resolved. "Everything will be fine."

"Yes," Miranda replied, clearly relieved. "I was so worried that I would overstep the mark by coming here and ruin everything. It's been so long since I've had a mother, I almost forgot what it felt like to have someone look out for you."

"Oh, my dear," I comforted her, hugging her tighter. It was curious, but I realized that only Miranda had made me feel like a mother, of any use. I struggled to remember the last time either Sebastian or Adora had ever needed me and, as I did so, any lingering doubts that I might be making a terrible mistake disappeared as my surrogate daughter nestled in closer to me, her head resting near my heart just like a child is supposed to.

Miranda

They called me the summer girl. "Oh, her?" one of my mon-eyed employers would say with a yawn, nodding ambivalently in my direction. "We always have a summer girl," they would conclude, shrugging their shoulders as if it were nothing, when-ever anyone inquired as to my place with the family. As if I were nothing.

I was never disturbed by their response; had my parents not died or dissipated the family wealth, I may have stretched indolently myself on a balcony in Cap d'Antibes or thereabouts one afternoon and uttered the same line as disinterestedly as my current employer. Circumstances, however, had contrived to place me on a precarious margin of society; one false step, one missed opportunity, one inappropriate reaction, and I'd be left in a hotel lobby somewhere, "no longer required," without the means to go home in any sense of the word. In such instances, there is only one way to find the path back to the hotel room and, after that, only more hotel lobbies beckon; the door to in-nocence is shut forever.

I wasn't supposed to be anything to write home about, the summer girl. None of us ever are: not attractive enough to distract husbands or make wives feel inadequate, not clever enough to challenge the authority of the household, sufficiently insignificant not to need to be entertained if seated beside someone at dinner. "And who are you?" they'd ask as we took our seats. "The summer girl," I'd reply and watch them turn away, relieved not to have to bother.

I was there to amuse their children, walk the dogs, provide companionship for the wives or the mothers-in-law while the husbands golfed and drank and sailed their boats. I was there to hold the tray of hors d'oeuvres when a maid could not be found on short notice, whenever we'd made an impromptu stop to drop in on so-and-so in a Mediterranean port. I was there to remind them of how superior they were in every sense of the word: superior to Fate, to luck, to life itself. Nobody had given up on them. People only are, they seemed to imply in their smugly dismissive fashion, if they are lacking, and we're not, they'd beam, triumphantly.

I used to wonder what it was they thought they'd won. Certainly not love, as most of the couples I knew could barely stand the sight of each other. I had no doubt that the wives couldn't care less about the knocks at my door in the early hours, after the whiskey was finished, after the cigars were left to smoke in the drawing room, ready to burn the house down if not for the attentive butler or housemaid who cleared them away. The same servant who threw a knowing look at the disappearing figure of the master, heading for the staircase to the summer girl's room.

If the wives ever did find out, they'd make quite a stink, but just for show, to prove they could. Then it was time to move along, to find the next family in need of exercising cruelty over the unfortunate. And that is why I was weeping in the square that day, because my time was up and I knew there were no aristocratic families left for me, not after my having been silly enough to truly fall in love with the drunk who paid my wages. If I'd been more like them, I might have won, or at least that's what I told myself bitterly in that café. I should have schemed instead of listening attentively to his terrible problems, which involved being unloved, being lonely, being all of the things that delusional men are when they're trying to convince gullible young girls to make them feel better, if only for the night.

When I looked up and saw Sebastian through my tears, I almost told him how much I would cost. After all, why would anyone as attractive as he ever look at someone like me? People are so fond of drawing the analogy that plain women come last in the race of love. Well, let me tell you, some people are so irrelevant that nobody remembers they even raced in the first place.

"Why are you crying?" he asked.

"What do you want?" I replied. I wasn't interested in games anymore. I wished he would just leave.

He looked frightened for a moment. "I don't want anything," he said. "I just want to help you. I like to help."

I didn't know anything then, but instinctively I sensed this incredibly handsome man might be able to. I could not perceive guile in him or cunning; he was immediately different from anyone I'd ever known before.

That was when I noticed her, watching us intently, the unfathomably stunning woman he had left for me. "Who's that?" I asked, pointing rather rudely at her.

I'll never forget the way he smiled, the depth of affection inherent in his expression, the wistful longing; I saw it all, and I prepared myself for the humiliation of being told she was his wife; not just that, the love of his life, infinitely worse.

"She's my sister," he said proudly. "She's the Summer Queen."

I remember how my spirits soared when he assured me that she was no competition in one breath and how they plummeted when, in the next, he confirmed that already I was back where I'd started—an also-ran. At best the handmaid to the Queen.

Adora

When you announced your engagement in August, I feigned perfect happiness for you. I was a constant companion to Miranda when you were not around, endlessly willing to discuss you with her for hours on end. Being with Miranda was the closest I could get to you. Yet although I knew you were smitten with her, the time we had spent together revealed how different she was from me in every conceivable way. Knowing you so well, I was aware of how unhappy you would eventually become when you discovered how incapable she was of pleasing you as I had, so I sought to teach her. I went with you everywhere, trying to show her how to handle you: never to frighten you, to follow the easy rhythm of undemanding conversation, to keep emotions quiet, never to upset you.

Yet I could feel that Miranda resented me. She wanted you all to herself, and I knew I should let you go, but I was so worried for you. We had always been together; I was terrified that, without me, you couldn't survive. I continued to go out with the two of you even though something told me to stop; the harder I tried to make her like me, the more desperate I appeared and the more she withdrew. But my pain superseded everything, Sebastian. You were leaving me for her, and all of the days of my life turned to nothingness without you by my side. I couldn't trust her to care for you as I did. While I knew it was inevitable we would both eventually marry, I never thought that our relationship would change. I thought you would wait for me forever, as I for you, to share everything the way we always had. Yet as soon as she arrived, you seemed to turn away from me, and it broke my heart watching you leave.

Despite your unhappiness, however, Miranda's suspicions, and the nearly constant fights that would occur after spending the evening with me, the two of you did not part. In fact, you appeared to need each other more. I was totally bewildered, little understanding that the idea of losing something so divine drives lovers to cling to one another in the face of trouble as if their lives depend on it. And then you ceased to join me in the evenings. I could not find you anywhere. I would search every bar and restaurant in the old part of town each night, but you were nowhere to be found. When I did see you at the house, you appeared more content than ever, but distant, especially Miranda, who found every excuse imaginable not to be alone with me. She had become a different person entirely from the defeated girl we first met. I didn't know who she was anymore.

Miranda

Most people have no concept of what it's like to have no hope, no tomorrow, just more of the same today. No, Sebastian wasn't who I had dreamt as my perfect partner when I was a child. How could he be? But I was fond of him, and I would never have deliberately hurt him. Everything I did, I thought was for the best, and I will say this: people who are supposedly madly in love when they marry hurt each other the most when they invariably disappoint each other; when they fail to live up to the idealized images their blinkered hearts once projected into the future. I knew the terms of the bargain I was striking, and I was equal to it. Sebastian was a good person, a willing companion, an easygoing, quiet man who needed only gentleness and good sense alongside him. I could provide that, I told myself. And if I did, a tomorrow I had given up on with each knock at my bedroom door suddenly could become a possibility and not a pipe dream.

Was it wrong to want to come first, though? It was all I asked. Would any woman, even a love-struck fool, have been able to cope with Adora's constant presence, the endless questions: "Do you think he'll understand that, Miranda? Look at me, watch how I deal with him. You need to always be soft. You need to always be ready to catch him if he falls."

Before I went to discuss my fears with Sophie, something told me to just give it up, to kiss Sebastian good-bye and leave him and Adora to it. If Sophie had not convinced me so completely how much he loved and needed me, I might have. As much as I told myself that Adora was no rival, everything in her behavior challenged what I so desperately needed to believe. I considered myself truly blessed to have found him in the beginning, once I had accepted the situation for what it was. I didn't need to pretend with Sebastian; he didn't know me, had no idea where I'd been, who I'd known. I was able to forget what I had become; Sebastian rescued me from that terrible existence, and that was the start of my love for him. He asked absolutely nothing of me; how many times can anyone ever say that? That they were loved without having to offer anything in return? Perhaps it's not so unusual why I was indebted to him.

Yet as soon as Adora started showing up constantly in our company, I could almost predict how everything would turn out. She wasn't his lover, but she might as well have been. She was as possessive as a jealous rival. I had seen so many similar women in my own brief life, flirting with the fathers of the families I lived with, making snide remarks to the wives delivered so sweetly that to react to them would only serve to make the duped wife look terribly petty, snide, not a very nice person at all, which of course was the intention. What I was absolutely convinced of, however, was that you could never beat such women; they were always one step ahead of the game, one sneaky trick away from winning.

I watched and learned that honest people react to such behavior, blatant as it is to those who are suspicious by nature.

By so doing, everyone thinks they are the ones who are at fault. Their partners, be it husbands or boyfriends, don't want nagging shrews constantly questioning their integrity. Eventually, such men tire and run willingly off to the seemingly undemanding and innocent souls who, unbeknownst to them, planned the demise of their existing relationship from the first meeting. There is no win over such women, least of all if you value truth above all things.

At first, I fought with Sebastian over Adora, until I realized that I was about to make a terrible mistake, just like all of the mistreated wives I'd spent so much time studying. I wanted Sebastian more than anything, loved the idea of our life together more than I thought myself capable. I wanted to come first for once. I was furious, in actual fact, that she had shown up to ruin everything. All of the years of watching people in my position lose fueled me to fight, despite my fear about the ultimate outcome.

I tried not to, but it was impossible for me; I couldn't keep myself from hating Adora. For Sebastian, I tried far harder to forgive and understand her than I ever would have with anyone else. I had seen from the beginning the remarkable love they shared for one another. And yet, I asked myself, what kind of sister would willingly try to cause unhappiness to someone she claimed to love so much? These thoughts and my own smarting humiliation brought out my pride. I couldn't trust her anymore, and the mere presence of her made me reel in disgust. I thought her nasty and manipulative for not leaving us alone, always contriving to exclude me from the conversations, reminiscing over situations I had played no part in. Everything she said or did seemed to scream "you come last." It was clear that she thought nothing of me, and I felt sick that I might have trusted her despite everything I had ever been taught growing up.

She had everything, absolutely everything; crowds of people practically parted like the Red Sea for Moses whenever she walked through town, whipping out fronds of palm trees to cool her if it was too hot. Why couldn't she just let me have the little I had managed to come by? She was so arrogant—what concept did she have of despair, of going unnoticed through life? The one time I was about to taste victory she tripped me at the finish line. My magnificent future was about to end before it started if I didn't do something to try to stop it, and so I thought about all of those women I had watched and learned from over the years and I knew what I had to do. I was desperate, an entirely unattractive quality in a woman. Fortunately, Sebastian didn't know any better, didn't understand that desperate people are the most dangerous because, for them, every day is a struggle in survival.

I had wanted at least something in my life to be special. I never wanted to feel again as I used to in the misty gray hours of the morning, having performed my unofficial duties, secure in my position at least for another day. Because of Adora, to keep Sebastian, I had to resort to the same game of trade and barter. It worked, but I lost what was left of my innocence and the quiet dream I had kindled somewhere at the back of my mind that had kept me going whenever I wanted to give up; the idea of a tomorrow, better than the last, ended right in front of me. It was just the same today, I realized, only the players had changed.

Adora

You became a stranger, Sebastian. Immersed in your plans for the future, you barely noted my presence in the house. Mama became your confidante, and I would frequently find the two of you deep in conversation during the hours when Miranda was out running errands—the things I used to do for you—my mother's face alive with possibility, with longing.

At the parties Mama constantly threw, Miranda and Mama would tolerate me in your company, but anything we discussed was purely superficial. If I tried to follow you, Mama's tight grip on my arm would stop me in my tracks. If I did find myself alone with you for even a second, it was always the same: your face knotted in thought, struggling to find the answers to what I asked, even though I knew I shouldn't trouble you with it. You knew very little about your wedding plans, which wasn't surprising, and Miranda always appeared vague whenever I asked about the engagement party or the wedding itself, when it would be. I had no alternative but to believe that Miranda had succeeded in turning you against me. Whatever she had done or said had worked. I became the third in the crowd where once I was the only person who mattered. But still, I had known you longer, understood you better. Whatever distraction Miranda provided, I told myself, could not possibly eclipse the love that existed between us.

It seemed to me then that I had been a hindrance and not a help to you as I had always imagined. As soon as you were old enough to escape me, you did. I was a child, emotionally stunted as a result of our isolation, but the more you and Miranda made plans to go away without me, the more I convinced myself that you did not love me and never had. Not even the bewildered concern in your eyes as I wept in your room while you dressed to go out could convince me that I meant anything to you. I relished the fleeting glimpses of your dismay, even if I thought that they were indicative of a need on your part for solitude that my despair continuously disrupted. I began to enjoy the pain my constant presence inspired in you. In my mind, you deserved no better. I knew I would never have left you; I punished you for growing up.

I allowed myself to be consumed by sorrow. I would spend hours alone on the beach, curled up on the sand, thinking only of you and of our shared history, which cast its net back to the beach of our childhood and the stories I told. I realized I had never witnessed anger in you or hostility of any kind, only the placid calm of your contented spirit.

Weeks passed. I became a specter of the happy girl I had been, even refusing to eat on occasion; Mama was utterly furious with me. I grew sullen and withdrawn, wasting away in the face of your growing independence, your refusal to submit to my childishness. I pushed everyone to breaking point, each act of defiance calculated to make Mama insist you take me with you everywhere. She never did, refusing to allow me to follow you on your travels. That was all I wanted, to be your companion again, for you to think solely of me as you once had. My only thought was for your happiness. And it was. In that, I did not lie.

I like to believe that something in you anticipated the end and led you to me. I like to believe that you sensed I was half a disappointment away from giving up on life entirely when you came to find me. For it was the morning in late August when I woke and realized I could not claim your heart any longer that you found me on the beach and lay down beside me, pulling me close to you. I had wept all night, knowing what I must do, aware that if I did I would have to let you go, aware that if I didn't I would lose you forever. I knew that the best was behind me; I wasn't being dramatic; it was an instinctive giving way in me; we are all born to love just one person, and you were mine. I had no thought then that I would never bear children, that I would marry a man who . . . well, that I would marry a man who was nothing like you. And in the end what hurt the most was that I had been grateful for every minute of what we had shared; not one second had I taken for granted, and I knew that I would relive all of our time together every day until I died because your future did not—could not—include me.

I'll never forget the ecstasy I experienced when I felt your arms engulf me. You had come back to me, and I felt foolish for ever doubting that you wouldn't. You had come home to me where I could always keep you safe; I took your face in mine and smothered it in kisses, so grateful for happiness again. I thought you would grant me whatever I asked of you. "Sebastian," I said, hugging you to me, "promise me you'll never leave

me." I let the moments pass, each one eroding the joy of the answer I expected, until finally you said, "No." It was the first time
in my life you had ever denied me. It was the first time I ever
felt the brightness of the world dim to a hopeless gray in the
face of an inconceivable loss. But you, my beautiful brother, did
not leave me there on the sand. You stayed with me still, your
actions directly contradicting your stated intent. We lay there
together for the last time, just as we had in days gone by, the
tears from your eyes falling into my hair until the sun set on
the last day of my innocence. It was as if you understood, even
then, that you were powerless in the face of what the future
held, that holding me was your way of saying good-bye while
you still could.

Miranda

When I saw them that day, together on the beach, like two lovers—the way they were wrapped around each other, Sebastian crying as he held her, how she covered him with kisses, how he let her—I wanted to believe that I was mistaken. But the intimacy . . . I couldn't dispute the intimacy or convince myself otherwise. I'd defy anyone to.

I had rushed from the house when I realized he wasn't there, knowing I had to find him. Sophie and I had been so successful in keeping them apart, and everything was going so well; he was forgetting her, piece by piece, or so I thought. Something told me to go to "their" beach—how many times had I heard Adora crow about that?—and, yes, they were there. I swallowed hard when I saw their two figures, experienced a familiar sense of rejection, of unworthiness. As soon as Sebastian could, as soon as I was out of sight, he had run to her. I saw my entire future open up; a witness to a greater love I could play no part in, a shadow in my future husband's life.

If she hadn't covered him with kisses, maybe I wouldn't have given in to the whispers I'd been privy to about them, whispers I'd ignored as ridiculous, disgusting. I went over and

over it in my mind, furious with bitter hurt. It was inconceivable; it was irrational to believe what I thought I saw. I felt discarded, irrelevant. Adora had triumphed again, although what
kind of victory she'd secured was lost on me. The more I gave
in to my feelings of rejection, the more I gave myself license to
see something else on that beach; the more I convinced myself
why Adora and Sebastian needed to be alone together. And
then it all crystallized in front of me: I was repulsed, but I knew
not to rebuke Sebastian; he would not have known there was
anything wrong. After all, hadn't Adora gone out of her way to
tell me of their unique bond, how deeply they loved each other,
how she felt they had been born for each other. The idea that
she could have lured an innocent into such a depraved situation was evil, I thought. Sebastian's entire world was her. And if
she stayed, it would never be mine.

I turned away. I didn't need to see any more, anyway. I knew
what must happen.

People are so fond of asking others to forgive them for they
know not what they do. I've always differed in that regard; I've
always believed that we know exactly what we do and, more important, what might happen when we do it.

I can only imagine what Sophie saw as soon as she opened the
door. There was no color in my cheeks; I think I looked wild as I'd
run in the baking heat all the way back to the house. She led me
inside and went to fetch me a glass of water that I couldn't drink
or hold, my hands were shaking so terribly. I watched Sophie
hover around me, so kind, so like a mother, before she sat down
opposite me. What was left for me if I didn't have Sebastian? I

asked myself. Who would love me again? I was so overcome that I rushed over and burrowed my head in her lap, unable to stammer an explanation of what I had witnessed, torn completely between revealing everything and saying nothing. Yet when I felt her hand smooth my hair, experienced the comfort of being cared for after so long, the affection she showed me spurred me to the ultimate gamble. I wish I could say that, before I knew what I was doing, I heard the words come out of my mouth as if someone else were speaking them, but that's not true. I had rehearsed my lines all the way back to the house and, like an actress following her director's cue, I listened to my desires and told Sophie that I was going to leave. "I was foolish to ever imagine that somebody like Sebastian could love me. I cannot be involved in this. It's incomprehensible to any decent person."

Sophie stopped smoothing my hair, her hand suspended over my head. I didn't know if she was deciding whether to strike or soothe me. A deathly silence fell between us. I couldn't see Sophie's face to read her expression, and I was too scared to move. Everything hung in the balance.

"What are you trying to tell me, my dear child?" she finally asked, taking my face and turning it toward her. There was something about Sophie as she studied me that was terrifying. Her expression had set into a grim mask. "Speak to me now," she insisted, not harshly but firmly.

"I saw them together on the beach," I began. I sounded like a child protesting innocence while caught in the act of stealing. "*Their* beach. The one they always go to together that they never take anyone else to—"

"And what was it that you say you saw?" Sophie asked, moving me aside perfunctorily, albeit gently, and standing up and walking over to the window.

"I sa—I saw them kissing each other. They were lying together on the sand."

It felt suddenly stifling in the room, Sophie's drawing room filled with pale silk draperies and refined furniture, so delicate it looked as if it might break if you sat on it.

"It's not possible," she finally replied lightly, as if ordering something off a menu. "My children are not capable of what you say . . ." And the way she glanced at me, as if I were nothing, the way I was so often regarded, turned something in me. I wasn't going to walk away from this. I was going to make her believe.

I sat there in bewildered, broken disgust. "I *did* see it, and everybody talks about it all the time," I answered defiantly. "All I have ever done is love Sebastian. I am devoted to him. You know this. Why would I lie to you and ruin my whole life by having to leave? I've come to you because you are like a mother to me because I don't have one anymore. I have been happier these past few months than I ever have in my life. Haven't you seen me patiently deal with Adora, her constant presence? I have never, by word or deed, tried to turn Sebastian against her. But her influence is clearly something that I can't compete with. Anybody else, Sophie, would be repulsed and run away, but I haven't because I know it's not his fault. You know that the only way he will ever lead the type of life you long for for him is if he marries me. If he marries me—" I paused, calculating whether to continue. I had watched Sophie soften during my speech. I knew she was engaged in what I was saying. "—And if Adora leaves." I let the words hang between us.

It was clear to me, however, that Sophie had never suspected any such thing, hadn't grasped the extent of Adora's devotion. Yet when I suggested leaving, she shuddered, no doubt contemplating the life Sebastian would lead if I was not there.

"Miranda, I don't doubt that you think you saw something," Sophie finally responded. "But they are so very close and always have been; perfectly innocent things can be misinterpreted. I know how difficult it has been for you to try to find a role in Sebastian's life, and for that I owe you so much. But this?" She gasped, incredulously. "My children involved in this? My dear child," she continued sympathetically, "I am his mother, and I can assure you that there has *never* been a woman in Sebastian's life." Sophie assumed a more maternal, patronizing tone and delivered her final line decisively, as if in no doubt of what she knew to be true about her son. "My dear Miranda, he wouldn't know how—"

"Yes, he does," I replied quietly, before she even had time to draw breath. I raised my eyes to look at her, steadily, unblinking. "Yes, he does know." I laid myself bare. It was shameful to admit I wasn't a virgin, but I could sense she didn't judge me. I stood up from my submissive position as dutiful daughter-in-law-to-be and contemplated her as an equal. "And if, as you say, Sebastian has never had a girlfriend, then somebody else must have taught him."

"Oh God," Sophie remarked, doubling over, reaching out a hand to steady herself on the chair. "Oh dear God. I can't— It's impossible to ask me to—" she protested, looking up at me almost in an appeal.

"If Sebastian is ever to marry for love and even raise a family, then I trust you can see that Adora must leave. It's for the best." It took all my courage to deliver my ultimatum but, as I have so often justified, what other choice did I have?

Sophie's eyes were screwed tightly shut against her surroundings. I'll never know what went through her mind at the unfathomable choice she was presented with.

"Poor Sebastian," Sophie wept. "He will lose you and Adora. I can't imagine what this will do to him. He loves you so very much, so much more than anyone else. I know I can't ask anything of you. I feel so terribly guilty for involving you, even though I can't stand to believe this. Tell me again, are you sure?" She opened her eyes and stared directly at me. "Is there a doubt in your mind, Miranda?" she begged, despairingly.

I had feared she might throw me out of her home when I first arrived that day, especially considering the harrowing news I brought with me. Yet as I sat there, studying her distraught expression, I could tell that she had not closed the door on me. It was still ajar, that promised world of security and Sebastian and her, a family such as I had never known, waiting. All I had to do was say the right thing. I saw two lives open up in front of me: one with them and the other as an indentured servant to the overprivileged, of dingy rooms on the top floors of country houses, of insipid knocks on the door after everyone was asleep; of having to open the door or being destitute again; of stale alcohol and emotionless unions and of breakfast-time charades pretending to be something other than the whore who lived in the attic, the summer girl who entertained the children by day and, when no one was looking, their fathers by night.

"Yes, I'm sure," I said, and I meant it.

As soon as I said it, a steely reserve came over Sophie, a seamless transformation from broken mother to resolute guardian. "Then I'll send her away."

I doubt she even knew I was in the room anymore; it was the last time I ever saw her when she seemed young. She didn't turn around when I assured her that it was the right thing to do for Sebastian. I actually stayed for some time, trying to offer some consolation, as if any could be found after what I'd told her. It was only after I left that I realized, throughout everything I'd said, Sophie's gaze had been trained on the olive grove outside. Her tears falling to her feet as she watched unflinchingly the only place, she had once confided in me, where her children had ever been truly happy.

Adora

I can still hear the sound of your footfall on the steep stone steps as you climbed up into the world we had shared for the last time, the white butterflies fluttering in and out of the bougainvillea as you made your way toward me. You wore a pale blue shirt and the face of hope as you ascended the stairs, your face lighting up to find me waiting for you, just as I always had.

I was being sent away. "For the best," Mama had said, although she wouldn't even look at me or tell me why. You hadn't witnessed the terrible scene or heard the atrocious things Mama said to me about how I was destroying you with my selfishness, how I had stolen you from her when I was a child, made your life miserable with my possessiveness. She wouldn't listen to me when I tried to explain that I had only wanted to help, that you hated the sound of her tears. She had hit me, slapped me across the face, something she had never done; she told me that Miranda was going to break up with you if I stayed, that the only way your relationship could survive would be if I left forever. Nothing I could say would dissuade her. I was to leave you, never knowing if I would ever come back.

I was supposed to tell you that I was going away for a long,

long time. Despite how I had betrayed you by not accepting Miranda as I should have, Mama trusted me to do this. "He will only listen to you. And haven't you played that to your advantage," she remarked bitterly. "You make sure, if it's the last thing you do, that you let him go in peace. Make sure," she pressed, frightening me with her intensity, "that he never misses you for a second."

Sometimes pain is so overwhelming that it almost goes unrecognized by those who experience it. In spite of everything, I felt very little as I sat on the edge of the bed watching Mama rush about throwing my things into suitcases. What was happening was incomprehensible. Now I realize that everything in me died as soon as she confirmed my greatest fear: that I could no longer be near you. I drew a line through my entire life, something to be endured, not celebrated. To live without hope is death anyway; you were hope to me, Sebastian. I only had to look at you to be reminded of that: that kindness did exist somewhere, that sometimes it is in the simplest, most ordinary places that we find our home.

Did I know then, as I stood at the top of the steps on that last day of summer, that I would always wait there for you? That I would forever search beyond the faces of the guests as they arrived at our house to see if, perhaps, you were the last visitor coming up behind them? That I would wait for the sound of your footfall on the steps, coming home to me, for the rest of my life?

I will never forget your happiness as you kissed me good morning. It was almost as if you had grown into a man overnight. The delicious delicacy of youth that haunted your perfect face was still there; you would always, I knew, be young like that. Yet there was something more; a pride had taken hold, an

expectation of the future and what it might give you, a realization that you were worth something because you were loved by
Miranda, and because of what that meant. You had arrived at
your future, and you seemed to stand in front of it in astonishment that you had ever accomplished such a marvel and gratitude that it belonged to you.

Nothing extraordinary happened that morning; we performed our rituals of breakfasting and playing with the dogs
just as we always had. It was exactly like any other day we'd
shared together. Yet as I watched you talk and laugh and look to
me for the assurance I would no longer be able to give you, I
prayed Miranda would always protect you, would never let you
hear the spiteful things people said about you; would know
better than to disturb you when you went off with our dogs
somewhere; would always greet you first thing in the morning
with the brightest of smiles, the warmest of good mornings;
would let you rest your head on her shoulder in the hammock,
allowing nothing of the real world to filter into your conversation, nothing of war, of death, of brokenhearted people. I hoped
she would keep you safe in the Elysium we had shared together—for there was no place for you in the real world, Sebastian. You could exist in all of your simplicity and grace only in
an enchanted realm protected by quiet angels, our dogs, whose
simple, defenseless souls asked nothing of you but the love that
shone from you in everything you did.

I said very little to you, Sebastian; I just listened for a
change. I thought I would die of love as you told me about what
you would do the next day and the day after that. I didn't travel
there with you; I stayed with you in the moment during which
we lived our last seconds together, admiring everything you had
become, mourning everything I would miss.

Yet I knew I would defy Mama. I couldn't tell you I was leaving and never coming back. All I had ever longed for was your happiness, Sebastian, and you were so content. How could I have upset you? I had only ever tried to save you from tears.

"I'm going to the beach later," you said. "Titania will come; she's like you, she goes with me everywhere. She swims like a dolphin too."

I smiled; I didn't tell you that Titania was nesting, about to have another litter of puppies. I chose to leave that as a surprise for you, after I went away.

"What are you going to do?"

I turned to the sea behind me, closed my eyes, and tilted my face up to the sun, drinking in our island, its fragrance, the touch of its particular breeze, the sounds I had thought always to hear. "I'm going to think of you, Sebastian," I replied, "and how much I love you."

I felt you come up behind me and give me a quick hug. I hadn't said anything out of the ordinary; you had heard me say such things every day of your life. This last day had to be like any other, so I let you rush off down the stairs to the car waiting to take you to the beach, and I wasn't going to watch you leave, but then I heard you call my name and I knew that I had to turn to see you in the driveway, that I would never forgive myself for avoiding a memory of you. You were standing by the car, the sun on your hair, the cool morning light enveloping you in a peaceful mist of pale blue and golden white. You were holding something in your hand. At first, I was unsure if you were beckoning to me or waving me off. What I did know was that you looked heroic, like a soldier ready to fight or rather, I realize now, ready to live. It was only when I looked closer that

I realized you were holding a stem of bougainvillea in your hand, holding it out to me. And unable to help myself, I rushed down the stairs to where you waited for me, Sebastian, and felt the incomparable blessing of your kindness as you placed it behind my ear with the care and gentleness of an angel for the last time.

And then the car took you away from me down the winding road to the coves of our childhood, which ended that day; to the blinding white beaches and the forgiving sea that once muffled the sounds of all our sorrows, that once cradled us together in the blissful silence of the deepest love.

Sophie

Sebastian had been my gift to myself. That I was trying to have a child, his father had no idea. The life of a politician's wife can be a solitary one. After the excitement of banquets and travel had dissipated, I longed for something for myself, something more substantial than lunches and dinners in opulent surroundings bedecked in jewels to sustain me. I had never desired anything more. When Sebastian was given to me, I understood why I had been born. That he was mine forever was my only thought.

Some people would have given him away when they realized. There were places, even then, for such children, where they could be hidden. He was late in everything he did: to speak, to walk, to pick out colors, to understand regardless of how slowly or carefully we spoke the simplest of requests. There are parents who would have turned away, unable to confront their own failure; but I defy anyone who ever saw my son to forget him. Had he not been mine, I would have begged his real family to give him to me. I have always believed that the souls of children like Sebastian find us, whether they are born of us or enter our lives through circumstance or need. And that a child as divine as Sebastian chose me to be his mother is the greatest honor of my life.

His life was commonplace, his tragic death a twist many others have suffered in an ordinary existence led by a very simple boy. And that was our secret, what his beauty made up for, disguised, what was not immediately apparent to anyone who met him; Sebastian was, like Adora said, born half asleep. He could count, he could read to a degree; he could sit amiably with guests and answer easy questions, attentively listening to all that they said; he could tell you every name and story connected to his dogs and carefully smooth the ground with his hands to provide a place for them to sleep; he could turn to you in the morning light with such abundant trust that made you flinch with gratitude that such a person existed in such a malicious, unfeeling world. He could, if the right, patient girl came along, perhaps marry and live an easy, undemanding life with someone who was grateful simply to find a gentle soul who would not hurt her, who was able to provide financial security, asking for nothing except her bright smile to comfort him in his confusion.

It was no great love affair, such as we conspired to make out; it was a deal I was prepared to broker for my son. I didn't blame Miranda, though; from what she had told us, the girl had led a dreadful existence before she met Sebastian. I didn't consider it a sin for her to grab what sliver of happiness could be found in her dismal life and cleave to it in the absence of any kind of real hope. In the final analysis, at best, her prize was a boy who would never be able to truly fulfill the role of a husband to any degree of complexity. But I believed that, although there were girls like Miranda around every corner—mistreated, dying of disappointment more quickly than the rest of us—she did genuinely love him, but as one might a damaged child, we both of us understood that. Her love was borne of being saved from destitution.

Some people have been horrified that I was so pragmatic. Yet what else was there for Sebastian? Part of him was just missing somewhere, in a place we could never find. He lost out on so much of life because he couldn't comprehend anything beyond his immediate environment. Had Miranda not met him, I knew that she would have been seduced and ruined, no doubt, by one of the drunken husbands who preyed on her like vultures; an easy mark, discardable, not really one of them anymore. I did not believe her to be an opportunist or an unkind girl; Miranda was unfortunate. I thought that the best she could ever do was to marry an uncomplicated soul, divine though he was, and make the most of it. And that is why I loved her, because she was grateful for so little and because, thanks to her gratitude, my little boy was afforded as normal a life as his limitations would allow. I couldn't have asked for more.

I held Adora entirely responsible for everything that happened. I don't know that it is so very unusual for daughters and mothers to be rivals, especially when it comes to love. I just think that very few people would be straightforward enough to admit it. For me, there is no point in acting coy now. I've come across a few who resent their daughters for being the apples of their fathers' eyes, yet I doubt any of them ever had to endure what Miranda had divulged about the depth of Adora's affection for her brother. What Miranda had told me was unfathomable, and even though I knew it was impossible I could have ever overlooked such a thing, I was forced to ask myself, what did I know of my children really? They were never with me, they were always away together and, although I had tried to intervene, I had allowed it, in a sense. As soon as I realized my own culpability, I recognized that, by trying to love Sebastian, I had harmed him. Miranda was right; the only way my son could ever enjoy a fulfilling marriage was if I sent Adora away. I had only Miranda's word to go on, but she had no reason to lie; as Miranda had beseeched, what would she gain if she left?

Yet more than that, as unpalatable as it is to admit, something in me wanted an excuse to be free of Adora, for Sebastian's sake as well as her own. Her love was crippling him. She didn't realize the pain she caused her brother; her self-pity was too acute. In her attempt to help him, she ignored the signs of his distress. At parties or dinners, Sebastian never lost sight of her, watching as if for a sign that she might accept his choice in Miranda. He needed Adora so. So much of the unhappiness of his relationship was caused by the fact that he could no longer share anything with his sister. I expect it was inevitable that, after the initial exhilaration of the new, he would turn to the past for stability. Yet Adora's constant meddling went too far, beyond the realms of decency apparently. I had no option but to send her away. Because I loved my son more. Because I wanted to keep him for myself.

After she left, he would often say, "I miss her. I can't find her anywhere. I shall just have to tell myself that she is hiding." As the days progressed, however, Sebastian really did come to believe this; he had poor skills when it came to remembering things, so I didn't doubt that he had forgotten what I had instructed Adora to tell him. However, it was more than that; he appeared to regress dramatically without her; often unable to

articulate even the simplest things, falling frequently into a bewildered state neither Miranda nor I could penetrate. I had sent
Adora to another island, quite close to ours, to stay with friends
from Paris, who would take her there at the summer's end. Sebastian had no memory of it, however, so Miranda and I used
to jolly him along whenever he asked; as he began to more and
more, "I still can't find her; where is Adora hiding, Mama?"

"Where do you think she's hiding, Sebastian?" one of us
would ask, playing a little game to keep him from becoming
upset. He would think about it for a while, but always he failed
to find an answer, and sometimes, he would say something terribly sad like "I don't know; Adora always used to tell me where
she was" or "Adora always knew where everyone was and where
I should be." And it was at such times that I would have to fight
very hard to convince myself that I had made the right decision.

On the occasions that he did manage to rouse himself from
his confusion, all he wanted to talk about with us was his sister.
We lunched every day as we always did on the veranda; the
only difference was Adora's absence. At first, I tried to engage
him, allowing little stories about Adora to be told, but Miranda
began to lose patience over time. She did try at first to present
a pleasant face whenever my daughter was mentioned, if only
for Sebastian. Yet Miranda was not a saint, and I accepted that
there was little reason for her to fondly reminisce over a girl
who had so desperately tried to destroy her happiness. I
thought her very much like me in that she could not conceal
her true emotions; the expressions on her face gave away everything as the memory of the hurt my daughter had caused blis-
tered to the surface over time. At the end, she would meet the
mere mention of Adora's name with barely concealed disgust. I

tried to appease her, but it was clear that my daughter had been no friend to Miranda, and it was impossible for me defend Adora's actions. Besides, I couldn't bear to have Miranda leave after everything. . . . For her sake, whenever Sebastian would start to say something about Adora, I would place a hand on his and quietly shake my head. "Later, darling. Tell me later," I would say. I could see that he didn't understand, and I actually thought that for the best too. Better to let Adora's memory fade by never speaking of her. But Sebastian was no fool. He was capable of so very little, but he did know that whenever I promised "later," it never came.

I live with the knowledge that I failed him entirely. As soon as Miranda and I excluded Adora completely from our conversations, indeed our lives, Sebastian's decline into that helpless state from which only my daughter had ever been able to rouse him began.

We tried everything to get through to him, frantically searching for things to do, our bright smiles frozen on our faces, terrified to switch them off for fear of what it might do to him. He became more and more withdrawn, uncommunicative, seeking out only the company of his dogs. And whenever we asked, "Sebastian, what did you do today?" he would invariably reply, "I looked for Adora, but I still can't find where she's hiding."

I had no sense of foreboding, only worry. Yet Miranda differed from me in that regard; she knew. She clung to Sebastian those last days of his life as if knowing she could not keep him, as if accepting that, as far as she had gone to remove Adora from his life, she would always be second best. As much as Miranda had permitted me to peek behind the curtain to her true self, we understood one another. I perceived a quiet acceptance in her, an innate comprehension of life's uncertainty, which made her always appear thankful for each shred of joy she was given. At best, the three and a half months of their affair was but a morsel in the feast of life. So few people would ever have undertaken such a thankless role. It is bittersweet to think that that was, for her, the best of it—of life. I know for a fact that she has been starving ever since.

I sometimes see young people, of the ages they were when they met, and they seem so much like children to me now, mere babies. Always I find myself mesmerized by the delirium of such lovers, able to recall the ecstasy of first love, the glorious prospects of a future. And then I experience the blow of realizing that what they need most is protection: older, wiser eyes and ears to guide them away from disappointment, everything, in short, that I didn't provide for my son.

From the fact that he knew such love before he died I can sometimes take comfort. It is like a salve on my burning heart. When he walked into the sea that day, he was surrounded by love in all the different guises it can assume: unconditional, intimate, obsessive. He was only a boy of twenty, not yet completely filled out, his face splendidly youthful. Had I been a better mother, had he never had a sister, he might not have gone off that day. But I wasn't a better mother. And I have lived with that knowledge ever since.

He came to me the morning he left us, terribly upset, and found me in my bedroom.

"I can't remember the rhyme, Mama," he said, his confusion evident in his uncombed hair and the rumpled clothes he had clearly thrown on. "I stayed awake all last night trying to remember it. Adora used to sing it to me, and I can't find her to sing it to me again."

"Sit with me," I said, opening my arms to him. He came and laid his head in my lap the way he used to when he was eleven, when he would come to find me even though I was mad and too unnerving for even his sister to be around. Yet still he came to me. I was his mother.

I knew what rhyme he spoke about. It was actually a poem, Guillaume Apollinaire's "*L'Adieu.*" He was five and my daughter three when I taught it to them. That I once thought such a sad, sad piece was appropriate for two babies I will never understand. So intense was my zeal to surround them with culture that I forgot how young they were; whenever they came home with paintings from school, I would pull out my art books to find something reminiscent of what they had created. I can still recall Sebastian's wonder when the sludge green mess of brushstrokes he presented to me with such pride was quickly compared to one of Picasso's early Cubist masterpieces. I wanted him to feel special. To accomplish that, there were other ways. If I had stopped thinking and loved them as I should have, I might have filled their minds with innocence instead of ruminations on death. Too late now to ponder all my shortcomings; only the poem remains, the one I sang for him, as Adora used to, the morning he died:

J'ai cueilli ce brin de bruyère
L'automne est morte souviens-t'en
Nous ne nous verrons plus sur terre

Odeur du temps brin de bruyère
Et souviens-toi que je t'attends

I've gathered this sprig of heather
Autumn is dead you will remember
On earth we'll see no more of each other
Fragrance of time sprig of heather
Remember I wait for you forever

When they were children, they thought heather was bougainvillea, as no such flower could possibly bloom in the heat of our island. I thought it so very enchanting when Sebastian brought Adora the fuchsia bougainvillea stem and placed it behind her ear, thinking it the flower from the poem, not understanding at all the significance. He was five years old. I reveled in the scene, experiencing that familiar, all-encompassing wave of love his simple, childish acts inspired in me. Adora refused to remove the flower from her hair, even at bedtime. When she awoke the next day, it was crushed and ruined. So he raced out of the house and returned to her with another one, like a young Lancelot, swelling with pride at her delight. Everything we had then, we had in abundance: love, flowers, the years of our lives stretching out into infinity until that terrible day when my son, without Adora to guide him, made his choice.

Immediately, he was relieved. The smile returned to his lips, the brightness to his eyes, and I recall feeling so proud that I had restored his happiness, at last. Everything would be fine, I told myself. The path we had struggled to find through his depression of the previous weeks became clear: now and then, when he needed me, as he so clearly did, he would come to me and I would help him. If I ever saw him fall into a somber mood, I would ask him—when Miranda was not around—what he needed me to tell him and he would be well again. I rejoiced that the spell was finally broken. Sebastian had been released from Adora's influence and, in her stead, he had sought me and I had succeeded in helping him. For so many years, only Adora had been afforded that privilege. Now it was mine.

"Oh, Mama . . . I know, I know, Mama," he said slowly, stopping at the door. "I *know*," he repeated with more excitement, as if he had come across the most important discovery he could ever imagine. "I know where she's hiding now!"

"You do, Sebastian?" I asked, thrilled that he'd finally remembered where she'd gone, softening at the wonder he exuded at having accomplished something all by himself. I wanted to jump up and smother him with kisses because he was so adorable, alive and young, with everything to hope for, but I knew he would be embarrassed, so I simply exclaimed, "You're so clever."

"That's what Adora says," he said proudly, smiling his final smile for me and taking Titania and going out through the hall. I assumed he was going to meet Miranda. But he wasn't. And it was the last time I ever witnessed wonder in Sebastian, the last time I could have ever held him to my heart and told him that he was the reason I was born.

That afternoon was perfect. Can anyone know what it is like for a mother to finally fulfill her role for her most cherished child? To feel of use again? For years, I felt as if I'd been forced to watch my son grow from behind a glass window, unable to call through it, to reach out and touch him. Such astonished joy filled all of that day. I even softened toward Adora when I realized that no real damage had been done. I couldn't wait for dinner: Miranda, Sebastian, and I all together, all united in the marvelous future we would share.

But Sebastian didn't come to dinner. And he didn't come home that night. And the next morning, he was still nowhere to be found. I tried to reassure Miranda that he used to do this when he was younger, disappear for days only to reappear, restored and alive, a new dog with him. Yet something in me, as much as I prayed otherwise, sensed this wasn't the same.

I remember experiencing a terrible sense of foreboding when a neighbor, who had met Sebastian on the beach shortly after he would have left me, remarked that he had asked him where he was going and Sebastian had replied, "To be with Adora. I know where she's hiding." The man had never seen him look so happy and had stayed watching as Sebastian ran into the sea and swam as far out as the horizon. The man had returned home for lunch quite buoyed by what he had witnessed and had enjoyed a lengthy conversation with his wife about the remarkable *petit voleur* who had grown up into such a superb young man.

I sent word to Adora immediately, hoping, although I knew it was impossible, that he'd found a way to her. Of course, Sebastian wasn't with her, had made no contact with her. I was beside myself. What have I done? I asked myself. And then it came to me as I caught my reflection in the glass, the why of everything, the reason he had run off, what I had said to cause him to leave us:

Remember I wait for you forever.

I heard Adora's voice in my memory that dreadful day when I sent her away; I heard her plead with me to understand how they used to hide in the sea because he could never bear to hear the sound of my tears, why she always used to say, "My brother lives in the sea, like a dolphin," to make him think that it was a lovely thing instead of an act of desperation to save him from me and my relentless grief.

Remember I wait for you forever.

It was one of the last things I ever said to my son. Clever me, I had thought at the time, marvelous me; I have saved my son from despair. Oh, but I had done nothing of the sort. I had ignored everything about my children—even the son I professed to love the most all of my life. What I had done by reciting that exquisite poem, just as he asked, was to lead my precious child to his death. Sebastian thought Adora was hiding in the sea, waiting for him.

The villagers rowed out in their fishing boats with lanterns, calling for him in the vain hope that he might still be alive, but I knew everything was over, all at an end. I realized the moment I discovered the dogs were not in the olive grove; I knew, without being told, that they had followed him. We found them lined up on the shore, framed by the sunset, watching the horizon as the light died as if guardians of my son's choice. They stayed at their post for two days. They kindled the wish, as I did quite in spite of myself, that the simple boy who loved them the most might come running out from behind the waves to greet them as he so often had in life. And that hope, like mine, drained from their trusting eyes, slowly but surely, as the minutes ticked by and the sea kept my son's new home a secret. As soon as Adora stepped off the boat from the neighboring island where I had sent her, she ran to their favorite beach to join the dogs in their vigil and, thereafter, the whole village came to mourn at the edge of the sea, behind Adora and her pets, for her brother who had drowned and the Summer Queen dying without him in front of them, tears spilling without end down her perfect face, which had seen and cherished only the best in Sebastian.

The dogs were all saying good-bye, their eyes trained on the waters that owned him, knowing that, when they turned away, all sight of him would be lost forever. But they did not all follow him as Adora had once promised they would; only Titania, his favorite, who died in her sleep at Adora's feet on the beach the day we gave up the search. In the aftermath of death, when consolation is most needed, I was left with the unbearable realization that his beloved dogs had not loved him the most, after all. It was Adora they followed back to the house, the body of Sebastian's beloved Titania in her arms, where they returned to the olive grove to wait for her each evening and her ritual walks to the edge of the cliff, watching over the sea that owned her brother.

I am a romantic woman. Like they did, I watch it, too, the shifting shape of the waves somehow reminiscent of my son. It is the only place I can be near him, because we never found his body. It is as if Sebastian willed himself to stay forever out of our reach but always in view, a part of the beauty that surrounds us, a reminder of the splendor that once was: a gift, waiting for us forever.

Adora

You died at sunset on a Sunday. That is when they gave up the search. The previous Friday you had walked out into the cool, still water of a September evening and swam until you were so exhausted the current pulled you under. You did not fight or struggle to resurface for one last look at the island you loved so much. You simply closed your eyes and let the waves close over your curls, their touch a comforting relief.

I convinced myself that I took the gift of life from you. Death was your only means of escape. Whenever I would think of you walking down to the beach we loved the most, it was as if a breeze blew through me, enervating my nerves, suffocating me with what I knew happened next. I would try to imagine what went through your mind as you walked down the road, understanding exactly what you were about to do, knowing nothing about what might happen. I later learned from kindhearted individuals that it takes an inordinate amount of courage to kill oneself. This awareness tainted my image of you on that Friday evening. I tried to imagine you as Hercules, striding forward, preparing to meet the destiny you had planned; in control, perfect, completely alive.

But then the image would die with the excruciating truth of my own actions, and I would be forced to accept that you approached that sea like a defeated man, yearning only for oblivion.

It is inconceivable that I should ever have left you alone. I still cannot bring myself to consider you as anything less than magnificent. To suggest otherwise belies the sparks of awe you inspired in all who knew you, despite your lapses into a sadness nobody save I could rouse you from.

Since I was a tiny girl and the inception of your changing moods that caused such worry to Mama, I had sought to heal you only with love, throwing my arms around you and clinging for as long as you would let me. As I grew older and more aware of the signs of your illness, I kept a constant vigil. It was not a trial for me to constantly watch you. I would have done anything for you, except leave you alone to discover a life beyond the narrow margins of the safety net I had spun around us. I could not allow it because I knew what might happen. The horrific episodes of your running away for days on end resulted solely, I believed, from my failure to protect you.

I realize now that you were not so ill that you could not survive without constant guardianship. You can perhaps forgive me for thinking otherwise. With being your sole companion, I had come to depend on you entirely. What had begun as sibling love grew to encompass an adult need never to be apart from you. Without you, I faltered or felt I did. I manipulated the lessons of our childhood for my own selfish gain. If I was prevented from witnessing my reflection in your blue eyes, from seeing the love you held for me, I had no idea who to be.

Nothing had ever changed for us on the tiny island that was

our home. We both should have known that things would. Perhaps if our world had consisted of more than the two of us, we might have been able to cope with the addition of the new. As such, we failed miserably, and my lack of maturity and worldliness resulted in my losing you forever.

Miranda

Later, after Sebastian died, when Sophie told me why, I couldn't cope. Everything we had ever shared, the recriminations, what I had put Sebastian through haunted me every minute of every day. I wept in Sophie's arms each afternoon, terrified that I simply could not stop crying or tormenting myself with what I had done. Sophie refused to let me destroy myself with regrets. We had done everything for him, she insisted, and that was what we must always tell ourselves: It was for the best, how could either of us possibly have known what would happen?

Besides, there was no doubt anymore that Adora had caused his death. She hadn't told Sebastian where she was going when Sophie sent her away. Typically, she had thought only of herself. That was why he went to find her; he thought she was hiding in the sea where they used to play. Oh, poor Sophie; when she had to tell me this . . . she could barely speak. Sophie told me that she had almost forgiven Adora, if such a thing were possible, until Adora confided her greatest regret. She actually asked her mother to forgive her for killing Sebastian, because she believed that was what she'd done; not because he'd gone to find her but because she'd left him in the first place; because her meddling, which she claimed was only to help Sebastian, had forced her mother to send her away, prompting her brother's terrible depression, which only she had ever been able to help him with. Arrogant to the end, Adora believed that Sebastian had killed himself because he simply couldn't live without her and would rather die. When I learned things like this from Sophie, my feelings of remorse waned. Adora was right; she had done everything to herself.

"You didn't tell Adora that he'd gone to find her in the sea?" I asked Sophie. She didn't reply at first, just shook her head slightly, no.

"She did kill him, Miranda. That's the point," she said finally. "It's all the same thing, her obsession, the nonsense she instilled in him about how they couldn't live without each other. If only she'd told him where she was going, he would never have gone looking for her and drowned. Let her believe that her dreadful behavior was the cause of his death, that she caused his depression because I was forced to send her away—it's all true! For years, I allowed her passion free rein, and I will forever reproach myself because it cost me my son. My every instinct told me to intervene when they were children, but I did not. Adora must own the guilt of Sebastian's death; she must never be allowed to do anything like this again. She must understand what her skewed devotion has cost everyone. I won't tell her, because if she knew the truth then she'd hold me accountable for sending her away. Adora would never see that I simply had no choice. I won't forgive her, Miranda. All of this is her fault."

If it were not for Sophie and her unwavering sense of justice after he died, I might have crucified myself for helping to push Sebastian to his death. Sophie made sure that would never happen, for either of us. Adora's confession exonerated us, and that was what we chose to believe.

I stayed on the island at Sophie's insistence. I didn't have anywhere else to go, and it was inconceivable that someone in my position would ever have found a decent home anywhere else.

I was pregnant, you see.

I was terrified to tell her, especially considering that I had known for around three months before Sebastian died and may not have been able to hide it much longer. Yet Sophie did not cast me out when I confided in her; she promised to care for my unborn child and me so that we would never want for anything. I was so relieved; I never wanted to leave Sophie, who was kinder to me than I had a right to expect. I was frightened that, if I ever did leave, I might not return, that I would be an exile. Every day we relived memories of Sebastian. We reminisced over everything we had ever done together, as short a time as it was. We smiled through our tears at everything he had meant to us. She became my real mother, not a substitute anymore. She told me that I would always be a daughter to her, even though Sebastian was gone.

I was spared from ever having to see Adora. Sophie sent her off the island immediately after Sebastian's death, despite how Adora begged to stay. She went to Paris, where photographers had clamored to photograph her ever since a local journalist had forwarded pictures of her when she was crowned the Summer Queen two years earlier. Adora had shown no interest in ever leaving the island, bound as she was to Sebastian but, after his death, Sophie insisted that there was nothing to keep

her there and Adora meekly submitted. She was an instant success, lauded right, left, and center. I learned all about her ac-
claim from the letters she wrote to Sophie—not that she read
them, preferring to rip them up and toss them in the bin,
where I retrieved them. Sophie never discussed Adora. Nor did
I. It was as if she no longer existed.

I never envied Adora for her good fortune. It struck me as
meaningless compared to what had been lost. She never visited, except for once around the Christmas after Sebastian
died. Sophie didn't want her back, which was a relief. It made
everything so much easier. She refused to allow her in the
house, meeting her in a café in town. I had not left the house in
a number of months so that no one would see I was pregnant.
As overjoyed as Sophie was at the prospect of being a grandmother, my child would have never survived the stigma of
being born illegitimate, so until she could decide what to do for
the best, I remained cloistered in the villa, with only her
trusted housekeeper for company.

Sophie did find a solution—James, whom she had met
while he was vacationing on the island. I never asked why she
considered him the best candidate, nor did she ever divulge
quite how she knew he would be amenable to what she was
prepared to ask. All I knew was that she found him, invited him
to the villa over Christmas, watched as a burgeoning friendship
developed between us, and then took care of everything. James
proposed to me in the new year.

I wasn't so naïve as not to think Sophie had some hand in
it, but I was so grateful I didn't ask any questions. Later, I discovered James had a price, a handsome one, it transpired.
Enough to help him set up his own law practice in England
and more than enough to enable him to lie about me to his

family. It wasn't a particularly pleasant story; no explanation about doing the right thing ever is. I was forced to accept that I would always be looked down upon by his mother and father for submitting, as the story went, so willingly to him when we first met and becoming pregnant immediately, forcing him to do the gentlemanly thing. So James stayed on with me — something that was not particularly difficult, as he had lost his job in England before he came to the island for a Christmas break — for almost a year, until we could feasibly return. We claimed that Genevieve had been born prematurely in July 1920, when, in fact, she was born in March of that year, but we waited long enough before leaving that the nearly four-month age difference wasn't as apparent and held our breath and prayed for the best.

Looking back to when I first met James, I thought him so affable and guileless; I was astonished when he was prepared to take me on. I almost felt guilty. James, so unlike me, saw the best in everyone and, in the beginning, his inability to judge people was a godsend. When I found out he had a price, I wasn't exactly disappointed, as my genuine affection for him was borne of gratitude, not love, and even the story we concocted didn't bother me unduly. After all, it was true; I had fallen in love and submitted quickly to Gigi's father, the only difference being who he really was and who we claimed him to be. Yet I did hope that James and I could have a good marriage. I wanted us to bring out the best in each other, for Gigi's sake above all things.

Yet Sophie was prepared to accept all of the luck that had come our way in the shape of James as a gift from Sebastian, protecting his child in some way, and I was happy to let her believe it. Naturally, there was more to my husband than met the eye—nobody just agrees to marry a single pregnant woman without some motive. While I feared initially he might be a sadist, tyrannical behind closed doors, the truth was rather more prosaic: He was hopeless with money and, beyond a few clumsy forays in the early years of our marriage, resolutely celibate. I kept this to myself; I never burdened Sophie with it, but I did often question if she had an inkling as to James' true proclivities, if that was why she picked him.

Of course, James's secret only truly became apparent to me when he agreed to Oliver's request that we not have more children, when I began to grasp precisely why he deferred to Oliver in everything—simply to be near him, to worship him under the guise of friendship, protected from suspicion by me, his wife. I let it go; what was the point in dwelling on it? After all, I had been desired enough in my life, and all it had ever led to was trouble, so it wasn't so difficult to live without that kind of affection, although it did take some time for me to accept that. Everything had worked out for the best. Of course, there was still the problem of Adora; yet Sophie promised never to tell her about the child. "My God," she exclaimed with a shudder, "can you imagine what she would do if she thought Gigi was Sebastian's child? It's unthinkable." I couldn't have agreed more.

It was time to move on. I had to put Sebastian away, although his memory haunted every aspect of my day. My time on the island with Sophie had helped me to deal with such a terrible experience. Remembering him, as painful as it had been, had kept me close to him. Yet I began to understand that, without Sebastian, I would never have found the peace I did with James, who asked nothing of me and whom I did not need to look after in the same way. I began to make plans for

the future again, relieved that the past was not going to affect
it as I had so feared it might. I had matured under Sophie's
guidance, learned to accept the things I could not change. I
thought I would never make the same mistakes again. I felt
alive again for the first time since I met Sebastian. I had spent
so long living in fear, however, that I was content to simply accept the luck that had come my way and enjoy myself at long
last.

The following Christmas, of 1920, just before we returned
to England, James's best friend wrote to say that he was returning to the island and would love to meet up with us both. I was
excited to meet Oliver, looking forward to sharing James's life
with him. James was so keen for me to meet him, too, and eager
to meet Oliver's new girlfriend, the "mystery woman" as he re-
ferred to her. He was always so full of stories about Oliver; they
were clearly as close as brothers. James seemed to worship
him. I found it sweet, at first, long before I knew precisely why.
James had been rather discarded by Oliver, who had taken off
after the girl he was still with the day after he met her the previous Christmas, leaving only a note to say not to worry and
that he would be back in a few weeks. Those few weeks had
turned into a year. That was actually how Sophie came to meet
James. He was at a loose end and went to eat in a café, which
was where they found each other.

I can still recall James holding the door to the bar open for
me and feeling a warm sense of safety as I walked in, waiting
for him to identify Oliver and introduce me, his new wife. And
then I saw Adora, and I felt ill at the terrible memories the
mere sight of her evoked. For a moment, I simply hoped that
she was there by chance. I had no intention of acknowledging
her. I remember the look of shock on her face, which she, as

ever, masterfully concealed when her boyfriend, Oliver, my husband's best friend, called over to James.

I noticed immediately the ring on her engagement finger as I walked toward where she sat, as stunning as ever. I waited for her to explain that she already knew me. But she did not. And neither did I. At the time, I simply thought that there was no fight left in her. It was only later when I realized that I had allowed her to dictate how things would be in our new lives. I had followed her lead. The future I had been foolish enough to consider a right receded before me as I finally assumed my original role as the handmaid to the Queen.

Adora

She did not leave, as I thought she might. Instead she stayed on over the winter and for the next year. I was saved from witnessing her sorrow because I was away, my career having taken off immediately after your death. There was no one I could turn to after your death, nobody who would forgive me. As with you, Miranda assumed my role as a daughter, replacing me.

They excluded me, Mama and Miranda. It was obvious that they didn't want me there. Why would they? I believed that I had killed you with my selfishness. If I hadn't made you love me so much, you would never have taken your own life. I made you think that you couldn't live without me, and so you took your life rather than live in a world where I was not near you.

The following year, when I learned that Miranda had married quite suddenly and would be leaving our island for what I thought would be forever, I'm ashamed to say I felt pleased. I cowered in the face of my conscience, wracked with shame for what I had stolen from her, the devastation I had caused. Her husband, however, turned out to be Oliver's best friend, James.

Unbeknownst to one another, we had been romanced by best friends. Neither of us could escape the other.

We never revealed that we knew one another. We simply neglected to mention your name. Your light receded from our present into the past of which we would never speak. Mama played along with us, refusing to do anything to jeopardize Miranda's happiness. Besides, she refused to discuss you with anyone except Miranda, even me, her own daughter, so it was unlikely she would ever have said anything in any case. Oliver was none the wiser.

We slipped you into a drawer, Sebastian, hid you behind a curtain, concealed you at our backs, the ghost of what had been our happiest days. Yet still you lingered in the glances between us if ever we found ourselves at a place we had once all visited together, or if a song played on the radio that we had danced to. The time to be friends had arrived; the appearance of which was crucial for us to uphold. It was seemingly easier for me than Miranda, because I had more. James was the ever-adoring servant to Oliver's regal presence and I, elevated to royalty by association with the hero of his peers.

We displayed such restraint over the years, careful never to create suspicion. I kept my silence about how I knew her because I was crippled with remorse at what I had done. I had killed my own brother; nobody would have wanted me had they known. I lived in fear that Miranda would tell James, who would tell Oliver, but it never happened. It was the secret Miranda, my mother, and I shared.

I never once blamed Miranda for not understanding how to help you. I accepted the responsibility for your death as mine alone. I did this for you, Sebastian; because you loved her and, were it not for me, you could have been happy. We had always loved the same things; I put my own feelings aside for you; I did everything for you. So you must understand, then, why I had to take Gigi, why I had to keep her near me. Because, in spite of the effort Miranda made to conceal the truth from me, I knew. And yet because of your love for her, I never told a soul.

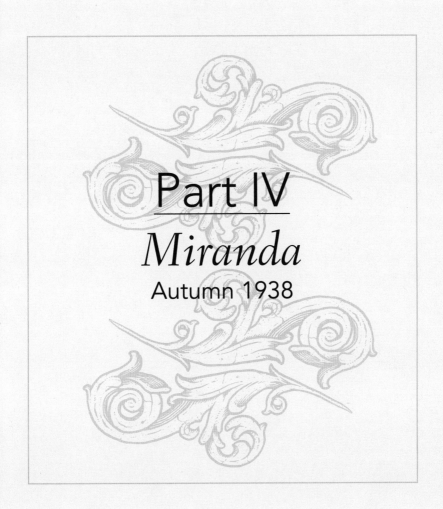

Part IV
Miranda
Autumn 1938

Sophie

As I concluded the tragic history of my family, it was evident that Genevieve mistrusted me, which was entirely appropriate given her love for Adora. For the hours or days or months it would take for her to reconcile everything I had sought to teach her, I cared little. That she knew the truth about Adora—how Adora had manipulated everyone so mercilessly and why she had stolen the boy Genevieve loved—was all that mattered that afternoon. For Miranda's sake, I was desperate that history not repeat itself. Yet in the context of the previous hours' revelations, nothing was straightforward. To brutally interrogate her past, to accept nothing had been real: that was what I asked of Genevieve. It was not inconceivable to me that she could not yet bring herself to believe that the woman she adored was capable of such malice.

To be loved as unconditionally by someone as beguiling, as passionate as my daughter awoke not only a desire in her but a lust for more. In her friendless world, all Genevieve had was Adora. She had learned to love within the walls of her Beloved Aunt's prison. Her inability to accept that the idol of her dreams could be anything less than perfect highlighted to me then only how well she had been educated by Adora.

For Miranda's sake alone, I revealed everything—up to a point. It would have served no one, least of all Miranda, to tell Genevieve that Sebastian was her father. She did not deserve to lose everything she held dear for a second time. How I pitied Miranda's isolation—what she had been forced to tolerate over the years: Adora's singular obsession with her daughter. Cruelly aware that Genevieve would never believe any criticism leveled at Adora, what Miranda must have thought when she met Jack for the first time defied comprehension; an agony I understood only too well.

Yet unlike her mother, Genevieve had not held fast to the man she did not yet realize how much she loved. She had inherited Miranda's pride, but she had taken it to an extreme, dismissing the boy who told the truth in favor of the woman who lied. It was apparent to me that Gigi lacked her mother's innate understanding of people and, again, having been educated to an exceptionally high standard by my daughter, had chosen to think only of Adora. I did not envy Genevieve the realization that would surely come when she put the pieces of the summer's puzzle together and recognized in Adora everything she loathed in people. Nor did I wish to think of her disgrace when she understood how completely she had betrayed her mother, who had loved her beyond words.

I told Genevieve what I knew of Jack: the look I had distinguished in my daughter's eyes, the reason Miranda had escaped my daughter's company as soon as they first met. I knew everything because I had lived it all before. As a consequence, my heart gave out from the shock and from the weariness of anticipating what would inevitably come.

During her earlier visits, when she thought I was sleeping, Genevieve had poured out her heartache. She would talk out loud for hours, poor girl; there was nobody else to whom she could turn. By so doing, she had provided practically all of the information I required to deduce the truth behind Jack's supposed silence when he was away in Monte Carlo. When my daughter finally admitted, however, weeks after Genevieve and Jack had separated, how she was trying to help this poor boy who had been spurned by his family and Genevieve, I held out hope that I was very wrong. My daughter simply wanted to be near him, which I found unbearably sad. We all had wanted the same thing over the years, but Adora again could not bear to share a boy who, in her addled mind, appeared to be the living, breathing embodiment of everything Sebastian had ever been to her.

Eventually, however, all the illusions I had fostered were destroyed when Adora, thinking I could not hear her, believing me to be asleep, too ill to awaken, confided everything. I learned of the phone calls she obstructed, of their meetings, of her despair at Jack's unraveling to the point where I believe she became unhinged, unable to distinguish past from present. Such is grief, I have learned, for those who have loved beyond the realms of all human comprehension. Yet after what my daughter shared with me, I was aware that my only recourse was to be merciless with Genevieve about Adora, sparing her nothing.

I considered both Miranda and her daughter to be mere innocents, incapable of loving as deeply as my daughter, but more fortunate than she in that they sought only to elevate the objects of their adoration to greater heights. Their love for others did not constitute a cell from which the only escape was death.

I held nothing back. I told Genevieve nearly every single

thing I understood about my daughter and the cruelty of the acts she had committed in both the past and the present. I relieved her of the responsibility of ever again regarding Oliver with awe, minutely detailing every indiscretion he had been guilty of. That my final revelation was what shocked her most was evident from her expression. She could not conceive that he would ever betray Adora with other women because, for Genevieve, there were no others who could possibly compare. I told her that all she had ever loved was a fiction. My daughter's existence was nothing anyone should ever try to emulate.

Genevieve

I thought the chore of packing might take my mind off Sophie's revelations, force them to a place to be confronted later, but what she told me wouldn't leave me. I did not want to believe a word of what she had said. I was only a girl, far too young to conceive of such horror. And yet I was a mere year and a half younger than my mother when she had lost everything, when you, my Beloved Aunt, had stolen everything from her.

I lost something vital in me that afternoon, a knock-on effect of the devastation your acts inspired in me, the girl who worshiped you. For the first time in my life, I lost the ability to remember how pure my love for you once was, Adora, untainted by the knowledge of your imperfections. I had learned that people inevitably disappoint. I did not need another lesson, least of all from you. What you had done to me and to my mother was so malicious, so cold, I felt as if I had never known you.

I so wanted to believe that you could not possibly have meant to hurt me, that I was perhaps being immature and should accept that everyone, sooner or later, become strangers, even those we believe we know the best. I tried to find comfort in rationalizing such thoughts, but I couldn't. I knew that, if I bought into forgiving you in any way, whatever shred of hope Sophie's revelations had stirred inside me about finding Jack again would be eradicated forever. No, realizing that you were capable of outright cruelty, indeed could instigate a charade of mass deception, completely destroyed me. The only thing I felt grateful for that day was that the impact was instant.

I had no thought that I would never return as I carried my suitcase down to the hall. I was still in shock, scrabbling for excuses that would somehow permit me to continue to love you as I always had, although I knew deep down inside such a thing was impossible. I was still your darling girl then, your summer daughter, pushing the plain facts of your deceit aside so that nothing might change, unwilling to concede that everything already had. You didn't know what I had learned about you. I might never tell you.

And yet, whenever Sophie's words played through my mind, I knew it was impossible: I couldn't hate you. I couldn't make that leap then or discard you from my life as I would have done with a friend. Your love had been the greatest, the most powerful I had ever known. To face the dreadful truth about you was too hard for me, although I knew that, ultimately, I would have to. Yet I also had to accept that I had learned everything from you, so perhaps what had happened wasn't so surprising after all. And in this way, I was still able to hold a morsel of affection for you. We were so similar, after all.

I was completely lost as I walked down the staircase. The rush of benevolence I was trying to kindle began to subside as Sophie's words returned to haunt me, as the memories of the summer began to unfold in my mind with vicious clarity: the times you had rushed out of the house to meet Jack, as I had learned that afternoon; the lies you had told me; how insensitive you had been in the face of the regret I felt after we broke up. I convinced myself in my rage that I had done everything for you, even started a relationship with Jack to please you. Everything had always been for you. And you had willingly deceived me, ignored me, taken away someone who you believed I loved more than anything. You had not thought of me at all. Your love was not remotely comparable to the loyalty I had shown you; I had not attempted to steal from you. I had accepted my place, second always to you. Yet you had treated me like you had my mother once, with contempt, thinking only of yourself. You had stolen everything from us. You were not the generous, loving guardian I had always loved. You were a thief, indistinguishable from a common criminal in your greed.

When Oliver appeared in front of me on the staircase, a knowing smile on his face, his arms stretched out between the banister and the wall so that I could not pass him, I didn't flinch as I used to. I didn't check first to see if you, my Beloved Aunt, were near. He wasn't my uncle anymore; he hadn't been that for quite some time. He was a man, one who had found your love lacking over the years. You had not not been enough for him. The growing resentment inside of me understood why, considering what I had learned. As he stood there, his hand draped over the banister blocking my way, engaging me in conversation, I heard nothing—only the voice in my head telling me to lean in closer, to follow his lead, to permit what I knew he wanted to happen, what had been happening for years.

A day before the idea of being caught would have been inconceivable, ghastly. We'd gone to such lengths—Jack, even—to ensure that you would never find out. The irony was that Jack had been Oliver's idea, not yours, to divert attention in case

you were suspicious. I didn't immediately do as Oliver implored me; I ignored Jack in the beginning, refusing to show
him any regard, because I was devastated that Oliver could
allow me to be with someone else. It was only when I realized
that I would truly lose Oliver if I didn't do as he wished that I
submitted to Jack, ironically the same evening that you, Adora,
instructed me to be with him. Do you know how easy it was for
me to tell myself I was doing it for you? Yet I did, ignoring Oliver's ruthlessness, his lack of regard for me. The one problem
was that I did truly fall in love with Jack, but only until Oliver
wanted me back completely, not that he made it easy. Not only
was I distraught, as you imagined, Adora, that Jack had not
contacted me while he was in Monte Carlo, my tears were reserved, too, for Oliver, who kept me hanging while he was away
in Italy as to whether he could forgive me for jeopardizing all
of our futures by not doing as he had asked me, simply using
Jack as a front, for falling in love with someone other than him.
Oliver and I had met on occasion during my relationship with
Jack—even though doing so made me uncomfortable because
of my feelings for Jack. But I was always powerless to refuse Oliver. Yet with Jack nowhere to be found after his trip to Monte
Carlo, I submitted to Oliver again to help mend my broken
heart, and we continued our affair right under your nose.

Initially, in the very beginning, we thought it would end.
Oliver certainly did; how often did he tell me that what we
were doing was so wrong, so terribly wrong, but that he
couldn't resist me, that I made him feel special? I had always
adored Oliver, just like you, ever since I was a little girl. I always
wanted you to put me to bed, but I never objected when Oliver
did; I always did what I thought you wanted. I once believed,
you see, that you would never hurt me or put me in a situation

that you did not believe was safe. I never realized that I was
flirting with him when we walked the dogs on a Sunday; it was
only later, when he would find me and point out, slowly, over
months, how I had given him no choice but to love me, to want
me so desperately, that I realized how I had been leading him
on. Had you taught me that? he asked. I seemed to know exactly what to say to make him feel loved. I was frantic at first; I
didn't want to because of you, but then Oliver made me see, although he never said so directly, that if I loved him like that, I
would be just like you, and so I did. I did it to become you,
whom I had always wanted to be. I was sixteen when I understood what a real woman did with the man she loved. Everything before that had just been practice. And yet, I remember
thinking afterward, although I never dared tell Oliver, that if
that was how you felt when he loved you, my Beloved Aunt,
then I felt terribly, terribly sorry for you.

Had anyone found out, his career and his life would have
been destroyed. When you found him that day in the olive
grove, he let you believe that he had tried to kill himself because you hadn't loved him enough; it distracted you, he
thought, from looking at our relationship. The truth was he had
threatened the same thing to me, saying that was what he
would do if I ever told anyone; he loved me so much that he
couldn't stand for anyone to separate us. It was my fault; unable
to cope with betraying you, I had tried to stop things from
going any further, but he wouldn't let me.

We had an argument in the olive grove, and I ran down to
the beach, down the hidden stone path behind the bougainvillea that he had shown me once; it was where we used to meet
in secret. When I came back, at the sound of your screams, I
realized that he'd meant what he said when I saw the noose in

his hand. I didn't dare leave him after that; I let everything go on because I saw what it would do to you if he died. Since it had begun, I'd told myself that I was pleasing Oliver to save you.

And then you turned against me. You had no time for me, Adora; sometimes you acted as if you didn't even like me. Everything I had done, although it was a betrayal of you and made me so unhappy, I told myself was for you. Oliver confided how difficult life with you was, how I helped him to love you more, to be more forgiving. I accepted my role as second best; I never asked him to leave you. I didn't even conceive that he might. Well, that's not, strictly speaking, true. I just couldn't help but imagine what a life with him would be like; you seemed to have everything with him. And yet you treated me as if I meant nothing to you. As soon as you could, you took away the one person who actually liked me for me, whom I so callously used and discarded the minute Oliver wanted me back. Because even though I knew Oliver was neither a gentleman nor a gentle man, I still could not escape the conviction that being loved by him must mean I was as good as you and so I let myself fall in love with him that summer, at first to see what it felt like to be you and, later, because I had no choice.

Standing on the staircase, I studied him and his seemingly impossible good looks, his lost eyes; that sense of sadness that hung about him sometimes; a fear that I might deny him, perhaps? I let myself believe that as I stood there, the gloves off. I thought only of myself, just as you had. And so I kissed him back, experiencing the rush of cruelty and its inherent power, right there on the same steps where Sebastian once waited for my mother. I betrayed you in your own home, as terrible an act as all of the lies you had told me while I stayed there. I paid you back that afternoon. I kissed him to experience all over again what it meant to be desired by someone so popular, so established, that no one would ever dare do a single thing that might upset him. Pitiful creature that I was, I still wanted to be you, to forget who I was for a brief moment, someone who seemingly meant so little that she could be mercilessly duped without remorse; to feel as secure as you did in everything; in your beauty, your love, your cruelty, your passion. As he pulled back, triumph in his eyes, I conceded defeat.

He turned away, picked up my bag, and proceeded down the stairs, turning once to look back at me; a man in love with the romance of embracing a child, to feel young, to know he could. It was then that I noticed you, gliding past, and all of my grandiose sentiments of the preceding minutes shriveled into ugliness as I realized how completely I had betrayed myself; the shock of shame, of having done something unforgivable, irrevocable, slammed into me, awakening me to the truth of who I was.

I could not know what, if anything, you had seen. Your beatific smile told me nothing as your bejeweled wrist glinted in the late summer sun as you turned the handle to the door, disappearing from my sight, taking all of your secrets with you.

Adora

There is an incomparable solace in remembering the moments before some quietly spoken, well-meaning friend or family member delivers the news of a tragedy. Those moments when one's breathing slows, when one's mind prepares to suspend disbelief, exults in its ignorance, before one is told categorically that nothing will ever be the same again.

I was picking flowers in the garden when I heard my mother's scream on learning of our father's death. I knew that to enter the house would change everything, and so I stayed outside, my eyes transfixed by the blooms in my hand until you, Sebastian, came to find me. When we could not find you that terrible day, I stayed on the beach watching the sea until the sob in my mother's voice behind me told me what I could not bear to hear; the search would not continue. I was reading *The Desert of Love* the day my mother telephoned from her hospital bed to inform me that she had told Genevieve about you and Miranda. I can still remember the ease with which I picked up the phone, the delirious expectation that my angel was at the other end of the line. And when I saw Genevieve appear at the top of the stairs leading down to the driveway, I remembered how I used to melt at her youth, the love that used to fill me with how special she was, how blessed I once thought I had been to have enjoyed her over the years in all of her innocence, and knowing with complete conviction that it was the last time we would ever see each other.

I walked up to meet her at the entrance to the olive grove, remarked immediately her face wet with tears, experienced a strange mixture of pride at how she attempted to resemble me in my dress and disgrace for having contributed to such misery, even though I had tried to save her from it. She resisted at first, but then she let me pull her into my arms, just as she used to, with total abandon. I breathed in the scent of my perfume on her hair, stroked her arms, which had turned golden brown from her summer in the sunshine, felt the weight of her head on my shoulder, resting there as if it were any other day we had shared, not the one which I knew, without being told, would change everything.

I allowed myself to enjoy perfect peace for those brief moments that she let me hold her. I closed my eyes and felt the breeze at my back, noticed how perfectly the late afternoon light illuminated the road behind her, listened to the rustle of the bougainvillea trees all around us. Held tight to me, I treasured the delusion for the last time that Genevieve was my child, born for me, forever mine. But when she pulled away, her eyes were devoid of love for me. They were no longer innocent or oblivious to all my imperfections, to all my selfishness. I saw only her confusion, her hurt and incomprehension at everything she had come to learn, as well as the fear that I had first noted at the beginning of the summer.

There was no one to blame. Everything had been my choice. For you, Sebastian, I stole from everyone—from Miranda, from my mother, from Jack and Genevieve. I could not erase the years, return anything unsullied by my touch. All I wanted was to be near you again, my darling brother, to relive the blissful years of our childhood, to sit opposite you in a café, to stand beside you, to surface from swimming underwater to find you splashing in the waves next to me.

I could not give Jack back to her. I had tried, but it was no use; I couldn't expose him to any more cruelty. Finally, I accepted that he had come for me, despite how I had tried to resist, unsure if I was ready yet to follow. This summer in his presence is the closest I have ever come to feeling as I did when I was a girl. Simply to look at him is enough. I can never expect people to understand or forgive, for they neither own my heart nor its history. The past that encompasses the beaches and the sunshine and you, my golden-haired brother, who gripped my hand as we walked as though your life depended upon it, who turned me away from the brutality of existence and offered me a refuge in your simple, unquestioning soul. This final chapter has constituted merely the briefest of time in the context of this life of ours, but for everything I have lost, I have reclaimed a tiny particle of the happiest time of my life. No one could possibly convince me otherwise. I would not allow it.

But there can also be no more grief for me, and that is why I sent her home. I could no longer look into the face of my girl, whom I had long lost, so I whispered in her ear to go and never come back, pushing her toward the driveway and the waiting car, turning my back on her as I walked up the steps to the house full of all of the exquisite things I have found on my travels, each one the keeper of a memory, a perpetual reminder of the beauty I have owned.

All my life, I thought that my love could provide salvation; everything—Oliver, Gigi—I considered penance for how completely I had failed you, my dear brother, when you needed me most. I tried to save Gigi from the pitiless and the unscrupulous, but I recognize now what a hypocrite I have been. The only person who Gigi needed to be saved from was me. For it was I who destroyed her from the moment I saw her in the crib. My love has destroyed everything. I have condemned myself to a life of purgatory. And I have been punished beyond words.

As I listened to the car pull out of the driveway, I knew that I would forever walk with her in my imagination through town; hold conversations in my head of an evening simply to hear her laughter; recall the joy whenever I turned from my nightly walks through the olive grove to see at the window her little face, which witnessed, for a time, only the best in me, wanting only my love in return; the reason I stayed longer on this earth than I might have. I sent her away because I couldn't bear to witness the disappointment in her: the one person, besides you, who never judged me, who loved with a child's innocence—unconditionally. Better by far that she be free from me and all of the misery I own and have brought to those I love. I have been generous with nothing in my life, except for that. I did it for her. I expect no one to understand. I taught her to love and, by so doing, I also taught her to steal. I will miss her every day of my life, but my heart has survived for only one person; you, my brother. I wish only to remember you now. I give back to Miranda at least something of what I took from her.

Genevieve

I didn't want him to but Oliver insisted on driving me to the port. He tried to make me understand how important it was to deny everything. Yes, he adored me, but Adora, Adora he had known for longer. *Everything will be fine, yes?* Those lost eyes, saying, *Please don't tell on me. It was you, how could I have resisted you, your youth, the way you look at me. I'm only a man. . . . Be a good girl.* I looked out of the window at my island speeding past, everything I had loved, where I would live in my heart forever, the olive trees and the pine walks and the sandy dirt tracks leading down to the clearest seas and whitest beaches, and I thought to myself, *Wasn't I always good, Oliver? Hadn't I always done exactly what you asked, ever since I was a little girl?*

I was deaf to anything he said to try to excuse himself. He didn't know what I had learned that afternoon about him from Sophie and actually poor Jack before her, and as I watched him try to charm me as he always had, I felt ill. All I could think of was you, Adora, walking away from me, up the steep stone steps back to the paradise that was forever lost to me. And it was then that something struck me—a simple, obvious fact I had never paid any attention to. It was only paradise because of you.

Otherwise, it was just an island; there were lots of those in the world with the same views and the same hotels and the same villas. All they lacked was you.

I glanced at Oliver and, with the blinders off, he suddenly seemed rather ordinary without you beside him, his skin a little damaged now from the sun, his face rather weak, not as strong as he'd once seemed. Would anyone have loved or wanted him if you hadn't? If the idea of being with Oliver wasn't tied to the knowledge that whoever did have him triumphed over you?

Of course, I understand, whatever you want; I wouldn't like to be in your position either. Don't worry about Adora and me, we'll be fine. I doubt she saw anything . . .

I listened to Oliver do everything to appease me. He did so love to please, after all. I considered what awaited him back at the house. To think that, after all of the years of being unfaithful to you, he should be found out in his own home with the woman you loved like a daughter. If I hadn't been so disconsolate, I might have laughed at the irony. Yet had you seen anything? I didn't know. If you had, you spared me from it.

I caught sight of the port in front of me and knew it would be the last time I ever sat in the departure area, waiting to sail back to the place I had never considered home; a temporary barracks where I dreamt of you.

The concierge who had known me since I was a baby opened the door into the waiting room with his ritual greeting: *"Ma pauvre, pourquoi les larmes? Vous reviendrez très vite, je vous le promets."* My poor girl, why the tears? You'll be back soon, I promise.

No, I thought, no, I won't. I didn't tell him that. I braved a smile. I stood patiently as Oliver held out his hand to him with his ritual "Sir, how are you?" and watched how honored the concierge felt to be included in Oliver's warmth, a friend almost. *Wonderful, isn't he?* the man's smile seemed to say as he turned to me. I nodded knowingly, complicitly, and as I walked away it struck me that that's what you did. Your ritual expressions when it came to Oliver; the *yes, of course,* with a knowing smile, the adoring gaze when you knew everyone was watching you, the slightly chastising, raised eyebrow if he said something silly; the more somber attention you paid whenever he tried to discuss something of import. And it was then that I realized what a brilliant actress you were, my Beloved Aunt, because the real you was the devastated woman who spent hours in her library, gazing out of the window at the sea; the brokenhearted woman who had stood in the olive grove and had seemingly forgiven me because you knew you had no right to judge.

I was leaving the island alone, something I had never done before; Oliver always took me home. He was scheduled to then, but it had become impossible because of what had just happened. I imagined my father's disappointed expression when I arrived in England, his best friend nowhere to be seen, having to make do with me, and I found myself thinking of my mother that day when I was eight years old, her child, the very essence of who she was, stolen from her. What must she have experienced during that trip home, what sadness had weighed on her of which, bound to silence for reasons I couldn't understand, she could never speak. Why had she never told my father she was engaged to Sebastian? Why did she choose to protect you to her own cost? I felt such remorse as I recognized her selflessness in allowing me to be loved in spite of everything that had happened to her, solely for my benefit. Why, though? After what you had done to her? I almost didn't want to tell her what had happened with Jack for fear of what it might provoke. Perhaps my silence would be my gift to her. My silence and my re-fusal, I determined, never to see you or Oliver again.

No, I wouldn't speak of Jack. I would avoid him even in my own thoughts because I dared not confront what I knew to be true: I had loved him. I had known when I was with him—despite the fact that I was, in many ways, playing a game for Ol-iver's sake—that what he gave me was genuine love and what he asked of me was nothing. It wasn't possible, I had told my-self at the time, that what I experienced with him was happi-ness. He wasn't the image projected by everyone of the perfect man: Oliver was and yet . . . And yet, I left that island knowing that nobody would ever love me more and that I had no right to be forgiven for what I'd done. My only saving grace was that I knew better than to ever ask.

Oliver refused to leave me, shadowing me as far as the steps up to the boat, like a jailer walking me to my execution. I expect that's what he thought. He would have been shocked to learn I couldn't wait to be rid of him. We stood there in silence as we waited for the other passengers to board; I wasn't going to say anything at all, but there was a question that niggled that, in spite of myself, I had to ask before I left: Had any of it been real?

"What was I to you, Oliver?" I asked, uncharacteristically straightforward, not smitten as I usually was, ecstatic that he'd even glanced at me.

I watched him soften at my question, doing a poor job of concealing his relief that I wasn't going to cause a scene. He reached out his hand to touch my face as if I was a flower, a practiced move he must have performed a million times before. "You, Genevieve, I will always remember you as . . ."

I waited; for a split second I thought he might surprise me.

That thing came over him, the Oliver thing; the sadness at all of the things he couldn't change, the empathy for others, or so we thought. When he finally answered, I recognized that the sadness was fear of how inferior he was; the fear of a con man at being found out.

"Genevieve, I will always think of you as my summer girl."

He beamed at me, a melancholy, winsome smile, a slight wince of his forehead at having to give me up; he would probably congratulate himself on it privately later, the morsel he'd given to me to secure my eternal affection. How could I hate him or tell on him with such a touching sentiment to remember him by?

I didn't say good-bye. I just turned away and walked up the gangplank to the waiting cruise liner. I was leaving as I arrived: the summer girl, not the Queen. My mother's legacy had endured.

She was waiting for me at the harbor when I arrived home, the mother I had abandoned. How many times would I ask her forgiveness to excuse my atrocious behavior? I would have to learn to be her daughter all over again, if she would only let me.

As I walked closer to her, I could see that she had been crying; her eyes were bloodshot. My mind flew to my father; where was he? She took me into a corner and, clutching both my arms so tightly they hurt, told me what had happened: how my father had been arrested, how Oliver had been taken to jail mere days after I left the island.

Adora

I stood and watched him leave me from my library window, my husband with the police who came for him. I stood there for hours as the day died, the room growing darker with each second. It seemed to me that everything that had led up to his arrest—the experiences, the love, the terrible grief—lurked within the four corners of my library with me. They were the shadows in the eaves of the bookshelves—the light receding.

All I had left was your love: the splintered shards I clutched to my chest, despite the pain. I felt suddenly very old. I knew it was because hope had left my house. Gigi took it with her when she left.

I knew that I should walk down the stairs, turning left into the kitchen to speak with my staff, to perform the ritual of my days and nights. But the view before my eyes, in the dying twilight of an empty day, seemed to anchor me there. I just wanted to think. I accepted that my words had no meaning. Nothing I had ever said in my life had altered a thing.

In front of my window, the white heads of the waves barely visible in the darkening distance, I remembered that people used to say my eyes were the color of the sea. And the agony of what once was felt like a cleaver in my chest. My eyes were bright then because hope shone from them like a searchlight, the hope that had eroded to a speck, barely visible in even the brightest of light.

The last of it had been taken that day on the stairs, when I looked at Gigi and she at me, both of us knowing in the piercing surprise of the moment that she would betray me in a heartbeat. That she already had, with my husband.

I have felt my heart break. It is a dull sensation, your heart breaking, like the sound of a pebble dropping on the sand . . .

And yet I had known long before. Suspected at the start of the summer, when I saw her run up the hidden stone path, knowing there was no way she could have discovered it unless Oliver had shown her. Confirmed when I started to look more closely: everything they thought I couldn't see, the intimate glances, the suddenly ambivalent attitude around one another. I loved them both more than anything in the world. From me, they could keep nothing, despite how clever they thought they were.

And so Jack. When I finally understood why he was with us—not for me, as I had originally thought, but to save her—I recognized that I could put right what I did wrong that summer all those years before with her mother and you, Sebastian. It was a test. I pushed Gigi to Jack to protect her from Oliver; I wanted to believe she was too young to know what she was doing. I thought that's what you wanted me to do, Sebastian, despite my own instinct, but it didn't work. Genevieve and Oliver continued to surreptitiously meet on our tiny island, deviously using Jack as a means to distract me, I presume. Yet still I tried; I kept pushing, forcing the issue with Jack, and then he came to me that afternoon and everything changed; everything became clear again.

This life of ours has taken its toll. All of us imperfect creatures, we have all stolen from one another: truth, mercy, forgiveness. Somehow, these qualities have eluded us. And we have all paid a price, all of us betrayed, whether by love or intention; no one has been spared.

There is no hiding place for the heartbroken. No shelter for those of us who caused the break ourselves. Our perfect life had merely been a façade. After you, Sebastian, I thought Oliver was my salvation; I did everything to please him, even keeping silent about my love for you because it displeased him. From the day we met I loved him, refusing to allow anything to cloud his days. I even thought that my love had saved him that day he tried to take his life. Later, when I realized how mistaken I was, I wanted to believe he did it because he was so ashamed about Gigi. But I know now my husband has no such shame, because my husband has killed people to give me this exquisite life.

Gigi and Oliver were the final disappointment I could endure; the last of my faith was spent. As soon as trust is questioned, each tomorrow shared seems darker. The hint of a burden where once there was innocence is forever implicit. I felt what was left of my heart disintegrate when I realized how completely I had failed in this life, how there was no one left to whom I could turn and not find myself lacking in their eyes.

But just when I was about to drown, my love, you rescued me.

Sophie

God has not yet decreed it is my time, in spite of how often I have begged him to take me. I have the days, always the days, to think, to remember. My punishment, it seems, has no end.

Somehow I never believed I would see my daughter again after I telephoned to let her know what I had told Genevieve about her mother and Sebastian and, of course, herself. The truth about Adora, as terrible as it was, was unforgivable and my voicing it equally criminal. The betrayal of a daughter, one's blood, has been condemned through the ages as the most hideous of sins, punishable by death. But still I live with the bitter aftertaste of what I have done.

Adora came to me the night Oliver was arrested, her eyes finally cleared of the blindness that had permitted her to love him without question. She was incomparable, standing in the doorway to my hospital room, barely altered by time, almost like a statue, preserved not by happiness but by sorrow. It was the first and last time we ever looked at one another without the mass of lies and unspoken resentment a barrier between us. We saw each other exactly as we were: a mother and a daughter unable to love one another completely because of the

loss of a son and brother we had spent the residue of our shattered hearts longing for.

I moved over so that she could sit beside me on the bed.
Instead, she curled up next to me, her head on my chest, her
hand gripping mine. It was an act of trust I had never received
from her before, not even when she was a child. That I would
experience such love for another human being again I had
thought impossible, but it is often said that the heart is the
most resilient organ we own. My own rallied again for the final
moments we shared. We had all failed each other: Sebastian for
leaving us; my daughter for worshiping him without thought
for anyone but herself; me for denying myself to her when she
most needed my guidance. In the face of her passion, I realized
that night how insignificant a person I really was. A monster of
obsession and unfulfilled longing that had destroyed everyone
she loved, that is what I had created. Even so, I envied her the
capacity to still display such affection, to love so ferociously, despite how misguided her choices.

The weight of her beside me was overwhelming. It was the
weight of her very soul, the unfathomable reaches of desire and
longing and deep, inexplicable love. She was born of me; the
burden of responsibility for her nature was mine alone. She resembled a newborn curled up next to me, a paragon of trust,
dependent on a mother's words, a mother's love to guide her. I
had failed her as completely as she had failed me; she for never
needing me, and I for turning my back on her, for believing
what I was told, for cursing the day she was born.

I took her face in my hands and kissed her forehead, her
eyes, her perfect nose, her mouth, unable to prevent tears of regret from coursing down my cheeks.

"Gigi has gone," she said. "She's never coming back."

"I see," I replied. "You understand why I had to do it, Adora, don't you?"

She seemed in shock, unable or unwilling to speak. I looked at her and felt an agonizing pang. "She was Sebastian's child," I implored, revealing the secret Miranda and I had kept for years. "I couldn't allow it to continue or have Miranda suffer anymore. You must see what you've done, the same thing that you did with Sebastian. You stole that boy from Genevieve just like you tried to steal Sebastian from her mother. I had to intervene before it went too far. I had to do it for Sebastian and poor Miranda. Do you really think she deserved this? She is such a kind person, Adora; after everything, the way she allowed Gigi to stay with you every summer, thinking nothing of herself . . ."

She didn't move; I was unsure if my words had even penetrated. I told her the part I had played in James and Miranda's marriage, how it had all become possible, why even James was bound to silence with Oliver about how he met his wife—the bargain I had struck for the sake of Miranda and Sebastian's child, Gigi, the reason for the elaborate charade we had all played a part in. Still, she remained expressionless.

"You must send the boy home to his mother. Can you imagine what it would have felt like for us had someone kept Sebastian when he was alive and refused to give him back? Adora, *Adora,*" I pressed, trying to make her understand, but nothing seemed to rouse her. "She was *Sebastian's* daughter, Adora," I repeated, hoping for a reaction. I almost asked her then if she knew; I had so often speculated on whether the secret we had so closely guarded was something Adora had already uncovered, although how I had no idea. Was that why she took Gigi all for herself, destroying Miranda, years before? Yet she didn't

even flinch, and I stopped myself, returning to the pressing
need to make my daughter see what she must do: "If you don't
let Jack go, it will be like you're hurting your brother, and you
know how he loved you."

"But Sebastian died because of me; he killed himself because I wasn't there to look after him," she said finally, slowly
sitting up and moving away from me.

After the first terrible days following Sebastian's death, we
had never discussed it again. Yet at the sound of her words, the
full force of what I had allowed her to believe undid me. I
couldn't let it continue; all of the lies had to end. I had punished her by never telling the truth about why Sebastian went
swimming that day, blaming her, happy to. I was tired, though,
exhausted; I just wanted everything to be over, and I couldn't
have Jack on my conscience. I had to do it, too, for Miranda and
Genevieve.

"Sebastian didn't kill himself, Adora," I said. "He thought
you were hiding. After you left—after I sent you away—he
thought you were hiding, and he grew terribly ill trying to find
you. I thought he had simply forgotten that you had told him
where you were going. You know how poor his memory was,
and one day he came to me because he couldn't recall the
words of the rhyme you used to sing—the one that goes *Remember I wait for you forever* . . . So I sang it for him, like you
used to, and I'll never forget how thrilled he was when he told
me that he finally knew where you were; the poem had jogged
his memory. I thought he had simply remembered where you
told him you were going, but I didn't know then that you
hadn't done that. He thought you were hiding in the sea,
Adora. He wasn't trying to die; he was looking for you."

When Adora turned to look at me, I was momentarily astonished. Somewhere in my mind, I had kept her as a little girl, and yet it was a woman whose enormous eyes met my own; eyes that contained a world of experience and secrets I could never mine, not even if I lived forever. I mourned those lost opportunities as I drank her in, that exquisite face almost imperceptibly worn by age and grief, the light woolen sweater she wore pulled over her slightly slumped shoulders, her magnificent curls. My child, one I had longed for, who I never could have imagined would end up that lost woman sitting on my hospital bed, unable to speak. What might have changed had I loved her more? What could she have become had I not closed my heart to her?

I was never to find out. Those were the final words I ever spoke to my daughter. They were the last rites.

Genevieve

I have idealized Jack over the years. He has become the single memory that encapsulates my youth—of a promise that never came true. When I was eighteen, there was something impossibly romantic about a broken heart, about a girl walking away from a devastated boy in a picturesque Mediterranean café by the sea. Except the broken heart did not belong to me then. I imagined myself just like you: adored, beloved by two men; making the ultimate sacrifice; turning away from youth toward maturity, because I wouldn't listen to Jack's lies. How defiant I was, refusing to believe a word against Oliver, and yet, I knew, I knew. Even then.

I thought that everything in life was recoverable. I didn't truly believe that I would never see Jack again, that he would fade from view. I thought that he might always wait for me, that I had the same effect on men as you, Adora. I believed it because of Oliver; if he could turn away from you to me, then perhaps, as outlandish as it once had seemed, I might even be equal to you, yet never better. I never allowed myself to go that far. It is only now, with the benefit of experience, I can recognize how extraordinary Jack was, how he tried to save me from harm.

He had found out everything, uncovered the secrets behind Oliver's enormous wealth: the prostitution, the racketeering, the
drug dens hidden behind whitewashed walls; the abysmal truth
that led to Oliver's arrest. And Jack paid dearly for it when Oliver blackmailed him by threatening to tell me about his brother
and how he died, playing on Jack's weakness, fully aware of why
Jack had been sent to the island in the first place.

Jack had tried to kill himself several times and had even been
institutionalized at one point. He had developed a crippling ad-
diction to drugs and alcohol, of which he was thoroughly
ashamed and which he had tried desperately to overcome. But
the slightest thing could upset him; he could only cope in a calm
environment, and that is why his father had pulled strings for
him to come to the island, hoping the more sedate pace would
settle him. And for a time, while I did Oliver's bidding so that you
would never suspect a thing, when I genuinely fell in love with
Jack, despite my fear of upsetting Oliver and moving away from
him, Jack was happy. And Oliver saw that and, jealous at being
usurped by someone infinitely superior to him in every regard,
he reeled me back in, and I let him, because I had known him
longer and because I wanted to be you.

And so, after I left him, Jack sought solace in the opium
dens of the island, which Oliver provided but pretended never
existed, and that is when you rescued him. Many times you
were seen together on the beach, Jack resting his head on your
shoulder, you clinging to him as if your life depended on it. It
was said that the two of you seemed locked in your own private
world and that you, my Beloved Aunt, appeared to follow him.
Wherever he went, there was concern for him; it was clear that
he was suffering from some of kind of wasting disease, but
there was never any doubt that he would be safe with you.

Many were the evenings when you were seen trying to feed him or calming him when he grew agitated, and it was said that he submitted to you willingly, like a child; that a smile from you sated him as much as his love seemed to console you.

If I had not betrayed you, none of it would have happened. I would never have gone to visit your mother and broken my promise not to burden her with my problems. The events of the past, guarded so brilliantly for nearly twenty years, would not have resurfaced, and I would maybe today be free. But I'm not.

Now, when I recall the things I was so frightened of that summer, they seem so inconsequential; I was scared of not living up to you with Oliver, of you ever finding out what I'd done, of Jack seeing through me for what I really was. That first afternoon when Jack came to us, I thought I might pass out from nerves. And now, if I could, I would live that afternoon every day of my life, for I know how extraordinary it is to feel like that, to be sure that someone else feels the same way. I would reach across the table and place my hand on his to calm his nervousness; I would relish every word he spoke; I would help him, instead of turning my back on his innocence, his kindness, untainted by spite or selfishness. I would love what I could not understand: simply that to sit opposite Jack in the blissful heat of a Mediterranean summer, against a backdrop of sea and sand and bougainvillea, was one of the happiest times of my life. I would understand, without waiting for the disappointment of years to teach me, that such an experience is the exception, treasured deep within us for its rarity. Yet for years now I have lived with the crippling awareness of what my actions caused, the multitude of things I loved about Jack that he will never know.

Like you, my Beloved Aunt, I hanker after yesterdays.

Adora

The olive grove, an island in the Mediterranean Sea, 1938

After I left Mama, there was only one place to go, one thing left to do. I walked here to the olive grove, where I found Linford, patiently waiting, and he joined me, falling immediately into perfect unison with my step; Linford, who has guarded the gates of this limbo, where all of our forsaken souls have waited for the sound of your call. Jack was waiting for me here. I came up behind him and wrapped my arms around his slender form, rested his head on my shoulder, cradled him like a baby. And here I have stayed with him—and you—as I have relived our history, telling you both my stories just as I used to when I was a girl.

All my life I have waited for him. I know I deserve no blessing such as this, but I have been given one, because of you, Sebastian. All these years I prayed that you would forgive me. I am with Jack as he fades into slumber, permitted to give him the love I couldn't show you the day you went to find me. I hold him tighter to me, wanting all of the love of the years that have passed to course through him, to become a part of this boy who in every characteristic and deed is so completely you, my brother. I close my eyes to his familiar face and I feel as if I am with you again, Sebastian, holding you near as I wished I could have the day you left us forever. I allow the moments to pass, together with you again on the sands of our youth, loving a boy whom nobody else loved, someone heartbroken, exiled from peace, as I am.

Everything has led up to this moment, the light fading, the two of us wrapped up in one another, the sensation of his golden curls against my cheek, the weight of his hand in mine, his acceptance of my presence. It is enough.

"Adora," he murmurs, stirring from his sleep, "it's late, so late. Can we go home now?"

Whenever life has become unendurable, Sebastian, I have gone blind to reality and imagined myself with you, as if we were hiding again underwater. Every step of my life, my love, I have walked with you. I have taken you with me everywhere. Sometimes, I have sat with you at our table, surrounded by guests, watching you in my memory, where you used to sit, remembering how you used to smile at me. And I have found home again, safe from the sound of malice.

The nights I let you go; I never let you follow me there. In the early evening, the day dying, we walk together to the olive grove, to the edge of the cliff with our dogs where you leave us until morning, when I return to find you, always there. And I have waited all these years for you to let me travel to where you live, to forgive me; to send the angel to walk with me to my death.

And when I heard his footfall on the step at the start of this last summer and saw you in that boy, I knew I could die now, that you had reached out and touched his soul so that he would lead me wherever you need me to go to find you again. And I have followed him like a devoted pilgrim because I know you have shown him the way to paradise.

The brightness of the world has not yet dimmed, but soon we must sleep and so I smooth the ground around Jack with my hands, like you used to, so that he can rest. As I lay him down, I see the stem of bougainvillea he has clutched in his hand, and as I lower my head to kiss him tenderly on the lips good-bye, he places it behind my ear. And it is then that he anoints me, I who never held any child in my arms I did not have to give back. "You are my mother now," he says, granting me a blessing in death that I was never afforded in life. His eyes fill with tears as he turns toward the sea, and I finally understand where I am going. And I lay him gently down to sleep before I stand up to walk to where you live.

The dogs gather around me, my back to the house where I paid for all my sins, my eyes fixed on the sea that owns you. I take my leave of the olive trees, the bougainvillea, the distant white houses dotted down the hills, and the streets where we walked together, kissing the memories good-bye. So long ago, such unsurpassed pleasure so catastrophically ruined it could never be reclaimed.

I find myself remembering the first time our mother brought us here to the island, how I held your hand, Sebastian, on the edge of the sand, facing the wonder of it all. What joy we had in our hearts then, we two golden-haired children; how the future seemed inevitable, the two of us together always, silhouetted against the immense world beyond. You gripped my hand that day, frightened you might fall if I let go, but I didn't let go. I never have. *Remember I wait for you forever,* we sang, oblivious to how true the simple rhyme would be.

As the dusk moves in, I look out to the sea that owns you and I know that you have kept your promise to me. From the safety of the marble balustrades where I stand, the sea below me, the breeze kissing me good-bye, I hear your call and open the gate to walk to the edge of the cliff.

I look behind me one last time to the house that played host to such enormous love over the years, the love that made me stay, but her little face no longer peeks out from behind a curtain. All gone now, the child I tried to save, just as I watched over you, Sebastian, while you lived. Instead, I see the angel who walked with me this far sleeping under the falling leaves, his soul safe in our refuge. I glance down at Linford, who is watching me, his knowing, gentle face upturned to mine, understanding that we are leaving. And it is then that I turn back to you, Sebastian: my brother, who lives in the sea, like a dolphin, safe from the sound of the tears of those who weep for you, searching for where I am hiding.

Forgive me, my love, for having left you so long.

Sophie

After she died, I found the books. All those years I never asked her what she was doing in that library of hers. She was writing to Sebastian, the story of her life, of the dogs who lived with her. Telling him stories, just like she always did. And in those tomes I found my daughter, far too late beloved by me, and realized how terribly I had misjudged every single thing she did.

They found tears in his eyes, the young man's. The doctor told me at the hospital. He had been found in the olive grove, his face turned to the sea. I was discharged the day they brought his body to rest there. It was how I learned that my daughter had left us. There was a crowd gathered around the entrance, mourners such as I had never seen. *La petite voleuse est morte,* the little thief is dead, a woman wept, as I should have. They consoled me, but I had not even begun to grieve; I didn't even know how then. Later, when I discovered everything, that is when I truly learned what sorrow is.

But the tears in Jack's eyes preoccupied me. And I remembered a line from Baudelaire: "The dead, poor things, have sorrows of their own." And when I read my daughter's diaries, I accepted that Jack had been right, the dead are heartbroken to leave just as his heart had broken to leave her.

"Is it possible that the tears started after his death?" I inquired of the doctor. I didn't care for him. He regarded me as an irritant; all he wanted was for me to sign the papers releasing Adora's body, which had washed ashore.

"It's not possible," he remarked curtly, trying and not succeeding to muster a whisper of compassion. I didn't say anything at first, appraising him with my eyes, letting him know that I knew his type, had come across ordinary, insignificant people like him all my life who sneered at the exceptional, who sniggered at difference. "Well, you would say that," I said proudly. "You never knew her. You couldn't possibly fathom how unbearable it would be to leave her." And I turned on my heel and walked away, leaving him bewildered and infuriated that I hadn't signed the papers, that he couldn't just dismiss my daughter the way I had all her life, to get her out of the way and carry on with the day.

It has become part of the myth of the island now: that even the dead wept to leave her, the Summer Queen. That and the story of how her dogs all followed her off the cliff, one by one, because they loved her the most and couldn't bear to leave her. The legend has it that her brother, who lived in the sea like a dolphin, told them to stay when he was called to paradise, to comfort her in her sadness, because, without him, she had no friends in this life. But there was an angel who asked to be exiled from heaven because, when the gates opened to let the dolphin in, he had seen the Summer Queen weeping as she watched her brother leave and had fallen irrevocably in love with her unfathomable beauty at first glance.

Every day, she would beg him to take her to where her

brother was hiding, but he was never allowed to return. If the angel even so much as approached the gates, he would die and be left behind. Yet she was so kind to him in her sorrow that he experienced a happiness he had never known, and the angel accepted that he could not deny someone so rare. And so he walked her to the gates, knowing the guardian would open them for him, and he asked that she be allowed to enter, offering his own life as the sacrifice. The Gods of the island were so distraught that the angel had died they granted the Summer Queen immortality so that she could watch over all of the lost souls of the island. And that is why all the stray dogs of the island gather in the olive grove. It is so they can be near to where the Gods buried the angel who gave up his life so that the Summer Queen could join her soul mate. It is why she watches over the grove, keeping bad weather and famine away from its gates, because of her endless gratitude to the angel who comforted her in her grief.

I suspect that the story developed because the truth was unbearable: that with the gate left open, all the dogs ran away, some of them claimed by kinder souls, most of them left to starve on the streets where my two children, the patron saints of lost souls, had once rescued them and kept them safe.

As with all myth and legend, there was some credence to the story. One dog did follow my daughter: Linford, just as his grandmother, Titania, had followed Sebastian, dying at Adora's feet when he didn't emerge from the sea. And far more than anything else, it was this knowledge that finally broke me: that Titania's death was not simply chance, as I believed at the time, but that Adora had happened upon the truth with her story that enchanted Sebastian when he was a little boy, and it was far too late to ask her how on earth she could have known such a thing, as well as all of the other things my daughter kept cloistered in her rare and vibrant heart.

Not a single member of his family came to claim him. His mother did not want him back, and his father was too ill to make the trip. Jack's mother had never been able to forgive him for the car crash that killed his brother four years earlier, when he had been driving the car, far too drunk to manage it. His brother, she wrote, had been the light of her life, and she was not ashamed to admit to me that she had loved him far more; in fact, she was defiant. I remember sitting in Adora's library and laying the letter down on her desk, knowing I should be appalled, yet accepting that I had no right to judge considering what I was guilty of doing for Sebastian, the son I, too, loved beyond the realms of comprehension.

I knew. I knew that Miranda lied to me about what she had seen on the beach that day. And I sent my daughter away, knowing that I was punishing her for a lie. I did it because it provided me with an excuse. I wanted Sebastian for myself and because I thought that Miranda was his only possibility for a normal life. I did it because I resented my daughter more than I cared to admit, because he loved her far more than me and always would. I destroyed her happiness because I was jealous of her, because I wanted to be her, just like Miranda, just like Gigi. It was only later that the impossibility of my ever assuming her role became apparent when Sebastian chose to give up his own life searching for her rather than staying with Miranda and me.

And I didn't tell her the simple truth, not because I was afraid she would follow him, but by blaming her I excused myself. She hadn't told him where she was going; that was why he died. Not because I forced her to leave and destroyed both my children in the process. I sacrificed her for the sake of my conscience. And the rub is that it was all for nothing. Sebastian could not live without her. It was the inescapable truth. Without her, he would have died long before. I was never equipped to provide him with the love that could sustain him. From the instant she was born, he had lived and breathed only for her. In the final reckoning, Sebastian's life had been beautiful only because of her. And I am left with the unbearable awareness that as my son was drowning he held out the hope that, at any moment, he would see her face and that, for my precious child, that joy never came, because of what I'd done.

I buried Jack in the olive grove. I know that's what Adora would have chosen; after all, she brought him here, where she brought all the other lost souls nobody wanted, to keep them safe.

The ghosts of their souls live alongside me now: of Linford, of Titania, of Adora, and of two perfect boys, separated by years but completely alike in every other regard. They are everywhere I turn; the vision of them with the sun on their hair and the sea in their eyes is sometimes so acute, so real, it is as if I can reach out and touch them again. I believe now that both boys knew they would not be permitted to stay on this earth; something deep inside of them understood the instability of their lives and how valuable each moment was. And it consoles me to think that it was my daughter's face they chose to commit to their souls as they left. I am humbled that they chose her and that they watched over her while she lived, offering the love everyone else withheld.

After her death, I moved back here to the island. It wasn't as if Oliver could object, considering that it was always my house. I gave it to Adora when she married, telling myself that I wanted to be rid of the excruciating memories contained within the walls but, in truth, unable to cope with what I had done to her and Sebastian. It was here that I read Miranda's letter, in which she confessed that she had lied about both the nature of what she saw that day on the beach and Sebastian's role as father to her child: Gigi was not his or mine; she was the child of the father whose family Miranda was working for at the time. If Sebastian had not approached her in the café on that afternoon, she would have been destitute. As it was, he provided her with the alibi she needed to restore her reputation, and I let her.

I am left with the terrible knowledge that Adora died not knowing the truth. I cannot imagine her thoughts as she realized that her cherished brother's child had so completely betrayed her. And to think I only told her for Miranda's sake; all those years, I'd thought Miranda a saint for letting Gigi stay with Adora, unable to understand such selflessness. "Let her keep her, for Sebastian," Miranda would reply beneficently. What an extraordinary girl, I would say to myself, newly resentful of Adora for everything that we had lost. Now, considering what I have learned about her, I wonder if Miranda didn't raise Genevieve to usurp my daughter as some kind of perverse revenge.

It's curious how certain things from memory jump out at

you. I remember an occasion that first summer Gigi stayed with Adora, just before Miranda and James left. We had all spent the day at the villa, and Gigi wanted to stay the night. Of course, I sided with Miranda against James, who didn't mind, and I refused to allow it. My goodness, how she wept. The child was inconsolable, and she ran off to the olive grove and wouldn't come out until Oliver went to collect her. I remember how he picked her up in his arms and sat with her, telling Gigi that there would be other nights, that she must be a good girl for her uncle Oliver and he would see her first thing the next morning and they would take the dogs for a walk on the beach. And Gigi replied, "If I'm a good girl, what will I get?" And I watched Oliver wrack his little brain and come up with the best treat he could think of: "Well then, young lady, I will marry you when you grow up and then you will be just like your aunt Adora."

As with all things in my life, I should have paid more attention to how her eyes lit up, how she tightened her grip on his hand, displaying a child's lack of guile in failing to conceal her joy. I remember turning to my daughter and being surprised at what I witnessed; oh, the beatific, unreadable smile was still there, but there was no mistaking the expression in her eyes: a mixture of sadness and pity, although why I'll never know.

I find myself often now thinking of Gigi and Adora together, reflecting on what it was that impelled Adora to love her so much. After all, my daughter didn't know until I told her that Sebastian was supposedly Gigi's father, so it must have been something else, because I can never forget her cries of delight whenever Gigi ran into her arms and the way she draped the girl in her jewels and strolled with her through town, calling on everyone to admire the child and share in her joy; how she made everybody laud Gigi as a beauty when, in truth, she was quite the plainest little thing anyone ever saw.

I wonder if Gigi remembers everything Adora did for her now; the insignificant girl who nobody liked; how my daughter made her exceptional by loving her. I wonder if she hangs her head in shame whenever she recalls how hideously she abused my daughter, as I do. And yet I have learned to stop questioning why Gigi forsook such enormous love. I believe that what haunts her heart these days is punishment enough.

Genevieve

You died on a Tuesday, my Beloved Aunt. We learned from your gardener that you threw yourself from the cliff into the sea below. They discovered your body a few hours later, washed up on a nearby beach. The poor man who had been forced to watch you, the woman he adored, dive into the water from the grove he had tended with such love was too far away to hurl himself after you. He was haunted by the sight of you turning for one last look at your house, but what he could never ever recover from was the vision of Linford, who followed you, without hesitation.

Sophie refused to bury you. You were cremated and cast to the sea. To be with Sebastian, she said. I did not return to the island for the memorial service, nor did a single member of my family. For years I have pretended that it never happened. For me to find you again, I convince myself, all I have to do is board a ship and there you will be, waiting for me on the dock, your white-blond hair perfectly bobbed, your aquamarine eyes alive with love as you take me in your arms and whisper into my ear: *Darling girl, you've come back to me. The summer is ours.* Off we will go, in your car, and up the hill to that beautiful house. I will change into my summer clothes, lovingly picked out over the weeks before, and find you there in the olive grove, watching over the sea, waiting for something, waiting for me.

Immediately following your death, there were so many things I could not fathom. There were times when I thought I had never known you at all. Yet there was one thing I learned that made perfect sense: I knew exactly why you had turned back toward the house one last time before you killed yourself. I asked you once, when I was about ten years old, if I had been yours, what would you have called me, and you replied, "Hope. You are Hope to me." I remember being disappointed. I didn't like it; I thought you might have named me something grander, like Serena or Arianna. Hope sounded like a name my mother would have chosen. She was so traditional in everything she did, I never could grasp why she had given me such an unusual name. Of course, as with so much to do with you, my Beloved Aunt, I missed everything. I represented possibility to you, innocence, a dream that tomorrow might be better, and when you would walk your dogs each evening through the olive grove to the edge of the cliff, it was only the sight of my face at the window that made you leave the edge and stay one day more, because I was hope to you.

You taught me that there are people who enter our lives who possess a magic that transfixes our souls, that pulls us toward them, awakening a need and a passion we never knew existed. For me, you were that person. I remember the days of my childhood when you poured lemon juice on my hair, told me stories as I curled up in your lap, smiled your incomparable smile whenever I appeared. In the final reckoning, I keep the best of you inside of me. To let it go would be to lose something priceless.

Still, it is inconceivable to me that you killed yourself; I know you died because of me, because I destroyed the last of your faith. The only way I can stand it now is to tell myself that the day you dived into that blue, blue sea you were long dead inside. I have been forced to alter the details of your suicide in my memory. Instead, I imagine you walking into the sea, and I picture you slowly submerging, your curls the whitest blond, the diamond necklaces you treasured twined and glinting in the sun around your neck. In your arms you carry bundles of fuchsia bougainvillea, which float away as the sea claims you, inch by inch. But it is your eyes that transfix, for they bear the same expression of greed I first saw as a child, as if death were a bountiful feast and you were the guest of honor. As the water reaches your chin, you take your last breath; a deep, all-encompassing breath that draws all the loveliness that was inside of you, and I am left only with your eyes, indistinguishable from the sea as the water closes over you, the sodden bougainvillea the only evidence you ever existed.

I am thankful that you did not live to see what happened next with Oliver. Not for you to have to witness the complete destruction of everything you held dear. Besides, you'd seen enough. Such things are reserved only for those who can bear them. You were not one of those people, my Beloved Aunt. Yet the irony of your death is not lost on me. When I think of you, I, too, feel as though I am drowning. And I, unlike so many sage psychiatrists, know for a fact that time erases nothing, heals no wound. Time merely takes me away from the last cherished moments when I knew where to find you, my beloved, my sad, my cruel Aunt. Cruel because there is no possibility that anyone who was loved by you could ever escape your devotion; life faded after you died, and we were all returned to normal; irrel-

evant people once made special only by you. And I know I
shouldn't, but I do, despite the hollow pain that ensues whenever I make this request of the Gods. I ask them for just one
thing: that they give you back to me, if only for a second, so that
the last thing you ever see of me is how much I love you and
not how I betrayed you. For a moment, merely the asking con-
tains a shred of hope subsequently destroyed by the logic that
such a request will always be refused; the ensuing nothingness
that is life with you erased from it returns me to my sorrow.

And so you haunt me. Always with me, you are the invisible
diner at our table, the constant presence that trails me as I go
about my daily routine. There is not a person in my family un-
touched by you; there is no dress I own that I did not imagine
wearing on your island; there has never been a season of my
life when I was not waiting for you. I can shut my eyes and
imagine you gliding past, feel myself beside you on one of our
walks. In the darkness of a closed-lidded world, you are alive
and vital, unchanging, mine. You are the ghost of everything
that once was lovely, everything that I helped to destroy, a
shadow that casts its majesty over everything that remains, reminding me of what a poor imitation I am.

We shared the greatest of love, you and I, for each other
and for a young man whom we could not keep, whom we both
played a part in destroying. Would others deem it tragic that all
I have left of you now is a stem of bougainvillea I pressed between the pages of a book? Or would you tell me, as you so
often did, that the opinions of other people mean nothing,
what matters is who you allow to leave the touch of their fin-
gerprints on your soul?

Yours are forever imprinted on mine. I have afforded no
one else the privilege, not even my future husband. We are all

born to love someone totally and utterly. For me, it was and will always be you.

I can love you now because I know everything. There was a time when I did not—had not yet received Sophie's uncompromising letter, informing me of everything she had been wrong about, condemning me for my conduct and what I was about to do.

When I first arrived home from your island, I found safety in my mother's embrace. Lost in my inability to understand who was right or wrong; my mother helped me to see that you were a woman who had stolen everything from her and from me, an abominable, despicable creature capable of acts of calculated cruelty. She immediately forgave me for what happened with Oliver. I was so young, she told me, so, so young. How could I possibly have known what I was doing? How could I have known that Jack was so unstable; it wasn't so wrong to love a charming, older man. It wasn't unusual to be led astray by sophistication and wit and flattery; I certainly wasn't the first young girl who had fallen prey to the promises made by lonely husbands who fall under the spell of youth with all of its allure. "Men don't stray, Genevieve, for no reason. Oliver clearly was very unhappy with Adora; he evidently found what he was missing in you," she said. "Adora is entirely responsible for not loving him enough and for so despicably using you."

It was easy to believe her, because I wanted to. Compared to what you had done, I was hardly as bad, I rationalized. I was really only helping Oliver, and he was lonely; my mother was right. How many times had he clutched my hand from across a table and said, "if only," with such plausible longing that I lost myself in him and the promise of a life I could never dare contemplate because of what it would do to you. And yet you had not thought of me when you ran off with the boy you had been so desperate for me to love; why did you do it if not to deliberately hurt me by spiriting him away to make yourself feel young again? Finally, my mother made me see that you were a very jealous woman, jealous of her and of me. You had taken me away from my mother because you couldn't have children of your own; you couldn't bear to see anyone have more than you. And so what I had done became forgivable, justifiable, even inevitable in my mother's eyes; after all, you had been my teacher, and look at the example you'd set for me. You betrayed me and I you, but only because of how badly you had let me down; a pitifully tit-for-tat analogy, so inferior to the riot of emotions we held for each other. And yet I believed it.

Of everyone in the sorry situation we found ourselves in, my poor mother was the real victim. I could never escape the guilt I felt for loving you more throughout my childhood, for making her feel lesser when all she had ever done was love me and want the best for me.

That is why, despite my reservations, I told the lie that exonerated everyone. It was really the least I could do. I did it for my mother and for my father, who didn't deserve to be punished, especially not after the sacrifices they'd made for me. Why I said that Oliver was with me the evening he was apparently seen and photographed exchanging an enormous sum of money with a notorious drug trafficker, which led to his arrest. It was part of a sting that had been planned by the largely irrelevant island police for many years to expose him as the premier facilitator and go-between for the drugs that were ritually funneled from China and Morocco by traffickers, via our island in the Mediterranean Sea, to mainland Europe and Britain. Yet until that evening, the authorities had never been able to catch him in the act. My father, as his lawyer, was investigated to find out if they could tie the money to Oliver's legitimate businesses, although my father was entirely innocent of any wrongdoing and refused to cooperate or even acknowledge a word against his best friend, resolute that Oliver would never have involved him in anything that might potentially harm him. Yet my mother assured me that if I lied for Oliver the entire case might crumble, and it's funny how things like photographs can be misplaced, especially when so much money is involved. And so I lied. It wasn't difficult, because I thought the accusation was the most ludicrous thing I'd ever heard and because Oliver was so plausible in his letters—letters that first begged me to help him and then grew more intimate as time went on and I would find myself reminiscing about how charming he was and, soon, I allowed him to come to visit.

Of course, I said yes. Yes to everything, the new life, the partnership, the possibility of it all. Everything happens for a reason, my mother rationalized. And the way people talked of you, Adora, made it very easy to excuse myself; it was quite a scandal, and fewer and fewer were the people who had a kind word to say about you. Oliver, on the other hand, was an innocent man, although there were those acquaintances who never quite accepted that fact, which is why we all moved. My father was content to follow Oliver wherever he suggested, and Oliver so needed a fresh start, especially after everything he'd been put through.

It was only when I received the letter from Sophie after she was informed of my wedding that I was forced, once again, to accept that I had placed my trust in all the wrong places, choosing what was easier to believe because it exonerated me. I went to my mother and demanded to know if it was true, because if it was, then you were innocent of everything she had suggested and what I had done, during your life and after it ended, was unforgivable.

She didn't even try to deny it. No, I wasn't Sebastian's daughter. Yes, she had lied to save herself. No, I couldn't possibly back out of the wedding. If I did, she would disown me. The man I had always believed to be my father was not as astute a businessman as he made out; he was mired in crippling debt. They needed the money my wedding would bring, considering my fiancé's extensive fortune. Oliver was marrying me, she elaborated, because of a deal my mother and he had brokered, of which my "father" was kept resolutely in the dark: I would provide Oliver with an alibi and, in return, he would not destroy my family's reputation by revealing what he had learned a few years before from someone close to the aristocratic family my mother had worked for the summer she met Sebastian—namely that I was a bastard, conceived out of wedlock, passed off ultimately as another man's child. Nor would he suggest that, much like my mother, I was a whore who seduced married men; he would instead do the decent thing and marry me.

"He doesn't love me at all?" I asked, something in me accepting, even as I posed the question, that I deserved this, what was happening. "Why did you do it?" I asked.

"Sometimes, Genevieve, it's necessary to make compromises in order to survive," she replied ambivalently.

"And am I the compromise, Mother? Why would you do this to me?"

She laid down her sewing with a frustrated sigh and cast an

appraising glance over my appearance. "That's a bit hypocritical, Genevieve, considering how little you ever thought of me. I
never compared, did I, to your idol, Adora? Did you think that
you could ignore me, relegate me to second best for years on
end, and then come home and just expect that I could forgive
you because you're my daughter and the bond that the relationship implies? You were my daughter when you ran away
from me every summer to worship my antithesis without a single thought for my feelings," she replied coldly, and then she
said something so simple, but yet so devastating, it ruined me:
"I did it because I could."

"That's it?" I queried, astonished. "Because you could. You
have no other reason than that?"

"That's the way it generally works out; an opportunity
arises, and then there are those who are prepared to take it. It's
why I called you Genevieve, because Adora once confided in
me that, if she ever had a daughter, that's what she would name
her. You were born first, so I took the name away from her because of all the trouble she'd caused me and because I could.
And I really don't think the irony was lost on her at the beginning or in the end. Do you, Genevieve?"

I couldn't see for my tears; the full responsibility for everything I had done washed over me like acid. "I don't know you,"
I said. "I don't know who you are."

"Oh yes you do, my dear," she replied, amused. "You're very
much my daughter. Ask yourself this: when you flirted with Oliver and let him have his own way while your 'Beloved Aunt'
was alive, why did you do it? Was it not precisely because you
could? Or am I wrong in that, my darling?"

I almost wished she'd killed me, because I couldn't disagree; there was no protestation—of being young, tempted, cu-

rious, everything I had bought into to excuse myself—that would ring true. Everything—the cause and effect—crystallized in my mind as I stood there, immobile, as if I had been turned into a statue, trapped in a moment forever when I realized exactly what I had done and how the responsibility for your death was mine alone.

I watched my mother pick her sewing back up as if we'd just been discussing something inconsequential, forgettable, and I marveled at how she could possibly justify her actions. It seemed to me there was an art to what she'd done, and then I realized exactly what it was; it was the art of malice—the ability to destroy someone and their happiness and to justify it as survival. And as I stood there, soundless tears rolling down my face, the bitter realization dawned that there was not a shadow of a doubt that, in everything I had done, despite how you had loved me, I was my mother's daughter.

Epilogue

Miranda

New York, 1940

I've told two lies in my life, and I stand by each of them. Sometimes it's necessary to make compromises, essential in order to survive. And I have when many others would have decided against it because I've been prepared to do so, and I'm not going to apologize for that.

No, I saw nothing untoward on the beach, but I said I did because I had no other choice. If I didn't marry Sebastian, God knows what would have happened to me. I was pregnant by the father of the family I was working for when Sebastian first introduced himself to me in the outdoor café. Adora found out; that's why I made up the story about her and Sebastian. She was told by my lover's wife—told to stay away from me, apparently. She came to me to ask if it was true.

Of course, I denied it, but I couldn't trust her not to say anything, so I did what I had to do. There wasn't any other choice anyway. I couldn't ever run the risk of her changing her mind and telling the truth about Genevieve's father. Besides, if only she had stayed out of things that didn't concern her, everything might have turned out differently.

My only regret is that Sophie had to find out. There was no

keeping it from her, especially when the wedding was announced. There was not a prayer that she would have allowed
Genevieve to marry Oliver if she still believed Sebastian to be
her father, especially after losing Adora. To be fair, it was more
than time to sever the tie. We had a new life to look forward to;
I felt it best to leave Sophie behind in the past, but doing so
did cause me some anguish. After all, if it weren't for her . . . I
mean, let's face it, she did convince James to take me on with
the generous dowry she offered, and in return he kept his silence. I owe practically everything to her but, in the end, it was
her choice to believe me. Certainly nobody made her, although
I can't conceive of ever doing anything like that to my daughter.
Everything I've done for Genevieve, or Genny as we call her
now—so much more traditional and reliable than the silliness
of Adora's name for her—has been for her own good. But then,
we are very different people, aren't we?

I know people will think me hypocritical considering that I
was never his greatest fan, but Oliver and I get along rather
well now—better than well, actually. He is quite charismatic, I
must confess, and we've had the opportunity to talk, to really
get to know one another, and I'm not too proud to say I was
wrong about him. We have rather more in common than we
thought, and it is so important we be friends now. Fortunately,
all of that dreadful business has been put aside. The most hideous mistake by the police on the island; I haven't pressed to
find out what made them believe such a thing in the first place,
but I don't suppose there's much point in dwelling on unpleasantness now. Especially when nobody lost anything; luckily, all
of that hard work didn't fall by the wayside. Oliver didn't lose
the fortune he'd worked so hard for. The only unfortunate
thing was the scandal it generated along with Adora's suicide

and the dead young man found in the olive grove. It was why we had to leave England to live in New York, where Oliver was born.

I wasn't very upset, if you want the honest truth, and everyone in New York has been so welcoming. Of course, in the beginning, we were tainted rather by what had happened; a few Americans had visited Oliver and Adora on the island over the years, while others had heard of them, and questions were naturally asked. After I sat down with them, though, and put them straight, they apologized. Well, they were horrified, weren't they? I mean what kind of woman would ever steal a child from a mother who loved her so much, who had lost so much in the first place? And then, having an affair with the boy who was in love with my daughter, encouraging his addictions, leading him to his tragic death. Who could forgive that? Naturally, they always ask me if she was as beautiful as everyone said, and I tell them: "Well, it's like Oliver said to me the other day: it's what's inside that counts, and considering how cruel she was during her life . . ." And here I let the sentence die, knowing I have secured the victory I sought by the sympathetic, sometimes gleeful, nods I receive. And then I add, "And, of course, he would know."

I've often asked myself why she didn't tell on me. It was why I let Genevieve stay with her. I was terrified that, if I didn't, she would spill the beans, but she never did. That last summer, I thought that was her game with Jack. I mean he was practically identical to poor Sebastian. I thought she was torturing me, rubbing my face in her triumph, but I was wrong. Anyway, more fool her. Besides, it wasn't the wisest move she could have made, was it? Considering what happened.

I quite like being made a fuss of by Oliver; he's very good at it, very attentive. It's actually thanks to him that I've grown in confidence. He often tells me, when I dismiss one of his compliments about how attractive he always found me: "There are all types of beauty in the world, Miranda. Don't underestimate yourself." And I don't anymore. People actually seek me out here, and I don't like to boast but I've found my way back into the social circles I was born into. People love to listen to my stories about the island, and I always make it a point never to disappoint them.

The funny thing is, for so much of my life I really resented Adora for everything she had. But the other morning, just after I woke up in our marvelous new apartment on Fifth Avenue, invitations jamming the letter box, I thought to myself, Well, she didn't win, did she? As I felt the warmth of the sunshine filter through the huge picture window facing Central Park, I realized something that set me free: I wasn't the summer girl anymore, made to linger in the corner until I could be of help; people want to know me. And Adora, for all of her beauty and wealth, is remembered as an unbalanced woman, the subject of an illicit scandal, who once lived on an island that most people here have never heard of. I sat down to my coffee, a huge weight off my shoulders. You see, it finally dawned on me that there was absolutely nothing left to envy her.

Genevieve

New York, 1940

I feel as though I have been here for hours, transfixed by the vision in front of me that has pulled me back to a place I no longer speak of, which haunts me still. They are still there, the perpetrators of this shadow on the sweeping staircase in the Grand Marble Hall of the Metropolitan Club. He stands a few steps down from her, his arm resting on the banister, blocking her way. Her eyes are downcast as he speaks in hushed tones.

What is he telling her? I wonder. Is he suggesting a nightcap at "21" or the Rainbow Room—later, when he can get away? Is her heart pounding with the anticipation that someone so worldly and handsome is interested in her? I wonder how long it took him to mark her in a room full of people, the most insignificant, overlooked, wholly ordinary girl. Has he even mentioned me yet? I suspect she has limitless family money, everyone here does; perhaps he is sizing her up for when things don't work out with me. Regardless, I know he has chosen her first and foremost because nobody else would and because she will be grateful and he will feed off that until he tires of her.

I won't say anything; what would be the point? In truth, I

rather pity him. Everything he does now seems to smack of desperation. I'm curious what approach he's brooked with the young girl, barely seventeen by the looks of it. Perhaps today he's playing the role of grief-stricken widower about to embark on a new life, but one unable to forget the devastation of his exquisite first wife's death. During the course of the conversations I've overheard, he vaguely hints that this marriage to me is not exactly what he wants but he has to do the right thing, which usually elicits gasps of concern, and it is then that he allows whatever woman he's with to place a consoling hand on his. "Will you ever go back?" the sympathetic listener inquires. "No," he replies, nursing his drink, somberly shaking his head. "Too painful, you know," he continues, glancing up, just, as if he can barely raise his head because of the weight of agony he lives with.

He's had to work harder, it must be said. It's not quite the same here. There are many people who don't know him, so the adoration he was accustomed to proves somewhat lacking. Here in New York, he has money but not history, and so, for the first time in his life, he has really had to try, and several times he has asked me, genuine fear in his eyes, if people might think that we're ordinary. "I mean, surely, they can't think that, Genny, can they?" I take him in my arms and pat him on the back, like a child. "Of course not, darling," I soothe, "how could anyone think such a thing of someone as remarkable as you?" And for some reason, he always believes me.

I have no friends here, not so unusual considering I never had any except for you. I find myself with so much time on my hands, the spare wheel at parties, relegated to a corner, unable to rise to the spirit of the occasion. I've learned a lot, though, about what people think, and in a perverse way it amuses me.

I've learned what a disappointment I am compared to you, whom most know of only by reputation, despite how hard my mother has tried to make them believe otherwise.

"I imagine she'll get pregnant straightaway," a woman remarks. "She'll have to, if she's to keep him interested. I can't fathom what he sees in her; she's so bland, but then he's getting older now too. Do you remember when he was married to Adora, how stunning he was? My God, it was all I could do not to . . ." "I thought you did, my dear," her counterpart insinuates cheekily. "Well . . . ," the woman remarks, a sly smile on her lips, "between you and me, he was something of a disappointment . . ." And I listen as their voices trail off as they move to another room, and it's at such times that I think to myself: Yes, we are ordinary now, Oliver. We always were.

I cope by immersing myself in a world that I can only describe as blind, as if I am drowning in a sea of memory where everything was once perfect, a sea where you live. I recall the bougainvillea in your hair and the Frenchman who sailed all the way from Cannes just to see you: *Are you very annoyed, chérie*, I hear him ask as you, bathed in gold, the light sparkling off the water, lead him away to the house. I see your white silk dresses and glinting diamonds and hear your lyrical, enchanting voice as you call my name, pulling me down, further and further, into a blissful state where all I can hear is your voice, all I can see is you. And I willingly follow you into that blue, blue sea, as if it were paradise and you the keeper at the gate.

I feel like the child who spies on the adults in the lounge from a perch on the stairs when the girl, startled, suddenly sees me

emerge from behind the curtain where I've hid. I watch my fiancé turn toward me without a hint of surprise, his practiced
smile broadening as he moves with that indolent grace of which
I was once so fond, his arms outstretched. I think not of him
and our future life as I go to him, but of the young girl on the
stairs, her moment of importance at an end.

You are with me as I move to meet him, my Beloved Aunt,
your golden arm slightly touching mine, and I can smell the
sea and feel the sunshine as we glide toward him, an impassive smile on my face, and I almost give in and return to that
blissful state when it was always just the two of us. Yet I know
I can't. And it is then that I falter, because I am not you, because I suddenly see the people, guests who have arrived for
my wedding to Oliver tomorrow, looking at me and finding
me lacking. And I know that, if I am to survive this, I have to
let you go.

I can barely bring myself to say good-bye, to wrest your arm
from my waist, and yet I accept that the time has come for you
to leave me forever. There can be no more moments in my life
when I cast my memory back to you or the white beaches and
aquamarine seas reflected in your incomparable eyes and long
for them. I can no longer dream of islands where you live,
where I could once find you, for I understand that to do so
would root me to a time and place that must be put away; because life is unbearable without you, made worse if I think of
you and how I destroyed you. And although my heart breaks, I
will no longer call your name to bring you near once more. Beloved of my youth, let me go now.

But you refuse to leave; you linger beside me, ever on, a
constant reminder of the beauty and love that were once mine
alone. And so I finally concede the battlefield, my Beloved

Aunt, as I fold into Oliver's arms with a curious mixture of acceptance and defeat. And I am consumed not by him, or by the future, as he holds me there, but by the memory of the sun and the sea and your blond, blond curls trawling behind me like a vapor, the tarnished glow of a light receding, and the sound of your voice calling my name.

Sophie

An island in the Mediterranean Sea, 1940

They are there in front of me on the beach. A tiny boy and a tiny girl bronzed from the sun, their hair white-blond. They are my children.

For each of us, there is a moment . . .

When I was a young girl and would read a story with a tragic end, I would mourn not for the disaster that befell the characters but for the matter-of-fact acceptance that life must proceed, that there was no other choice. I cannot imagine such a thing possible; I am always there, willingly imprisoned in a moment of recollection, of happiness, of pain. I cannot bear to leave them. The mundane insistence of every day that I must get up and do this or that means nothing to me; my choice is to stay behind. They have not grown old with me, would not understand the world as it changed, so for them I froze my heart in time so that I can linger unchanging with them, so that they will know me again.

I kiss these pictures in my memories, of Sebastian's little hands, plump with childhood, smoothing the ground for his dogs to sleep on; of Adora's lilting voice enchanting him with the story of Geordie sailing to Sebastian in a basket made of cherry blossoms; of the immeasurable depths of her misunder-stood eyes, which searched for kindness and found it in a boy whom nobody wanted but who was accepted by my daughter because she saw only his soul. And I sometimes find consola-tion in accepting that I am evolving, not further and further away from them the longer I live, but closer to them; because I know they will wait for me, and I am ready to ask to be forgiven.

This is my refuge, my one place of solitude and peace. It is to this spot I come each day, to the edge of the cliff in Adora's olive grove, the vast expanse of sea before me, to imagine them again. It is the only scene from their childhood that I replay, the only one of any import. I hear the sea in my memory, the clatter of teacups and cutlery being laid by the waiters sur-rounding me, the buzz of conversation, the fluttering of my dress at my ankles, the weight of my hat as I watch them. I see them jump and laugh together, bask in the admiration of tour-ists who have never seen the like of them before, or ever will again. I call to them that it's time to come in, and Adora turns to me, and that is when it happens, when I understand what eluded me then. It is the look in her eyes, the one I so misun-derstood when she was four years old. I thought then that her gaze was defiant as she clutched my son's hand more tightly, disobeying me. Yet what I see there now, in those profound aquamarine eyes, is a simple plea, something I would never have understood had I never loved her. Her eyes beg of me, *Please. Please let me keep him.*

Have we all not wished for the same thing in our lives? To keep forever the one person we love the most? Far luckier than most, my daughter always understood that there would never be a love to equal their own. And so, on this late afternoon, their memory dancing in front of me, I give him back to her:

Adora, my love, I say, *he was never mine; he is yours to keep.* I used to believe that part of Sebastian was missing, somewhere we could never find. But now I know where he is; he was hiding in his sister's soul, kept safe there, and that is where I look for him now.

For an infinitesimal moment, before my eyes shut tight to stem the tears that will flow without end until the next morning, I see my daughter's exquisite face flood with relief that I have understood her fear. I have not taken away the one person who would never betray her, and I feel such intense love for her that its strength almost overwhelms me. My children leave me then, and I can almost bear to let them go as I watch them recede into the horizon, together again, united in youth and innocence, their blond curls aglow in the light cast by the sunset, their laughter the music of the dusk. I know that they are leaving me for somewhere better, where they will never ache with regret or longing again, and for just one moment, as I accept the things I can never change, it is as if all of the world's malice has never touched her, and my daughter's life is full once again of infinite possibility.

Such is the gift I bestow in the twilight of each day.

For each of us, there is a moment.

My beloved daughter.

Mine.

Gallery Readers Group Guide

Introduction

Filled with secrets, love, betrayal, obsession, and deceit, *The Art of Devotion* is a beautifully rendered window into one family's dark and complex history and the heartbreaking reality of love's true power. Told from the shifting points of view of four women, the story explores the psychological effects and emotional damage within a family led by a matriarch who was tragically widowed too soon; the fragile, almost inappropriately close, relationship between her son and daughter; and the reckless deceit of an outsider.

The secluded beaches of a sun-drenched Mediterranean island are the perfect playground for young Sebastian and Adora. Emotionally adrift from their mother, Adora shelters her sensitive older brother from the cruelties of the world. Sophie does not question her children's intense need for each other until it's too late. Her beloved son's affections belong to Adora, and when he drowns in the sea, she has no one else to blame.

Still heartbroken years later, Adora fills her emptiness with Genevieve, the precocious young daughter of her husband's business associate and his jealous wife, Miranda. Thrilled to be invited into the beautiful and enigmatic Adora's world, the child idolizes her during their summers together. Yet, as the years progress, Genevieve begins to suspect their charmed existence is nothing more than a carefully crafted illusion. Soon she, too, is ensnared in a web of lies.

Discussion Questions

1. The opening lines of the novel suggest that "For each of us, there is a moment: what we see at the last, before God closes our eyes forever; an entire existence distilled to one perfect memory." Do you agree with this sentiment? Discuss what each character's "moment" might be. Discuss what yours might be.

2. There are four different narrators, and the novel switches viewpoints frequently. Who do you consider to be the most reliable narrator of the four women? Or are they all, to varying degrees, decidedly unreliable? How did your perception of their trustworthiness shift as the novel progressed?

3. With which character do you most identify? Why?

4. Adora "steals" Genevieve from Miranda and appears to mold the young girl in her image. Given what you know ultimately transpires and the rationale behind her seemingly manipulative and cruel decision, can Adora be forgiven? In the context of this act, is her choice barbaric or benevolent?

5. What does the character of Jack symbolize for Adora and what impels her immediate desire never to let him go? The subsequent relationship between Adora and Jack is ambiguous and its nature unclear. How do you perceive their bond? What role do you think each plays for the other? Contrast Adora's relationships with Oliver and Sebastian

to what she shares with Jack. What are the differences/simi-larities, if any, between them?

6. There are many recurring symbols in the novel: bougainvil-lea, the olive grove, the sea, and the stray dogs. What does the bougainvillea signify to each character? What does the olive grove symbolize? Are the dogs symbolic within that context? Finally, what does Linford represent to Adora?

7. The role of the mother is one of the central themes of the novel, specifically the attributes that might define a "good" one. Discuss the notion of maternal guidance/sacrifice in relation to Sophie and Miranda. Are the decisions they make for their children justified or self-serving? Could it be argued that Adora, although barren, is actually the most selfless "mother" of them all?

8. Throughout the novel, Adora inspires a cross-section of emotions ranging from adoration to hatred, yet none of the characters appear able—or willing—to ignore her. Why is this? Beyond her beauty and wealth, what is it about Adora that proves so compelling to others, even those who despise her? Why can't anyone seem to escape her influence?

9. The ending of the novel challenges nearly everything the reader has been led to believe throughout the book. Were you surprised by what was revealed? In rereading earlier passages, do you see any foreshadowing of what would ulti-mately transpire?

10. The nature of idolatry is at the heart of the novel, specifi-cally Genevieve's desire to emulate Adora in everything.

Given what happens, does Adora condemn Genevieve to an equally tragic life by indulging her in this whim? Or is Genevieve to blame and Adora merely an innocent victim of a crush that turned into a dangerous obsession?

11. Discuss the title, *The Art of Devotion,* as it applies to each character in the book. Under the guise of "devotion," all make decisions that have profound, sometimes tragic, repercussions for themselves and others. Examine the varying types of devotion each character displays.

Enhance Your Book Club

1. Bougainvillea is a recurrent symbol of the novel. Stop by a flower shop and purchase some of their fuchsia blooms for book club members to wear during your discussion!

2. The story is set on a French island in the Mediterranean. Consult a map or look online to help you better visualize the story's setting.

3. This novel has many similar themes to F. Scott Fitzgerald's *The Great Gatsby.* Read that classic novel and compare the two.

Author Q&A

1. **What inspired you to write your first novel? You've worked for the BBC and as an editor; have you always been a writer at heart?**
I would say that I was always passionate about literature. For me, it's all about the book. Obviously, my background in the editorial field fueled that interest, yet the desire to

write emerged only after several years working in that environment, perhaps because the nature of the job requires writing "on demand" to a certain degree. Working so closely on promotional materials, as all editors do, gave me the confidence to try to write something for myself. So I took a year to attempt to come up with something: I wrote two pages a day for five months, and at the end of that period I had a first draft of *The Art of Devotion.*

2. **Where did you come up with the idea for this story in particular? The character development is fantastic—are any of the characters based on real people?**

I can't speak for all authors, but it is a general truism that those who desire to write are often counseled to write only "what they know." Of course, there is a little of what I know in this novel. I, like many writers, delve into a world of memory to find inspiration, and I am lucky in that the memories I have amassed are peopled by such exquisite souls. Yet, for me, the pleasure of reading has always derived from being able to project my own imagination into the life of a story—envisaging people I know as the characters, creating their world as I see it based on what the author suggests. As a consequence, I wouldn't dream of imposing the facts of the inspiration of this book onto any reader. The book belongs to whomever reads it, to interpret as they wish, so that it becomes "their" story, personal and unique to them and founded on their insights and experiences.

3. **The novel has some very surprising twists. Did you have**

the ending planned when you began writing, or did the character's relationships develop as you wrote?

In essence, the novel crystallized in my imagination when I accepted that Adora would die at the end of the summer in 1938 — and, most importantly, that she wanted to. As soon as the choice became "hers," everything else — the nature of the betrayal, the history with Sebastian, her relationship with Jack — formulated in my mind and a clear trajectory from start to finish emerged.

4. **You've set your novel in paradise. Have you visited the Mediterranean islands for inspiration?**

Until I was twenty-one, I spent all of my summers on an island in the Mediterranean Sea.

5. **Did you have a "favorite" character in this novel? Was there one you related to more than others?**

I pity Genevieve — in fact, she haunts me. I wrestle with Sophie, still unsure whether to forgive her. I grudgingly acknowledge Miranda's strength. Yet, ultimately, Adora is always with me. Curiously enough, I have no idea where she came from. Who she is — her motivation and passion — never fails to take me by surprise, as her personality is revealed throughout the novel. Truthfully, she took on a life of her own, and it is a life that still fascinates me to the point that, even as I reread her, I am still trying to make sense of who she is and why she proves so compelling. Even so, she never fails to break my heart.

6. **Which point of view was easiest to write? Which was the hardest?**

Miranda proved the easiest voice to write. Yet, contradictorily, she also proved the hardest in that I found it literally devastating to write her "final" speech. Originally, I had thought to grace Miranda with a rather poignant, almost redemptive, closing scene, but it occurred to me as I sat down to the task that the very last thing Miranda would be, in reality, was sorry. Something about this awareness just felled me—it was like being punched in the stomach. As much as I didn't want to—and maybe this is because, in some ways, Miranda is my "offspring"—I accepted that she had to be judged. I could not intervene as an author to try to "save" her or offer up a reprieve. It was up to readers to decide how they perceived her conduct. I didn't change a word from the first draft to the last: I knew exactly what Miranda would say, how she would justify her actions, the delight she would take in her circumstances, and, although this scene took only five minutes to write, hours later I was still deeply affected by my decision. Yet I also recognized that everything about the story had led up to that moment; it was the twist the novel required, the bitter rub from which there was no escape: a dark interpretation of devotion—the art of malice, if you will.

7. **What writers have you been inspired by? What were you reading while writing this novel? What are you reading now?**

For inspiration, F. Scott Fitzgerald, Edith Wharton, T. S. Eliot, Virginia Woolf, Kazuo Ishiguro, Louis de Bernières, Françoise Sagan, Émile Zola, François Mauriac, John Cheever, Graham Greene, Ian McEwan, Ian Rankin, Evelyn Waugh—the list is endless.

I couldn't read at all while I was writing the novel. I started several books, yet I found that I couldn't concentrate on them and, even more counter-productively, I began to compare my writing—unfavorably—to those authors and found that I stalled creatively. As a consequence, I stop reading altogether whenever I am writing, as I find it extremely difficult to have another voice in my head, beyond the "voices" I need to find for the characters.